Maya Blake's hopes of becon̲
born when she picked up her f
thirteen. Little did she know h̲
come true! Does she still pinch herself every now
and then to make sure it's not a dream? Yes, she
does! Feel free to pinch her, too, via X, Facebook
or Goodreads! Happy reading!

Tara Pammi can't remember a moment
when she wasn't lost in a book—especially a
romance, which was much more exciting than a
mathematics textbook at school. Years later, Tara's
wild imagination and love for the written word
revealed what she really wanted to do. Now she
pairs alpha males who think they know everything
with strong women who knock that theory *and*
them off their feet!

Also by Maya Blake

Enemy's Game of Revenge

Diamonds of the Rich and Famous collection

Accidentally Wearing the Argentinian's Ring

A Diamond in the Rough collection

Greek Pregnancy Clause

Royals of Cartana collection

Crowned for His Son

Also by Tara Pammi

Fiancée for the Cameras
Contractually Wed
Her Twin Secret
Vows to a King

Discover more at millsandboon.co.uk.

SEXY RICH BOSSES

MAYA BLAKE

TARA PAMMI

MILLS & BOON

First published in Great Britain 2025
by Mills & Boon, an imprint of HarperCollins*Publishers* Ltd,
1 London Bridge Street, London, SE1 9GF

www.harpercollins.co.uk

HarperCollins*Publishers*, Macken House, 39/40 Mayor Street Upper, Dublin 1, D01 C9W8, Ireland

Sexy Rich Bosses © 2025 Harlequin Enterprises ULC

Out of Office Nights © 2025 Maya Blake

His Forgotten Wife © 2025 Tara Pammi

ISBN: 978-0-263-34476-9

08/25

MIX
Paper | Supporting
responsible forestry
FSC™ C007454
FSC
www.fsc.org

This book contains FSC™ certified paper and other controlled sources to ensure responsible forest management.

For more information visit www.harpercollins.co.uk/green.

Printed and Bound in the UK using 100% Renewable Electricity at CPI Group (UK) Ltd, Croydon, CR0 4YY

OUT OF OFFICE NIGHTS

MAYA BLAKE

MILLS & BOON

Dedicated to Carly, my editor,
who always challenges me to DIG DEEPER! :)

PROLOGUE

Teodor Domene shook his head, a bark of disbelieving laughter escaping as he raised the crystal tumbler of premium cognac to his lips and drained it. The spectacular view before him and the sounds of revelry at the wedding of the decade blurred to nothing beneath the red haze of impotent rage threatening to swallow him whole.

He really should've gone ahead and called his bookie to place a bet on himself on how long he'd last at his brother's wedding before the inevitable storm of belittling, indifference and outright mockery eroded whatever good mood he'd managed to cobble together. Despite knowing what being in this place, this *palacio*, did to him.

Hell, he deserved a medal for enduring a single minute, no matter how much he loved his oldest brother.

Better yet, he should've taken the easier way out and avoided his father altogether, royal protocol be damned. Then he wouldn't be caught in this relentless maelstrom of seething, helpless rage.

It'd started, as always, with the little things. A too-long sideways glance from a member of the king's inner circle here. An uncontested scoffing remark there. Jabs wreathed in humour and false smiles. Then travelling up the food chain to the throne, where it slowly spiralled into frigid, uneasy silences from his father, the king. Culminating in downright dismissal.

As a creative, the part of Teo he'd wrestled hard into emotional detachment quite admired the intricate, hived framework of it all.

There was a time when he'd talked himself into believing it wasn't about him, that he was overthinking things, being *too sensitive* as his mother had liked to taunt him with when he'd done the utterly astonishing thing and complained.

These days he never allowed it to get to that stage. Where the blatant rejection got too acute for even him—older, infinitely wiser and securely cloaked in his beloved armour of deep insouciance—to make excuses.

He felt the weight of familiar scrutiny but didn't turn around. He was well enough attuned to his twin brother to know Valenti lurked somewhere behind him, casting one of his brooding stares his way. Teo fought the dual sparks of resentment and shame.

It wasn't fair to shove Valenti beneath the tent of his discontent when his brother had chosen a path in life that had earned their father's respect but had also brought horrific tragedy that Teo wished he could have spared the brother he loved. He was much better off working harder to sluice off this oily sensation of worthlessness that slicked him when he visited his father's palace. A place not very many welcomed him to despite his grudging title of Prince of Cartana.

The Playboy Prince.

The reminder brought another sordid twist of humour but not the smug satisfaction he usually derived from his carefully cultivated persona. He knew the source of that dissatisfaction. Words strewn about with little care, as sharp and stinging as had been his bad luck to avoid overhearing them all his life. Including just five minutes ago.

'One successful union, King Alfonse. Perhaps you can work on Valenti next? Or the wild playboy? Surely it's time he curbed his disgraceful ways?'

'I have heirs coming out of my ears now, hopefully with

more on the way. I trust Valenti to do the right thing when the time comes. As for Teo...'

There had been a charged silence, mirth siphoned from the air.

'Perhaps it is as well that I might not be around for much longer, eh? There are some things a father can be excused for sparing himself from, *no?*'

Sparing himself from...like the failure of a son?

The tightness in his diaphragm was just indigestion, he was sure. He'd overindulged in the—

'Excuse me... Your Highness?'

He tensed at the husky voice but didn't turn around.

He'd mastered masking his feelings, but even he reached saturation point eventually. And the owner of that voice, the woman he was increasingly struggling to place in an appropriate box, possessed eyes that saw far too much.

Her throat cleared pointedly, challengingly, and with a silent grimace he discarded his glass and turned. 'What is it?' His tone was harsh enough to draw a flinch, but he couldn't bring himself to care. Not when he was positively roiling in being aggrieved.

Sabeen El-Maleh's eyes narrowed for a nanosecond before her proud chin went up, highlighting a regal beauty that wouldn't have been amiss in this grand, history-drenched palace. 'I need to talk to you. I need—'

His caustic laugher stopped her. Wasn't this the very contrary story of his life? Those who had zero use for him and those who always wanted *more*? 'You *"need"*? I handed you the commission of a lifetime not a handful of months ago. You had the honour of making every stitch of the Queen of Cartana's wedding dress and trousseau. You're the envy and talk of the haute couture scene. What else could you possibly need from me, Miss El-Maleh?'

Her chin notched up higher. 'I need to know why I'm still just your *temporary* creative director. I deserve to—'

The feral sound working from his throat stopped her flow of words. 'Now is not a good time,' he interrupted. 'You should leave.'

'Really?' she scoffed. 'What could possibly be occupying you? You've been standing here, alone, for ten minutes.'

'And you took that as an open invitation?' he taunted. 'Fine, if you're going to impose your presence on me, then dance with me.'

'What?'

Dios, even frowning her face was perfect. 'You heard me.'

'No,' she replied coldly. 'I don't dance.'

He didn't bother tempering his mocking laugh. 'Nonsense. Everyone dances. And I've seen you dance with my own eyes.' And *sí*, he'd been more enthralled than he cared to admit.

'What's wrong with you?' she demanded.

'Right now? Very many things.' He prowled towards her as he spoke. She stepped back in sync with his movement, initiating the very dance she'd refused. Then her back met the wall, the darkness closing around them.

His eyes swept down her body, fully aware he was using this distraction to allay the turbulent emotions flaying him but unable to stop himself from admiring what he saw. The flawless cut of the gown she'd created for this wedding. The faint notes of purple in honour of his brother and the bride's chosen theme colour.

Sabeen El-Maleh's talent was undeniable.

His gaze snapped up to catch the censure in hers. But alongside was another expression. One he'd caught faint tendrils of in their past interactions. One he'd recognised because he'd also felt the undercurrents of it, there beneath the river of his denial. Heat. Desire. *Lust*.

'Right now, though, I can pinpoint one very wrong thing.' Her breath hitched, pushing a puff of air over his lips. Propelling him closer. 'Or is it deliciously *right*?'

Her tongue slicked over her lips. 'I… I don't know what you're talking about.'

He laughed. 'We both know that's not true. Question is, can I be bothered to prove you wrong, Sabeen?'

Teo told himself he would've behaved himself if she hadn't let out that barely audible moan. If she hadn't writhed like a shameless siren against the wall. If—

He captured her mouth before reason could take hold. Reason had failed him spectacularly tonight. It'd tricked him into believing he could remain unaffected by his father's indifference. That the old king would be mellowed by illness and the reality of staring mortality in the face.

Well, reason could take a flying jump!

Instead he welcomed the illicit pleasure that stole through him as, after a moment's resistance, she melted in his arms. Her arms wound around his neck, her gorgeous greed mounting as she strained closer, her mouth opening in ravenous need beneath his.

He moulded her supple hips, dragging her closer to his body, her pelvis over his raging need. Tongues duelled in aggressive challenge, their sampling of each other building hunger on top of hunger. She tasted divine, her scent heady, as he'd half feared she would. The addicting, mind-numbing kind he craved. When the need for air forced them apart, he buried his mouth in her neck, licking her warm skin as she moaned.

'That's it. This is the only need I'm interested in fulfilling.'

She stiffened, and he cursed inwardly. Then she was pushing at his shoulders, her face a picture of regret and horror. 'If you think you can have your way with me just because you've heard—'

'Heard what?'

Her lips pursed, her gaze dropping from his. 'This was a mistake.'

He'd heard the rumours of her affair with a certain photographer and how she'd been jilted. Had listened to uncouth speculation from his own circle about the possibility of another stepping in for a chance to be the recipient of a rebound fling.

Teo hadn't dwelt on why the notion had riled him then and continued to do so now. Somewhere buried deep, he registered that within his aversion lurked a layer of carnal desire he should repel. If for no other reason than her position within his professional empire.

'Prince—'

The reminder of his position frayed the temper he'd fought to keep under tight control. *Santa cielo*, anyone with a lick of sense could see he wanted to be left alone. If they didn't, then they deserved the lash of his tongue. 'Save the false outrage, Sabeen. We both know you weren't unwilling.'

The scorching look of contempt she gave him should've been sobering. But all he wanted was to drop to his knees and beg for another kiss…he who never begged.

It was this place. His father. His mother. The whole infernal lot of them. He needed to get away. He suspected not even the love of his brothers could make the trapped scream in his soul remain throttled for long.

'Whatever you need, the answer is *no*, Miss El-Maleh. If you're that unhappy you can end your contract now. Otherwise, we'll both forget this little…lapse in judgement happened. Agreed?'

He watched her fight for composure and win where he'd failed so miserably. Spike him a look filled with regal attitude. 'I couldn't agree more. Goodnight, *Prince*.'

He turned on his heel and left the terrace, the knots in his gut tighter than ever. And if her scent and taste lingered long after he'd boarded his private jet, discarded his clothes and stepped beneath his shower to angrily take care of the erection that wouldn't subside, well, no one knew about that offensive loss of control but him. And if he threw himself naked on his bed knowing that the problematic areas of his life had just expanded from his father to include Sabeen, and that he didn't intend to rest until they were both resolved once and for all, well, the first step of overcoming adversity was acceptance.

Wasn't it?

CHAPTER ONE

Six months later

'EITHER SHE GOES, or I go!'

The statement was accompanied by the flamboyant snap of a colourful kimono and much jangling of eye-catching jewellery.

Teodor managed to stop himself from rolling his eyes and forced in a deep…deeper breath. To remind himself that melodrama in the high fashion industry was as cheap and abundant as air, and that like a child's tantrum, sometimes you just needed to let it play out.

So he throttled his impatience, his focus shifting from his overly expressive creative director to his more subdued one, his stomach clenching slightly as he gauged the *she* in question for her reaction. And saw, more interestingly, the first sign that her usually impressive composure wasn't as ironclad as she wanted to portray.

Her eyes widened the smallest fraction, drawing attention—as if any more was needed—to the dark honey irises, currently framed by thick kohl that highlighted her breathtaking beauty.

The face of a goddess. That was one of many accolades thrown at her feet when she'd been acclaimed as the hottest supermodel twelve years ago.

The world had mourned Sabeen El-Maleh's departure from the runway eight years later, her pivot into fashion design hailed with equal parts enthusiasm and sneering in the cut-throat fashion business.

To her credit, she'd proved her sceptics wrong. At least for the first two years. Her last two hadn't been as stellar—save for the brief flash of inspiration for the Queen of Cartana's wedding that she hadn't recaptured since—paving the way for the haters to crow with glee. It was also unfortunate that for part of those last two years, she had been with Teo's special edition fashion brand, Domene X.

The haute couture brand, House of Domene, was thankfully under his complete control and thriving, without any of this side drama he was currently witnessing.

He tightened his jaw now as Cristobal, the fashion genius he'd poached from his competitor five years ago, continued his tirade. Having two directors was unusual, and yes, he knew he should've cut his losses with Cristobal the second time he'd checked himself into rehab. But Teo hated admitting failure, and he was also aware it had everything do with the old king.

Especially when he intended to prove a point to his father once and for all before the year was out. Before it was too late!

Teo's disgruntlement grew when Sabeen remained unruffled, the picture of haughty, *sexy* regal poise. Almost as if *she* was the one with royal blood flowing through her veins, not him. He shifted in his seat as the very stimulating picture she made stirred his manhood, reminding him once again of *that kiss.*

There was a reason the Playboy Prince of Cartana, as the media had jeeringly labelled him, didn't date where he worked, a reason the House of Domene continued to excel despite the studied carelessness with which he treated other areas of his life. He wasn't about to start messing with it.

Especially not now.

His belly clenched tighter at the reminder that time was running out. That his father's health was further declining every day. That the need to prove himself as worthy as his brothers was slipping through his fingers. 'Are you not going to defend yourself?' he asked Sabeen, a little more sharply than he'd intended, betraying that he wasn't as laid back as he was projecting.

Sabeen's head swivelled slowly towards him, as if she had all the time in the world to grace him with her interest. By the time their gazes connected, Teo's belly was fully clenched in anticipation of her full impact.

And what an impact it was.

In his line of business, outward beauty was almost nauseatingly commonplace, a feast he'd often seen men fall into stupid raptures over.

But even a gluttonous fool would recognise and fully accept that Sabeen El-Maleh's brand of beauty happened only once in a lifetime. That it went beyond skin-deep. Resided in her very bones with a kind of mesmeric presence that left deep impressions long after she'd left a room or the runway or the pages of a magazine were closed.

Her slim, bare shoulders sheened with some lotion that made them positively glow, lifted in an easy, unaffected shrug. 'I was merely waiting for him to wear himself out or be done with his exhibition, whichever came first.'

Her delivery was as cool as her burnt-orange halter dress was hot. Had he not spotted that momentary flash of panic, he would've believed she didn't care a single jot how this meeting went. Whether he was finally going to make a decision about the temporary status she'd broached, triggering those unforgettably decadent, *disastrous* minutes on the palace terrace six months ago.

'You see the way she speaks to me?' Cristobal ranted, his patched mosaic kimono flashing in the late-afternoon New York sunlight as he continued to pace the loft space Teo used as his one of his studios in the city. 'Once upon a time, people knew their place in the order of things.'

'By *people* you mean *women*, right?' Sabeen taunted, again with barely a raised tone. But the edge was there in the tiny flare of her beautiful eyes. The minuscule twitch of her sharp masterpiece-worthy cheek bones, highlighted to perfection with barely there make-up.

Teo, equally intolerant of the sexist remark, tensed.

Cristobal spluttered, his eyes darting to Teo as he tried to gauge whether his blatant sexism had offended. 'That wasn't what I meant.'

'Thank goodness for that,' she replied. 'But pray tell, what did you mean?' she invited in cool challenge.

She uncrossed and recrossed her mile-long legs, angling her body to face Cristobal and, in the process, drawing Teo's focus like an uncouth schoolboy to the breathtaking outline of her body, starting with the yards of hair currently secured in a neat bun at her nape.

He'd only seen Sabeen with her hair down once. At the party celebrating her early retirement from modelling. He hadn't known until then that besides being a leg man he was a hair guy too. Or maybe he wasn't. Because he hadn't experienced that rampant, control-destroying impulse while fantasizing about anyone else's hair.

Irritatingly, that preoccupation had only grown over time, despite the painstaking distance he'd placed between them since *the incident* in Cartana.

Hell, if it hadn't been for the complete meltdown happening right before his eyes, the start of which had necessitated his visit to New York, he would've been back in Milan, his chosen home base. For now, until he achieved his goal once and for all, he was staying away from San Mirabet, Cartana's capital city. A place he was welcome now, but hadn't always been. In the past, the palace officials had warned that having the twin bastards of the king under the same palace roof as the crown prince, together with their mothers—unknowingly impregnated by the king during his wild-oats-sowing days—would court too much scandal. Especially when that assertion was sustained by his mother's and the former queen's past and current vitriolic antics and his father's apathy.

Dios, was it any wonder he stayed clear of the palace?

While a lot had changed since his older brother, the former crown prince and now King Azar of Cartana, had ascended the throne, some things hadn't.

He suppressed the bereft sensation and anger and instead allowed slivers of fondness to stir through his impatience, lowering the level of his intolerance. He and his brothers would be reunited soon enough.

Being with them mildly eased the knot in his chest. Although these days, with Azar nauseatingly happy in his new role as husband, father and king, and with Teo's twin even more closed off and sullen than usual, the glaring desolation in his own life was hard to dismiss.

Whatever. Their reunions were an immovable tradition, and with his and Valenti's joint birthday celebrations coming up, Teo intended to delve neck-deep into the oblivion it promised, even if it killed—

'Look, can we accept that the experiment has failed? Two creative directors in the same house was never going to work,' Cristobal griped.

'I agree,' Sabeen said calmly.

Cristobal pivoted towards his nemesis, eyes wide. 'You do?'

She shrugged. 'My time is better spent taking full control of a collection, rather engaging in a collaboration that's akin to flogging a dead horse. I can't remain a stand-in for ever. One of us has to go.'

Teo's gut clenched at the pointed response, disgruntled by the dread that she might be serious about walking out on him. Or, worse, that she might be playing him.

His days of being overlooked, undervalued until it was time for his mother to use him as a pawn against his father, were far behind him. The reminder filled him with even more bitterness and regret because now he had finite time with his

father, what with the old man battling a debilitating illness
that was slowly marching him towards the grave. Teo despised that while his mother's inability to handle being a parent to King Alfonse's spare and *other spare* had cost them a
lot, his father's ultimate indifference to the toxic atmosphere
his twin sons had inhabited had sounded the death knell for
any hope of a relationship. And that he continued to perpetu-
ate that indifference…

'Are you choosing to be the one to leave, Miss El-Maleh?'
he asked, the silky deadliness in his voice flowing like venom
around the room, making his irksome subordinates fidget.

Satisfaction oozed through him as her façade slipped another fraction, granting him a further glimpse of her panic.
A second later, the composure was back in place. But it was
enough.

Twice she'd shown her hand.

So he sat back and watched, aware that he was seeking a
specific reaction. Perhaps even projecting. He wanted her to
fight for what she wanted. The way no one had ever fought for
him. The way he was fighting for what felt like a lost cause
every day.

'You're the head of this house,' she said eventually with
that huskiness to her tone that tunnelled more unsettling sensation through him. 'I stand behind the work I've done. And
I've made my sentiments clear. It's time for you to choose.'

Her challenge was also clear. Teo held up his hand as Cristobal wound up to launch another voluminous objection. Genius or not, the older man had fallen far short of expectations.

'You're right, this isn't working. We have four months until
the pre-season shoot is scheduled to start. You each have six
weeks to finalise your collection. The collection that doesn't
make the cut will be excluded and the director fired.' His tone
was a blade, his intent unwavering.

Domene X might be secondary to his rabid devotion to the
revered House of Domene haute couture brand, but they both

carried his name, represented the legacy he drew pride from, despite everything his mother had done to make him and his twin detest their surname. To make them feel worthless simply because they'd had the misfortune of being born after the heir. Despite every detestable slur she'd bandied about to make them ashamed of who they were, how they'd come to be born. A situation which she'd puzzlingly clung on to and luxuriated in materially with every bone in her body.

He pushed those chaotic thoughts away as his flamboyant creative director rounded on him, face florid with outraged horror.

'You are pitting us against each other, like some common reality show?' he spluttered, his thick accent turning his words hoarse.

Teodor's jaw gritted. 'Against my better judgement, I'm giving you one more chance to do the job you were contracted to do. If you find that objectionable, the door is behind you.'

The older man's gaze flickered to the door, then jumped away, as if alarmed he would be transported through it against his will. Teo hid a tired smirk as he waited for inevitable capitulation. Cristobal had few options, and they both knew it.

Sabeen on the other hand…

The quiet pride she wore as close as her gorgeous dark honey-gold skin might get in the way of her accepting his terms. If that happened, he had other cards up his sleeve. But while he was almost looking forward to the challenge, he wanted her easy capitulation too.

He watched her already formidable posture straighten further as she finally locked her gaze on his. The battle he'd anticipated had arrived. Parry and thrust. Her rancorous expression of *How dare you* and *You'll regret this* as sharp as that look of contempt she'd meted out that evening on the palace terrace.

Groin heating, he met it with an arched *Take it or leave it* brow.

She capitulated with an infinitesimal nod, faint colour staining her cheeks and giving away her own recollections of that evening.

He laid out his expectations to them both, barely waiting to finish speaking before his gaze returned to her.

To see her eyelids dropping as if hiding her true expression from him, right before the tiniest flutter of her delicate nostrils and unwavering stare ended with a brisk but husky 'Accepted.'

Then she rose fluidly to her feet.

The burnt orange clung to every perfect inch of her. The hands she smoothed over her slim, supple thighs the very essence of elegance.

Teo's belly tightened all over again. Right before he cycled through his mental list of which of the beauties to summon tonight. Because he needed this years-long preoccupation with Sabeen El-Maleh to end. *Now!*

This little professional storm in a teacup was over. Time to put it in his rearview.

Time to bring out the playboy.

Entrench himself in the comfortable skin of the persona that had been his lifeline since his mid-teens. Part of him freely accepted that yes, he wasn't averse to being fussed over by members of the opposite sex. That far from tarring all women with the same brush that his mother fully deserved, they were the solution to the deep hollow in his soul.

He wasn't like Azar before his oldest brother had found his soulmate. He didn't despise *all* women simply because of the failing of one.

So what if the most important one had turned out be a vile manipulator? He'd used his mummy issues to his advantage. Sought solace where others would've avoided it under the cowardly banner of trauma transference. And it'd worked a treat. *Hadn't it?*

Acutely aware that he was staring at the only woman who'd called their one sizzling kiss *a mistake*, then proved she was resistant to his charms by treating him like a plague in their brief meetings since his brother's wedding; that his gaze had strayed unprofessionally far too many times over her svelte body; and that Cristobal was still in the room, watching Teo's unwilling attraction unfold, he shot the other man a sharp look.

'Since you're still here, I'm assuming you're on board too?'

Cristobal struggled to his feet, thrusting out his double chin in pitiful defiance. 'If there is no other way, then I'm on board, as you say.'

Teo waved at the door. 'Shouldn't you get on with it, then?' He couldn't halt the snap in his voice, his fingers drumming the desk as Cristobal exited.

Proving her insultingly easy aversion to him, Sabeen pranced away on six-inch heels, throwing over her shoulder, 'I'll get on with it too, shall I? See you in six weeks.'

Fresh irritation sparked in his belly. *She did that to him. Every. Single. Time.* 'Aren't you forgetting something?'

She froze, then turned in a pirouette he'd seen a thousand times on the catwalk and yet still made his blood rush through his veins.

A small crease dissected her smooth forehead, right before one elegant brow arched. 'I don't think so.'

'The Fashion America Gala is in two days. You're coming with me.'

Her frown melted away, replaced by displeasure. 'Wasn't Cristobal going to be representing House of Domene? With your blessing?'

Was there censure in her voice? He refused to acknowledge it. 'I had plans to be in Milan, but since your antics have brought me here instead, I'll be attending. With you instead of Cristobal. Do you have a problem with that?'

'And if I have plans of my own?' she parried.

Tension tightened, an unwelcome dissection of what those plans could be, attacking him. What the hell was wrong with him? 'Cancel them. And before you object further, remember what you have to gain. Or lose.' He allowed himself a ruthless smile that made her stiffen ever so slightly. 'Need I remind you that earning a permanent place as my creative director isn't just about compiling a collection? That it's also about being a team player for the brand as a whole?'

The threat hung between them, as he'd fully intended. His passion for creating exquisite designs might be his driving force, but he was also a businessman. One determined to win at all costs, but specifically for this vital next project. His chance to earn the rightful respect he deserved and his place in the Domene family tree.

Several seconds of tense silent contemplation later, she nodded. 'I'll attend. If you insist.'

'I shouldn't have to. It's your job, so I expect you to be there.'

Her lips pursed, and Teo was astonished by how much that display of temper pleased him. *Dios mio*, she would be glorious in full rage. Not that he planned on stoking that sentiment in her any time soon. Or ever.

That moment on the terrace where he'd nearly lost total control was an aberration. *Never to be repeated.*

He skimmed feverishly through that mental list of available women again, sucking in a disgruntled breath when not a single name snagged his interest.

'I know it'll sound annoyingly cliché, but since you've sprung this on me at the last minute, I hope you won't need me tomorrow. I'll have to hunt around for something since I have nothing to wear.'

Absurdly that, too, pleased him. He really needed to have his head examined. 'No need for a hunt.'

'What?'

He sagged deeper into his chair, his eyes coasting professionally, he assured himself, over her once more. Now the idea was planted in his head, he itched to see her wearing his latest one-of-a-kind creation he'd been working on. 'I'll have something overnighted from Milan. I'll send a car for you in the morning. You can try it on then.'

Damn it, damn it, damn it!

This was supposed to have been a short, decisive meeting.

Meet with Teodor Domene. Deliver the unequivocal ultimatum she'd been withholding—and dreading—for months. Leave.

Instead she'd been locked in a room with him for over an hour. Forced to breathe him in. To listen to that rich, raspy sensuality that dripped with every syllable that fell from his too sexy mouth. Forced to parcel out the handful of times she'd allowed herself to look at him—because any more would seriously risk her equilibrium. Relive that exquisite, mind-shredding kiss. Berate herself severely when she'd failed.

She'd tuned both men out just to try and collect herself, catching words like *fortnightly* and *contact*, then regretted it when ignoring him had only drawn his attention, a question clear in his narrow-eyed look. She'd nodded and said *yes* stupidly without knowing exactly to what she was agreeing.

Her belly churned now as she walked in painfully measured steps to the door, the deplorable weakness she'd experienced since their very first meeting on the night of her retirement party—a reaction that had sparked a heated argument—evoking a sense of fury and helplessness that made her yank the door handle far too hard, risking him seeing the further deterioration of her composure.

Damn it!

Shutting the door behind her, she sagged against the wall and sucked in a deep breath. She hated that he did this to her. That it was so effortless, the way he affected her. Like that abandoned kiss, which had triggered such horror in her and a volcanic gleam in his eyes that had only made her...*hotter!*

Her single saving grace was that her hard-earned composure worked most of the time, and she could only hope that he continued to remain clueless how she suffered in his presence. She hated it enough that the one personal area of her life she'd sworn to overcome, he obliterated so obliviously.

But that was a good thing, she assured herself as she straightened and exhaled. Because she'd discovered, to her emotional cost and annihilation, that men like Teodor Domene—who believed they owned the world and everything within it—only needed to smell weakness to pounce on and devour their prey.

And she was no one's prey. Not any more.

Not after Nathan Gray.

Even thinking the name shot acid into her throat. Sabeen gritted her teeth and breathed through it. Then ruthlessly forced herself to focus on the problems in front of her.

The truth she'd admitted to herself only recently and still grappled with.

She'd lost her mojo.

She waited until the executive lift door completely shut before she wilted, swallowing hard as the words rolled frantically through her brain once more.

Her creativity had terrifyingly deserted her.

Despite the confidence-boosting support and friendship from Eden Domene, the new Queen of Cartana. Despite the stunning coronation and wedding trousseau Sabeen had put together under Teodor's direction. Despite the multi-page spread she'd earned in *Vogue* magazine in the aftermath of those achievements.

Hell, even despite the fact that she'd attended the royal wedding with Teodor, and had been the subject of more media scrutiny than she'd wanted.

Because, sadly, those comments had been of a snide nature, weighing her value only by who she knew and not her professional worth. And as always, the stench of her past association with Nathan Gray had followed, reducing every ounce of hard work into one salacious, scandalous, *dismissive* soundbite.

For heaven's sake, they'd even stopped using her name for those stomach-hollowing column inches.

Notorious Nathan Gray's Ex's New Collection Is a Flop!

Gray's Ex Faces Axe from Domene X!

But by far the most devastating of them all:

Supermodel to Super Mistress to Super Nothing!

Despite the euphoria of creating the wedding collection and the despair of the negative press, Sabeen attributed her current condition to two things. Grief. And *that kiss*.

Both had sent her running to the beloved remote house on the hill on the outskirts of Essaouira, Morocco. The house her grandmother had loved with every fibre of her being and which she'd passed on to Sabeen when she'd died shortly after the wedding. A refuge where she'd licked her wounds and thought she'd managed to get herself together enough to tackle her next project.

Only to be confronted by failure after failure.

She pressed her tongue to the roof of her mouth and blinked rapidly against the pressure behind her eyes as the lift opened and spat her out.

The steely warning in Teodor's unique Domene grey eyes had been unequivocal. Another failure and she truly would be a *super nothing*.

But…as much as she wanted to rail at the heavens for depriving her of vital support in the form of her grandmother, Sabeen knew she had loved and supported her. For the most part.

Yet you disappointed her too…

She pushed that harrowing thought away, leaving her wide open to the naked truth of her other problem.

The kiss she couldn't forget. The kiss consuming her, possibly to the detriment of her creativity.

And yet…she hadn't chosen to walk away given the chance. Had instead accepted Teo Domene's challenge. Because he and the House of Domene were a combined once-in-a-lifetime opportunity she would be insane to walk away from.

Is that the only reason?

Stepping out into the sunshine and electric vibrancy of Manhattan, she plucked her sunglasses from her purse, slotted them into place and breathed out.

Over her dead body would she allow this to carry on much longer.

Jida would be ashamed of her wallowing. Her grandmother would tsk repeatedly at even the faintest hint that *a man* was behind this knock in her confidence. But she wasn't totally blinkered enough to recognise that she'd sustained severe emotional scars after Nathan.

He'd—

No. Enough.

She'd wasted enough heartache on him. She flagged a cab, taking the tiniest of wins when it slid to an eager stop before her. She basked in it, ignoring her overly raspy voice which always sounded that way when she was agitated, and gave her Greenwich Village address.

She had six weeks to turn the last six months—or two years if she counted Nathan—of her life from a disaster into something remotely salvageable. No. Not just *salvageable*.

A raging success.

One that would right every wrong turn she'd taken in her past once and for all.

Better still, it would be six weeks free of Teodor Domene's electrifying presence. Free from having a million butterflies swarming to life in her belly at the mere sight of him.

Best of all, she wouldn't have to be constantly on guard about falling under the spell of another devastatingly handsome, emotionally bankrupt playboy who would so carelessly toss her emotions into a wood chipper just to sit back and raise a glass of champagne as he watched her bleed.

History repeating itself through her grandmother with her grandfather, her mother's turmoil over her father, then her through Nathan was quite enough. Karma could take a flying leap into a boiling volcano.

She would break the El-Maleh curse. Claim every *corner of her life back.*

All she had to do before that was get through the gala with Teodor Domene.

CHAPTER TWO

A ONE-HOUR DRESS FITTING.

A thing he'd done countless times in the past but was now reserved for the very select few.

So why the hell was he on his fourth espresso before eight o'clock?

He'd already reconciled himself to the possibility of shutting down Domene X if things didn't work out.

Si, but failure is still failure. And while Mama's sneers wash over you these days, evidently you're still not immune to Papa's opinion. Are you?

He jerked his fingers through his hair, cringingly grateful when the doorbell interrupted the recollection of what he'd overheard his father say at Azar's wedding. Teo loathed to admit it, but more than the apathy and indifference to his and Valenti's plight of being subjected to their mother's attention-seeking manipulation, it was hearing that his father would rather face the consequences of his ill-health than interact with his third son—*that* was a pill that both chafed and angered Teo.

And if he did nothing else, he would get the old man to eat those words.

Setting his cup down none-too-gently on the pristine marble console, he waved the butler away from the door, ignoring the knots in his belly.

An hour today. A handful tomorrow night.

Then he'd be free to work on the most important project of his life.

Teeth set, he yanked the door open, causing the statuesque beauty's head to rear up. And just like that, another knot strangled into being.

A part of him wondered abstractedly if Sabeen was a witch. If she'd been sent by the devil himself to torment him. Because surely no one—besides himself of course—had the right to look so effortlessly perfect at this time of the morning, with her hair neatly knotted once more, the barest hint of make-up highlighting every inch of flawless skin. He granted himself the smallest glance at her cream thigh-skimming wraparound jersey dress. 'You're late,' he snapped.

'I'm not,' she replied with calm so serene it was like watching a still pond at sunrise. 'I'm actually a whole minute early.'

He wanted to toss out the trite retort about early meaning being on time but stopped himself. He was projecting. Again. Exposing that she was burrowing deeper under his skin when he knew most of what he was feeling wasn't even her fault.

Or was it?

Wasn't she the only one who'd been able to achieve that besides his parents? He would struggle to name any of the parade of beautiful women who'd graced his bed in the last year. Yet, a three-minute indulgence with this creature—albeit an intensely sizzling one—had taken seemingly permanent residence in his consciousness, resisting any effort to remove it.

'Coffee?' he tossed over his shoulder as he strode back into the living room. Then felt disgruntled all over again when she shook her head. What the hell was wrong with him?

'No, thanks. I've had my one cup of the day. More and I get the...' The faintest frown momentarily marred her forehead. 'I'm fine, thanks.'

He stifled the urge to demand that she elaborate. That it had risen in the first place was irritating in the extreme. He never asked a woman about her thoughts. He'd learned very early in life, much to his cost, that that way lurked landmines ready to annihilate him.

His mother had only needed the slightest prompting to launch into a vicious diatribe, outlining every source of disappointment, disgust and fury that her twin sons by the former king had had the audacity to arrive a few weeks later than the current King of Cartana, thereby depriving her of the coveted position of Queen of Cartana. Decades later, her intense resentment for that slight still burned just as bright.

At times, Teo wished he could be like his twin: aloof, unruffled, insults and overdramatic recriminations bouncing off his wide shoulders as he moved through his quiet, if angst-filled life. At some point Valenti had even offered the excuse that their mother's behaviour stemmed from her inability to handle her twin sons as a single mother. But Teo had tolerated that opinion for five minutes. His mother was capable of love. Unfortunately that love only encompassed power, recognition and deeply material things.

Never him or his brother.

'Come,' he commanded, aware of the un-playboylike gravity of his tone. He barely bit back 'Let's get this over with' before heading down the hallway of his penthouse.

Her heels clicked briskly behind him, his shoulder blades tingling at the sensation of her watchful gaze on his back, perhaps even puzzled by his mood.

You and me both, he mused bitterly.

Throwing open the doors to the room, he strode to the mannequin positioned in the centre of the room, draped with the outfit that had arrived first thing this morning as per his instructions.

For the umpteenth time he sought out flaws, his critical gaze seeking ways to elevate perfection into a masterpiece.

He made no apology for achieving the impossible repeatedly through his career. It was what had earned him endless accolades, a rabid following and more billions than he would be able to spend in six lifetimes.

He exhaled, slow and deep, his roiling senses settled, *finally*, as the throbbing pulse that fed his first and only love slid into place.

Some people bandied about, tearing their hair out over what their roles in life were, whether they were on the right path or not. He had known from the very first time he'd slid a swathe of silk between his fingers that this was what he was born for. Not even the brief stint in the army with his brothers, when their deep bond had solidified and his twin had been co-opted into special ops, had tempted Teo to change paths.

Disparaging, sneering, downright mockery hadn't dissuaded him. These days he had the last laugh. His own mother begged him, when she found the grace to drop her perennial animosity, to create signature gowns for her, which she would then boast about—out of his earshot, of course, because heaven forbid a word of approval should fall from her lips.

And depending on his mood, he either sent her away with nothing or tossed something her way. He curbed a jeering smile.

Yes, he was aware that some would deem him a disrespectful son. He had earned many more unfavourable labels than that in his thirty-five years. Hell, these days he collected them like trophies.

'Are we doing this?'

He tensed, then forced himself to relax, to drag himself into the present. 'By all means, but you will need to—'

His words dried up when he turned to see her already shrugging out of the wraparound dress she had arrived in.

Dulce cielo.

He clamped his jaw to keep it from dropping. And yes, for the first time in his life he yearned for the strength to resist staring at a beautiful woman like an uncouth schoolboy. But he couldn't have stopped himself if the world was ending. Because even dressed in underwear that covered more than most bikinis, Sabeen was simply magnificent.

Serene, composed and so utterly unaffected by him that he wanted to ruffle every last edge of her. To watch her come undone, in a way that would both shake him out of this entrancement he found himself in and teach her that he wasn't to be trifled with. To eject this despised, curious tongue-tiedness that held him speechless as she finished undressing, clad only in a pair of chocolate French knickers, balconette bra and stylish heels, her garments thrown over her arm, one eyebrow raised as she waited for him to collect himself.

'Where do you want me?' she muttered.

Dios. Was he completely out of line to deem some words forbidden between a man and a woman striving to remain professional? Just for *his* sanity's sake?

'Where do you think?' he threw back at her and then almost laughed beneath his breath. At this rate they would descend into childish taunts and hair-pulling before the hour was out.

Ignoring him, she went to the nearest armchair, dropped her dress over it then, after spotting the tailor's platform behind the mannequin, calmly stepped onto it and simply…waited.

Teo ignored the faint shaking in his fingers as he plucked the garment off the mannequin. Watched instead as she focused on what he held in his hands. The stretched crepe-and-silk blend had been produced to his exact specification, sifting through dozens of combinations before settling on this. And as he'd envisioned, the fall, feel and texture elevated the garment to incredibly special.

'Turn around,' he instructed.

When she did, he assured himself the head-to-toe scrutiny was to judge which adjustments were needed but mocked himself silently when he lingered far too long on the dramatic dip at her waist, the flare of her hips, the glorious texture of her skin and, of course, her flawless, endless legs.

Jaw clenched, he inhaled deeply. His control back where it

needed to be, he draped his creation over her head, secured the discreet zip, then stalked around her, scrutinising every inch of the gown. 'Turn,' he commanded once more, indicating the walls of mirrors.

Pride stalked through his veins as he watched her eyes widen at her first glimpse in the mirror that bordered the room on three sides.

'It's…' She sucked in a breath, her composure satisfyingly fracturing as she altered her pose, angling for a different look.

'It's okay,' he stated. 'I'll wait while you find the perfect words to heap praises on my head.'

Her awed expression didn't change. Something heated in his belly and rose to his chest. It was far too warming, too *needy* to be tolerated. So he stamped it beneath ruthless feet.

'It's incredible,' she offered simply in the end, her rasp deep. Sincere.

And there he went clenching everything again to stop the relentless battering at his senses. To stop himself wishing for that voice to belong to a different individual. *Like his father…*

Dios, what the hell was this?

'Not quite,' he disagreed. 'Since this dress was created for someone shorter, the hem will need to be taken down, as will the sleeves.'

Striding to the tablet containing his sketches and ideas, he quickly made the requisite notes and sent it off to his three New York assistants.

Then he returned, stalking around her three more times, gauging further adjustments until he was somewhere near satisfied. He looked up then and caught the peculiar look on her face which she quickly attempted to suppress. 'Something wrong?'

'Who did you make it for?'

From the colour staining her cheeks he suspected she hadn't planned on asking him that. She confirmed it a moment later with a single wave of her elegant hand. 'Actually, never mind. It's not important.'

'Are you sure?'

She blinked, most likely at the bite in his voice, entirely produced by the weight of knowing everything he did from now until his goal was achieved was of crucial importance. That he couldn't afford a single slip.

'Is it part of your upcoming collection?' she said after a stilted silence.

He aimed a narrow-eyed glance at her. 'You should know better than to ask since I never reveal my creations beforehand.'

Again a dart of something fractured her composure. And heaven help him he wanted to dig at it, to bare it to the light. See what made her tick.

He didn't need to know what made her or any woman tick. All he needed was sex when the need arose, then distance when feelings risked getting in the way. He'd learned a long time ago that seeking solace elsewhere only brought disappointment and the same grasping demands his mother craved. Keeping his entanglements in emotion-free zones suited him perfectly.

'Arms up,' he instructed.

Her slim arms rose to exactly shoulder height, displaying how the draped sleeves fell. Satisfied he nodded and held out a hand. 'Walk around, show me how it looks in motion.'

She took his hand, stepped down, then withdrew her fingers with insulting haste, before starting her signature strut that had held millions in her thrall during her modelling years. Teo couldn't have pinpointed why her walk was mesmerising if his life depended on it. All he knew was that, like the unfathomable depths of the passion for creativity that flowed in his veins, hers was an intangible gift.

If only it didn't succeed in scrambling most men's brains. *Men like Nathan Gray.*

The scandal-courting photographer's name made thunderbolts rumble across his already roiled senses.

She froze. 'Is something wrong?'

'Not with the dress, no,' he drawled.

'Does that imply there's something wrong with me?' she pressed, her cool tone sliding into chilly territory.

Yes. What on earth did you see in an imbecile like Gray?

'We're done here for today, Sabeen. Take off the dress,' he said curtly, aware of an alien spark that absurdly resembled jealousy.

She remained motionless for a stretch longer, then swayed towards him with that same distant composure that made his fingers itch to unravel her. To reenact that kiss just to feel her melt in the helpless way that attacked him far too often. With admirable strength of will he resisted.

She reached him and pivoted, silently directing him to lower her zip.

The second he did, she shimmied out of the dress, handed it to him then with glorious confidence, and a complete lack of self-consciousness, strutted back to where she'd dropped her dress.

Teo just about managed to keep his libido from exploding, shaming him thoroughly as he walked her in silence back to his front door. Watched as she sailed out, nose in the air after his instruction to report back the next evening to ready herself before leaving for the gala.

And if he cringed beneath the cold shower he had to take after the departure of the woman who occupied far too much room in his thoughts, it was worth it. Mastering his control around Sabeen was essential. Because nothing could derail his plans.

Nothing.

It felt like a blink of an eye had passed before Sabeen found herself back in front of Central Park Tower. She didn't bother looking up. Making herself dizzier than she currently felt wasn't a wise choice when she was about to fling herself into Teo's cyclonic presence again.

But she was vividly aware of the stratospheric sensation of dealing with Teodor Domene, a reality pounded home when she stepped into the fastest elevator in the world and was whisked up with stomach-dropping speed to the Domene residence.

Of course he lived in the most iconic building in New York City.

If only she wasn't unequivocal about punctuality, abhorring those who blithely went with the fashionably late rule. But, she grimaced inwardly, neither fifteen seconds nor fifteen minutes would calm her shredded nerves.

She still couldn't believe her behaviour yesterday, flinging off her clothes in front of him like the supermodel she'd once been. Telling herself it was his fault for answering his door in a deplorable mood, triggering her own recklessness, hadn't stopped her agitation for the rest of the day, nor her tossing and turning last night.

And the voice whispering that she'd wanted to see him ruffled again, maybe even display a feral gleam like the one after their kiss? Well, that voice could take a long walk off a short pier because it didn't help one iota.

She'd stayed within touching distance after the fitting, breathing him in, revelling in that heady scent of sea-breeze and smoke. That rusty vault she'd locked tight had cracked open, allowing a sliver of craving to escape. Shaming her as she relived that kiss for the thousandth time.

So yes, she deserved to be suffering now, boiling in remembered disgrace. Suffering through her body's reaction to Teodor's undisguised virility. Maybe this was the control-mastering test she needed to pass before regaining peace and inspiration? To honour her promise to her grandmother never to let a man hold sway over her independence and future?

She was saying a feverish prayer when the double doors to the most breathtaking residence she'd ever seen were thrown open, a finely dressed butler nodding in courteous greeting.

'Miss El-Maleh, welcome.' He gestured her into the spectacular living room, little of which she'd noticed in Teodor's presence yesterday. 'His Highness is just finishing up with a phone call in his study. You'll be attended to shortly.'

Hell, no, she was not disappointed that Teo hadn't greeted her himself.

'Thank you.'

'May I get you something to drink?'

Summoning a smile, she shook her head. 'No, thank you. I'm fine.'

The lingering look the middle-aged butler cast her she was used to, dismissing it as she surveyed her surroundings. She'd been subject to every expression under the sun when it came to her physical features.

Long before she'd crossed the challenging threshold between girl and woman, she'd been labelled everything from *goddess* to *witch*, *angel* to *Jezebel*. And while a thick skin hadn't ultimately protected her vulnerable heart, she'd learned better composure and poise in the face of others' reaction to her.

So she ignored the hovering butler and took in the black-trimmed cream elegance and comfort of the luxury furnishings she knew would feel heavenly to touch and relax in, the priceless art she recognised from some of the most renowned artists both living and dead and the gorgeous hints of soft-toned veined marble. Then she feasted her eyes on the pièce de résistance, the iconic landscape spread out like the most exquisite banquet beyond the floor-to-ceiling glass walls.

Central Park was the perfect rectangle surrounded by glittering lights in the early evening, kissed by the spectacular orange sunset over it.

She was so absorbed in the breathtaking vista, she didn't

hear the footsteps approaching until they were feet away. Bracing herself, she turned. Only to feel another hollowing in her belly.

'Mara, Gio, I didn't know you were here.' If her tone faintly reflected her disappointment at Teodor's continued nonappearance, she fervently hoped they didn't pick up on it.

Mara, one of Teo's dozen-strong assistants who worked at his flagship House of Domene base in Milan, quirked one carefully plucked eyebrow, her expression hovering between mild amusement, condescension and barely disguised jealously that immediately made Sabeen's tense up.

'Of course I'm here. We're always on call for whatever Teo needs. You know that.'

The familiarity with which she addressed her boss invoked the intended speculation that Sabeen absolutely despised herself for. Berating herself more sharply, she smiled coolly, switching to look at Gio, only to stifle her frustration at his equally unwelcome expression of amusement and heated appraisal of her body.

'Right. I see.' She flicked her gaze past them, letting the obvious question hover in the air. She wasn't going to ask, risk it come out wrong and be forced to deal with their attitude. She was unsettled enough as it was.

Gio stepped forward, hand outstretched, forcing Sabeen to reluctantly place hers in his, grimacing when he weaved his fingers through hers. 'We've been here all day, slaving away to ensure your gown is perfect. Now it's time to transform you from *bellissima* to *magnifica*,' he crooned, kissing her fingers.

She tugged herself firmly from his hold, ignored his patent disappointment as she followed them both down the familiar hall. Her heartbeat picked up when she heard deep tones behind one of the closed doors, but Sabeen kept her focus rigidly straight, aware of Mara's watchful gaze. She had zero interest in being drawn into any drama from one of Teodor's acolytes. Or was she more than that?

Tightening her grip on her fraying emotions, she followed them into the room, and her breath whooshed out with wonder all over again. Admittedly, she'd been too busy making wrong choices yesterday to fully appreciate his creation, even though she'd been speechless when she'd tried it on. She'd been mildly alarmed that he might see how deeply affected she was by his raw, unbridled talent, that tinge of envy that his artistry wasn't stunted in any way by doubt or whatever demons seemed to be stifling her.

Now she fully appreciated the breathtaking design of the unapologetically feminine and confidence-endowing strapless gown with a long back slit, embellished with glittering crystals banding the waist. But what elevated the ensemble was the detachable caped sleeves, which fell to the floor to end at the precise length of the dress's hem, embellished with the same crystals that formed a wide collar to hold the sleeves in place.

And in the centre of that collar, instantly recognisable and formed entirely of studded diamonds, was the opulent *D* signature logo.

Long before she'd met and experienced the befuddling secret attraction to the shameless playboy behind the House of Domene label, Sabeen had fallen head over heels with Teo's sublime talent.

Here, now, she could put her mortifying personal feelings aside and bask in the utter glory of Teodor's design, allow herself the thrill of knowing this masterpiece would grace her body, that she might even rediscover her own inspiration simply by wearing the stunning gown.

She barely registered setting aside her handbag and undressing, her only focus on opening herself up to that possible inspiration as Mara and Gio fussed about, cinching her into the gown and presenting her with silver stilettos and a velvet, crystal-studded clutch.

She'd worn her hair up and done her make-up in shades of

silver beforehand, and she was fastening her simple diamond bracelet when she heard the muted indrawn breath behind her.

Eyes snapping to the mirror, they collided with the molten silver searing gaze of Teodor, decked out in a silk-lapelled tuxedo so sublime on his gladiatorial body it was positively blasphemous.

'Leave us.' The gruff command electrified the space as she was conducting a helpless once-over that he was mirroring so belly-hollowing effectively then added, when his assistants didn't move fast enough, 'Now, please.' His gaze darted to Mara then to Gio, with a nod and a flash of a supernova smile before adding, 'Thank you for your hard work.'

Again, since he'd snatched every crumb of attention, Sabeen barely registered Mara preening at his praise before his focus was back on her.

On his creation.

The harsh correction didn't stop the careening butterflies from turning her belly into a rollercoaster as he sauntered closer her, brazenly trailing a third appraisal, then going one better to circle her, bringing that formidable presence and intensely evocative scent with him.

'You look exquisite,' he stated after his second circuit.

Her fingers convulsed around her clutch at the throaty offering. 'You mean your gown looks exquisite,' she forced out.

She couldn't afford to be lumped in with others. Not when her very skin itched to preen just like Mara. Just like the many hapless women—and men—out there who only needed to set eyes on this man to fall into throes of adoration.

She was not and never would be one of them.

Her one disastrous relationship with Nathan Gray had taught her that it would be pure folly to tangle with another playboy. Or any man for that matter.

From the corner of her eye, she saw his nostrils flare at her crisp correction. Then his eyes narrowed a fraction.

'A gown is simply a gown until the right woman breathes

life into it. But if you insist, then, *sí*, I'm much impressed with how it's turned out.'

The right woman…

She had no business experiencing a tinge of pride. She knew without a doubt that had she not been available, he would've found a hundred others to take her place. Just like Nathan Gray did after—

'I'm ready. Shall we go?' The query was sharper than she'd intended, but when she peered at him, his gaze remained on the gown, bringing relief that he hadn't noticed the tiny slip in her composure. Because, curiously, he seemed to have slipped into creative mode.

'Not just yet,' he murmured.

She watched him stride across the room to the tablet he'd used before, pick it up and return, the stylus flying over the screen.

'What are you doing?'

He didn't answer. The fierce grasp of concentration held her reluctantly rapt, her sudden craving to know what he was doing making her take a half-step towards him, only to freeze when he frowned at her.

'Stay still, if you please.'

She opened her mouth to snap that she wasn't a dog to be ordered to heel, but again she held her tongue, that bite of envy returning more sharply when she saw that he was sketching a whole new design along the lines of what she wore.

'Should I bother asking if that's for your next collection, or are you going to shut me down again?'

His sketched for ten more seconds before he holstered the stylus. Only then did he meet her gaze. Making her immediately regret the impetuous question when his gaze probed deep. Deeper than she cared for. 'It wasn't important to you before. And yet you ask again. Why?'

Because I need a crumb of that inspiration.

She pressed her tongue to the roof of her mouth to stop

those words from spilling out. Then forced a shrug. 'I'm just making conversation.'

The blatant lie garnered cynical arched brows that punched heat into her throat and up into her face.

'You expect me to believe you're interested in conversation when every look you fling my way drips with disdain?' he said, clearly unaffected by the thought.

Cringing, she pivoted towards the door. The quicker she got this night over with, the quicker she could shut herself away from all the glitz, temptation and histrionics of existing in Teodor's world. Perhaps she could console herself with the fact that her true feelings about the type of man he was hadn't shone through after all.

'It's not personal,' she threw over her shoulder.

His mocking laugh drilled twin tunnels of fire and ice through her.

Nathan, too, had laughed at her.

More frequently and over more serious matters than she cared to recall. The fire disappeared, leaving behind icy goose bumps that thankfully the long sleeves hid.

'It seems I've struck another nerve,' he drawled, because apparently, he could see through her façade to read her just as effectively.

'You don't seem too concerned about it, so I'm sure offending me means nothing to you.'

A slight flaring of his nostrils amplified his displeasure. 'Careful there, *cariña*,' he murmured as they walked side by side towards the living room. 'Convince yourself that you know even remotely what makes me tick and I'll be forced to prove one or two things to you.'

She just about caught herself from stumbling at the words spoken with the harshness of crushed glass. When she examined his fallen-angel features, she was met with the formidable wall of granite that reminded her of his centuries-old roots and his brief stint in the army with his brothers in his early twenties. How the Spartan savagery that had birthed his ancestors flowed through his veins. That simply because he'd chosen a career dedicated to dressing and undressing women didn't mean he was in any way soft or affable.

Burning awareness flowing from her elbow and demolishing that ice she'd lamented just moments ago dragged her gaze down to discover he'd wrapped his hand around her arm to halt her stumble.

He didn't hurry to release her. And a part of her wasn't in a hurry to demand it either.

The shocking realisation triggered a visceral reaction. Before she could act on it, a dramatic gasp diverted both their attention.

Gio was staring at them, mouth agape. Eyebrows raised. A puzzling reaction, because he'd already seen her in the gown.

'What—?' Sabeen started to ask.

Mara interrupted, her focus fixed squarely on Teo. 'Did you need anything else, Teo?'

He dropped her arm, striding briskly for the door. 'No, *gracias*. I'll see you both in Milan in a couple of days. Have a safe flight back.'

His back was turned so that Teo didn't see the longing on Mara's face. Sabeen saw it, though. And something unpleasant flipped in her belly.

It was yet another thing she was wrestling to dismiss when they stepped out of the limo and onto the red carpet leading into the X-Ceed Heights Building in Lower Manhattan twenty minutes later.

'Do you realise your employee is in love with you? Do you care, or are you arrogant enough to simply take that as part of your due?' she blurted.

His head snapped sharply to hers. *'Scusi?'*

Her desperation for the earth to open up and swallow her whole brawled with the need to discover his reaction to this bout of madness she couldn't seem to stop. Heaven above, what was wrong with her?

'I...' She shook her head, ignoring the flashbulbs igniting giddily around her as the eager paparazzi caught their first glimpse of their beloved Playboy Prince.

'You what?' he prompted, a sharp edge to his voice. 'I'm learning a few things about you. I can't quite decide whether I want my frosty creative director back or if I should delve deeper into just what is behind this curious turn of events.'

'I... I'm not frosty,' she argued far too weakly.

The corner of his mouth twitched with a barely there smile. 'Indeed. I've seen you deign to laugh with my sister-in-law.' He leaned close. 'And let's not forget that kiss, hmm?'

Heat pounded her. 'I thought we weren't going to talk about that?'

'You threw this door wide open, *cariña*. So tell me, is it simply a case of my being tried and convicted of offences trapped in that beautiful head of yours?' he parried.

'It's not... I'm not...'

He bent towards her, ignoring the even more frenzied snapping of media photos she knew with stomach-dropping certainty would wing their way around the social media universe before the hour was out.

'At least be brave enough to admit your truth, Sabeen. Maybe that would unblock all this...tension that's holding your creativity back.'

CHAPTER THREE

HOW DARED HE?

Of course, her outrage arrived far too late.

Long after he'd stepped coolly away from her, leaving her to face shouted questions about the gown she didn't have answers to. Leaving everyone to salivate over the possibility of catching a glimpse of a House of Domene exclusive while he sauntered to another batch of the press and charmed them with smooth soundbites that had them laughing.

She was still bristling when he returned five minutes later, suavely offering her an arm she had no choice but to take or risk further rabid speculation. 'For your information, I'm not blocked,' she defended hotly. *Belatedly.*

He plucked two glasses of chilled vintage champagne from a passing tray and offered her one before slanting her a mocking glance. 'Really? Then, why haven't you produced anything worth the talent I know you have in over six months?' he demanded, his voice a lethal blade wrapped in silk.

She wasn't addressing the Playboy Prince now. She was talking to her boss. The man with the passionate drive and talent that repeatedly left his competitors puzzled and in awe. But since the same question dogged her, and she absolutely refused to attribute it to *a man*, she raised her chin. 'Every designer goes through a slow phase.'

'Should I even bother to laugh, or shall I go straight to pointing out that we both know that's a load of nonsense?'

'How dare you?' she snapped, lowering her voice because if she hadn't wanted undue attention from the paparazzi, then she most definitely didn't want the people at this gala to see her remotely ruffled. Designers were worse than fishwives when it came to spreading gossip.

'I won't bother answering that either. But whatever or *whoever* it is you're working through, work fast. My patience isn't infinite.'

Her insides shook at the ruthless delivery. 'Is that a threat?'

He held her in suspense, quicksilver eyes wandering over her face as he raised his glass to sip from it, as hers dropped to his strong Adam's apple, a flash of heat invading her pelvis. 'By all means. Take it as a threat if it helps focus you.'

Searching his face didn't show any signs that he didn't mean it.

Her agitation intensified. Even as she'd thrown down that gauntlet two days ago during the meeting with Teo and Cristobal, she hadn't quite let herself consider whether her professional demise was imminent.

Now she was forced to stare into the abyss of possibly losing the one solid thing in her life, the only thing that brought true meaning despite her having seemingly lost her way temporarily, and her heart constricted.

'You can't fire me. You've renewed my contract for another six months, not to mention we agreed on the six-week deadline.' Her voice was thankfully poised. Strong enough to paper over the continued quaking in her belly.

Except a sardonic smile still hovered over his sensual lips. Those eyes were still probing far too deep for her to celebrate her composure.

He shrugged. 'Suing me for whatever imagined breach you cobble up will only make one of us unhappy. And it won't be me.'

His unfailing conviction wasn't even needed.

She knew how powerful and influential he was. How

quickly and mercilessly he would bring that to bear on any grievance she might make made her insides churn with unease. Not to mention…she already knew from her own exacting standards that she needed to step up her game.

Hating him for having the last word, she pursed her lips as, with a droll look, he said, 'Now it's time to mingle and show off my spectacular creation. Let's pretend we're not at odds, hmm?'

He didn't wait for her to answer.

One hand in the small of her back propelled her into the nearest group, who turned as one to hail the Playboy Prince with obsequious welcome. Between one breath and the next, all traces of the hard-edged billionaire boss had evaporated.

In its place a breathtakingly charming Lothario who draped kisses on the backs of feminine hands, offered jaw-dropping largesse to panting acolytes, graciously accepted the reams of accolades when eyes turned to the gown Sabeen wore and delivered borderline-risqué jokes that had everyone falling over themselves with laughter.

Everyone except her. She stood rigidly throughout, ignoring speculation and envy from both men and women alike.

At the very first opportunity, she excused herself to the ladies' room.

Then proceeded to give herself the talking-to of her life. Right up until the murmured conversation outside her stall froze her frantic self-flagellation.

'Did you see his latest creation? It's unbelievably fabulous. God, I'm so jealous!'

'That you didn't create it, that you're not wearing it or that you're not the one he'll be tearing it off when the night is over?'

'Can I say *All of the above, but especially the last one*?'

Laughter rang out, then trailed away on lusty sighs.

'Maybe you shouldn't be so quick to want to step into her shoes. Remember what happened with Nathan Gray?'

Sabeen's breath hitched.

'God, don't remind me. I'd feel horrible for her, but seriously, she should've known better, shouldn't she?'

Ice clogging her veins, she clenched her fists and stayed put. Going out there now would turn the gossip mill into a veritable gossip bullet train. They'd speculate about what she'd heard and how it'd affected her. They'd pretend to soothe while examining her for battle wounds.

So she waited until they left.

Then she exited with her head held high. To endure another hour of weighted scrutiny until Teo deemed the torture over.

And as they headed to the car, he turned to her, his face rigid.

'To your earlier, unwanted point. As to whether my employee is in love with me or not, it's irrelevant. As long as she fulfils her role efficiently, she's welcome to feel whatever she feels whenever she feels it.'

She shook her head, her chest tightening absurdly. 'You really have no scruples, do you?'

A look passed over his face, uncharacteristically solemn. One she recalled only seeing once, at his brother's wedding when she'd approached him on the terrace. Before he'd summoned the lethal Lothario.

Before the kiss that still made her toes curl whenever she recalled it.

'I can't afford to,' he stated, that hard edge back in his tone.

'What does that mean?'

He frowned, then waved the driver away from the door. He saw her into the limo, lounging with one hand over the open door, the regal epitome of a man confident and content in his skin and with his world. Then he lobbed another twisted smile her way. 'Looking for another reason to flee back behind your wall of ice?' he asked, evading her question.

'I don't need to. Everything about you makes me glad I'm not foolish enough to find you remotely attractive.'

That grave look returned then was instantly replaced by

a sardonic laugh. Lower. Deeper. Setting off unwanted fireworks within erotic parts of her body. 'You were right to stay away from me, *belleza*. Because now I see why you fight so hard to keep that wall all the way up.'

Strains of ominous music started at the back of her brain. 'I don't know what the hell you're talking about,' she replied with more heat than she wanted, further revealing his infuriating effect on her.

His hand came up, slowly. So mesmerically, she wasn't sure whether to stare into his unbelievably sexy face or watch that hand drawing ever closer to her cheek. 'You're absolutely terrified, aren't you?' he murmured.

A wild dip in her belly blared danger as the tune's tempo ramped up. If this was a movie, she would've been screaming at the hapless victim to run. But this wasn't a movie, and she was absolutely no victim. Nevertheless, she would be foolish not to heed the shrieking warning for self-preservation.

She modulated her breathing long enough to ignore the elegant finger hovering tantalisingly over her skin and the traitorous part of her that yearned to feel his touch once more.

Staunchly gathering her scattering composure she raised a brow. 'Terrified? Of what, exactly? That a man who thinks he's a god and therefore spreads himself about waiting to be adored and greedily laps up attention is trying out his weak charms on me? Keep living in that illusion, *Prince* Teodor. Far be it for me to burst that giant ego of yours by reminding you that there are hundreds—perhaps even thousands—of your kind littered between here and the French Riviera.'

His face shut down. His hand dropped away. But those ferocious eyes remained locked on hers. And…heaven help her, she couldn't miss the glint of battle that lit his eyes for a furious instant, like a supernova ripping through a quiet galaxy, before he regained his composure.

She didn't need a PowerPoint presentation to know she'd

struck a very active nerve. And, yes, that in her haste to shore up her defences, she might have laid it on too thick.

And even when yet another sycophant huskily called his name and he ignored them and kept those molten silver eyes pinned on her, she knew deep in her bones that, in her haste, she may have won a small battle, but she'd succeeded in starting a war.

That the gleam in his eyes had been the equivalent of an alpha war cry she might need every inch of armour to live through.

Determined footsteps approached.

His name was trilled again. But still he watched her, a predator sizing up how best to deliver a kill strike.

'It's going to be truly delightful to watch that ice wall of yours melt, *cariña*. If for nothing else, for the chance to expose the hypocrisy that lies beneath the surface. *Buenos noches.*'

He shut the door and walked away, leaving that relentless quaking behind as he slipped so effortlessly into the crowd he commanded like everything else around him.

Sabeen told herself she was relieved. That it wasn't mild nausea from trying to decipher what exactly he'd meant chasing her through a restless night and a bleary-eyed morning, when a courier arrived to reclaim the gorgeous gown for its return to Milan.

And no, she was most definitely not dwelling on Teo when she stepped off the plane in Morocco twenty-four hours later for what she hoped would be the beginning of the most important six weeks of her life to salvage her career.

There was only one thing that should be claiming his attention: perfecting his next collection.

Ensuring his father had no choice but to admit his worth.

Nothing else should be permitted precedence. And yet once again, he'd let his most primal emotions vanquish him.

What the hell had he been thinking throwing down that

gauntlet to Sabeen? Especially when he knew that having done so, he would be unable to walk away.

He'd held himself rigid, refusing to look back. He'd gritted his teeth, forcing a charming smile as the socialite who'd helped herself to his left arm draped herself all over him. He'd stopped himself from snarling at her to remove herself. He had an image to project, after all.

An image that'd emboldened Sabeen into throwing around insults. He knew very well it was the reason he'd issued the challenge. She'd scored a bull's-eye, and he couldn't let her get away with it.

How many times has his mother called him *useless*? Taunted him with his unimportance, ridiculed him for not even being the spare? Of course, it was entirely his fault that he'd hitched a ride in her womb when she thought herself pregnant with only one child, only to discover his existence on the birthing table. And from then on it seemed his only worth to his mother had been as a punchline and a verbal punchbag.

His belly clenched as his thoughts swung from one parent to the other. The former king for a time had striven to accept the son he didn't really need, having two exceptional specimens ready to carry on his legacy. But gradually, as Teo had watched his father and learned to build his armour more solidly around himself, he realised the truth.

He would always be the extra spare part no one wanted.

But had he tried too hard to appear invincible? Arguing instead of adopting Valenti's stony silences that had seemed far more effective at catching his father's attention? Being the first to shrug off an insult or a slight?

Dios, did it even matter now?

Because whatever he'd tried he'd remained third-best, pitied and disregarded at every turn. Now he was vilified for revelling in the lifestyle he'd chosen for himself. For the joy and decadence and, yes, sometimes debauched pleasure he squeezed out of every second of life.

She dared to mock him.

Bitterness swelled in his gut. Hypocrites. Every last one of them would jump at the chance to experience a slice of his life even while clutching their metaphorical pearls.

'Your Majesty…is that the right way to address you?' the far too shrill voice had asked, jarring him out of his internal reviling.

'Not quite.'

Alarm had darted across her face at his curt tone, but she'd rallied admirably. 'Well, I was just saying I'm having a few friends over at my place for drinks. You should join us.' She'd leaned even closer, flaunting a shameless amount of cleavage, with copious amounts of eyelash batting should he be thick enough to miss the extras on offer. 'You can teach me the correct way to address you.'

Her after-parties were renowned for delivering the right amount of debauchery that would wipe his mind clean of every scrap of disgruntlement and bitterness he'd endured in the last twenty-four hours.

And yet his usual rousing rejoinder had raced to the tip of his tongue, only to wither and die an agitated death. Not even the promise of oblivion was enough to sway him.

Pasting on a smile that only had her eyelashes fluttering faster, he'd disentangled himself from her surprisingly tenacious hold.

'Not tonight, my sweet. You will need to find someone else to tutor you in the art of courting royalty.'

Before her disappointment had fully formed on her face, he'd turned away and was striding towards the door.

At least one thing had been successful. With that gown Sabeen had so stunningly modelled, his competitors were primed for another excellent trouncing. He'd ignored the envious glances cast his way, the sycophants eager to blow smoke up his behind.

He was running out of time to salvage at least one crumb

of the respect and acknowledgement due to him. His father couldn't leave this earth without acknowledging his youngest son's value. And Teo intended to earn that praise if it was the last thing he did.

But first, he had his and Valenti's birthday party to attend.

'To wild oats and mummy issues. The first brought us into the world, and the second has kept us on our toes and made us the men we are.'

Valenti, his twin by a handful of minutes, and Azar, their older brother, exchanged puzzled looks before eyeing him suspiciously.

'I'm way too young to be losing my marbles, but I could've sworn you made the same exact toast last year,' King Azar said with a wink.

Teo smirked. 'So?'

'So you can't even be bothered to find new words now?' Valenti drawled, the corner of his mouth almost curling up, but his expression was as militant and bored as it had been since Teo could remember. He was almost certain his twin had been born looking intensely dissatisfied with the world. Not even the old man's continued expressions of pride could ease Valenti's perennial bad mood. In some ways he envied his brother. Valenti had his walls so heavily fortified not even a sliver of emotion bled through. Whereas *he* lately seemed to be haemorrhaging bitterness and rancour.

He shook his head then realised his brothers were still staring at him with various degrees of baffled amusement. Digging deep for his suddenly elusive joie de vivre, he plastered a smile in place. 'Why mess with a good thing? If I recall, it was just right after my toast last year that you saw your future wife, no?'

Azar's eyebrows shot up. 'Are you telling me you're looking for a wife on your birthday?'

'Hell, no,' he denied, the very idea making an itch scramble beneath his skin.

The King of Cartana swirled his cognac, grinning—a habit he'd taken to far too often since his marriage—as he eyed Teo.

'If I remember correctly, that female journalist you dated a while back quoted you as saying that you'd rather pluck your eyeballs out and use them as golf balls than settle down. Am I right?'

He had indeed said that, but for some reason, having his words quoted back to him grated, the disgruntlement that resided far too close to the surface, dragging sharp talons over his skin.

So what if he was firmly against the trappings of matrimony? Could anyone blame him? The risk of inviting even a fraction of the acrimony he'd witnessed between his parents into his life left him stone-cold.

Azar was newly married and entrenched firmly in his honeymoon phase. Teo was happy for him and Eden and for their relationship with the beautiful son whose existence Azar hadn't known about until a year ago. His nephew was a cute little devil. His sister-in-law was equally decent. But that was where Teo intended his feelings on attachment or permanence to end.

'Since you seem out of sorts, allow me to make the toast this year. It is your and Valenti's birthday after all.'

Before Teo could protest, Azar raised his glass, the wicked glint in his eye making the hair on Teo's nape stand up on end. Slanting a glance sideways, he saw that Valenti was equally tense, as if he, too, suspected he wouldn't like what was coming.

'To immersing yourselves completely into the still and deep waters ahead, and emerging triumphant with the greatest prize of all.'

'What the hell kind of toast is—?'

'Are you drunk?' Teo cut across his twin, frowning at Valenti. But even as he made the demand, he was dismissing it. His brother rarely drank. Hell, the only time Teo had ever seen Azar lose control was in Arizona four years ago, when he'd lost his head over the woman who was now his wife and queen.

Azar merely smiled, leaving the toast hovering ominously in the air.

Teo diverted his gaze before his brother looked into his eyes and somehow made the disturbing discovery that his first thought at the mention of prizes had been Sabeen, the woman who'd invaded his mind and taken residence there for the past two weeks.

The woman who had seemingly fallen off the face of the earth, leaving him no choice but to order his security detail to hunt her down. The woman who'd ignored his every communication, forcing him to concede that for once in his life, having someone play hard to get was somehow shockingly effective. That the thrill of the hunt had fired him up unlike very few things had in the last decade. And yes, he intended for her to pay for that too. She was his little project. Until her lustre wore off. Then he'd have no choice but to pursue his next high. But first…

He made a show of looking around at his invited guests, picking out a blonde bombshell who eagerly sashayed over the moment he caught her eye.

'If you're done spewing nonsense, maybe we can get this party underway? I have a clutch of eager women to seduce.'

He was most definitely going to ignore the reproving frowns that comment produced. Even if he had no intention of acting on it.

Not a single soul could tell the Playboy Prince what to do. Especially on his birthday.

CHAPTER FOUR

SABEEN LOVED EVERY corner of her grandmother's little house in Essaouira. The thick bricks that kept the room cool in the oppressive heat, the specially painted mottled walls in warm ochre that were as earthy as the sand on her favourite beach.

The pops of colour in the backsplash in the kitchen and in the mosaic walls in the bathroom all soothed her spirits and grounded her in a peace she'd never found anywhere else.

And yet now, as she rose from the sea and trudged onto the beach, the deep reluctance to return home seeped into her bones. And even that shamed her. Her mouth twisted. It seemed she couldn't turn around without being confronted with the heavy weight of her own failure.

She'd hoped the early-evening swim would relieve the burden, but wringing the water out of her hair, she accepted that it'd done very little.

A glass of her favourite Moroccan tea. Maybe that would help.

She closed her eyes, raised her face to the dying sun and pleaded with whoever would listen for a flash of enlightenment.

The turmoil of New York was two weeks ago.

She had shut down all communication in the hope that being here, in the home that her grandmother had had built for herself, would be the key to unlocking her creativity. That perhaps guilt would erode her secret, yearning attraction for Teo. But each day he'd dominated her thoughts and despair seeped ever deeper into her marrow.

For two weeks she'd roamed the rooms in her grandmother's house, then the alleys she had played in as a child, and had tea with friends and acquaintances. Then she roamed even farther for longer, searching for inspiration in places she'd never visited.

Nothing.

Had her previous success merely been a flash in the pan, a self-delusion that she could make a life as a designer? Or was it really what she feared the most?

No. She wasn't going there. Nathan had been bad enough, but Teo Domene? No way was she accepting that a man was responsible for this.

Except, like clockwork, Teo's face flashed before her eyes.

She gritted her teeth tighter. *Enough.*

Deep breath in, letting the scents of spices and earth and dark coffee soothe her as she navigated the narrow alleys back to the house on the small hill. Sleep would be non-existent tonight, but come hell or high water, she would break this block on her creativity.

She was mentally cycling through two weeks' worth of discarded designs, her gaze lowered to familiar cobblestones as she neared home. That was why she didn't see the powerful motorcycle crouched outside the house or the equally powerful man leaning against the wall next to her front door until she nearly stumbled into him.

She reared back, heart leaping into her throat. 'What…? How…?' She sucked in a quick breath to gather her composure. She had sacrificed way too much of it around him. That nonsense ended tonight. 'What are you doing here? And how did you know where to find me?'

Teo slowly straightened, his massive shoulders blocking out the narrow strips of sunlight slanting into the alley.

'It wasn't without effort, I'll grant you that. You've given me quite the runaround.'

She frowned. 'I have no idea what you're talking about. And you haven't answered my question.'

She looked around, unsure whether she was seeking deliverance or some clue as to what he was doing here, in this sacred place that had welcomed her but was now beginning to feel like it housed another monumental task she needed to overcome.

His head slowly tilted, those sexy silver eyes narrowing on her. 'You have no idea why I'm here?'

She huffed, dismissing the sparks igniting in her belly, spreading outward to engulf her whole body. 'If I did, I wouldn't be asking, would I? We're not supposed to see each other for another four weeks.'

Irritation lit his eyes before his expression changed, his gaze dropping down her throat, her collarbones, over her breasts and down her body before rising again. And when it did, it was with a different expression, sizzling commencing within those quicksilver depths that billowed heat into her own body, making her supremely conscious that she was only wearing her bikini with a damp shirt over it, and an equally damp sarong tied around her hips.

For the longest time, they remained in that fog of awareness. Until she snapped herself out of it when his face hardened.

'It's time to make some changes.'

Heat evaporated, his stark words leaving her ice cold. 'Meaning?'

Every trace of indolence left him as he folded his arms across his chest. 'We made an agreement. Back in New York.' His eyes narrowed to fierce slits. 'That you have either forgotten already or are refusing to acknowledge it leaves me very little choice.'

Her heart constricted tighter this time out of raw fear. She couldn't...wouldn't lose the lifeline of her work. 'No choice about what?'

He sucked in a control-gathering breath. 'You really don't remember what you agreed to?'

He wasn't talking about the night of the gala.

She'd painstakingly, unwillingly relived every minute of that night. Right down to her own questionable behaviour. So he had to mean the meeting with Cristobal and those final few minutes while Teo was still talking, when she'd spaced out because of his infernal effect on her.

In the face of so much failure in the past two weeks, she was unwilling to admit one more, so she kept her jaw locked, boldly meeting his gaze as he probed her expression. Whatever he saw there made his own jaw tighten.

'Right, we're playing this game, are we?'

She remained silent.

'You agreed to send me the first batch of sketches for my approval, and you also agreed to keep in touch regarding your progress. Both of which you have failed to do.'

She knew she'd given herself away with the surprise that sparked through her when, one eyebrow arched, his mocking mingled with condemnation. Then with fierce disapproval.

Swallowing, she glanced at her door, wanting refuge now more than ever. Because it was clear that Teo had come here to put the final nail in her professional coffin.

'Enough of this. Invite me in.'

Her eyes snapped to him, her heart constricting tighter. She couldn't. Not here. Not into the space where she'd sworn to her grandmother that she would stay away from men like him. It would be the worst insult.

She shook her head. 'No.'

Seconds ticked by as the air thickened with tension. 'Sabeen...'

'I can't.' She closed her eyes, desperately hoping he'd missed the thread of panic in her voice. But even blocking him out, she felt the forceful surge of emotion from him. Her eyes flew open just as he stepped closer.

'You have someone in there? A lover?' The words seethed from him, like a dragon preparing to rain fury on her. 'Is that what's been occupying you? Rolling around in the sheets with your lover when you're supposed to be working?'

Shock erupted in stunned laughter, making his face darken even more. Until harsh reality sobered her up. 'Not everyone is like you.'

'I won't disagree with that,' he agreed with unabashed conceit. 'I'm one in a billion. But unlike you, sweetheart, I don't let work get in the way of my ambitions.' His gaze returned to the door, his glare incandescent. The more he stared at it, the more Sabeen wondered if he had X-ray vision. And the more she wondered if that fury was laced with…jealousy?

Her insides twisted, knotting with unnerving excitement which should've been positively nauseating and yet…wasn't.

Starting to ask herself what was wrong with her, she abandoned that too. She was absolutely exhausted with what she felt around this man. 'I…'

'You what? Despise me? I'm aware. But it's not as simple as that, is it? You hate yourself even more. I'll leave you to unload just why I affect you so much in your own time. For now a simple *yes* or *no* will suffice.'

She toyed with saying *yes*, just to get rid of him. But then she remembered his ultimatum. Realised that she hadn't held up the end of a bargain she couldn't fully recall. Because she'd been occupied with reliving her kiss with the Playboy Prince.

Shame simmered again, and she shook her head. 'No, Teo. I haven't been indulging in wall-to-wall orgasms when I should've been slaving over your precious collection.'

'*My* precious collection?' he echoed with soft deadliness. 'Is that detachment I hear? Because if it is, be brave and own up to it now, and I'll hand the whole thing over to Cristobal.'

She tensed, the very idea anathema to her.

He saw her reaction. Raised that eyebrow again. 'There it is. You're not so detached are you, *cariña*?'

She gritted her teeth. 'Don't call me that.'

His smirk, so sexy, so infuriating, made an appearance.

It seemed now the matter of her non-existent lover had been clarified, the Playboy Prince was making his long overdue appearance. But even as she was ogling it a little too eagerly, it hardened with purpose.

'Invite me in. Or don't. But bear in mind that if I leave here without some evidence of progress from you, our association ends immediately.'

The sense of circling crows coming home to roost pressed down hard on her. She had a decent nest-egg from her modelling days plus the small inheritance her grandmother had left her. But she couldn't live off that for ever. And if Teo Domene, the king of haute couture, fired her and after that scandal with Nathan, she could kiss any chance of finding a job in the fashion industry goodbye.

She was poised on that precipice again, staring into the abyss.

Could she bring herself to appeal to his better angels?

She almost snorted under her breath. This man was no angel. Even the devil would fear him. But she couldn't keep him waiting any longer.

She opened her mouth, unsure what she was about to say.

Her hand, moving towards the door handle, made up her mind.

Unlocking it, she pushed it open, stepping into the cool, welcoming interior. Goose bumps covered her skin, and her heart continued to rap urgently against her ribs at the thought of inviting him into her grandmother's precious home. Sacred ground.

This was professional, she reassured herself. Nothing was going to happen. Well, nothing except the possible demise of her career.

Dropping her beach-bag onto the cushioned bench slotted into the hallway alcove, she turned, just as Teo stepped into her home.

The sight of him there felt all wrong…but also incredibly profound.

In no way did she want to think that this was a momentous occasion, but watching him turn, slowly nudging the door closed, she couldn't stop the way her lungs panted.

He faced her and froze, his eyes narrowing again. But this time they weren't filled with mockery or censure, they were filled with...concern.

Lunging forward, he grabbed her arm as she swayed, a frown pleating his forehead. 'Do you really need me to state that I've never forced myself on a woman?' His voice was thick with shock.

She shook her head, a pulse of anxiety pushing her to reassure him. 'Of course not.'

A layer of tension left him. 'Then, what is this?'

'There's never been a man inside these walls.' *Dear heaven.* Did she really say that aloud? His frown reversing into surprise told her she had.

She clenched her jaw tight as if it could reclaim the words. He released her, stepping back to take a good look around.

Surprisingly, his expression grew neutral and then slid into shades of appreciation as he took in the terracotta walls, the pops of colour she loved so, the white timber table where she'd spent many meals with her mother and grandmother. The rugs painstakingly sourced from merchants across Morocco, a pastime her grandmother had dearly loved to indulge in when she could afford it.

And then the Afghan knitted blanket tossed over the well-used armchair before the fireplace. Sadness and fondness moved through her as she remembered sitting at her grandmother's knee, listening to her stories as that blanket was knitted over many nights.

She wasn't going to think about her what her grandmother would've thought of Teo right now. Having him here, within the walls of the place her *jida* had poured blood, sweat and tears into making a home for her daughter and granddaughter after her own life had been fractured, felt like a betrayal.

But as long as she didn't put any of these traitorous thoughts and feelings concerning Teo into action, surely it was fine? The quicker she got this unscheduled meeting out of the way, the quicker he would leave. 'How did you find me?' she asked again.

He faced her after several more seconds taking in her home. 'Valenti can work miracles when he's incentivised.'

If Azar Domene, King of Cartana and Teo's older brother, was intimidatingly formidable, his twin was icily terrifying.

They'd barely exchanged a handful of words, but Sabeen had felt during each interaction that the other man could read her every secret. Perhaps, she mused a little anxiously, it was a trademark Domene trait. And as a highly sought-after security expert, she wasn't surprised Valenti Domene had been the one to find her.

She cleared her throat and took the bull by the horns. 'You're right, I don't recall the finer terms of our agreement. I wasn't expecting to see you for another four weeks.'

His eyes openly mocked her. 'You mean you weren't paying attention because you were preoccupied? With what, exactly?'

She fought the heat that rose, turning away so he wouldn't read her expression. He trailed after her as she went into the kitchen, filled the kettle and lit the stove. Then with nothing else to do, she faced him. 'Yes. And it doesn't matter.'

His eyes glinted for a moment then he leaned against the kitchen wall, a picture of masculinity that rudely captured her attention, refusing to let go.

'You agreed to keep me updated with your work, checking in at least once every two weeks. You missed the first check-in four days ago. Cristobal didn't.'

He'd dropped her rival's name just to rile her, and predictably, her belly clenched. But she wasn't going to waste time asking about her competitor. Not when she had pathetically little to show for herself.

Her gaze slid to the dining table where she'd left the remnants of her attempts about a week ago. He tracked her glance, straightening.

'No.'

'Why not?' he fired back.

'It's…not ready yet.'

'Evidently not, or you would be in a much better mood. But we are where we are. We have no choice.' The delivery was soft but just as deadly as it'd been at her door. The Playboy Prince had receded again, and the consummate creative genius was firmly in place. 'You will show them to me.'

She opened her mouth to refuse just as the kettle whistled, making her jump. 'Tea?'

He watched her for a few beats then shrugged. 'I'm not going anywhere. Go ahead and make your tea.'

Her hands shook through the process, but she made it, carried it over to the living room coffee table and set it down. 'Help yourself. I need to go and shower—'

He was shaking his head. 'You're stalling. We're going to get to the bottom of this. Now.'

'Because you've got other places to be?' she bit back, stung because he'd accurately guessed she was desperate for a breather.

He raised an eyebrow. 'What if I don't? Are you inviting me to stay?'

'No.' That came out much harsher than she'd intended.

His face tightened. 'Then, let's get on with it, by all means.'

To buy herself more time, she poured tea into two glass cups and pointedly held one out to him. 'As much as I don't want you here, my grandmother taught me to be courteous. Tea?'

The corner of his mouth twitching, he accepted it, his fingers grazing hers before he raised it to his lips and took a healthy sip. Then, his gaze still on her, he took another drink and emptied the glass.

'Now your obligations as a good granddaughter have been fulfilled.'

She sipped hers much more slowly but inevitably the small glass was soon finished and she had no choice but to face the music.

Breath held, she walked over to the dining table, supremely conscious of his intense presence. She'd thrown a light table-cloth over her drawings a week ago, more in despair than to protect anything she'd done. Grabbing one corner of it, she drew it away.

She watched him saunter to the other side of the table, his gaze searching hers for a handful of seconds before they dropped.

Sabeen couldn't breathe, couldn't even look as he reached for the first one. Then the second. Coolly examined each sketch. When he was done, he flattened his hands on the table.

'Do you need me to say it?' he murmured.

She swallowed the boulder in her throat and still couldn't speak.

'Sabeen,' he pressed firmly.

'Say it,' she implored hoarsely. 'If you're going to fire me, just do it.'

A ripple went through his jaw. 'I wish I could say Cristobal was faring any better than you,' he said.

Absurdly that didn't make her feel better. 'So that's it? We're both out?'

For the longest time he didn't speak. He examined the sketches even more thoroughly the second time, flinging several onto the floor. Leaving only a dismal handful. Only then did he look up. 'These ones are salvageable. Barely.'

'And?'

His masculine hands returned to the table, now resting on her sketches. The sight of them so close to her work flipped her belly.

'And this collection is too important to leave to your whims and feelings,' he said with a gravity she'd heard in his voice in New York, exposing the startling truth that this wasn't just a new season's fervency. For whatever reason, *this* collection held some kind of reverent importance to Teo. She was busy searching his face for a clue when he continued. 'I can fire you right now, as you seem to be craving, or I can stay and help. But you're going to have to ask for it.'

'Don't do me any special favours,' she bit out, unable to help herself.

He exhaled roughly. 'Sabeen, I have just come from two extremely trying days with Cristobal. Do not push me.'

That surprised her. And he saw.

'You continue to think the worst of me even while you're drowning and I have a lifeboat.'

She held back the words that would damn her, probably for ever. Swallowing her pride was a huge effort, but what choice did she have if she didn't want to fail?

Besides, there was a reason she'd wanted to work for Teo Domene. The king of haute couture was matchless in talent. She'd been thrilled and stunned when he'd picked her as a protégé, then a temporary replacement when Cristobal went on his sabbatical. Having it all fall apart, admitting failure and inviting more scandalous whispers especially after Nathan, wasn't an option.

Sensing her internal battle, he leaned over the table, bringing his indomitable will to bear on her. 'Ask me. Ask for help.'

'And you'll give it?' *Without strings?*

Something twisted in his face, gone too soon for her to decode it. 'It's my name. My line. Failure may be acceptable to you. It isn't for me. Ask for it.'

Her mouth dried, a deep tremor rising from her belly. 'Help me.'

If she'd expected Teo to immediately produce a tablet and begin salvaging her mediocre offerings, she was in for disappointment.

He stepped away from the table, strode over to the coffee

table and poured two more cups of tea. Clearly her surprise showed because he sent her a droll look.

'The hard task-mastering will start soon enough, don't worry,' he drawled. Then his gaze trailed leisurely over her. 'You still want to shower?'

Why that conjured heated images of their bodies sliding together like that night on the terrace, she refused to contemplate. 'Yes.'

He nodded, drawing out his phone. 'Have you had dinner?'

She blinked then warily said, 'No.'

'Neither have I. Let's do something about that,' he said then after a moment speared her with a hard look. 'Time's wasting, Sabeen. I don't work well on an empty stomach.'

A little dazed, she hurried down the short hallway to her bedroom. Shutting the door behind her she blinked at the tea in her hand, set it down untouched on her dresser and went to her bathroom. A quick rinsing off while she ruthlessly stemmed the tide of uneasy excitement churning inside her. And because she absolutely wasn't going to deem this anything but another work meeting, she chose a simple knee-length orange-striped white dress and matching orange heeled slippers with gold buckles, adding hoop gold earrings before securing her almost dried hair in a firmer knot.

A quick spritz of her favourite oud scent—all without meeting her eyes in the mirror—and she was exiting her room.

Teo rose from the sofa at her entrance, and she was thankful he hadn't sat in her grandmother's chair. His gaze trailed over her before dropping to his phone. 'My assistant has sent me a list of restaurants, but you'll probably have a better idea.'

'Can I see the list?'

He walked over and displayed the screen. Completely unaware, she desperately hoped, of what his scent did to her. *Focus!*

She dismissed the first one. 'The food doesn't live up to the overpriced hype. Same for the second.' She pointed to the fourth one on the list. 'That one is run by a mother and daughter. It's small and out of the way, but the food is excellent. And you don't need to call ahead.'

The hint of his sardonic smile reminded her that that wouldn't have mattered. Even in her little corner of the world, men like Teo would command red carpet treatment even without trying.

Putting his phone away, he gestured silently at the door. 'Shall we?'

Senses still jumping wildly all over the place, she headed towards the front door. He stepped out as she locked up.

'Do you ride?'

Her breath caught. 'What?'

'There are very few places I can go these days with total freedom. I couldn't resist the chance to indulge that freedom. Such as it is.'

Movement beyond his mile-wide shoulders clued her into what that last statement meant. Two bodyguards hovered twenty feet away, alert and quietly menacing. Beyond them, a dark, armoured SUV too wide to fit into the narrow alley, idled with more bodyguards spaced out near it.

Of course he hadn't come completely alone. He was third in line to a powerful Mediterranean throne after his twin brother and King Azar's newly discovered son, Max. And while he could probably handle his own safety, protocol dictated he receive twenty-four-hour protection.

'Which do you prefer?'

'What?'

Without taking his eyes from her, he pointed to the powerful Ducati.

She'd never ridden one. The thought of her first time being with Teo Domene in singeing proximity had her shaking her head before the shiver, stupidly commonplace now, had rushed down from her head to her toes.

'Not that, thanks.'

Again, he hid whatever sentiment he felt about her adamant refusal well, easily pivoting towards the larger vehicle.

In silence they walked to the end of the alley, where she discovered another SUV behind the first. Sabeen cringed at the thought of the attention this would attract.

'Something wrong?'

'Besides you giving my neighbours endless hours of gossip fodder?'

Expecting a mocking quip, she was surprised when his jaw tightened. 'You should've listened better to the agreements you made then, shouldn't you?'

She deserved that, but it still stung.

The handful of miles to the restaurant passed too quickly.

The owner, Farah, looked up from an animated conversation when they entered, her wide smile growing wider as she threw out her arms. 'Sabeen! Good to see you. And you brought me a handsome guest too.'

That shameful sting of jealously disarmed her, but Sabeen kept a smile on her face as Teo smiled in greeting.

Of course they were given the best seat in the house, and the most expensive wine was produced in record time before Farah retreated with a promise to make every dish herself.

She was batting away the stings when Teo's gaze pierced her.

'Why here? What's the significance of coming to Essaouira to work? And think before you say it's none of my business. Knowing where your head's at is as important as wherever you go to tap into your creativity.'

She knew that. It was why she'd come here, after all. So why was it so hard to admit that to him?

Because it's personal. And personal is dangerous.

And yet she found herself replying. 'Because this place is more than just a workspace. It's home. My safe place.' A part of her very being. The admission was thick with emotions she couldn't readily contain.

Again, expecting some glib comeback, she was stunned when he nodded with gravity. 'Go on.'

Her eyes widened. He wanted more? 'It feels like every important point in my life is rooted here.' It was where she'd defied her grandmother—while secretly being spurred on by her mother—to accept the modelling scout's invitation to audition for her first gig. It was where she'd celebrated after her first, second and third appearances on the cover of *Vogue*. Where she'd sought refuge in grief, yearning for closeness after her grandmother had passed away.

And it was where she'd come to heal after Nathan—

Nope. Not him. Not here.

She was saved from further rumination about her ex when their food arrived. Fragrant couscous with a thick chickpea sauce made her mouth water. Fish *chermoula*, *kefta* tagine and a heavenly chicken pie dish made with thin pastry and saffron. And *zaalouk*, a platter of chips with an aubergine purée and hummus.

Sabeen was forced to shake her head firmly when Farah tried to foist more dishes on them. At this rate, they'd only manage to eat a fraction.

Teo tucked into it with gusto, his groans of appreciation making Farah beam. And Sabeen squirm in her seat.

Surprisingly, a companionable near silence passed, Teo occasionally asking the origins of a dish. But she couldn't let her guard down.

When their meal was cleared, she ordered gunpowder and mint tea. He ordered the thick Moroccan coffee.

Then he sat back, all bridled power and intense focus. She knew her brief reprieve was over when he tossed back the first tiny cup of coffee.

'For this to work, we need a few rules in place. We will work for as long on this as I deem fit. And you will do it all without attitude. Agreed?'

His domineering, boundless confidence should've been infuriating, but Sabeen couldn't forget that it was the reason he was who he was. Never mind the royal blood running through his veins. He had reached the pinnacle of his profession by honing his passion into creating countless masterpieces, some of which hung in museums across the world. A chance to refine her own design skills under his tutelage was why she'd originally applied to be part of his team.

And why, since she'd asked for his help, she needed to swallow her pride now. 'Okay.'

His eyebrow rose. 'Just *okay*?'

She shrugged. 'Would you rather I nitpicked the issue with you just for the sake of it?'

'No. But feel free to bring up any opinions you feel strongly about.'

'Don't worry about that. It may be your line, but when I succeed, it will be my name on the collection as well, no?'

He reached for the coffee-pot, poured himself another cup and tossed it back eyeing her the whole time. 'What you created for Eden for the wedding and the coronation was exquisite. What has happened between then and now?'

Her insides clenched hard. Yes, she'd lost her grandmother and that'd been devastating, and for a brief few days she'd had her mother around for comfort before she'd returned to the other side of the world.

But Sabeen couldn't honestly lay all her problems at grief's door. Especially not when her emotional compass kept pointing to one man…one issue.

Playboys and everything about them spelled disaster for her and yet she couldn't seem to distance herself from this one in particular. She shook her head. 'Why does it matter?'

His nostrils flared with a hint of displeasure. 'Because until you confront what it is that's standing in your way, you'll only be courting further roadblocks.'

Irritation and slivers of panic whistled through her. 'I didn't realise this was a therapy session. Are you saying that your every collection has been born out of carefree abandon?' she challenged purely, she knew, out of self-preservation.

Shadows drifted across his face before he effectively banished them. 'No. But I'm a master at compartmentalising. Clearly you are not.'

It wasn't an insult. It was a fact confidently stated, infuriatingly accurate. Because for as long as she could remember, her every emotion had bled into a well of sensation that she'd tried hard to suppress over the years. Until recently she was sure she'd succeeded.

Now it felt like all those bottled-up emotions were threatening to explode. 'Does missing a loved one count?' she asked then cringed a little at throwing her beloved grandmother up as a shield to hide behind. She could already feel *Jida*'s disapproving glare.

'Who?' It came with that sharp edge she'd heard a few times now.

'My grandmother.'

He watched her closely for several seconds, his gleaming gaze telling her he knew she was hiding more. Surprisingly, the edge softened. She exhaled with gratitude and relief.

'When we get back, you will tell me what about your grandmother you feel when you look at the sketches.'

Another knot inside eased but didn't fully disappear because she knew it wasn't as simple as that. There were other layers to her problem. Nothing came easily, not like it had for the Playboy Prince.

The Playboy Prince who's currently helping you.

She ignored the flip in her chest and examined him closer, attempting to see beneath the surface.

The cynical glint in his eyes intensified. 'What's on your mind?'

'Someone else would've fired me by now. So...'

'You believe there's an ulterior motive?'

She bit the inside of her cheek. Held her silence. But the truth was a writhing current between them.

After a tense beat he set down his cup with a sharp clip. 'My reasons are my own.'

'That's not—'

'Fair?' he bit out when she trailed off, then more shadows chased across his hauntingly captivating face. 'Perhaps I'm stubborn enough to chase after an illusion. I won't be dictated to over my ultimate goals. Or maybe I see something I'm not willing to let go. Yet. Including you.'

Her inner turmoil escalated, her breath whooping out softly. With relief? With gratitude? With unwarranted excitement? With deep curiosity, because she wondered if that had been aimed at something besides his next collection? But even if she'd been inclined to give in to curiosity, the subtle but imperious gesture to one of his bodyguards signalled the end of their meal.

A beaming Farah pleaded for them to return soon as she pocketed an astronomical tip. And when the older woman winked broadly and whispered in Arabic for Sabeen to *hang on to this one*, she smiled her way through the heat engulfing her whole body, her feet hurrying to the waiting car.

She was aware of Teo's penetrating gaze on the ride back.

'I would've thought you'd hurry to correct her.' His voice was desert-dry.

Surprise snapped her head in his direction. 'You speak Arabic?'

'Enough not to be hoodwinked by market vendors.'

She felt her eyes widen further. 'Market vendors?'

'You'd be surprised what inspiration can be found in the colourful alleys of Marrakesh.'

She knew that. Of course she did.

She'd frequently lost herself in the fabric stalls of Jemaa el-Fnaa market and the smaller, out-of-the-way ones as a young girl dreaming of a life in fashion design. It was at one of these very stalls that she'd been talent-spotted.

Somehow, though, she hadn't pictured Teo in that setting. It made him too familiar. Too accessible. She didn't want that because…

Aware of his keen stare she struggled to retain her composure. 'There was no point responding to Farah. She's an incurable romantic. She'll see what she wants to see.'

His mouth twisted again, eyes staying on her. 'Perhaps you shouldn't be so quick to dismiss that illusion.'

'Meaning?'

'If that is what she wants to see, create it for her.' A handful of words, tossed out with bold challenge.

Her breath caught. Possibilities rose sluggishly from an ashen landscape. Hazy then slowly taking form. The earthy, vibrant colours Farah loved, the loud jewellery that announced her arrival long before she appeared, like a percussive soundtrack to her existence.

For the rest of the journey and after they'd returned to her house, Sabeen scrambled to gather drips of inspiration. After examining her sketches one more time, he turned and leaned against the dining table.

'Tell me about your grandmother,' he prompted.

Sabeen swallowed. Shook her head. 'Not tonight.' The reply held faint pleading. One she hoped he'd miss or, if not, heed.

He stunned her by nodding and heading to the door.

'You're leaving?'

'Get a good night's sleep. Your taskmaster will return early. And Sabeen?'

Her belly performed yet another unhinged flip. The way he said her name was positively sinful. 'Hmm?'

'Be warned. I give very little unearned latitude.'

He waited until she nodded. Accepted his caveat.

Then she trailed after him, telling herself she was merely

being polite. Walking a guest to the door. The disarming truth was that she wasn't entirely ready to see the back of him.

With a handful of words, he'd awoken something inside her tonight. She'd expected the pushy prince and received the enigmatic man who'd unsettled her with his peculiar questions and observations. A mere three hours in his company, and he'd muddied the waters of her conviction, rearranging himself just so he wouldn't slot so comfortably into the pigeonhole she'd created for him.

As she'd accused him of doing to her in New York?

She leaned against the doorway, still unable to definitively dismiss him as he crossed the narrow street, swung one leg over the powerful bike and straddled it.

He didn't glance her way, but a live-wire awareness throbbed between them. As much as she hated herself for this admission too, Sabeen couldn't help but appreciate the sexy figure he cut astride his motorbike. A jolt of disappointment went through her for not accepting his invitation earlier but…

No. Hell, no. What the hell was wrong with her?

Stepping back abruptly, she grabbed the door, ready to shut it, just as his head swung her way, his gaze snagging her.

'Buenos noches.'

'Goodnight,' she murmured.

She stood there, her feet refusing the order to turn around as he gunned his engine and roared out of the alley.

CHAPTER FIVE

TEO PULLED UP at the villa he'd rented seven miles away from Sabeen's house.

For endless moments, he remained in the saddle, earning himself puzzled looks from his security detail.

He'd already made them nervous enough when the motorbike had been delivered. They had no doubt reported him to Valenti, their boss. Teo would bet a hefty slice of his fortune that his twin would text him with strident views about his recklessness before morning.

That was Valenti's clinical way of coping. Teo didn't begrudge him that. But neither could he live his life by his twin's strait-laced standards.

Especially when he knew his father would sooner shuffle off his mortal coil than show his own son an ounce of regard.

Acid churned in his gut at the recollection of his father's words at the wedding. He vehemently suppressed it, begrudgingly glancing up at the property his assistant had secured for him. It was beautiful, of course, as befitting a man of his status. The mellow stone blended well with the arched Moorish windows and the yellow light spilling from within.

The interior was equally welcoming.

Except he didn't want to be here, *seven miles away*. He gritted his teeth as visions of another room, and the person occupying it, filled his head.

Dios mio. He was going out of his mind.

Every reason he'd conjured up for pursuing this thing with Sabeen disarmed and disturbed him.

You should cut your losses. Let it go and move on.

But…instinct insisted that unlocking her talent would be vital to his goals. Plus, hadn't he vowed to make her regret those assumptions about him? Wasn't that why he'd jumped straight into the hunt when she'd finally been located?

His skin tingled with anticipation. With the thrill of killing two birds with one stone. Taking a dire situation and turning it around so he wouldn't be deemed so…superfluous? So worthless to both his father and Sabeen.

'Your Highness?'

'What?' he snarled.

His head bodyguard took a step back.

Teo sighed. 'What is it?' He tried modulating his voice. It didn't work. That hollow sensation stalking through him only intensified. Cartana was a mere two and half hours away by air. He could be there before midnight. He could confront the old man, demand to know why it was so easy to be discarded. Then maybe he might be free of this…this burr in his side he refused to admit was corroding something inside him.

Except, could he live with causing his father's condition to worsen? Some bored deity was toying with him, because every time Teo and his brothers believed their father was on a definite road to recovery, he would suffer a setback. Keep them dancing on their toes.

Would he even hold on long enough for what Teo had planned?

'We're just checking…if everything's okay?'

Teo glanced past the guard to the stunning, *empty* house. And just because he could, he smirked at himself for the frivolous notion. 'No, it's not. Contact my staff. Tell them to find me another villa. Closer.'

The man stared at him, wary and befuddled. 'Closer…to what?'

He jerked off the bike, tossing his helmet at the guard who, to his credit, expertly caught it. Teo would endorse Valenti giving him a raise.

He and his crew had only given him minimal hassle. Not so much the four previous teams, who seemed to object to Teo's occasional penchant for going AWOL without warning. Advising Valenti that he needed to hire men who could keep up with him hadn't gone down well. But his twin had eventually heeded that advice.

'Your Highness?'

Gritting his teeth at the reminder of the royal blood running through his veins, he stalked to the front door. What had the man asked? Right, about the relocation...

'Closer to her!'

His mood wasn't much improved when he woke up five hours later. A run on the beach followed by a swim in the chilly North Atlantic invigorated him enough. But the tightness in his chest as he knocked on Sabeen's door thirty minutes later unsettled him anew.

She opened the door, wearing a simple short-sleeved white linen top and a pair of orange shorts meant to keep her cool in the hot temperatures. Except it left her miles-long legs on sinful display. The deep *V* hinted at mouth-watering cleavage, visible turquoise straps hinting at the bikini beneath it. Which of course conjured up images he couldn't easily banish from his mind. Of her in his arms, her sublime taste in his mouth.

He really should've spent twenty-four hours in Monaco. Still could. Except the idea left a sour taste in his mouth, enough to draw a grimace.

Seeing it, she tensed, and her face, not entirely beaming in welcome but composed enough, turned a touch chilly.

'*Buenos dias*,' he greeted her, a little rougher than planned. 'Sleep well?'

'Yes. But maybe I should be asking you that?' Lushly lashed

eyes swept over him, and every inch they travelled left a trail of heat he wanted to growl at.

The urge to rile her up struck hard. And yes, he wished for someone to be in the same irate mood he was in. But *Dios*, even he wasn't that childish. 'Nothing another coffee wouldn't fix.'

She studied him for another few seconds, then stepping back, pivoted on the balls of her feet. Sure enough, that drew his attention like a shark to prey, and heaven help him, the sight of her bare legs and feet did something to him. Every inch of her taunted and tempted.

Monaco. Next stop. As soon as he was done here.

But maybe not for sex. It would please him greatly to spend a night at his favourite Monte Carlo gambling table, taunting some pompous CEO into losing a few million or his most prized supercar. Speeding up and down the hills of the French countryside with a newly won sports car always cheered him up.

He shut the door behind him then paused when that hollow sensation in his middle instantly lessened. Valenti would tell him he was losing his mind. Teo wouldn't fight that assertion.

By the time he prowled down the hallway into the living room, she was returning from the kitchen, a mug of coffee in hand.

'Black, no sugar?' she asked, her gaze stalling on the rim of the cup before rising to his.

He shouldn't have felt a sliver of satisfaction that she knew how he took his coffee, and yet there he was, basking in it.

He took it, nodding his thanks. Then tensed at the disarray on the dining table. 'You started without me?' Teo abstractly registered that he generally experienced three settings with her. Vexation. Taunting. Temptation. None of them reaped benefits satisfying enough to please him. The unwelcome truth was that Sabeen unbalanced him in a way he didn't enjoy. And it was a failing he needed to work out of his system.

'You were supposed to get a good night's sleep so you can start with a clear head.'

She stiffened then moved away from him to the table. 'I never sleep past dawn. I didn't see the benefit of just idling in bed when I could be sketching.'

He drained his cup just for something to do besides picturing her in bed. 'There's a reason delayed gratification produces indescribable benefits.'

The surge of heat in her cheeks pleased him far too much. 'You want me to bottle everything up until I'm at the point of explosion?' she tossed out, then groaned softly under her breath. 'I won't be reduced to making sexual innuendos as part of this process.'

Santo cielo, neither could he. Not if he wanted to keep his sanity.

'Then, let me put it simply. You need to dig deeper. Go bolder.' When she blinked her incredible eyes at him, he pushed on. 'Tell me what you were feeling when you created Eden's wedding gown.'

'Mainly? Deep irritation with you because you couldn't stand your brother's anxiety about his wedding so you decided to share your ill temper with everyone else!'

True, but there'd been the underlying reason, the perennial one that demanded perfection so he couldn't be seen as flawed. Only valuable. 'Be that as it may, what you created was far from hideous. It most definitely wasn't angry. So?'

'Friendship?'

'Is that a question?'

She huffed. 'Fine. Friendship. She was…*is* beautiful and kind, and after what she'd been through, she deserved something memorable and gorgeous. Something unique.'

He nodded, picked up one sketch to examine it. 'Good. Now, forget Eden. Pick someone else equally important to you. Find something that has made an equal impact on you. Put your own unique take on it.'

* * *

Sabeen watched him, a little intimidated by how easily he cut through obstacles. By the electrifying presence he conjured up just by *being*. 'Is that what you do?'

The chameleon morphed again, an eerie mixture of resolve and bleakness washing over his face. He didn't disguise it. Hell, he almost exulted in her seeing it. Openly warning her she'd fail if she attempted to define him. 'No, *cariña*. My demons feed me all the inspiration I need,' he drawled without a hint of humour or cynicism.

He meant every word of that.

Shock shortened her breath. His gaze dropped to her mouth, instantly spinning awareness tighter, more urgently around them.

If Farah was sunshine and smiles, embracing love and light with a loud, full-throated voice, Teo was turning out to be multilayered, the thickest of which was the Playboy Prince persona he'd fully mastered. The one which she needed to guard herself against. Because while she understood now that he was deadly on all fronts, that was the one she knew would be most potent. She'd seen him wield it in a three-minute clinch that still sent shockwaves through her every time she thought about it.

But…that didn't mean she couldn't use whichever persona he presented as fuel. Explore it. Her senses jumped in that familiar and oh-so-welcome way it did when she was on the right path. It wasn't as potent as the euphoria of creating her very first collection, but it was a start. And she would cling to it with everything she—

'Tell me what's going on in that clever brain,' he invited silkily.

She resisted excited flutters at his compliment. 'Nuance. Layers. Blinding light and deep shadow.'

Several beats of silence, when he leaned closer, not quite invasive, but near enough to make her painfully aware of every inch of his perfect face. 'And what brought that on?' he asked, even silkier, his eyes drilling holes in her.

You. She bit her tongue before that fell out. It would stroke his already over-inflated ego. And worse, she would reveal her unsettled feelings about him.

'I've learned it's best to just invite the muse to make herself comfortable, not to question her too much in case...' Silly superstition made her bite her tongue again.

His brows rose, the beginnings of humour lighting his silver eyes. 'Surely you're not afraid of your own muse?'

'We're not all equipped with the power to command them at will.'

'No, you're not,' he tossed out with pure conceit.

He stepped away, and she immediately wished him back in her space, filling her senses with his intoxicating scent. Because when he was doing that, she didn't have to think about the fragile transition of transferring her thoughts and elusive vision into reality.

He retrieved the sleek tablet he'd brought with him. Then, striding over to the sofa, he folded his towering figure into the sofa. Again, he'd avoided her grandmother's chair. Again, Sabeen was secretly grateful. And a little disarmed at his unconscious sensitivity.

'Well? What are you waiting for?' he taunted without looking up from his screen.

Curbing the childish urge to roll her eyes, she pulled out a dining room chair, and for the first time in a long time, pure anticipation and adrenaline poured through her veins as she picked up her sketch-pad.

Her first inkling of time passing was when his shadow fell over her. Even then, her pencil raced over the sheet. She felt his fierce intensity. Tapped into it shamelessly with breath held. Almost there.

Almost...

She startled when his hand dropped over hers, stilling her fingers.

'Time for a break,' he said firmly.

'No! I just… Wait, what are you doing?'

The pencil was plucked from her fingers and tossed onto the table. Only then did she notice the cramp in her hand, the bites of discomfort in her back, hip joints and neck.

Redirecting her gaze, she winced as a spasm twitched in her shoulder. That earned her a raised brow.

'It's been four hours. It's time for lunch.'

Her gaze darted to the window. The shadows cast by light through the windows had shifted significantly.

The scent of food then caught her attention. 'You ordered food?'

'If Farah's influence is reaping results for you, I'm not going to hold back from it. My security picked up our order ten minutes ago. Time to eat,' he insisted, his gaze raking her face for several seconds before shifting to the sketches.

Sabeen held her breath, her senses jumping as she waited for his verdict. He withheld it. Turning, he went over to the wicker basket covered with a folded chequered tablecloth, picked it up and headed for the small, walled courtyard outside the living room.

Throttling her disquiet, she followed, her surprise increasing when she saw the set table, complete with a small carafe of wine. He'd done all this while she'd been lost in her work.

It's merely for expediency.

She stressed that to herself repeatedly as he pulled out a chair, saw her seated before taking his own and dished out another lavish meal.

Sabeen couldn't fault the food, her appetite voracious as she ate.

But her gaze repeatedly strayed from Teo to the sketches she could see from where she sat.

Eventually, her frustration outed in a pent-up breath. 'Are you going to keep me in suspense?'

Like last night, he took his time to answer, sipping his coffee. 'Did you not agree on delayed gratification being a good thing?'

'No. I didn't,' she said through clenched teeth. 'Do you get off on riling me up?' she blurted before she thought better of it.

'*Get off*? Not entirely. But it makes a difference from that tiresome cloak of equanimity.'

So you like your women spirited?

She thanked heaven the question remained locked tight inside her. Why did she care how Teo liked his women?

'So *order through chaos* is your mantra? Or are you more of the pressure-makes-diamonds school of thought?'

His eyes glinted. 'Tell me what you're feeling right now.'

She suspected he wanted another unbalanced admission. She wanted to scream because right in this moment, he held all the answers.

'Like I have more to uncover.' The state of panic and inadequacy had lessened but not dissipated. And her heart jumped at the thought of reclaiming her sketch-pad.

'Deeper?' he prompted.

Her heart flipped. For some absurd reason, her gaze dropped to his mouth. It wasn't twisting with sardonicism. Or twitching with cruel mockery. It would always be intensely sensual, and she admitted she couldn't look at it without remembering that torrid kiss.

But right now it was lightly pursed. Contemplative. *Expectant.*

'Yes.'

'*Muy bien*,' he said then pushed a mouth-watering plate of honey-drizzled almond tarts towards her. 'First, finish your dessert.'

Just to stop herself from growling her frustration at him and because they were simply divine, Sabeen ate the dessert.

* * *

'Two? Are you kidding me?'

Fury sizzled over her skin. Consternation too.

She'd just watched him burn all but two of the sketches she'd painstakingly spent the whole day working on. That urge to scream spiked again.

She swallowed it down. How had she thought he was anything but what she'd labelled him? He'd been toying with her emotions all along.

Just like…

She speared her fingers through her hair, more to dislodge thoughts of Nathan than anything else, but there was disappointment as well.

'Are you going to say something or just sit there?' she threw at him.

He studied her, arms folded across his chest as he perched with one hip propped against the dining table, watching her unravel.

'Are you taking pleasure in this?'

'Pleasure? Not entirely,' he repeated the phrase from before, annoying her even further.

A rough sound escaped from her, unable to be bottled.

For some reason that made his eyes glint, almost encouraging as he watched her pace. Sabeen forced herself to stop and face him, mimicking his posture with arms folded. 'What the hell is going on?'

'You're upset because I'm not hailing your first venture as some extraordinary breakthrough.'

Yes, she wanted to snap. Her gaze swung to where her sketches were now nothing but ash. 'I sure as hell wasn't expecting that,' she said, anger destabilising her voice.

He remained unmoved, not even bothering to glance down at the two sketches he'd deigned to keep. 'I spent seven hours sketching them.'

'And in those seven hours, all you did was welcome your

muse to take a seat and put its feet up and then refuse to make it work for you. Besides all you're doing with these barely adequate offerings is indulging the fear gripping you.'

Her mouth dropped open, words failing her at how shockingly intuitive he was. 'It still doesn't excuse you burning my work.'

'No? How else will you do what you promised? How else will you stop wasting time on the surface?'

She gathered her anger like a protective cloak. Her euphoria was completely extinguished, but the panic hadn't returned with it. Instead determination burned through her. Determination to prove him wrong. Determination to be able to throw her brilliance in his face.

'The next time you burn my work, we're done.'

'Next time you produce mediocre work, I won't need to burn it. You'll burn it yourself,' he predicted in that soft rumble that so mesmerised her.

'It infuriates me that you think you know me on any level.'

His mouth twitched. 'I'm aware. Right now, you're torn between slapping my face and getting back to sketching, just so you can show me how brilliant you are. You're going to do neither.'

'Wanna bet?'

Silver eyes turned molten. 'Will you risk slapping me, knowing what might happen if you did?' he queried gruffly.

Anger turned to desire. Which she pushed far away, ignoring the fireworks fizzling through her.

She forced her eyes to roll in exasperation. Then froze when he slowly straightened and ambled over to her. His arms unfolded to brace his hands on his lean hips.

He wasn't going to kiss her. She didn't want him to. Did she?

'If you're about to ask me how I feel, then you must be blind,' she hastily said.

'As much as this show of temper intrigues me, I'm more interested in the appetite it's worked up.'

She frowned. 'I'm not—' She stopped herself.

Because, in fact, she *was* hungry. The hours had sped by again after lunch, and it was approaching sundown when he'd inspected her sketches before casually strolling across the room, lighting a fire in the hearth, and to her shocked anger, burning her work right before her eyes.

Now she watched him turn away.

'Come on. Our reservation is in fifteen minutes.'

'What makes you think I'm coming with you?'

'Because you agreed to do whatever I say, *tesoro*.'

She pursed her lips, refusing to honour that with another outburst. She'd already exposed too much emotion around this man.

He stopped in the hallway, lancing her with a narrow-eyed look. 'Are you reneging on the agreement?'

'You'd love that, wouldn't you?'

His mouth didn't twitch as she expected. In fact, his gaze was deadly serious as he looked into her eyes. 'No, I wouldn't. Come. Or don't,' he taunted with deadly ferocity.

He wasn't calling her bluff.

Whatever was driving him—and she sensed it was something bigger than just perfecting his next collection—would only accommodate her so far. She could lament her burnt work, or she could step up to the next challenge if she truly wanted this. He opened the front door and stepped out. Out of view.

Sabeen fought that invisible tug pulling at her for a mere second. She arrived to find him leaning against his motorbike. Holding two helmets.

'I find riding releases tension,' he stated. 'Unless you wish to hang on to it, of course.'

'Stop doing that!'

'What exactly?'

'Pretending you're giving me choices then reminding me I'm under your royal thumb. It's annoying.'

His eyes narrowed. 'There's barely any food in your fridge.

I checked. So unless you planned on going to bed on an empty stomach just to spite yourself, we're going out.'

Striding forward she snatched the helmet from him and slotted it over her head.

'It's on backwards, *cariña*.'

That sound escaped again. He didn't react. Merely took control, readjusting the helmet and securing the chin strap. Then securing his own, he mounted the bike.

Up close, he looked even more magnificent atop the powerful machine. Dragging her gaze from him she belatedly registered she was still wearing her shorts and top.

At some point, she'd slipped on a pair of flats. But her hair was loosening from its morning knot, and she had zero make-up on. 'I need to change.'

He treated her to another head-to-toe scrutiny that left tiny fireworks in their wake then reached into a hidden compartment and brought out a leather jacket. 'No need. You're perfectly fine as you are.' The slight thickness in his tone sent more sparks through her.

Those sparks sizzled faster when he held out his jacket. 'The wind can be uncomfortable if you're not used to it.'

She stared from the soft, expensive leather to his face, frustration joining the soup of sensations bubbling through her. Sabeen seriously wished he would just pick a lane and stick to it, so she would be free of this rollercoaster. Or maybe that was what he wanted? To keep her unbalanced and at his mercy? Why did that send an unwilling thrill through her when she should be shoring up her foundations, ensuring there were no cracks leading to temptation?

Determination kicked her harder, firming her own resolve. She'd sworn in New York she wouldn't succumb. She would see this through, no matter what. She reached for the jacket. He shook his head.

'Turn around.'

Determination wavered for a single moment, but she powered through it, turned and let him tuck her into the garment that'd graced his body. Smelling the scent that only grew more heady with each encounter, she wanted to give up and let temptation take her where it desired.

A loud scooter blaring down the alley jolted her out of the insane notions circling her brain. 'Can we go, please?'

He studied her for another stretch then pointed to a pedal. 'Step up here.' She followed his instruction and swung one leg over the seat. Its slant instantly angled her body forward. She'd known she would have to hold onto him for the ride, but faced with reality, every sense shivered with the power of the fireworks erupting inside her.

Pursing her lips, she perched her hands over his shoulders, only to feel his muscles moving beneath her fingertips. It took a moment to register the low rumble of his laughter…directly inside the helmet.

'That's not going to work, Sabeen. You need to put your arms around me.'

'Is that absolutely necessary?'

He turned his head and hooked her with a penetrative stare. 'To ensure your safety, *sí*. It's non-negotiable.'

She glanced over to where his bodyguards waited in a perfectly safe, *roomy* SUV. Before she could voice her change of heart, he'd turned the ignition. The machine vibrating between her legs made her gasp. A thrill of excitement she didn't even know she craved until that moment slamming into her.

'Arms. Now.'

Tilting her hips forward, she slowly slid her arms around him. He was warm. Hard. His six-pack rippled beneath her fingers. And…did he just tense? Or was that her? It didn't matter. They were moving. Another gasp caught as they rolled to the end of her narrow street.

'Hold tight. Follow the motions of my body. Lean into the corners with me. Okay?'

'Okay.' Surely it was the helmet's acoustics turning her voice husky.

He took off, and Sabeen got why people went crazy over motorbikes. Why he'd rebelled against his usual transport for this.

The unfettered freedom was exhilarating. The smooth, coiled power of his body as he manoeuvred the bike almost theatrically beautiful.

It was when she felt her nipples pebbling, her belly dipping and heat pooling between her legs that she knew she was in trouble.

Because after they reached their destination and Teo helped her off, his gaze watchful, emotions continued to roil through her.

CHAPTER SIX

FOR THE NEXT three days they went through a similar routine. She would sketch for hours. Teo would inspect her work in painstaking detail. In complete silence. Then burn all but one. Two if she was lucky. Each time she swung between anger and despair. Each time he watched her with clinical expectation for several minutes, then retreated to the sofa and his tablet, where he would furiously resume sketching.

Gradually, Sabeen realised that there was a sort of catharsis in watching her precious work go up in flames. But if she was being reborn, it wasn't without a ferocious struggle.

After burning her morning's work, he would feed her lunch. After burning her afternoon's work, she would pick where they ate dinner, and he'd drive them there on his motorcycle.

She would hang onto him, her front pressed to his back, feeling every shift and contraction of his muscles, feeling illicit lust steal through her as she slowly lost her fight against just experiencing it. Then she would spend the duration of their meal fighting her every wayward emotion.

The sound of his bike trundling down her alley on the fourth day excited far too many butterflies in her belly. But even as she dismissed them, she was striding to the front door, throwing it open with cringeworthy eagerness.

Expecting him to step off after turning off the engine, she withstood his usual searing scrutiny, his eyes lingering on her legs before meeting her eyes.

'Change of plans today.'

'What? Why?' When he simply stared at her, she folded her arms. 'I didn't agree to a dictatorship.'

'Is it one when I'm proposing that we take a break?'

She shook her head. 'I'd rather not. I want to push on.'

He raised an eyebrow. 'And waste more paper?'

'It needn't be wasted if you don't burn it. I don't see you burning your work,' she taunted.

The wave of savage disquiet rushed over his face before he expertly throttled it. But she'd spotted it, and her heart lurched. 'For every one of your sketches I burn, I destroy a dozen of mine,' he rasped, then his face closed tighter. Clearly he hadn't meant to disclose that.

Her arms dropped, her heart pitching harder with a strange kinship at gleaning this flaw.

The perfect Playboy Prince isn't so perfect after all.

'You do?'

He braced his arms over the handlebars, his gloved hands dangling free. 'It may not be as dramatic as sending yours up in flames but…yes. So you see, your fireplace is turning out to be a source of rebirth…for us both.'

She swallowed, the notion a little staggering and perhaps too soul-saving to digest right now. 'Do you do that with every collection?'

He turned, presenting her with his profile as his gaze fixed in the middle distance. 'No.'

Sifting through their previous conversations, she recalled a snippet. 'You said this collection was important. Why?'

His nostrils flared, and his fists tightened for a moment before he exhaled. 'I have a specific point to prove, *cariña*.'

'To whom?'

He redirected his gaze to her and pierced her with silver eyes that held deeper shadows. 'Do you care?'

'Of course I—'

He waved her away. 'I'm beginning to think you enjoy me

making you step out of your comfort zone just so you can blame me when you have a good time.'

His means of evading her questions was annoyingly effective. 'Of course I don't.'

Sensual lips twisted. 'You wasted two weeks before I got here. I'm reclaiming one of those days so we can make better headway. Get your swimsuit, Sabeen. I leave in three minutes.'

She could stand there, arguing with him on her doorstep. Risk him riding away. Or she could pursue this path she was already on. And yes, the thought of watching him burn another load of her designs withered her spirits. So maybe a break was what she needed.

Still, she took her time packing away her work and washing her breakfast things before tossing the items she needed into her beach-bag. It irked her that only five minutes had passed but she took it as a win when she stepped out and locked her front door.

'What am I supposed to do with this?' She held out her wide bag.

Without taking his eyes off her, he gestured. A hovering guard stepped forward, took the bag and headed for the SUV.

She pursed her lips, knowing she'd run out of time. Knowing deep down her senses were already leaping with glee at the thought of riding with Teo once more.

Helmet in place, she took her seat behind him.

'Are you going to tell me where we're going, or is this another of those delayed gratification things?' she asked as they hit the road.

His deep laughter filled her helmet. 'Who's dwelling now, *tesoro*?'

Her mouth twitched, veering dangerously into a smile. She hurriedly killed it. She absolutely *wasn't* enjoying this push-and-pull between them. He might possess other intriguing layers, but he was still the Playboy Prince.

Nathan Gray shattering her trust and her emotions had taught her never again to become a slave to them.

She was playing that reminder on a loop when they passed through cast iron gates and up a long driveway.

The property was ten times the size of her grandmother's.

Flat-roofed and single-storeyed, like most dwellings in the area, it sprawled wide in intriguing squares, rounded layers and coloured Moorish windows both small and large. Towering date palms, begonias and bougainvillea swayed in the breeze, offering refreshing pops of brightness against the backdrop of the terracotta villa.

Swinging off the bike, she pulled off her helmet and followed Teo to the open front doors. No staff greeted them—intentionally, she suspected.

It freed her to absorb her surroundings to her heart's delight.

A wall of shelves made of uneven-sized stones pulled at her to inspect the artefacts displayed there. Small pots and Moroccan-made statues vied with other gorgeous pieces from sub-Saharan Africa.

But what really drew her attention and delighted her senses was the dome in the middle of the living room. Built in the shape of a sphere with rough walls, its summit was a glass opening the size of a bathtub, drawing the gaze up to the gorgeous blue sky. It would be a spectacular thrill to lie beneath it at night, staring up at the stars through it.

Sabeen had visited countless luxurious residences in the world but hadn't felt as restful as she did when she stepped into the large foyer.

It took several moments to realise why. It wasn't the two giant vases filled with long-stemmed white lilies she knew cost several thousand dollars a bunch. It wasn't even the faint hint of the ocean or the mint tea and culinary delights happening out of view.

She didn't want to freely admit it, but Teo's presence in her grandmother's home had layered tension on her she thought she'd reasoned away as professionalism. But being here now, with no need to be on her emotionally fraught guard, she breathed freely for the first time in…a long time.

Setting her bag down, she toed off her flats, eager to feel the cool tiles beneath her bare soles, unable to contain her deep sigh.

She turned to find Teo watching her, as he'd done so many times in the last several days. As if he was attempting to decode her. And effortlessly succeeding.

She turned away sharply, fearing what he would see: a woman shattered and still bearing scars from her one and only serious attempt at a relationship, flailing to hang on to her professional lifeline while dealing with grief.

Open French doors drew her outside to a wide terrace, a long dining table easily seating twenty and wooden lampshades that would be glorious at night too.

Light and dark green tiles lined a sparkling, inviting pool, reminding her that she hadn't gone for her customary ocean swim since Teo had arrived on her doorstep.

'There are two things on your agenda today. The first is relaxation,' he said from just behind her right shoulder.

She glanced over, meeting his imperious silver gaze and the imposing aura that easily eclipsed even this spectacular place so that he was the only thing she saw.

'By order of the prince?' she tried with a little heat in her voice.

His face shadowed momentarily then shrugged. 'If that's what it takes.' He nodded at the view. 'Swim first. Pool or sea?'

She forced her gaze away, to the sea then to the glittering pool. If she was doing this, she was doing it wholeheartedly. 'Why choose?'

She caught his flash of surprise before she went back in to retrieve her beach-bag. 'Is there somewhere I can change?'

Still watching her, he pointed down a long hallway.

Walking away, she felt a punch of satisfaction that she'd

surprised him. In the grand scheme of things, it wasn't much. But considering she was the one constantly on the back foot, it felt good. A change from the self-esteem shredding she'd felt when she was with Nathan. And…she wanted more of it.

In another stunning masterpiece of a bedroom, she changed into her all-white bikini, knotting a matching short sarong around her hips. Snapping up her sunglasses and sunscreen, she was back outside and halfway to the beach in minutes.

The tingling in her shoulders when her feet sank into the warm sand said Teo was right behind. Two muslin-draped cabanas were set up on the sand, complete with towels and refreshments. Tossing her glasses into the nearest one, she untied the sarong.

His sharp inhale peppered her skin with tingling aware-ness and not an insignificant layer of desire. Wanting to dis-tract herself, she raced down the sand and threw herself into the incoming waves. Two Jet Skis were tied to a buoy about a hundred yards away.

She beelined towards them.

Barely twenty strokes in, she heard his faster ones. He over-took her easily, cutting through the water with streamlined prowess that was insanely beautiful to watch. She arrived at the skis as he straddled the first one. He held out his hand and helped her onto the other.

The second she was astride it, she flipped the ignition.

'Sabeen!' The bark of warning only made her bolder. 'Wait!'

She didn't. The spark of magic and the absence of despair fizzed in her blood. She might have resisted taking a break, but now she was here, she accepted it was exactly what she'd needed.

Her gaze on the horizon, she gunned the throttle. With a daring glare, she shot off, laughing with a freedom she hadn't felt in for ever when his eyes widened.

He followed immediately, of course.

Teo Domene wasn't in the habit of letting anyone best him.

But she squeezed every ounce out of their little game, speeding up when he did. Circling him when he slowed down but never letting him close enough to risk her upper hand.

He watched her, his face set in increasingly frustrating lines. Until finally he conceded. 'We're going back. Now.'

'You're giving up? Was it not enjoyable for you?' she asked, unable to hide her pleased smirk.

'I have to. I can't risk you doing anything foolish on my watch like breaking that beautiful neck.'

Her body reacted wildly to those words, her nipples hardening while her thighs clenched with the sensation pulsing between them.

The moment she reached the cabana, she snatched up a towel and held it against her body in a bid to hide and alleviate the turbulent feelings.

'Did you enjoy your little adventure?'

'You wanted me to relax. That was me relaxing.'

He raked a hand through his wet hair, completely—hopefully—oblivious to what the sight of his tight, bronzed body was doing to her. 'Evidently. I've never heard you laugh before.'

'Whereas I've heard you laugh far too many times.'

He remained sombre, watchful in a way that reminded her of his twin. In a way that made her insides jump because Teo in this mode was a little frightening with his incisive intuition.

'Speaking of which, you said the first thing on the agenda was relaxation. What's the second?' she asked after wrapping the towel tight around her body.

His gaze probed hers for several beats before taking a seat on the beach lounger next to hers. Pouring from a pitcher of ice-cold fruit punch infused with dates, cinnamon sticks and mint, he handed it over to her.

She took it and sipped, nearly rolling her eyes at the heavenly taste.

'Your grandmother,' he said.

Her heart lurched, but the hot objection she'd intended cooled far too rapidly and died altogether. Buying herself time, she took another sip, then stretched out on the lounger.

With her gaze on the horizon, she replied, 'Why do you want to know about her?'

'It's undeniable that she had a huge influence on you. Still does.'

She flicked her gaze away for a quick reprieve before his sheer will pulled it back. 'She wouldn't have approved of you.'

One corner of his mouth quirked, but his face remained serious. 'I'm aware that you think she might not initially have.'

She frowned at the puzzling response. 'How?'

Those incisive eyes probed even deeper. 'Among other things, you tense up every time I walk into your living room. That armchair was hers, wasn't it?'

She inhaled sharply then nodded jerkily.

'Tell me the significance of it.'

'It was her favourite chair. But it was also meaningful beyond its comfort. She used it whenever she wanted to have an important talk with me. I… It feels like every significant turning point in my life has involved that chair.' Tears pricked her eyes, but she rapidly blinked them back. 'Since she died, I only sit in it when I miss her counsel and her warmth. I couldn't let anyone else sit in it.'

He nodded and surprised her again by saying, 'And you shouldn't.'

Something tight inside her eased, and Sabeen found she could breathe even easier. Which triggered a fresh smarting of tears. What the hell was he doing to her?

He's the Playboy Prince, damn it.

He shouldn't be this considerate. This in tune with compassion. He should be pushing his sexual aura on her so she could storm off in a huff, pull the protective cloak tighter around her precious emotions. Not unsettling her with the dangerous idea that this connection developing between them could be as wild as his quicksilver eyes promised. Insanely beautiful, even. But above all and most importantly: non-toxic. Solid. Strong enough to withstand past devastation.

'Tell me of your time with her.'

Was it her imagination, or did he sound wistful? Jealous, even.

Her belly clenched for several seconds. Then tension eased out with her next breath. 'She brought me up as much as my mother did. *Jida* felt she had to be strict over certain things where my mother was more…chill.'

'They clashed over that?'

Sabeen nodded, the memories a little bittersweet. 'Repeatedly. I like to think I got the best of both worlds. And they loved each other, so it wasn't too disruptive or dysfunctional.' She caught his mouth tightening at the clarification, reminding her of the rumours swirling around his family. Rumours she'd paid no heed to but now triggered her curiosity in light of the shadows that haunted him. The test of fire he'd spoken of.

'You loved her, and she loved you. So why are you so terrified of that chair?'

Her head swivelled to meet his shrewd gaze. 'I don't know what you're talking about,' she said hotly.

'It goes beyond grief, *dulce*.'

Her heart banged against her ribs, hammering at her throat. Drowning out the sound of the waves crashing to shore.

He was unravelling her. With a shocking comment here, a sceptical glance there, a simple command to *relax*. The more she struggled to deny him, the looser the reins on her emotions became.

She was sure it was why she blurted a stupidly unguarded question. 'Why are you helping me? And don't tell me because it's in my contract.'

'Fundamentally, yes, but if you're seeking deeper meaning, I thought that was obvious, *cariña*. You've achieved the impossible height of intriguing me. And I sense that once you shed that baggage you're lugging around, the wells of talent will gush like the proverbial river. I'd be a fool to let all that potential go to waste.'

So…this was solely a professional advantage he sought to gain.

Her reeling heart berated her for being a fool. She turned and faced the glittering horizon, willing the free fall of dismay to stop. Lifting her gaze higher, she followed the vapour trail of a jetliner for a full minute. Then she shook her head, a peculiar but unstoppable certainty striking deep. 'That's not all. You think you know me so well, but I see you too. This whole process isn't just about me.'

Stealthy tension crept over him. He presented her with his regal profile as the silence stretched taut. Just when she thought he'd ignore her, he spoke. 'You're right. In a manner of speaking.'

'Explain,' she insisted. He'd delved deep beneath her foundations. Just why she needed to reciprocate she wasn't sure, but it felt imperative.

His jaw rippled. Then he exhaled. 'I have doubters. In Cartana. Doubters I intend to make eat their words. Is that satisfying enough?'

A month ago, she would've been stunned. But she recalled the shadows, his solemnity and bleakness. 'Who would doubt you?' she asked because it felt…absurd. He held more talent in his pinkie than most tapped into in their entire lives.

'I'll give you three guesses.'

She frowned. She'd seen him with his brothers, had seen their pride during the wedding. She'd barely encountered his mother. Or seen him interact with his father, for that matter, even though they'd both been present. 'Your parents?' she whispered.

The tight clench of his face verified her guess.

Before she could press for more, he bit out, 'Now answer my question, Sabeen.'

She scrambled to recall what he'd asked. Her grandmother.

The chair. 'She didn't entirely approve of my modelling, but she was on board with the new direction of my career.' She shrugged. 'I care about not disappointing her.'

'That's not all. You've been so brave. Don't stop now.'

She stifled a growl. 'This is the furthest thing from relaxing. You know that, don't you?'

He merely arched a brow. Waited.

'Fine. Her worry and disappointment went deeper. She was…scared for me emotionally too. And some of her predictions were realised. I haven't been able to bring myself to seek her forgiveness or counsel. Or sit in her chair. Are you satisfied?'

He treated her to that heavy silence until she wanted to squirm. 'Moderately,' he eventually said.

She cast her gaze around for a distraction, realised she'd left her phone behind. Then she saw him recline, his eyes drifting shut.

He was giving her the reprieve she desperately sought. It should've eased her disquiet. Instead, she found herself examining him. Tracing his aquiline nose, those sensual lips that still haunted her dreams. The dark mole she hadn't noticed before. The corded power of his arms. His ridged torso rising and falling in steady breathing, thick thighs she wanted to run her hands over. *Repeatedly.* To the visible bulge of his shaft beneath his damp swim-shorts.

She swallowed the sudden warmth in her mouth as heat stung her, tunnelling deep to rest, urgent and delicious, between her legs.

'Look your fill, *tesoro.* I'm not going anywhere,' he drawled, then his eyes still closed, he let loose a wickedly devastating smile that had her surging off the lounger, his rich laughter following her as she threw herself into the sea once more.

For the next two hours, Sabeen remained on her guard while she sipped cocktails which appeared as if by magic, and snacked on exquisite Moroccan hors d'oeuvres. But when it became clear Teo wasn't waiting to pounce again with his invasive questions, she truly relaxed.

Did she believe his probing psychoanalysis was at an end? Not by a long shot. But perhaps he'd truly meant for her to relax today.

So she did.

She dozed by the sparkling pool after a sumptuous lunch, explored the villa properly to discover there was indeed a housekeeper and her assistant that came with the property.

In a surprisingly large study, she gasped in delight at two floor-to-ceiling bookshelves holding hundreds of books. Plucking a bestseller that had been all the rage months before, she found a nook in a smaller living room and lost herself within the pages, looking up in surprise to see the sun had moved significantly, that early evening was falling.

And Teo was walking towards her.

The sight of her sarong caught between his fingers sent fresh waves of unstoppable heat over her skin. Unlike her, he'd changed clothes since their time on the beach, and dear God, the loose white linen trousers and the white T-shirt stretching over his broad shoulders and torso was so mouth-watering she was terrified of drooling.

'Dinner will be ready in an hour. Come. There's one more room you haven't seen yet.'

Clearly the glorious day of doing next to nothing and worrying about even less had mellowed her. Because she set her book down and rose without argument, not even battling her body's reaction to Teo watching with rapt attention as she wrapped the sarong around her hips.

The flicker of heat in his gaze made her breath catch. Made her intensely aware of the forbidden attraction consuming her whole as she followed him out of the room and across salons, through hallways and into the last room on the other side of villa attached to the far terrace.

Every room so far had been a delight. This was one reserved for the full exploration of one's senses. She pondered if it was why he'd saved it for last, when she was the most relaxed she'd been in years.

On one side were jaw-dropping works of art steeped in Moroccan heritage. Contemporary paintings by Benecerraf, scenic landscapes by R'bati, abstracts by Abecassis. Plush sofas, Berber rugs and wide floor cushions were strewn about, arranged to face the wall and pay homage to the artwork.

She drifted towards the display, but Teo brushed his fingers over her hand, redirecting her attention to the other side of the room.

It smelled of expensive cigars and ashes from a hookah. The walls were a darker mottled clay, and on the farthest side a long bar made entirely of distressed copper hammered into place with large rivets displayed dozens of colourful liquors.

Like the wall of art, this side of the room was equally eye-catching, enough to pull her in for a closer examination. Sliding behind the bar, she ran her fingers over the cool surface, studiously avoiding the sexily tousled prince who'd sprawled out on the long coffee velvet sofa facing the bar, with his bare arms flung wide to rest on the back of the seat.

His bronzed perfection was wreaking havoc on her senses, and she intended to keep a level head for as long as she could stand it. Then when she couldn't, she would simply leave.

'This estate isn't familiar to me. Which means it's new.' His gaze stalked her as she walked her fingers down the bar. 'Usually, individuals who think they're important and special gravitate to the more prestigious enclave ten minutes from here.'

'Is there a question in there, *tesoro*?'

She bit her cheek to stop herself from telling him not to call her that. It was clear he didn't intend to heed her. Plus, the endearment, however carelessly flung, was growing on her.

Still avoiding his gaze, she stopped to examine the copper sculpture at the end of the bar. 'Why did you choose this villa?'

'Because it was closer to you,' he said with brutal simplicity.

Her eyes flew to his. His molten gaze dared her to challenge that. To put a slant on it that wasn't savagely conscripted by him.

'Teo…' She wasn't exactly sure what to say, what she *could* say without betraying the maelstrom of emotions rampaging through her.

'Make me something,' he drawled, with the kind of assurance that said he expected his wish to be fulfilled.

And since Sabeen couldn't find it in her heart to challenge that assumption, especially because he'd gone out of his way to ensure she was fed noon and night for the past four days, she shrugged.

When she managed to tear her gaze from his, a quick glance showed the ever-present mint tea in a carafe set beneath the wall of liquor. The remaining ingredients were easy enough to locate. And despite her senses still churning all over the place, she strode over five minutes later with two glasses of Marrakesh Mule and handed his over.

He rose to accept his and sipped it while staring at her. Then gave that lopsided half smile. '*Excelente…gracias.*'

His hand brushed hers again, directing her to the sectional sofa directly opposite the art wall. 'What do you know about these artists?'

She shrugged. 'Not very much. All I know is what I've seen of them in art shows and museums. I do know they're exceptional. And these are…exquisite.'

'Indeed.' He sipped his drink again then pointed to two of the paintings. 'What you may not know is that those two went through periods of personal strife and public excoriation—and came out the other side stronger than ever.'

In other words, what *she* was going through. Before she could allow herself to be touched, he was pointing to another two. 'Those two, however, crashed and burned after a single burst of illumination. *One-hit wonder*, I believe, is the term?'

She stared at him long and hard. 'You want me to decide which of those two camps I want to belong to?'

His eyes drifted down her face, trailing warm caresses along the way. '*I'm* certain to which you belong. What you need to decide is if you want to fight for now or fight for life.'

She blinked, the movement curiously slow as the tumult of emotions distilled into one powerful sensation: desire. For the electric promise in his voice. For the heady belief that she had what it took to reclaim her power.

Teo Domene was a master beguiler, each word and deed projecting impossible dreams and cravings that tempted her closer to a flame she accepted she couldn't live without. Curiously more so now that he'd admitted that her success ultimately played into his own ends.

'You can reclaim the woman your *jida* was once proud of,' he murmured, eyes still boring deep. Seeing straight to the heart of her.

'And you can slay whatever demons need slaying back in Cartana?'

His nostrils flared, but he didn't tense as before. And the bleakness, while making another appearance, wasn't as acute. 'Look at us, so in sync.' The merest hint of cynicism pulsed through his gruff words.

We're in this...together.

A heady sentiment, exposing her to more earthy, elemental cravings, making her sway towards him, a soft moan escaping her.

He freed her glass from her clutches with minimum effort. She felt every octave of the deeper moan released from her throat when his fingers spiked into her loosened hair and gripped it tight. When he used the firm hold to nudge her close. *Closer.*

'What do you want, Sabeen?' It was a firm demand that dared her to meet him without fear or pretence. To be bolder in seizing her desires.

And what she wanted, above all else, was to relive that first and only kiss. Ignoring the imprudence hovering in the distance, she embraced the risky abandon of *more*. 'I want you to kiss me,' she whispered. Then more firmly, 'Now.'

The smug surprise in his eyes was doused almost immediately by a blaze of lust when he grunted. And swooped. Seizing her mouth with his in a fiery assault that made her gasp and part her lips eagerly beneath his. Firm and luscious and reigniting her memory, Teo's kiss was indescribable. Ravening.

His tongue swept between her eager lips, unhurried, decadently savouring her, sliding over the tip of hers, sending arrows of lust straight to her core. A disgraceful little whimper left her throat, her fingers scrabbling against his chest as she surged closer. Need built as he took his time in sating her. With an impatient groan, she dragged him closer, eliciting a dark chuckle before he deepened the contact.

In some infuriating part of her mind, she understood *why* women fell all over themselves for him. He could so easily slide beneath one's skin, take residence, carve his very will on one's soul. A sorcerer with every potent spell at his disposal.

One of those spells could mean her risking so much more than a handful of a few moments' pleasure. That warning finally tore through the dizzying effects of their kiss, spoiling the soup of bliss drowning her.

She pushed him away, almost resentful when he so easily let her go to retreat to the far end of the sofa, his hooded eyes slowly turning pensive as his arms returned to the top of the seat in a picture of regal indolence.

If not for the reddened swell of his sensual lips, and the very visible bulge between his legs, she would've thought the last few minutes was a fever dream conjured up by her overheated imagination.

'That was… That shouldn't have happened.'

There. This was the perfect opportunity to draw the line she'd been faintly sketching, firm and resolute, in the sand. To stand, hurry to the other room, reclaim her things and leave. But her body refused to move. Her mind rebelled against detaching herself from this magic.

'Shouldn't it?'

She shook her head to clear the lust fog gripping her. 'I got carried away...'

'With the intoxicating possibilities available to you?'

Her gaze flicked from her twisting fingers to his face, down his body, lingering where it really shouldn't. 'Whatever those are shouldn't include...this.' She waved a hand over him, a gesture almost comical in its frantic insistence.

But she wasn't laughing. She knew where giving in to one's senses too conclusively led. Without perception or discernment and far too trusting, the way she'd been with Nathan. She wasn't going back there again, even if this Playboy Prince was proving to have far more appealing depths than she'd ever imagined.

Theirs was a collaboration with an end goal of rebirth and redemption. She would do well to remember that.

He opened his mouth. And suddenly she was afraid. Terrified that he would ascribe some perfectly reasonable meaning to this too.

'Please don't trot out some cliché that it's for my own good or it's part of my journey or whatever,' she griped.

'No, *tesoro*. I'll let you marinate in that beautiful chaos all by yourself. What I was going to say is that dinner is ready.' His pointed glance over her shoulder snapped her gaze to the door, just in time to see the housekeeper disappearing.

'Are the staff trained to be ghosts?' She cringed at the husky disgruntlement in her voice.

'Hmm,' he offered noncommittally. He rose, held out his hand.

She rose on her own, not trusting herself to touch him again so soon.

Wryly amused, he led her outside and around the villa to

the largest terrace next to the pool, where a feast awaited them on the pristinely laid table. Sabeen hastily pulled out her own chair before he could, earning herself a less amused glance.

She accepted the glass of Château Latour Bordeaux just to curb the incessant tingling in her hands. Then she pre-empted him when he sent her a probing look once their fragrant chicken *rfissa* was served and cleared her throat.

'You've pushed and prodded enough. It's only fair that you answer a few questions too.'

His face hardened. 'This isn't about me.'

'Are you sure, Teo?'

His face hardened a touch. 'An inch wasn't enough? Now you wish for a mile?'

'If it'll help in mutual goal achievement, why not?' A light query, yet it immediately weighed like an anvil, linking them together that way, plucking at emotions she needed to keep far away from this exercise.

His nostrils flared at the clear challenge. Picking up his wine, he swirled it as he watched her, a deadly viper staring down its prey. 'Very well. You get one chance. Ask your question.'

CHAPTER SEVEN

'THERE'S A RUMOUR that you—'

'I don't deal in rumours. I go to the source if it's important enough or not at all.'

She paused, gathered her breath. 'Is it true you seduced your friend's older sister into teaching you fashion design?' she blurted. Then cringed as his eyebrows slowly rose in clear derision and flames devoured her face.

Had she gone insane? Of all the questions, she chose to ask him this?

His gaze dropped to his wine glass for a long pause. 'You've been reading the tabloids. I wouldn't have pegged you for a gossipmonger.'

She scrambled to regain composure that'd fled in acute mortification, her cover-up shrug almost disintegrating when his gaze dipped to her bare shoulder. 'When you hear the same story repeatedly, it's hard not to believe there's no smoke without fire.'

His quicksilver gaze rose, unapologetic, to lock hers in place. 'First of all, he wasn't a friend. He was the arrogant son of an aristocrat who believed himself better than me because I was born out of wedlock.' He paused, smiled humourlessly. 'I would've let it go if he hadn't dragged Valenti into his denigrating slurs. *Then* he needed to be taught a lesson. I chose the most effective one.'

Her breath strangled in her throat. 'You seduced her as payback for whatever her brother did?'

'You sound surprised. And yet you don't hesitate to look down that sexy nose at me for being an amoral playboy.'

'I—' She bit her tongue to avoid stating a clear untruth. Her hesitation earned her another derisive stare. It raked her face, exposing her every thought before he took a lazy sip of his wine.

'I promise you she wasn't an unwilling participant. Turned out she was equally peeved about her brother's antics. So we collaborated.'

'Then carried on collaborating?'

Another flash of pristine white teeth in a smile that didn't quite meet his eyes. 'Indeed. It was a productive summer that turned out to be life-changing.'

Something sharp and poisonous lanced low in her gut. That infernal jealousy. 'Because you discovered you had an affinity for reducing women to pools of lust? Or was it more a challenge to see if you could give Lothario a run for his money?'

The glint in his eyes sharpened. Turned dangerous and ominous. 'You seem entirely fixated on my epic sexual chronicles. Some might even say you're obsessed.' His mighty regal head tilted, and she wanted to hate the way the golden terrace lights poured over him, casting him perfectly in that fallen-angel illusion of light and shadows that had mesmerised her from the moment she'd first set eyes on him. She wanted to rail at the unfairness of it, but if life was fair, she wouldn't be in this position. Wouldn't be tolerating this insufferable situation.

Tolerating? *Really? Drinking fine wine in a gorgeous villa with even more breathtaking company?*

She pushed the droll taunting away. 'You've foisted relaxation on me. The least you can do is make conversation. If you're too scared to delve deep, then I'm happy to sit in silence.'

'*Delve deep*?' he enquired, the weighty silkiness draping his questions layering every inch of her skin in gooseflesh. It didn't help that the words projected wildly carnal images in her mind. A searing reminder of how long it'd been since she'd permitted sex to come within a whisker of impeding her thoughts or life.

'Is that what we're doing? Are you sure you want to go there, *cariña*?'

Heat surged higher, engulfing her whole being. And while it wasn't the wisest thing in the world, she couldn't back down from his blatant challenge. 'It isn't the strangest thing in the world to want to know a little bit about your boss after working for him for this long, is it? I don't even know your middle name.'

She'd expected another one-two punch of derision, maybe even a flash of his spine-melting but empty smile. She wasn't prepared for the wave of icy chill that spilled over his features, the dimming of the glint in his eyes or the tension that gripped and held him for a handful of heartbeats before he visibly slouched against his chair.

For the longest time, he remained silent until she thought he didn't intend to answer.

'My middle name is Alfonse, after my father,' he eventually offered without a single inflection, his gaze rising to track a flock of birds racing across the horizon. 'By deliberate and trenchant intention on my mother's part.'

'Why?' she asked, acutely aware of the deepening rasp in her voice. The stiffness in his body. But she was helpless to push the implications back. She cared about his answer. Cared about why a middle name had peeled back layers of the veneer she was used to seeing, granting her a hazy glimpse beneath. A glimpse of…anguish?

A muscle twitched in his cheek as his gaze moved from the swimming pool to the dark expanse of the sea a hundred yards away.

'Firstly, she mistakenly thought it would sway my father into changing his mind about his choice of bride. Then it was so she could shame him over what she deemed his promiscuity. Flaunt his misdeeds to the world just before he married someone else.' He settled deeper into his seat, but the indolence he'd displayed all day was markedly missing.

The tension riding him was familiar now, similar to his tension that evening of the wedding. Notably reappearing over these last few days. Today.

And it led directly to his parents.

'Why would she want to do that?'

A mask of bitterness etched his face in mesmerising marble. Even his eyes were pools of bleakness as he stared into the middle distance. Then rousing, he exhaled long and slow. 'Because my father committed the crime of choosing another woman over her. He chose to marry the mother of his firstborn son. A choice she, who had birthed twins and nearly died in the process, therefore believing herself to be saint-adjacent, took great exception to.'

'But… I read that he hadn't planned to marry at all. That he was…' She drifted to a stop, reminded by his comment about rumours.

He didn't rebuke her this time. '*Sí*, he believed himself to be infertile from contracting an illness in his late teens. It turned out he was wrong.' Again bitterness flashed hard. 'For the sake of the throne and royal protocol he had to marry one of the mothers of his children.' He twirled his glass without sipping. 'But it didn't matter to her what his initial plans were. She only cared that she wasn't the one chosen. And in true melodramatic fashion, everyone had to suffer the consequences of her thwarted destiny.'

She sucked in a breath, knowing she was catching a glimpse of just what made his depths run so deep.

'What did she—?'

He halted her with a wry head shake. 'You've strutted well past your mile now, Sabeen. And I'd rather not spoil the meal with indigestion.'

She examined his set profile, the unbending steel in his

eyes just as a memory shimmered across her senses: a video she'd seen of him giving a toast at one of his birthday parties. Something about mummy issues.

Pieces fell into place, but he'd shut the door on her curiosity, so she curbed her questions and ate the sublime food until she couldn't eat another morsel.

And when a mobile phone rang nearby, she was almost relieved when he excused himself to take the call. She rose and padded to the edge of the pool, almost tempted to dip her feet in it to cool herself down.

Large swathes of today had been relatively uneventful. Yet somehow she'd kissed Teo again…*and liked it*. Had confirmed his past wasn't as uncluttered with issues as his Playboy Prince persona indicated. And she'd uncovered a different sort of craving. The need to delve beneath his surface. Venture closer to the flame she now wasn't so sure would decimate her.

Was she insane?

She bent her knee and dipped one foot in the pool. Then switching over, she started to dip the other.

'You shouldn't—'

'Argh!' The unladylike yelp at the sound of his deep voice, so close, triggered a sideways tumble and a loud splash before the water swallowed her whole. Chlorinated water went down the wrong way, sending her spluttering as she broke the surface. Only to be submerged again when Teo dropped into the water next to her.

Arms seized her, yanking her flailing body upright.

One hand dragged wet strands of hair off her face before he frowned down at her. '*Madre de Dios*, you could've hurt yourself.'

Planting her hand on his chest, she shoved him away. He remained immovable. 'Whose fault would it have been? You sneaked up on me.'

Jaw clenched, his hands wrapping tighter around her, he kicked towards the edge. 'Are you okay?'

'Other than ruining a good meal with an unwanted night-cap of chlorinated water? Sure, I'm peachy.'

His eyes glinted. 'Your fire, *tesoro*. It's remarkable,' he rasped.

Fire morphed from combative…to something else. No, not something else. A replay of what had happened in the art room. But more potent now.

He drew another wet strand off her cheek to tuck it behind her ear. His touch lingered on her earlobe, sending shivers dancing through her bloodstream, her breath strangling in her lungs. Under the terrace lights, she watched droplets of water trickle over his chiselled cheekbones, into the divot above his upper lip, down his strong jaw.

The craziest urge seized her. To lick one of those drops. Maybe more. Wash away the chlorinated embarrassment with the storm of his kiss.

When her gaze flicked up from staring so damn longingly at his mouth, he was waiting for her. Molten silver cut into her, exposing her cravings to the moonlight. And again… *daring* her.

A sound born from frustration, from this insane yearning she couldn't excise from her soul rippled over the water, circled and returned stronger, probably because he'd also made a similar sound.

'This is stupid. I don't… I shouldn't…' She started to shake her head. The touch lingering at her ear curled over her nape, stopping the action.

A droplet ran down the corner of her mouth. She caught it with the tip of her tongue. Another sound left him, zipped directly into her veins.

'Teo…'

He surged closer, bringing his towering temptation to bear. 'No one else controls your fate or your desires. Only you do. Own it, Sabeen. Don't falter now.'

'Even if what I want is crazy?'

His mouth quirked, but his eyes remained ferocious, penetrating her feeble objections. 'The best things are born from a little chaos.'

'You have an answer for everything, don't you?'

That flash of bleakness returned. 'No, *tesoro.* I do not. But as I've made abundantly clear, I don't let that stand in the way of what I crave. The question is, are you woman enough to do the same?'

The Playboy Prince psychoanalyst was back, taunting her with a shiny vision of the impossible that somehow felt within reach. And since *he* was right there...within reach...

'Teo...'

His chest heaved on a mighty breath. Then that hand on her nape was moving. Along her jaw. Caressing her collarbone. Lingering on the pulse frantically beating at her throat. Pausing, his eyes meeting hers. Gauging her reaction. Smiling that triumphant smile when she swayed closer, the water moving over her skin causing waves of sensual delight she wanted to drown in.

Then his hand closed over one breast.

A moaned 'Yes...' drifted out then a more frantic 'Yes!' jerking free, her head falling back as his thumbs deliciously tortured her pebbled nipples. Fiery pleasure arrowed with unerring accuracy between her thighs, plumping up her sex, making her legs thrash in the water.

Teo's leg captured hers, pinning her to the side of the pool. He roughly pulled one bikini cup to the side and sucked one eager nipple between his hot lips.

'Oh!' Her eyes rolled back in her head as her fingers clutched his hair, held him captive against her as he rolled his tongue over her flesh.

After an eternity and not nearly enough time, he dragged his head up. '*Dios mio*, you're so beautiful.'

Joy sang through her. Then need pounded hard on its tail. Perfectly in tune with the clamour devouring her, he returned to teasing her, his other hand delving beneath the waist-band of her sodden shorts. Anticipation screamed through her, then she was shuddering as he found her swollen nub, flicked it with his thumb as his teeth grazed her nipple. Between one heartbeat and the next, Sabeen was flying high. Her nails bit into his shoulders, futilely fighting to stay whole even as she surrendered to being ripped apart by pleasure.

One finger breached her core then another. Her visions fogged, incoherent words peppering the charged air as Teo, his gaze now pinned on her face to watch her every reaction to his sorcery, joined her with a litany of praise.

The combination of the water lapping the underside of her breasts, his thumb wreaking sweet havoc and the fingers thrusting into her heated channel sent her over the edge.

'There you go, *hermosa*. Take it. Own it.'

Her scream intensified with the fierce onslaught of a seem-ingly unending release, the mouth trailing over her throat, lightly biting her jaw, before sealing possessively over her mouth, devouring her desire, granting her the most prolonged bliss she'd ever known.

Far too soon, though, reality impinged on it. She'd fallen under Teo's spell once more. And not just that, she'd done it out in the open, where any staff member or bodyguard wan-dering past could've seen them. Hell, any cunning paparazzo with a powerful lens could've taken pictures, splashed another scandal all over social media.

She'd set herself up to experience shades of the tumult she'd endured nearly three years ago—tangling with Nathan Gray, the notorious player who it turned out was merely toying with her. Even if Teo was different— No. Pushing aside the shock waves of residual pleasure, she tugged her bikini back into place, sidling away from him.

Aware he was watching her with hooded eyes, probably ready to ridicule her protesting way too late, she struck out for the pool steps.

'Sabeen—'

'No. It's…it's late. I need to go.' Hurrying out of the pool, she snatched up a towel and high-tailed it to the guest bedroom.

Tugging off her shorts and throwing a sundress over her bikini took ten seconds. She was shoving her things into the beach-bag when he appeared in the doorway.

He hadn't bothered with a towel, and in that moment, he looked every inch the Playboy Prince, destined for a centrefold magazine piece. Or the most decadent Christmas perfume ad.

Her pelvis tightened as she fought resurging heat.

'What are you doing?' he rasped then shook his head. 'You're staying here. Neither of us are in a fit state to drive. I've given the bodyguards the night off.'

She gritted her teeth, knowing it would be selfish and in-sensitive to insist she be driven back to her house. 'You really need to stop thinking I'm your puppet to command. Or believe that every woman who lets you within a foot of her wants to jump into your bed.' Dear God, why had she said that when she'd just willingly participated in a sexual act that still trailed magic in her blood?

'*Santo cielo.* You're standing in a perfectly adequate guest room. You should wait until you're invited into my bed before you make assumptions one way or another.'

Heat enflamed her from head to toe. Snatching up her bag, she shoved her feet into her flats and headed for the terrace, ignoring the heavy footsteps thudding behind her. Two steps down the stone slabs leading down the beach, she heard his sharp inhalation.

He caught her arms, turning her to face him. 'What the hell do you think you're doing?'

'What does it look like? I'm walking home,' she replied.

A frown clamped his brows. 'That's out of the question.'

'Watch me.'

She sailed past him as he dragged his fingers through his

hair. Less than ten seconds later, she felt his domineering presence behind her.

'Should you be out without your bodyguards, Prince Domene?'

She felt more than saw the bone-dry glare he threw at her back. 'What they don't know won't hurt them.'

'Are you sure?'

His longer stride easily propelled him closer. 'Someone in the palace will throw a fit at some point. Not to mention my twin brother will flay me alive. I'll happily blame you if I'm thrown into some dungeon.'

Her feet slowed, a spike of worry catching her middle even though she suspected most of that was nonsense. 'Teo, seriously, this is ridiculous. You forget I grew up here. I know my way home.'

He walked past her then waited for her to catch up. 'Good. Then, we'll make good time. Come on.'

When her feet refused to move, he rounded on her, ruthless resolution etched deep into his face. 'I'm seeing you home safe, *cariña*. And that's non-negotiable.'

'Is being an infuriating, domineering alpha bred into you at the palace or taught from birth?'

That sardonic twist of his mouth again. 'I wasn't brought up in the palace, so it's safe to say it's in my DNA.'

'Oh joy,' she muttered.

Glinting eyes drifted over her face. When that wave of simmering heat threatened again, she quickened her steps. The effect of her climax still lingered, a thrilling reminder and a throbbing demand for more.

Both conditions she was going to fiercely deny, battling it all the way to her front door.

Her hands shook as she slotted the key in the lock.

She knew she should've drawn a line under the whole day then. Just as she knew she wasn't going to the moment her gaze drifted over him.

'Your clothes are still damp.'

He arched a brow. Said nothing. Don't say it…don't—

'Come in. I'll dry them for you.'

Somewhere in the cosmos, Sabeen was sure deities were laughing at her as she did her utmost not to stare at a half-naked Teo, wearing only a towel and sitting at her dining table.

Molten silver eyes watched her restless pacing. 'You're wound up.'

'I guess your relaxation day failed after all,' she snapped then the fight fizzled out of her. Courtesy forced her to continue. 'That's not true. I… Parts of it were great. Thank you.'

His wry look intensified. 'But?'

'But…the pool thing…that shouldn't have happened.' At his silence, she huffed. 'This is where you say you agree with me.'

He shrugged. 'It happened. I'm not going to waste time debating what should or shouldn't have been. There's no point.'

She resumed pacing, stuck in the curious no man's land of wishing the dryer would ping quickly so he'd leave and wanting him to stay. To volunteer morsels of his life so she could justify this sudden urge not to push him away and protect herself. For him to deliver another insightful analysis that cut away more of her self-doubt and show her a clearer path to the centre she'd lost. The solid ground she hadn't felt for a depressingly long time.

Her feet slowed as she passed the sketches on the dining table. She felt his gaze on her, steady but savage. Willing her to do…what, exactly?

It was nearing midnight. The right thing to do was see to his clothes, bid him goodnight and go to bed.

But…the right thing had gone out the window the second she'd invited him in. So she pulled out a chair. Watched him stride into the kitchen and set the kettle on the stove.

'What's this?'

She turned sharply, her chest squeezing when she saw him

holding a white wooden box instead of the tea she'd assumed he was making.

The delicate but distinctive sound when he set the box down gave away the state of its contents.

'My grandmother's favourite teapot. It broke the day she died.'

'May I?' he asked, a curious thickness in his voice.

Sabeen nodded, even though her heart was caught tight in a vise whose origin she couldn't quite fathom. Or maybe she could. Maybe she wasn't ready to admit she was exposing herself again, granting him access to places she'd kept under lock and key since Nathan.

She watched his long, elegant fingers slowly unravel the knotted cheesecloth. Her heart jumped at the further rattle of broken crockery. He caught her pained look and, mouth flattening, stopped.

'No. It's fine.'

He nodded, but when she reached into it, he caught her wrist. 'Careful. I don't want my mood ruined by seeing you hurt yourself,' he said, his voice deep and sombre.

That sombreness weaved through her, moved her in a way that terrified her. Because she wanted him to understand. Wanted him to know without cynicism or condemnation what her connection to her grandmother meant to her. 'I know it's silly to keep something that's worth almost nothing.'

His scowl admonished her. 'We both know it means more to you than its monetary value.'

The chiding shamed her. But also buoyed her. When she padded over to him to look into the box she hadn't opened since she'd buried her *jida*, she did it by drawing strength from him. 'I don't know why I kept it.'

His recrimination deepened. 'Don't do that.'

'What?'

'You don't owe anyone an explanation for what you feel when you feel it. You know why you kept it.'

She pursed her lips, shame deepening a touch. Right along with the disconcerting feeling that he saw right into her soul.

'The real question is what you're going to do with it. How are you going to honour her with a box of broken memories?'

She blinked, her throat clogging with a swarm of thoughts and emotions. One of the prominent ones was that she'd vastly underestimated Teo Domene. He was the very last thing from shallow. His hedonistic tendencies were truly legendary, sure. But his layers were also fathomless. And it should've been a relief to know that he was different from the man who'd devastated her in the past.

Unfortunately, this new discovery placed him, the man she'd exposed her inner self so thoroughly to in the last few days, in the unique position of being exceptionally intriguing to her.

'Are you familiar with the Japanese art of kintsugi?' she murmured.

He nodded. 'It's a particular favourite of mine.'

Had she known that? Collected that nugget at the back of her mind and forgotten about it, only for it to resurface now? The idea of that, coupled with what she was thinking of doing, sent flutters rushing through her heart. And when his eyes went to the box and took on a determined glint, the butterflies raged harder.

'Tell me what you need,' he said, reaching for his phone and weakening her knees all over again.

The supplies arrived within the hour. By which time she'd cleared the dining table of everything and spread a protective sheet over it. Her hands shook as she spread out the shards of the broken teapot, and she was a little thankful that Teo, whose phone had been increasingly pinging with messages, went out into the courtyard to make what turned out to be a series of calls.

This felt like a final, cathartic act. One that was intensely personal, even if she was only laying the groundwork for the final concept later. She'd just finished setting out the sixth iteration of how she wanted the pieces to be joined when Teo entered.

His hooded eyes rested on her, then after several seconds he gave a curt nod. 'A good start.'

Like a valve released, she moved to her sketch-pad, her fingers closing over her favourite pencil. Just as the dryer pinged.

One imperious hand came up. 'Stay.'

She didn't bother railing against the command. But she couldn't help following his glorious form as he rose to retrieve his clothes.

'There's a perfectly adequate guest room down the hall,' she repeated his words to him then, completely compelled by forces she couldn't stop, added, 'You're welcome to use it for the night too.'

He froze, his eyes boring into her.

Too frightened to examine her true meaning underlying that common courtesy, she redirected her focus to the sketchbook.

She jerked awake at the sensation of something slipping through her fingers.

The sketchbook. On which she'd drawn nineteen sketches before her back and fingers cramping had forced her to join Teo on the sofa.

He hadn't taken up her offer to use the guest room. He'd merely relocated to the sofa after dressing and made a few calls to his twin and his head bodyguard to avoid inciting an international incident when he was discovered absent from the villa.

The only time her attention had been distracted was when he'd tensed during the phone call to Valenti. But she'd been unable to follow the rapid-fire Cartanian language which was so close to Spanish in many ways but also contained marked differences.

The charged look he'd sent her after hanging up, silently questioning why she'd stopped, thrilled her more than she wanted to admit.

She'd resumed sketching, sipping the mint tea Teo offered her in the witching hours. And…that was the last thing she remembered.

She started to stretch now, then froze, shock and desire-tinged awareness zipping through her when she realised what she lay against.

The solid column of Teo's upper body cushioning her back. Her lower body tucked between his splayed legs. Her cheek on his chest. His heartbeat thumping steadily beneath her ear.

The savage desire to remain exactly where she was.

'*Buenos dias*,' he drawled, the rumble transmitting all the way to her toes. 'Before you berate either of us too severely for what you think is another misstep, take a beat and tell me how you feel.'

The prompt dried up her knee-jerk urge to mitigate the disaster of finding herself in his arms and the even more terrifying silent admission that had followed it. Her breath eased out, biting back a soft moan when his fingers threaded gently through her hair.

'I feel…satisfaction. Like I've accomplished something important. In a way I haven't felt in a while.' The admission was hushed. Filled with overwhelming relief. She blinked back the sudden onrush of tears. Then, dragging herself back from temptation, she sat up and rescued her sketchbook from the floor.

The rush intensified as she leafed through the pages. Like her previous offerings, it started off tentatively, before quickly morphing into…more. Brazen. Fearless. Poignant. Her heart jolted with sparks of joy at achieving what she'd despaired of only weeks ago.

But…while she was immensely grateful, she wanted… *needed*…more than sparks. She was greedy for more. Fourth of July fireworks on top of New Year's Eve extravaganzas.

Rising, barely feeling Teo's lingering touch on her arm fall away, Sabeen approached the fireplace. The embers were banked, a blatant metaphor for her current state if there ever was one. Tossing more wood onto it, she watched the flames catch then roar to life.

Her heart in her throat, she tore her sketches from the book, held them to the fire and watched them burn.

She felt him crouch behind her but didn't turn. But she blinked back a swell of tears when he brushed his lips, soft, lingering, over her temple. '*Bravo, tesoro*. Now it's my turn,' he murmured.

Still perched on her knees, she watched him reach for his tablet. Saw the exquisite designs he was about to consign to the digital trash-bin. Her hand flew to his. 'No, don't! Those are incredible.'

'Perhaps. But the fire isn't quite done with me either, *tesoro*. Because *incredible* is good, but they need to be…' several beats elapsed before he added '…perfect.'

The way he said the word made her heart lurch. 'Why?'

His gaze remained forward, tormented eyes reflecting the flames dancing in their dark depths. 'When you're surplus to requirements it's easy for others to believe the worst of you. And if that status grates enough, the need to counter it by proving yourself becomes as imperative as breathing. And the quest for perfection never stops.'

She frowned. '*Surplus to…*' she echoed then froze, a shaft of anguished, shocked empathy moving through her. 'You? Why?'

His eyes flickered darker. 'Why do you think? My father went from having no heirs to having three in the space of twelve months. Something or someone was bound to fall through the cracks. I'll give you three guesses who that someone was.'

'Teo—'

He shook his head and surged to his feet. 'Save your pity, *tesoro*. I relish the challenge.'

She watched him leave the living room. Only then did she let herself exhale. To let the tears fall.

To warily approach the possibility that this feeling moving through her wasn't just about her work. That this rebirth very much involved her emotions too and specifically Teo Domene's visceral effect on them.

CHAPTER EIGHT

HE LEFT SOON after bringing her coffee and freshly made crois-
sants, delivered by his staff. She told herself she welcomed
the reprieve.

She gathered the ashes from the now dead fire and dis-
posed of them. Then she showered, napped for three hours
and cleaned her little house.

The first few buzzes of her phone she ignored, revelling in
this rejuvenating peace. But the buzzing continued, insistent,
until she snatched it up to turn it off only to pause.

At first, she wasn't sure what she was looking at. The image
on the screen preview was grainy at best, taken at night with
the figures unfocused. A blessing, she realised when it dawned
on her what she was looking at.

An image of her and Teo. On the beach last night.

The Playboy Prince's New Plaything?

Ice froze her veins, her heart dipping to her toes. But just as
she was wading through worst-case scenarios, another thun-
derbolt struck.

Playboy Prince Axes Creative Director

No. *No, no, no!*

It took three tries to click on the article, then anguished
seconds to realise the article wasn't about her.

Teo had fired Cristobal at some point in the last twenty-four
hours, without telling her. Before or after he'd kissed her? Be-

fore or after he'd dared her to let him touch her in ways that still took her breath away?

Was she next on the chopping block? Her insides dipped and dived as she read the article one more time. If the picture on the beach was accurately identified as her, old gossip would be given new life.

Questions were straining to bursting point when Teo knocked on her door just after sundown. She yanked the door open, barely able to contain herself. 'What the hell did you do?'

'Specificity is a skill I value greatly, *cariña*.'

'You fired Cristobal?'

His eyes narrowed as he stepped in and shut the door behind him. 'I didn't realise you were so attached to him.'

'Stop it. You know what I'm talking about!'

'I don't. Are you under the misapprehension that I should've consulted you first?'

His chilled mockery stung her hard. But she kept her chin up and her hands on her hips as she faced him in her living room. The place where he'd made her feel more special than she'd felt in an aeon. Had it all been an illusion?

'Consulted me? No. As you've reminded me infinite times, this is your show. But would it have killed you to tell me so I didn't read about it on the news?'

'It wasn't meant to be announced yet,' he stated laconically. 'Someone obviously leaked it.'

She exhaled, feverishly gathering her composure as his gaze zeroed in sharper.

'That's not all that's bothering you.'

She'd given up being astounded at how well he read her. 'There's a picture…'

He waited, a tower of infinite control.

Her heart still banging against her ribs, she pulled it up and showed it to him. He examined it for several beats, then handed her phone back.

'Forget about that. They'll lose interest in it soon enough.'

'And if they don't?'

His eyes narrowed, his tension growing. 'It bothers you that much?'

'That everyone will assume I'm sleeping with my boss to get ahead? Within the same time frame that you fired Cristobal? Of course it does!'

She was too het up to cringe at her screechy voice. She stopped and took a breath. 'Surely you can see how the timing of this looks?'

Conceit built in the slow arch of his brow and the pitiless look he flung her way. 'I don't live my life according to the timings of tabloids spewing nonsense.'

'Well, lucky you. The rest of us don't have the same freedom to be so laissez-faire about things!'

He prowled closer until he was at arm's length. 'Cristobal hasn't produced a single sketch since I last saw him. He's been on a friend's boat on the Riviera, indulging in drink and drugs. It's clear he didn't intend to meet any deadlines or even try to complete this assignment, so I wished him well on his next venture. The official press release announcing my new *permanent* creative director will be in a couple of weeks. Is that a problem?' he queried silkily.

'Yes. No. I don't know.' Grimacing at that, she whirled away, distancing herself before she did something stupid. Like demanding to know what all that meant. *For her.*

Stepping outside into the small courtyard, she walked along the wall to the almost hidden stone stairway that led to her second favourite place in her grandmother's house then climbed up.

The rooftop terrace spanned the entire square footage of the house, with loungers, a clay wood-burner, a mosaic-inlaid table with matching chairs and a raffia-woven awning to alleviate the worst of the day's heat.

She tried to blank her mind, lose herself in the smells of mint tea, spice-tinged air, wood fires and the sea.

The tall walls on either side ensured the utmost privacy, and she basked in it now, not surprised at all when, lifting her head to the soft ocean breeze, she felt his overwhelming presence behind her. 'I'm guessing we're not done with the deep excavation?'

He didn't respond immediately. He came close. Closer. Braced his hands on either side of her on the stone wall. Sabeen barely managed to resist the wild urge to lean back against his hard front. Savour his heat and let it fill all her cold places.

For a full minute, they remained caught in their charged silence, their eyes fixed on the horizon.

'What was Nathan Gray to you?' he asked with a hard edge, chopping her off at the knees with this question out of left field.

Spikes dug into her skin. Shoving one arm away, she freed herself from his force field, going over to the small iron table and cushioned chair set where she'd spent many hours and meals with her grandmother. It didn't hold the nostalgic, poignant gravity of the armchair downstairs, but she still clung to it as she boldly met Teo's narrowed eyes.

'None of your business,' she replied sharply, self-protection vital.

His expression returned to mockery, deepening with each passing second. 'I thought we were delving deep?' he challenged.

Sabeen swallowed, wondering why she wasn't ordering him to leave. 'I'll answer anything else besides that.' Heavens, could she sound any more desperate? Bare her soul any wider?

For reasons she couldn't fathom, his gaze morphed from sardonic to chilled and censorious while it probed deeper than she would ever be comfortable with. 'You're either hoping to stoke my curiosity or you're disappointingly not as brave as I thought you were.'

She needed a few breaths to get through the sting of that one. 'I won't be goaded into satisfying your curiosity, Teodor.'

He stiffened. Then his mouth twitched. 'Very few people

call me that. And never in that prim little voice that makes me want to see you in a starched uniform and sky-high heels with a whip in your hand.'

She gasped then cursed every single nerve-ending that melted into carnal subjugation at the image he evoked.

He laughed, low, husky and so sexy she clenched her thighs to prevent the urgent throbbing that started between them. Dear God, he was shameless. And so rampantly virile that she couldn't think straight.

'Does that turn you on?' he drawled as she was scrambling to regain her fracturing composure.

'No. It does not. So if that's what you're into—?'

'Oh, no, no, no, *tesoro*,' he interrupted, his tone amused. 'You've got me on guard now. You won't be using that sexy voice to taunt me into divulging even more snippets while you keep your torrid little secrets tucked close to your chest.'

'I don't have any torrid secrets,' she replied far too hotly.

'No?'

Hard eyes dug into her, evicting emotions she needed to hide.

She dragged her gaze away, staring at the same spot he'd watched minutes ago. The glittering sea she'd swum in as a child, watched over by the strong, strict but loving grandmother who'd done everything in her power to stop her daughter falling into the same pitfalls she'd stumbled into. And having failed at that, her even greater efforts to prevent the same from happening to her granddaughter.

Sabeen's heart squeezed at the remembered heartache of the toughest confession of her life: telling her grandmother that she'd tangled with a playboy and got her emotions crushed by Nathan Gray. Of the tears and disappointment, then the entreating that this cursed legacy of falling for undeserving men ended with Sabeen. Her own vow to get her life back on track after *Jida* was gone.

No way was she about to disclose any of that to Teodor Domene.

She swallowed past the aching lump in her throat. Focused on changing the direction of these probing questions. Then stunned herself with her next words.

'My grandmother gave me my love of fashion.'

She felt his ferocious focus then, a laser beam drilling into her. She kept her gaze forward, so she wouldn't be completely annihilated by this perilous path she couldn't seem to abandon.

From the corner of her eye, she saw his nod. 'I've seen some of her old sketches among yours.'

She started. She hadn't gone out of her way to hide them, thinking he wouldn't care. That he was too self-absorbed to pay attention to anything that didn't directly involve his two passions of sex and fashion.

'I thought they were yours until I saw the dates on some of them. She was clearly talented.'

Completely floored, she forgot her vow to avoid looking at him and met his sizzling gaze. There was no trace of mockery or amusement.

'She was also very beautiful. She came from a line of beautiful women.' She paused, remembering the brief but significant moments when her *jida* had revisited her own painful past. The raw anguish of her plea for history not to be repeated. 'Unfortunately, she also came from a line of women who'd been betrayed by men.'

He stiffened, his lips flattening in a displeased line. But he said nothing, his sheer force of will prompting her to continue.

'My grandfather was like you. A shameless Casanova.'

She heard his sharp intake of breath but didn't glance at him. If he was offended by the truth, she wasn't here to spare his blushes.

'He left her at the altar, pregnant and alone. Then had the gall to make an appearance years later with a proposition for her to live in luxury…as his mistress. She cut off all contact with him and moved to this house with my mother. Then she felt like she was reliving her worst nightmare when my mother fell into a similar trap.' She ventured a glance at him, saw his tight jaw, the incensed expression and told herself she didn't…couldn't care whether it was on behalf of the women she'd cared deeply about or not. Redirecting her gaze to the moonlit sea, she continued. 'Do you see where I'm going with this, Teo?'

'The tapestry is becoming clear, *sí*,' he drawled. 'Where's your mother?'

The vice tightened around her heart. 'She emigrated to India a decade ago. We talk often, but I don't see her as much as I'd like.'

He nodded then waited, silently compelling her for more.

'I think she moved away to escape the judgement of falling short of my grandmother's expectations of her.'

'Which were?'

Feeling too agitated to remain still, she moved to the far side of the low stone wall and leaned her arms over it. The sun-warmed stone offered temporary comfort and a reprieve, but Sabeen was acutely aware he watched her every move.

The short sundress she'd put on after her shower was entirely see-through, and her body was on show. It was a good thing, then, that physical nudity wasn't what bothered her. It was the inability to stop baring her soul that disturbed her the most. Yet she stifled the urge to run and hide. Or better yet, to boldly state that she had no intention of further exposing herself to his idle curiosity.

She did none of those things in the end.

Because it seemed no amount of jaw-clenching or internal stern talking-to was enough to stop the words from spilling out, independent of her will.

'Which were that she was never to put her trust in a man. Never hand over control of her emotions in the belief that she'd fallen in love. And, at all costs, never hand over her agency for the sake of pleasing a man. My mother failed on all those counts. She returned home with me, broken. She loved me, but I grew up watching their love-hate relationship turn increasingly sour because my grandmother, despite loving her daughter, was reliving the worst period of her life, while my mother blamed her for what she believed was an emotional flaw passed on by genes and beauty, compounded by my *jida*'s threat of withdrawal of support if she so much as looked at my father ever again. A father who also happened to be a Lothario himself.'

When she was done, she turned, leaned her hip against the cool wall to see him better. Just in time to see a curious expression being wiped off his face. Her belly clenched. Surely that hadn't been…hurt?

She attempted to probe deeper, chasing after the expression, only to watch him lift his molten silver gaze, as if almost daring her to believe such an emotion would floor him.

'So she judged your mother for making the same mistakes she did?' Sharp slivers of bitterness coated his question.

'You think she had no right to do that after doing everything in her power to warn my mother of the risks?'

He spiked her with a censorious look. 'You presume your grandmother held the golden key to happiness. A path that only involved your mother not repeating her mistakes. What if your father had proved to be both a playboy and the man who granted your mother the greatest happiness, given the chance to reconnect that he apparently wasn't allowed to have?'

She frowned. 'Do you hear yourself? That's a contradiction in terms.'

'Is it? You think your mother would've only been happy with a staid, excitement-averse nobody who would flog himself for so much as accidentally smiling at another woman?'

Memories of rows and tears after her grandmother had attempted to force just such a procession of supposedly safe suitors on her mother reeled through her mind. Her mother had hated every one of them, pleaded with her grandmother to stop. It'd reinforced the acrimonious belief that the El-Maleh women were doomed to love only one type of man.

She refocused on Teo to find him looking at her. Daring her to admit the truth. She licked her suddenly dry lips then cursed herself when he followed the action with blazing eyes. 'So you're saying she should've chased playboy after playboy until she found one willing to reform just for her?'

'I'm saying no one has the right to inflict their expecta-tions—or lack thereof—on others, even if they themselves have failed in their own endeavours.'

Layers of bitterness in his tone made her heart lurch for him, tugging her close to the dangerous flame of their shared sense of misery loving company.

She watched intently, spellbound as he went over to the table, picked up the wine he'd brought with him and two wine glasses and returned to where she stood. It was another bottle of the exquisite Château Latour she'd so enjoyed last night.

His gaze still on her, he slowly filled the glass, set the bottle down on the wall and held the glass against her lips.

Despite the way she looked and the constant barrage of sex-centricity generated because of it, she'd never considered herself an especially sexual person. She suspected years of watching and hearing what beauty had done to her family had diminished any desire to explore her sexuality until it'd receded to the back of her mind, buried—but apparently not dead.

In her innermost thoughts, she'd often wondered whether it was that lack of exposure which had made her gravitate, naive and oblivious, towards Nathan's overtly carnal existence. The charm he'd exuded so freely.

And whether it was why she was so fearful of being caught in Teo's erotic vortex. Of losing herself so entirely in it that she wouldn't be able to see top from bottom. And while knowing Nathan's other deplorable characteristics had been what had eventually devastated and soured her emotions, she didn't feel the same danger when she was with Teo.

No, his was a different sort of peril. With him she sensed a deeper entanglement, a fathomless yearning she'd never once felt with Nathan. A certainty that emotional annihilation with Teo would be apocalyptic.

'Isn't that the very definition of learning from one's mistakes?' she asked, unable to stem the river of sensual delight flowing through her veins. Thick and heavy as she took a large, indelicate gulp of wine, spilling a drop that dripped to her chin and landed on her collarbone.

Her breath strangled completely as he followed the red trail, his eyes turning hot and mercurial.

'But it wasn't your mistake. And taking on literal generations of tribulation and carrying it on your back, no matter how much you love your family, won't get you very far if you're so weighed down.'

She swallowed, resisting that pull he so effectively lassoed around her. 'You wouldn't be asking me about Nathan if you didn't know that it's not just others' mistakes that have affected me, Teo.'

His nostrils flared in a visible, primal act of temper and slivers of jealousy. It shouldn't have thrilled her so much. 'You know I despise rumours. Tell me what happened with him,' he breathed the order.

She resisted. The humiliation might not burn as searingly, but it was lead at the bottom of her soul, weighing it down.

Maybe it's time to let it go, then...?

She jolted, that internal voice sounding so distinctly like Teo's it was disarming. She set her glass down with a sharp clink. 'God, get out of my head,' she blurted before she could stop herself. 'I don't need anything from you,' she forced out, more in hope than belief.

A trace of his displeasure receded, replaced by a bleakness that signalled she'd touched a sensitive nerve.

He raised his glass and sipped his wine then set it on the wall next to hers. 'If you insist, then so be it, *tesoro*. To hell with everyone else. It's time to be your own muse—'

She launched herself at him, threw her arms around his neck. 'Stop talking! Every time you do I feel... I feel...'

'What?'

'I'm not sure whether to slap you or thank you. It's driving me insane.' Her fingers dug in, her reaction matching his primal one a minute ago.

A tremor charged through him, and a jagged sound left her throat.

'If it helps, you drive me insane too,' he replied, eyes raking over her face to settle on her mouth, another fine tremor transmitting through her. 'And you're welcome to do either. Both even,' he added hoarsely.

It was the most alive she'd ever felt. And like yesterday and all the days before...she wanted more. So when the words fell from her lips, they felt like the most natural, seismic phenomenon in the world. 'Make love to me, Teo. Let's shake the crazy loose and be done with it, yes?'

Her defiant hunger and hope intensified the free fall he'd been in since he made that knee-jerk decision to move closer to her house. Hell, Teo suspected it'd been in existence before then too. This confounding instinct to plough ahead, the intangible certainty that within her renaissance was the key he needed to succeed with his own goal—that, for the first time in his life, he was discovering he needed someone else—was awakening feelings Teo didn't know what to do with.

Now, given the option of shedding the galling lust that came with this unwanted emotional discovery? He'd be a fool to refuse, *si*? Particularly when, after tasting her again, having her in his arms far too briefly yesterday had driven him out of his mind for the rest of the night, even as he'd revelled in her blooming by throwing away her shackles?

He looked into her beautiful eyes, eyes the colour of the sand on his beach at sunset, and said the only words available to him. 'Your wish is my command.'

He speared his fingers into her hair and gripped hard, the way he knew she liked. Her enthralled gasp drew his lips to the exposed line of her neck. Trailing kisses on the delightful erogenous zone, he went to slide his other arm around her hips, to pick her up.

'No. Right here.'

He pulled back, examining her expression. This went deeper than a titivating request. Barely ten minutes ago she'd been distressed about a grainy picture in a tabloid. Either she was taking back her power, thumbing her nose at those who'd caused her distress, or she wasn't ready to accept him within the walls of her grandmother's home.

The possibility of it being the second siphoned his breath from his lungs, awakening a familiar rejection. Enough to stall him, though? *Hell, no.*

If he was wrong and her decision was based on the former…well, he was no stranger to kinky requests. He released her hair, watched it tumble down like a seductive river, then grabbing the thin sundress barely covering her, he ripped the fabric in two, tossed it away so he could marvel over her stunning body. Fall on his knees in worship of her.

'*Dios mio*, you take my breath away. I'm so damned greedy for you.'

She gripped the wall behind her, thrust out her chest, her toffee-coloured nipples tight and proud, and splayed her endless legs, a sultry invitation dripping from her liquid eyes. 'Then, take me. Pound me until I tell you to stop,' she demanded boldly, a brazen command that hooked straight into his desires and latched on tight.

So tight, that for the first time in his life, Teo found himself actually falling to his knees before her. He gleefully let the persistent phone calls from his brothers and the semi-urgent demands of his staff fall away. Let the gut-hollowing sensation that he was running out of time where his father was concerned fade to the back of his mind for once.

Because not thinking about it, silencing the shredding possibility that the outcome he sought might never be realised, was a welcome reprieve almost as addicting as the smooth, warm skin of the most beautiful woman in the world.

And when each caress of his fingers, each whispered kiss drew that awed gasp laced with tendrils of wonder from her, who was he to wish for common sense?

Drawing her thong down, Teo caressed up her inner thighs, first fastening his gaze on her, so he didn't miss one single reaction, then followed it up, after a leisurely caress of her silky wet sex, with placing his lips where he...*they*...both needed it most.

Her head fell back, her fingers spiking into his hair to grip hard, arousing him further as she held him in place, and gyrated her hips. Chasing her pleasure with an abandon that had him groaning and straining for his fraying control.

Her first release, when it came, was a sexy, throaty shout of his name as she shuddered above him then went beautifully boneless.

Teo caught her as she crumbled, then tossing her over his shoulder before rising, he hurried to the loungers. They weren't as sturdy as the ones at his villa, but he didn't care.

Tugging off his clothes, he only stopped long enough to sheath himself. Then he prowled over her, overcome by the primal need to claim her. Another first for him. He'd never encountered a woman he'd wanted to claim, to stamp his possession on, as much as he did Sabeen.

Perhaps she had the right idea. Best to rid themselves of this craziness so they could get back on an even keel as soon as possible. So he could return to Milan, finish the task of proving to his father once and for all that he was worthy of the Domene name. That he wasn't superfluous after all. That commanding a kingdom like his brother or protecting face-less individuals like his twin wasn't all it took to be a worthy human being. That sometimes, leaving one's mark on the world could be as simple as creating something stunning and unforgettable and—

'Teo!'

Her sultry demand reclaimed his focus, to the hand curled around her plump breast, the thumb teasing her and sending her into a frenzy. Her hands rushed up and down his back, digging in, then soothing.

'Already impatient again?'

'More,' she demanded. 'Now,' she insisted.

Her beautiful lips parted, probably to issue another edict, forgetting who the sovereign was here. Lips twitching with self-deprecation at how she'd so easily turned the tables on him, he leaned low and took her mouth, sliding his tongue in to snatch the next command from her, savouring it as he did her bidding.

One kiss tumbled into another until he was far too soon on the heady precipice. 'I need to be inside you.' It wasn't a sophisticated confession, meant to arouse. It was a raw need plumbed from his soul.

And when her eyes went liquid and she spread her thighs in sinful invitation, it was all he could do not to bow his head in supplication. Gritting his teeth to claw back more control, he positioned himself where he needed to be, where he craved to be more than he wanted to take his next breath, and he thrust home.

Her guttural shout rose as high as the tall walls, then caved back in on them in the sweetest surround sound, making his back bow in unadulterated bliss. '*Santo cielo*,' he grunted, his vision blurring with the sheer pleasure of possessing her.

A little terrified he would lose it if he wasn't careful, he blinked hard and fixed his gaze on her, taking note of what pleased her. What made her entire being shake. And when he found the key, he turned it in that lock, earning himself a treasure trove of wild passion.

'There you go. Is that what you want?' he demanded hoarsely.

She shook with the surfeit of pleasure ripping through her. 'Yes! *Jiyad jdaan…*' she wailed. *So good.*

He laughed a little raggedly. 'You think this is good? I'm not stopping until you scream yourself raw, *tesoro.*'

'Yes! God, yes!'

Time and pleasure and need blended into the perfect paradise, and he gave himself wholly to this moment. And when she tightened around him for the final time, Teo let himself be swept away, totally ignoring that lingering, taunting voice questioning whether he hadn't only opened the door to more madness.

One he might never escape.

CHAPTER NINE

SABEEN WAS SURE she'd misplaced part of her brain on the terrace in Morocco. Because very little could explain why she'd asked Teo to carry her down the steps and into her bedroom in the aftermath of the most sublime storm she'd ever experienced.

Worse, she hadn't done the sensible thing and shown him to the guest room or, better yet, insisted he return to his villa. Instead, she'd slid into bed, locked in torpor and lifted the sheets in eager invitation. After another soul-shattering round of sex, she'd dropped into a satiated sleep, only to be roused by a buzzing.

'Are you going to get that?' she'd murmured, concern building beneath her ribs when he merely slanted a blistering look at the phone.

Swiping it off the table he'd hit the button. 'Valenti, what is it?' Seconds passed, his face darkening with mild shock and anguish. 'When did it happen?'

Sabeen's breath had stalled as she'd tried to read his face.

'Claro.' He'd exhaled harshly, half-exasperated by whatever his twin was throwing at him, at the building urgency that made Teo's face darken with every second. 'I heard you the first time, *hermano*. I was already on my way. I'll see you in a few hours.'

He'd ended the call then veered to face her fully. Her heart had lurched, the raw need to allay whatever troubled him making her reach for him. 'Is it your father?'

'The old king's health has worsened.'

The old king. Not *Papá* or *Father.* There was a bite to it, a tightness around his eyes that she remembered last seeing when they attended his brother's wedding. Come to think of it, he'd displayed zero signs of the Playboy Prince then too, his mood almost brusque with a restlessness.

He exhaled then nodded sharply.

'Teo—'

'The fire isn't quite done with me yet, *tesoro*,' he bit out. 'I must return to Cartana. You will come with me, *sí*?' he demanded fiercely.

The madness had deepened. Because, heart squeezing for him, she'd responded immediately. Unequivocally. 'Yes.'

That was all he'd needed. With the ease of royal privilege, they were packed and on his private jet within the hour, the flight smooth and seamless, setting them down in San Mirabet just before dawn.

The last time she'd been there was to attend Azar and Eden's royal wedding and coronation. Eden's open warmth had touched Sabeen, and they'd stayed friends since.

On those occasions, though, she hadn't stayed on the Palacio Domene grounds. She'd enjoyed the comforts of a luxury five-star hotel in the centre of San Mirabet.

This time, however, the small motorcade had swung through the main palace's imposing gates and through an astonishing number of centuries-old cobblestone streets, all beneath the towering grandeur of the palace, to stop before a residence that looked like a smaller replica of the sprawling main building it was attached to.

Looking around, she'd seen it was one of six such buildings.

'They're the Royal Cottages. I have rooms in the *palacio*, but I find that I'm less…accosted by stuffy-suited councillors when I stay here,' he'd explained, his face set. He'd grown steadily more austere since his phone call and more tense with every mile they'd neared the *palacio*.

He'd thrown open his door before his bodyguard could and came around to hers. She'd taken his hand, still awestruck, both at her surroundings and the fact that Teo had brought her here.

This uncharted journey of theirs most definitely had an end date, but somewhere in the tumult of rediscovering herself, she'd also made the discovery that while it was an effective mask, and perhaps even a necessary one for him, Teo's self-centredness was only a veneer. Perhaps an overly efficient if self-sabotaging one.

And glancing at him as they'd followed the butler, her elbow caught in Teo's grip as they'd climbed one of the two sweeping staircases that led to the second floor, she'd yearned to tell him that. To offer the same succour he'd given her? In the hope that it was the gateway to giving him something… more? Like her heart?

The organ in question had lurched in alarm, but she held the panic at bay. Screeched that the timing wasn't right. Might never be. He'd come to Cartana for his father. And ultimately, she was here to finish the vital project she'd started.

And to offer more?

What if he didn't want it?

Could they slot back into their previous roles of creative director and creative genius, existing on separate continents?

A layer of unease had slithered over her emotions, a tiny spurt of gratitude following that she hadn't voiced her feelings so recklessly.

Keeping that in mind, she'd remained silent as the middle-aged butler swept open double doors that led to yet another exquisite set of rooms, with vaulted ceilings, handmade glittering chandeliers and a mix of antique and contemporary furniture that begged to be admired and appreciated. But her focus had remained riveted on Teo, who was watching her with that heavy-lidded intensity she yearned to break through. Right before he dismissed the butler and unceremoniously swept her off her feet and into an even grander royal bed.

Now, the mid-morning sun laid her actions bare.

She was plastered all over him, not fighting him at all when he'd dragged her over his body so she'd slept with her cheek on his chest, his fingers tangled in her hair.

'Your heartbeat just picked up. Should I be flattered into believing it's excitement, or should I anticipate a little turmoil in the light of day?' he mused with that slight edge that lined his voice so often now.

She remained silent, cursing him inwardly for his vexing talent. But it was probably a good thing if he knew the full extent of her unease. It would make things so much simpler.

Nathan had been entirely oblivious to her feelings, mocking her for being melodramatic whenever she'd pointed out his insensitivity.

She frowned. Why on earth was she thinking about him?

'Speak or I will be forced to act. Perhaps more of that madness you crave, hmm?' There was a lazy indulgence in his voice, but with a clear command too.

Raising her head, she caught a glimpse of wariness. And it occurred to her that he'd probably never been in this position. After all, every woman he'd bedded had probably begged to be there, protested at being shown the door when the time came. And while she'd stopped herself from avidly following his every move in the tabloids, from his tension just from being this close to his father, she highly suspected Teo had never brought a woman here before.

Was she being wildly naive? Secretly hopeful that she was unique?

'Or are you cured so soon?' came the drawled query, even as thick conceit mocked the possibility.

Sabeen wasn't sure if it was the urgent need for damage control—because no, she was far from cured; in fact she feared the opposite—or the need to keep barrelling down this path she'd taken with him that made her slide off him. Or at least attempt to.

He caught her easily, his hands spanning her waist to keep her in place atop him. Eyes turned quicksilver in the morning light burned into her. 'Stay. Use your words. I'm capable of many things, but I don't think I've mastered the ability to render anyone permanently mute, *tesoro*.'

'You asked me about Nathan before. Do you want me to talk about another man while I'm lying in your arms?' she asked, eyebrows raised.

He tensed. Jaw clenched tight, he released her, but he didn't move far away, following when she slid off the bed to go to the window.

The breathtaking grounds beyond the window barely caught her attention, the delicious thought that he clearly didn't want her out of arm's length stealing through her, burrowing into needy spaces that threatened to melt her resolve. Because she would've loved nothing more than to erase this aspect of her past with Nathan from her mind.

'We met on a photo shoot in Norway. The old clichés were eye-wateringly rife. As were the warnings that he was a womaniser collecting notches on his bed-post. And yes, I thought I could be the exception to the rule.' She slid him a glance then, gauged his reaction. Tried to see if she could read between his lines. Silver eyes challenged her to speak the words aloud.

She couldn't. Because…because…

She shook her head, terrified to finish that thought. There would come a time, pretty soon she feared, when she would need to face every emotion she felt for Teo Domene head-on. Not least because of the promise she'd made to her *jida*.

'I also did the unthinkable when he said that we were done. I chased after him. All the way to a small village in the far reaches of Norway. To discover he had a wife and the requisite two point five children who knew nothing of his other life. In the space of a half hour, I shattered four lives, plus mine.'

'Was he the reason you gave up your previous career?' The question was an icy blade, cutting through the thick emotions clogging the air.

She paused, not to choose her words but to bask in the small bubble of pride she felt then. 'No. I'd planned to give up modelling two months before I met him. The scandal that I'd seduced a married man and continued to pursue him when he wouldn't leave his wife and family for me was simply a cruel coincidence. Of course, that wasn't what was reported. It was a much juicier story for me to have crashed and burned over a man who didn't want me, who'd jilted me. A story he did nothing to deny, even though he knew the truth. I hated him for that, but I think I hated myself more for being so blind. For not remembering my family history until it was too late.'

She sighed, the memory of what came next slashing through her. 'I came home…after. *Jida* was already sick, but she was still my rock. I think…all this heaviness I'm carrying is because I helped her as much as I could, but if I hadn't been so preoccupied, maybe I could've done more.'

His silence when she finished speaking drew her to face him. His eyes were narrowed, his face set in enigmatic lines she couldn't fathom.

'You wanted to know. Well, that's the whole sordid saga. Are we done with this now?'

He closed the gap between them. 'Not quite, *tesoro.*'

She shook her head vehemently. 'No, I'm done with—'

His fingers brushing firmly over her lips stopped her words. Silver eyes burned into her as he quickly replaced his fingers with his mouth. The kiss was hard, tinged with annoyance. But it quickly morphed into something dangerous and familiar. A deep, unrelenting craving that dragged her arms up to wrap around his neck. That propelled her body that vital inch closer so she could plaster herself against him.

He reared back, strong hand gripping her shoulders. A

sound left her throat, embarrassingly resembling a whimper. She swallowed hard before another one could follow.

'Is it just misplaced guilt you're carrying around, or are you struggling to burn the past sketches of your life where he's concerned?'

'Misplaced?' she echoed.

'From what you've said about your grandmother, I think she was a tough woman, but she obviously loved you. She probably forgave you long before she passed. So *sí*, I believe your guilt is misplaced. Now answer the second part,' he pressed.

Her heart thudded dully. As much as she wanted to strenuously deny it she couldn't. Nathan had coloured a large swathe of her relationships since. Or the lack of them, in truth. 'Some things are imprinted too deep to burn away.'

His nostrils flared, his eyes hardening. 'Shall we see about that?'

'What—? Teo!'

He tossed her on the bed. Then launched himself after her while she was still bouncing on it. Strong arms grappled her into place beneath him, his eyes ablaze with lust and inextinguishable purpose.

Sabeen's mouth gaped when she read his intent. Teo meant to erase every vestige of Nathan from her mind in the most carnal way possible.

A way that had her thighs falling in open and shameless invitation, even as her inner self shook her head with mounting despair.

He pulled away at the last moment, dragging a frustrated objection from her throat. 'Beg me for it, Sabeen,' he commanded thickly.

Oh God. 'You think you're that irresistible?'

His eyes scorched her. 'I know it. So do you. Beg,' he insisted.

Eyes locked on his, she raised her arms above her head, pinning her own wrists together. His eyes flicked upward, his nostrils flaring at her willing subjugation. Next, she raised her knees, taking care to slide over every inch of his outer thighs on the way to wrapping her legs around his waist.

He thickened so he was even harder, bigger against her. His breath truncated, sensual lips she was dying to taste again parting on slow pants. Still he commanded the words from her.

When her chest started to rise, he wrapped a hand around her throat, stalling her. His nose brushed hers, but his eyes never closed. His will bore down hard on hers.

Then he employed sinful tactics of his own. With a deft angling of his hips, he brought the tip of his wide shaft to rest against her wet core. Decadent shudders drowned her at the wicked promise of being filled. Possessed. At the very thought that he could succeed in cleansing her of the remaining echoes of devastation and humiliation.

The very thought that she could finally be free… She swallowed then shuddered all over again at the possibility.

His eyes darkened on seeing her reaction. '*Dios mio*, you drive me insane. Do you know that?'

'Enough to give us both what we want without the royal theatrics?'

'You think this is mere theatrics?'

'What else can it be?'

He shook his head, brushing his nose across hers once more. 'Give me what I want, and you'll find out for yourself.' Then he wickedly eased himself in a mere half inch.

Another whimper completely disgraced her. 'Teo…'

'*Tesoro…*'

She bit the inside of her cheek, every inch of her body on fire. Deliverance hovered, one simple word away. And she wanted it…needed it just as much as she craved this delicious dance between them.

She squeezed her eyes shut.

'No. Open your eyes. Look at me. There will be no mistaking what this is. Who I am.'

She swallowed, feeling the imprint of his hand on her throat.

And moaned with helpless delight. In the end the word slipped out. Hot. Heavy. *Freeing.* 'Please.'

A shudder moved through him. 'Again.'

'P-please.'

Colour scoured his chiselled cheek bones, the first sign that he too was unravelling. 'Once more,' he croaked.

'Please, Teo. *Take me! Fuck me!*'

With a primal grunt he drove into her with all the purpose of a possessed man, his mouth swooping that last inch to claim the scream that ripped through her as he gave her everything she craved. The hand around her neck held for another moment, then shot up to grip her still-crossed hands.

Hard chest to soft chest, hips locked in sublime coupling, he made good on his vow and drove every last thought of the past from her head.

The despised churning sensation that had sparked to life with each update of his father's health grew as Teo stepped out of his residence. It was so much easier losing himself in Sabeen's arms.

But the last twenty-four hours had been intense, and while she made a stunning picture passed out in his sex-rumpled bed, he wasn't monstrous enough to interrupt her sleep.

Besides, he suspected his twin would invade his privacy if he ignored one more text. That sibling was waiting for him, silent and watchful as only a deadly ex-special operative could be as he tracked Teo's approach.

Valenti said nothing as Teo slid into the passenger seat of the Mercedes sports car his brother drove when he was in Cartana, but it didn't stop his brother from sending him probing looks on the short ride to the main palace.

'What?' Teo growled eventually.

'You brought her here?'

He didn't bother asking how Valenti knew. 'What's it to you?'

'You usually keep them far away,' Valenti stated the obvious, setting Teo's teeth on edge. He wasn't sure which annoyed him more: having Sabeen lumped in with faceless past liaisons or the truth that he'd brought her here, to the heart of every accusation of his flaws he'd ever faced in his life. 'You let her into your workshop too?'

He hadn't yet, but since he was unnerved by the very idea that he wouldn't mind letting Sabeen into his most sacred place, he kept his gaze pinned on the centuries-old façade of the place that had never truly felt like home.

'And what if I did?' His snap trumpeted his fraying control, but he didn't care.

Valenti's perusal sliced deeper. 'You won't even let me in there. Some would say you're letting the twin code down,' he said, his voice tinder-dry.

Teo's breath whistled out of a tight throat. Hell, his whole body was tight. 'Have you forgotten that she's my creative director?'

'Stop wriggling out of it. That place is your sanctum sanctorum. You flip metaphorical tables if anyone so much as looks at the door, never mind approaches it.'

Teo's teeth set tighter. Valenti's fingers drummed on the steering wheel for several seconds. 'You don't think I know what this is about?'

Teo tensed again but kept his lips sealed.

'You could've set up your workshop anywhere on earth. You threw everyone off the scent by setting up the second-best one in Milan. Because of him.'

Him. Their father.

Something burned at the back of his eyes. He turned his head away, blinked rapidly to disperse the impediment. 'You have no idea what—'

'Your soul is here, Teo. Because you want him to see you,' he said with such solemn conviction, the bottom fell out of Teo's gut. 'Did it occur to you that you made it easy for him by pretending not to want what you want?'

His gut clenched hard because hadn't that already occurred to him? That by assuming the very persona he had, he'd flipped the bird at the very thing he actually wanted? 'What's the fun in making things easy? Even absurd things my twin brother purports to think I want?' The joke fell as flat as the denial, both dying before they'd even been born.

'If you say so,' Valenti rasped as they arrived at the palace doors.

'I do. So drop it.'

Valenti sent him one last, hard look and opened his door. In silence they entered the palace wing that led to their father's residence.

Azar waited outside the double doors. When Teo reached him, his brother tugged him into a one-armed embrace. A fraction of his turbulent emotions settled. If nothing else, he'd always had his brothers' unwavering affection.

'About time you showed up. He's been asking for you.'

It took a moment to realise Azar meant *him*. Teo's heart flipped at the news then common sense reasserted itself. 'Nice try, brother.'

Azar frowned before his eyes flicked to Valenti. Teo ignored them both. 'Let's get this over with, shall we?'

His muscles clenched tight as the valets opened the suite doors.

Old King Alfonse was laid up in bed, exactly where he'd been the last time Teo had visited several weeks ago. Since then, though, his father's health had declined. It dawned on him then that with the old man's health having bounced back so often from death's door, their father's sheer willpower always defying the odds, he'd believed it would repeat that pattern this time too.

He took solace in seeing that illness hadn't diminished the former king's formidable character. Or changed him, apparently.

He fought his emotions when predictably his father's gaze

slid past him to Valenti. To Azar. Lingered there for a moment. Then...returned to Teo.

'You took your time,' his father rasped, an infinitesimal tremor in his voice that in no way belied its power.

Teo stiffened. Then forced himself to relax. 'I was giving you time to rebound so we could go another round.'

Both his brothers inhaled sharply, spiking him with shocked glares. But something unstoppable pushed him farther into the room to his father's bedside whereas normally he would've stayed near the door, ready to end another discordant visit. Something very similar to the bold vein of strength he'd seen in Sabeen.

Despite all the baggage weighing her down, she'd striven to rise above the challenges facing her. Her unquenchable courage was to be admired. Even emulated.

Her renaissance by fire had changed him too.

He would seek the truth here and now. But whatever the outcome, his self-worth was no longer in question. That admission punched relief through him, but decades-old anguish wasn't as easy to vanquish.

He knew it on closer inspection of his father's features, his heart lurching when he realised he didn't want to be running out of time.

A new, unfamiliar reason niggled at him, taunting him with its elusiveness. 'But it looks like you're letting this round kick your ass, Papá.'

'Teo...'

His father's hand rose, waving Azar's warning away. 'It's fine, *mijo*. Your brother has something to say. Maybe it's time to hear it.'

It was his turn to be shocked. To stare askance at his father. Dazedly he heard him ask after Eden, Max and his unborn second grandchild.

Unborn grandchild...why did that—?

He refocused in shock as the doors shut behind his brothers.

It was the first time they'd been alone in…for ever. 'What's this about?' he barked with more bravado than he felt.

His father's piercing stare rested on him in silence. For half a minute. Then longer still. And for the first time, Teo felt the naked blaze of being seen. Felt his heart constrict at the emotion flitting through his father's eyes. None of which was censorious. Or disappointed. He looked almost…remorseful.

'You're angry with me,' his father finally said.

A bark of bewildered laughter seared Teo's throat. 'What gave me away?'

He was being impertinent. While he wasn't entirely proud of it, it was either this, rant and rave like his overdramatic mother, or fall to his knees in despair. And Teo didn't do crawling. Well…maybe he did that for only one person. Sabeen. The woman he was accepting held more power in her soft, super-talented hands than she probably knew.

His father's droll smile added to his confusion. Then the whole thing intensified when he patted his space next to him. Teo approached warily, hands deep in his pockets. A stance his father didn't miss.

'This is decades overdue, but… I was wrong about you, *mijo*.'

Shock and anguish flayed him, certain his ears were playing tricks on him. 'What did you say?'

The old king smiled wryly. 'It sounds improbable after all this time, I know. And if you're suspicious it's a desperate attempt by an old man to come to grips with his mortality…well,' his withered hands weaved through the air for a moment, 'you wouldn't be entirely wrong.'

'Wouldn't I? Because I had the great fortune at Azar's wedding of hearing you say it was perhaps a good thing you wouldn't be around much longer to see your son disgrace you any further. A fine tune to add to the soundtrack of my life, *sí*?'

'*Dios mio*,' his father muttered, his face turning ashen.

'Is that remorse for speaking it within my hearing, Papá?

Or saying it at all?' he pressed. He needed this, more than he'd ever imagined. Teo knew it was an essential key to unlocking something vital within him. The bottleneck of emotions that felt like it would burst at the seams, decimate his life completely if he didn't keep it corked tight.

'Teo…*mijo*, this isn't easy to admit, but I lost my way with you a long time ago.'

'Bull—' He stopped himself in time before the uncouth word fell out. Whatever his feelings, this was his father. '*Perdonne mi*,' he rasped.

Again he sensed his father's sad amusement, but the old man who'd ruled his kingdom for several decades before abdicating had mastered the art of maintaining his composure, even with his sons. Perhaps to his own detriment?

His father patted the space again. '*De nada.* Can I explain?'

Emotion climbed into Teo's throat, but he sat and jerked a nod.

'It became clear very early on that your mother would fight me in every way where you and your brother were concerned. I had to learn to pick my battles very carefully. I was a young king with difficult roles and a kingdom to grapple with. In a blink of an eye, the future I'd imagined for myself had been turned on its head.'

Teo stiffened, anguish rising once more.

His father took a long breath. 'The truth was that while I welcomed three sons instead of none, I had a complex line to walk. Your mother's unhappiness grew toxic very quickly. Every time I so much as raised an opinion about your upbringing, she threatened to take you both away from me. And I know you're probably thinking I was the king and should've tossed around my power to make things go my way. But I suspected she was taking her…unhappiness out on you, so when I was advised to take a step back, I took it.'

'Let me guess. That advice came from your exemplary

council? The same council that advised that Valenti and I should be raised nowhere near the palace?'

His father flinched. '*Sí*. I was concerned about minimising your turmoil, but in hindsight I see they were more concerned about appearances. Insisting you and your brothers join the army so you could be away from the dysfunction your parents couldn't seem to stop creating was a way to solve the issue.'

The army. Where Teo and his brothers had finally forged the unshakeable bond their mothers had been so hell-bent on destroying. 'You did that? I thought...'

'I had Parliament push through the legislation requiring royal sons to serve. I thought if I couldn't be in your lives on a fuller basis, then at least you three should have each other. And you...' Silver eyes locked on him. Causing that bottle-neck to strain further. 'But long before that, I believed you didn't need me as much as your brothers, *mijo*. You were always so supremely confident. Self-assured and undaunted by whatever was thrown at—'

Arid laughter seared Teo's throat, the confirmation of one suspicion doing nothing to salve his desolation. 'I guess I did a good job of fake-it-till-you-make-it.'

His father winced again. 'Yes, I see in that, too, I let myself believe what wasn't true. But your brothers needed you. They weren't so—what's the in-vogue term?—in their own heads when you were with them.'

He raised a brow, although his insides twisted with the revelations. *His father had had a greater purpose?* Teo hadn't wanted to join the army. He'd gone so he wouldn't be left behind. And because a royal decree was one not even his mother could rebuff. 'So I was the comic relief?'

'No. You kept them balanced. And for that, you have my undying gratitude, *mijo*. But you deserved recognition too, not just as the bulwark for your brothers but in who you are. I failed to do that.'

Teo was struggling his way through this new revelation

when his father spoke again, tossing more boulders onto his pulverised senses. 'I've seen your workshop at your residence.'

For the umpteenth time in what felt like a relentless twenty-four hours, everything inside him flipped. 'What?'

'I also came to your first show. And I fought your mother when she insisted on you doing something other than what you loved.'

A spark of anger lit through him at the disarming news. 'That's all well and good, but did you at any point think it would benefit me to know all these things you did but decided to keep to yourself?'

His father exhaled, his expression pained. 'I watched you succeed *despite* me. You were so angry, and I was ashamed. Not an easy thing for a king to admit. For the most part, I thought keeping my distance would ease the toxicity your mother steeped you in.'

'You never once thought to remove us from it altogether? Seek sole custody? Or was that a scandal too far for your kingdom?' Teo bit out.

A tinge of shame coloured his father's pale features. 'It was considered. And rejected. And I agreed. Taking a child away from their mother should be the last resort, king or no king. I hope you never have to face that choice as a father.' His face fell. 'As for why I'm doing this now, I was too busy trying to get through to Valenti after his...' His jaw clenched. 'I'm ashamed to say I seem to have failed there too.'

The ordeal his twin had endured still cut them all raw. But Teo selfishly wished for a sliver of what his father had denied him. As for the quip about being a father himself...

The niggle came again. *Harder.*

Dios, why the hell couldn't he recall—?

'Your next show...you will move it here.'

A royal edict if he'd ever heard one. So what if it was the very thing he'd striven for the first time he'd picked up a stylus? 'And if I refuse?'

A wave that closely resembled pain moved through his father's eyes, quickening Teo's breath. 'I would be disappointed, but I would understand.'

'Would you?' he scoffed lightly, but his insides were slowly unknotting, the waves of emotion drowning him as he looked at his father telling him he was halfway to doing the very thing he'd wanted for as long as he could remember. Seeking—*and finding*—acceptance.

'Your Highness, your father needs to rest now.'

Teo's head snapped towards the doctor who'd just entered. He'd walked in here expecting another round of his expectations being disregarded, his emotions being turned to mincemeat with indifference. Now he'd survived the fire. The core of his very being sizzled with…rejuvenation. A rebirth that felt too big, too unwieldy to contain.

On stiff legs he went to the door and pulled it open. His brothers waited outside, concerned looks on their faces.

'Teo?'

He turned back to his father, aware of his brothers listening in.

'Whatever the reason is for you not being more…disillusioned with me than you are right now, you need to hang on to it.'

He frowned. Shook his head. 'I don't…'

'*Sí*, you do. It's important. Perhaps the most important thing of all.'

He suspected his father knew every detail of what was going on in his sons' lives, even from his sickbed. Without answering, because he didn't know how without shattering that ball of paradoxical dread and hope lodged in his middle, he shut the door behind him. And turned to find his brothers eyeing him with varying degrees of censure.

'He's trying to make amends,' Azar said. 'You must hear him out.'

'Is that a royal directive?' he growled without heat. A great chunk of the answers he'd sought had just been provided. He didn't know yet whether he was ready to forgive and forget. But a new, deeper urgency was rising. Demanding attention. Something to do with Sabeen.

Azar stiffened then exhaled. 'Of course not. But as much as we want to deny it, our father's time is running out. Don't waste time you'll regret.'

The ominous words ringing in his ears, he started to turn away.

'Where do you think you're going?'

Teo stopped, realising he was already halfway to the main entrance. 'Did we have plans?' *Dios*, he hoped not.

Valenti, eyes narrowed, accurately read his thoughts.

Azar beckoned to Teo. 'If you're hurrying back to your residence because of your…guest, I'm afraid I have been ordered to let you know that she's busy right now.'

His chest cracked open with fury. And fear. And unfathomable oceans of jealousy. 'What the hell did you just say?'

Azar's hands shot up in mock surrender, even as a wicked glint lit his eyes. 'Easy, *hermano*. My very pregnant wife, who's carrying twins by the way and is therefore not to be denied anything her heart desires, insisted on having lunch with Sabeen. Sabeen agreed. Eden told me not to expect her back until at least mid-afternoon. I'm just saving you the trouble of incurring the queen's wrath by interrupting her girls' date.' His keen gaze sharpened. 'But now I'm interested in what you think I meant because I could've sworn you were ready to rip chunks out of your king,' he teased.

Frustration unleashed an unfettered growl before he could stop it, casting a fond eye at the exit as it ate him alive. A quick glance at his Vacheron Constantin watch showed it was just past lunchtime. Stewing in this urgency and dread building in his chest was hell.

He exhaled and turned from the door. 'Two hours, then their date is over. Not a word out of you,' he warned his faintly amused twin then stalked past them both as Valenti's sombre demeanour reasserted itself.

'Where are you going? Or is it a secret?' Azar drawled.

'To drink your most expensive cognac. I believe you've taken possession of a Henri IV Dudognon?'

Azar inhaled sharply, hurrying after him. 'I dare you to touch that.'

Teo smiled without humour, the wild notion that he'd been rushing back to tell Sabeen about the conversation with his father, to seek her counsel about allaying the dregs of anguish and bewilderment within him because she alone could, escalating the churning consuming him.

Because he was beginning to learn what that truly meant.

And if that belief was valid, then he was in peril yet again. One that might utterly consume his heart and soul this time.

He was still stewing in that unsettling notion, sipping the finest cognac ever made when the niggle, powered by his father's last words, finally solidified in his reeling brain, sending him jerking to his feet. '*Dios mio!*'

Sabeen pushed her food around her plate, hoping Eden wouldn't notice she had zero appetite. That not even the presence of the pregnant Queen of Cartana beside her, the Michelin-starred chef Azar had sent along to cook their surprise girls' lunch—one of a million ways he spoiled the love of his life—could make Sabeen not wish for a simpler meal back at her grandmother's house. *With Teo*.

Or that the outcome of the last few hours spent in a transformative state sketching page after page was something she wanted to share only with him. Even now, her very skin tingled with the almost out-of-body experience of it, and the decisions she'd made when she woke up in his bed, to just lay everything on the line—

'What's wrong?'

Sabeen jumped, her startled gaze rising from her plate to meet Eden's shrewd green eyes.

'And before you pull some excuse out of thin air, know that I've been in your shoes. I was covering by talking your ear off but, sweetheart, you look downright miserable. Another emotion I recognise, but I'm thankful to say is in my past.'

Sabeen gave up the pretence of eating, setting her cutlery down and startling again when Eden's hand dropped down on top of hers, gripping it tightly in support before she let go.

'I hope you know you can trust me.'

Sabeen swallowed, warmed by the friendship Eden hadn't held back from their very first meeting. 'Of course.'

Eden nodded, her gaze encouraging.

'I think...' she started then grimaced as tears prickled her eyes. 'God, I'm a mess.'

'Take your time.'

She inhaled slowly. Let it out. Then summoned a smile. 'I'm grateful for all this. Sorry if I'm ruining it with my mood but—'

'But I'm not the one you want sitting across from you at the table right now?' Eden finished shrewdly.

Sabeen gasped then sighed. 'Of course you can read me like a book.'

Eden smiled. 'I told you I've been there. And that's why I should tell you not to be like me. Don't let whatever is bothering you stay an obstacle. Unfortunately, those gremlins have a way of growing roots and making you believe they'll be impossible to dig out without pouring your heart out on national television.'

An unguarded chuckle slipped out. 'You're the queen. It's only right your love declarations were epic.'

Eden grimaced, waving away the staff members who approached with more platters of food. 'It's great for everlasting love and all that, but I could've done with not becoming the world's number one meme.' She sobered. 'Do you want me out of your hair, or can you manage another half hour so I can introduce you to the most divine dessert ever created?'

Her response was easy. 'Dessert, please.'

She needed all the sugary rush of courage she could get to tell the Playboy Prince that she'd fallen in love with him.

Except courage was nowhere to be found when five minutes after the queen had departed, with a promise extracted from Sabeen to visit her in the palace proper before she left, Teo walked through the impressive mansion's double doors, his face a fierce, unreadable mask.

'We need to talk.'

For a moment, Sabeen wondered whether she should've kept the sordid details of her past with Nathan to herself. Whether Teo had hit his quota of dealbreakers with her. Finally.

She followed him across the breathtaking foyer with the familiar House of Domene coat of arms inlaid within the warm gold marble floor that led to a trio of hallways. The footmen who'd opened the doors smoothly closed them and quickly made themselves scarce.

The immaculately dressed butler, Fernando, who served them while the queen was present, stood out of earshot at a respectful distance.

The intractable look in Teo's eyes froze her in place a second before her throat closed in alarmed realisation. Of course, they'd returned to the real world. He had a life and magic to create outside of their ephemeral bubble in Essaouira. She just hadn't thought the end would be this abrupt. This soon after she'd thrown herself so shamelessly at him and, dear heaven, wanted to do so again—

'I need to remain in Cartana. My father's health remains concerning.'

Sabeen hated herself for the relief she felt that this wasn't about her. About what they'd done last night and this morning. It prodded her into nodding and approaching because the need to be near him in his time of difficulty wouldn't allow the distance. 'I hope he gets better soon.' Dear God, could she fail harder at disguising her yearning? 'Did you get a chance to talk to him?'

He nodded briskly. 'He clarified things,' he said.

She waited for more, but he didn't seem interested in elaborating. Instead the intensity in his eyes grew. She licked her lips. 'Did it not go how you wanted? Is he—'

'I don't want to talk about my father, Sabeen. There's a whole new set of issues that needs dealing with.'

Was he telling her their torrid little affair was over? Sabeen's heart lurched. The last time she'd been in this situation she'd let herself down. It wasn't happening again. As much as it hurt far worse this time, she lifted her chin. 'Fine. I'll let you deal with whatever it is. Guess I'll see you when I see you?'

His nostrils flared. 'Meaning?'

'Meaning I'm leaving. Isn't that what you want?'

He frowned. 'I didn't make myself clear, it seems. We're far from done. And you're most definitely not leaving Cartana.'

Fire and ice fought for supremacy within her at his steel tone. 'What does that mean? I'm not your prisoner.'

Shades of bewilderment and apprehension flashed through his eyes, gone before she could decipher the reason. 'No, of course you're not. But for starters, you asked me for my help. And you agreed to do whatever was needed to get that help. I don't believe a specific location for where that work would happen was baked into that agreement.'

Her breath shivered out of her at the resurgence of the domineering prince. But more than knowing every word he said was valid, and that she yearned to grasp the golden trophy she could see shimmering just out of reach, it was the shadows in his eyes that pulled harder at her. The burning desire to give him back a fraction of what he'd given her. And selfishly...carnally, the prospect of more nights with him, more bliss-filled hours experiencing the best lovemaking she'd ever been gifted.

Something of that last longing must have slipped through her composure. His eyes darkened, his aura swelling in response. 'Besides, we're not done with each other yet, are we, *tesoro*?'

Need dripped hunger straight into her bloodstream, drying up any weak objections before they could escape. But even with the unassailable evidence that she was growing so very addicted to him, that she stood on the precipice of risking the very emotions she needed to protect, she couldn't deny the truth. Even worse, she felt no inclination to step back.

But she could attempt to put a few guard-rails in place, couldn't she? Maybe? 'I'll stay here with you on one condition.'

Displeasure and disappointment flared in his eyes. 'Let's hear it.'

'I don't want anyone to know about us. I can't risk my reputation taking another hit if...*when*...this ends.' He was her boss. Whom she'd crossed the line with numerous times. She knew to her detriment how rabidly the vultures would pick at the carcass of another unfortunate decision.

'Your reputation?' he echoed stonily, a little perplexed.

She lifted her chin higher. 'Yes. And you should be pleased I want it this way. Keeping this under wraps helps both of us.'

His face turned marble hard. A minute passed while silver eyes drilled into hers. 'Are you sure about that?'

His tone was devoid of inflection, and she couldn't tell which she liked less: when he spoke with zero emotion or with his Playboy Prince voice. Especially now she knew how deep his waters ran.

Teo Domene wasn't a vacuous pleasure-seeker with a penchant for delivering exquisite masterpieces on a sickeningly regular basis and gaining billions of accolades and dollars for his empire. He possessed a wealth of layers wreathed in mysteries he shared with very few people. Being exposed to his true self had turned her inside out in a little over a week. What would a month...a year...a lifetime—?

No. That foolishness was out of the question.

But even while it bruised her to push closed a door he clearly didn't want to close yet, she knew not doing so would bring her more devastation than she'd known before. *When* this thing between them ended.

This time around, she would keep the fallout out of public view and judgement, thank you very much. So she summoned her strength and stared into his mesmerising eyes. 'Yes, I'm absolutely sure.'

Was it a trick of the light, or did he pale a shade? In the next moment, one corner of his mouth was tilting, his face morphing from marble into devastating charm as he sauntered towards her.

'Careful, *cariña*. You might revel in an illicit secret tryst right now, but the alternative might not be open to you when you change your mind.'

The warning cut deeper than she would've believed possible. But she'd picked her path. She would walk it. 'Then it's a good thing I'm absolutely sure.'

Too late, she remembered he only called her *cariña* when he was in full Playboy Prince mode. For another eternity, he stared at her. Brushed his finger down her cheek, along her jaw to the corner of her mouth, then over her bottom lip, his gaze scarily pensive.

Then he nodded. 'Very well. So be it.'

His whole life he'd fought to know where he stood. Regardless of whether he ultimately enjoyed that position or he was left with no choice but to create that place for himself, he'd always deemed it best to be equipped with foreknowledge.

For the first time in conscious memory, Teo wished for ignorance.

Because this panic bubbling inside him disturbed him only a fraction less than the giant crevasse of unnerving emptiness he felt.

Was it mere hours ago that he'd thought he'd made a giant breakthrough in his life? That in helping her overcome guilt over her grandmother and beginning to unblock her creativity once more, *he* had overcome the yawning sensation of inadequacy that he'd plastered over with his various caricatures for so long it'd almost become second nature to him?

Well, apparently, the stains weren't so easily washed away.

She wanted to hide him like an unworthy little secret.

And in the very place he'd hoped to make a fresh start while sipping cognac and waiting to tell her that he'd achieved his deepest desires, after all. He'd been found worthy of the attention and recognition that had long been denied him.

Where he'd hoped to erase the memory of his mother using his talent to drape herself in his masterpieces then happily forgetting he existed until the next time she needed a new wardrobe.

Teo had taken all that in stride. Hell, just like the magnificent haute couture he created, he'd mastered the art of making beauty and flaws, pleasure and pain coexist in one dazzling whole, so no one bothered to dissect where one ended and the other began. He'd become a master at breathtaking camouflage. *Sí*, he'd learned too late that he'd become too good at it and it had ultimately cost him time with his father. But that was all behind him now.

So why did this panic burrow deep into a soft and shockingly vulnerable place he hadn't known existed until she'd given him her condition about secrecy?

He exhaled long and slow, while his brain frantically rushed to provide clarity.

Perhaps it was a good thing he was here in Cartana. Slackening his guard beneath the Moroccan sun and in her fierce beauty and will had clearly made him soft. Sleeping with her, while intensely pleasurable, had further addled his senses.

Besides, there was a much more important reason he'd instructed Fernando to inform him the second the queen left, the reason he'd taken Valenti's car and rushed here. And if she paled at seeing the unabashed ruthlessness that rushed through his bloodlines, he didn't care.

'You've given me your conditions. Now let me tell you one of my own.'

Dread danced over her face, but to her credit, her chin remained high, her gaze unwavering. 'I don't see why you would have any.'

His hard, little smile felt starched. 'Patience, *cariña*.' He gritted his teeth at the careless endearment he'd used a thousand times with dozens of different women. It tasted…wrong with Sabeen. But the *tesoro* he'd taken to calling her felt… risky. Exposing. 'The possible seismic shift might require fortitude.'

'Don't drag it out, then,' she said.

His gaze trailed over her, lingering, his mouth watering in searing recollection, even while his heart hammered for a different reason. The thing that had jolted him in Azar's living room.

'We didn't use protection this morning.' The words shook through him, and he couldn't help himself as an image lit through his brain. Azar's mention of his pregnant wife had immediately conjured up a mental picture of Sabeen's belly swollen with his child. A vision he suddenly wanted to become reality more than he wanted his next breath.

And if there's no child?

Another lash of anguish flayed him, letting him in on another shocking discovery.

He wanted her to be pregnant.

Wanted an heir, treasured from the moment they first drew breath, not three regretted decades later.

'Until such time as we know the consequences for that oversight, you're not straying one foot from my sight.'

CHAPTER TEN

SABEEN FELT AS if she was outside of herself, hearing his words fall. Hitting her like vicious little darts. Some poisonous enough to weaken her legs, others striking her heart with...*elation*?

He lunged forward and caught her before she even realised she'd sagged dangerously. Her arms flailed, then latched onto his strong arms...because of course they did. Quickly dropping them, she stepped back, bumped into the table and scrambled further.

'Easy,' he warned, his voice stiff with suppressed emotion.

A hysterical little snort escaped her before she could check it. 'Easy?' She swiped her hands over her eyes, in a vain effort to calm herself. 'I feel like I'm in a damn wood chipper.'

Did he flinch? She shook her head, still rocked to her core that the slip hadn't even occurred to her. She'd been so busy craving when she could slide into his arms next. When she could have him inside her once more.

His eyes narrowed. 'You can't use this as one of your conditions to leave if that's what you're contemplating. There can't be any doubt that the child is mine. I'm sure you'll work out why.'

His meaning fell into place instantly. Eden and Azar. 'You think I'm going to somehow become an amnesiac and forget who impregnated me—if indeed that's even remotely on the cards—and live obliviously in some metropolis with your child for two years?'

Cynical humour twisted his mouth. 'Emulating my brother's and Eden's journey would be most unoriginal, and you and I are far from boring. That said, I intend to mitigate any chance of misplacing you by not letting you out of my sight. I haven't forgotten that you fell off the radar recently. That's not going to happen again.'

The sensation of walls closing in on her, where she'd only last night felt a rebirth, dredged disquiet through her heart. The idea that he was merely covering his bases, ensuring he knew to the second what their recklessness had produced, squeezed a vice around her heart. 'And if I say no?' she threw out, desperately testing turbulent waters.

Maybe she knew what it would achieve. Maybe she even secretly craved that primal reaction. Because his face turned to beautiful, forbidding stone, quicksilver eyes zeroing in on her with feral intent that sent shivers dancing over her skin.

'You're welcome to do as you please, of course. But it won't come as a surprise that the likelihood of you carrying my heir won't be one I'm going to be blasé about until we know one way or the other,' he finished with gritted teeth.

She dragged her gaze from his, recalling the steps he'd gone to find her in Morocco when it was merely his collection on the line. She wasn't foolish enough to believe she could just swan off while the possibility of carrying Teo's heir was up in the air.

The enormity of this new situation bore down on her. How could this be another chapter of history truly repeating itself in three generations? Except…just like her mother and grandmother before her, she couldn't find it in herself to feel shame or regret. Both women had proudly claimed the children they carried. So would she. The image of her grandmother's chair made her heart squeeze. Because she knew that if she was alive, her *jida* would've stood by her, given unwavering support if she turned out to be carrying Teo's child.

Teo's child…

A helpless moan escaped. Hands closed over her arms. Opening her eyes, she was compelled to look into silver ones.

'The fire isn't done destroying the baggage weighing you down. It's probably wise not to make hasty decisions.'

'Are you saying without you, I won't make it?' she challenged.

Expecting a harsh *yes*, he surprised her by shaking his head. 'Of course not. Your strength alone will see you through. But am I interested in waiting for that to happen in your own sweet time? When I'm not guaranteed you won't reverse all the progress you've made?' He shrugged, an eloquent expression of dismissiveness that cut her deep. But she knew he wasn't as aloof about this as he was projecting. Besides this new development, at the very least he had a vested interest in seeing her collection finished.

And damn it, so did she.

Besides, she wasn't ready to let this go, even though the faint ticking of a countdown clock at the back of her mind warned her that end was coming. Possibly sooner than she was ready for. That, again like the women before her, she might have to do this alone.

Her face flamed when she saw where his attention had moved to the hand she'd dropped to her belly.

Where his child might be growing.

'When will we know one way or another?' he rasped, his deep voice rumbling through her with more force than a jet engine.

She scrambled to recall dates and a fresh consternation washed over her. She couldn't have been in a more opportune window if she'd planned this to the second. Her teeth sank into her inner lip as a worrying thought struck. Surely, he wouldn't think she'd planned this? Examining his face, all she saw was grating impatience as he waited for her response. 'My period isn't due for about ten to twelve days.'

He stared hard at her, then his nostrils flared. 'You're in your most fertile window?' Was his voice deeper? Thicker?

Her face flamed hotter. 'Yes,' she muttered. His eyes stayed fixed on her. Until she fisted her hand in a bid not to visibly squirm. 'Teo.' She couldn't tell if she was warning or pleading.

This time when his gaze dropped to her middle, it stayed. Seared. 'How do you feel?'

'Not pregnant, if that's what you're asking,' she forced out. Then grimaced. 'Sorry. But this might turn out to be a non-event. Till then—'

'You wish to put it to the back of your mind, pretend like it doesn't exist until it becomes an issue?' Before she could reply to his acid tone he ruthlessly continued. 'I need an answer, Sabeen. Will you stay?'

The lack of the familiar barked command threw her for a moment, adding to her confusion. Then the Pavlovian response kicked in nevertheless, pushing her to give him what he wanted.

Which in turn disturbed her greatly, because it turned out that even after this bombshell revelation, what Teo Domene wanted also happened to be what *she* wanted. It would be almost parasitic, except at every turn she'd also ended up...fulfilled. Sated without trickery. Sated in a way she'd never been before. Professionally. Emotionally. *Sexually.*

In a mere handful of days, Teo Domene had turned her inside out in ways she could never have imagined she could be transformed.

And as he watched her with that almost sardonically smug expression, she wanted to go against the grain. Summon up a firm *no.* But who was she kidding? In this moment, besides her grandmother's house, with Teo, there was nowhere else she wanted to be.

'I'll think about it,' she hedged.

His nostrils flared with clear displeasure, but again he surprised her by nodding. 'I must return to the palace. I'll be back for dinner. As my guest you have free rein of the residence. If you need anything, Fernando will be around to provide it.'

Expecting him to leave immediately, she watched him hesitate at the door. Perplexity flashed on his face before he inhaled deeply and said, 'Come with me.' He held out an imperious hand.

'Why?' she asked warily.

'There's one more thing to show you before I go.'

Curious despite herself, she followed him up the grand staircase then down the long hallway to the opposite wing to the master suite.

Again he paused before the tall double doors then swept them open.

The room was easily twice as big as her grandmother's entire house. Her feet propelled her to the centre, where she spun slowly in wonder.

A designer's dream workshop, with a wealth of fabrics, six workbenches, mannequins and an entire wall dedicated to some of Teo's most celebrated designs. She'd mistakenly believed that his treasured workshop was in Milan, but this felt...special.

'I didn't know this was here,' she murmured then frowned. 'You didn't mention it when I was making Eden's trousseau.'

'Because very few people know this studio exists. And fewer are granted access. Or so I thought,' he muttered darkly.

'Why?' she asked before she could stop herself. 'And why are you showing it to me at all?'

That curious bewilderment flashed across his face once more. Then he shrugged. 'You showed me your grandmother's chair. This place is my equivalent,' he said, his voice rough and raw.

Perhaps it was a sweetener to keep her exactly where he wanted her. Or Teo exposing another layer of himself. Either way, her heart lurched, her emotions frantically scrambling not to bubble over.

'Use the space as you see fit.' Striding to a workbench that turned out to be automated, a switch lit up the whole table. 'Place your sketches here, and they'll be converted into a 3-D version, and you can continue creating from here...' A flurry of instructions followed, most of which only half registered.

She'd remained old-school with her designs because it was a custom of her grandmother's she'd wanted to honour. But this, Teo letting her into his inner sanctum, showing her a part of himself others rarely saw…

'Thank you,' she whispered, the near-terrifying sensation of brimming with too much emotion choking her again. 'Teo—' She stopped when, with a perfunctory knock, the doors swept open.

Valenti Domene filled the doorway. His gaze passed briefly over her and the studio before settling on his twin.

'Everything okay?'

'Why shouldn't it be?' Teo asked.

Valenti didn't answer. The two men watched each other, peculiar expressions weaving across their faces. *Twin-speak.* After several moments, Valenti nodded gruffly at his brother, his dark silver gaze moving over her before he turned.

'Thanks for checking in. But maybe next time use one of the many phones you've got next door?' Teo teased a little tensely.

'I would if I was sure you'd answer' came the grouchy reply as Valenti left as abruptly as he'd arrived.

'What was that all about?'

Teo shrugged. 'It's not every day I find out I might become a father. My emotions are somewhat…amplified.' The edge had sharpened, shards of bitterness cutting through his voice.

'And he felt that too? Does that happen often?' she asked, stunned.

'Very rarely. So it's…meaningful when it does.'

Her heart did that dipping thing again, her eyes desperately searching for a sign that this wasn't all a proprietorial claiming.

That *she* mattered in this too.

But his gaze was efficiently shuttered when it raked her face before he nodded. 'I'll see you later,' he said crisply.

Then he was gone, taking the very air with him. Leaving her amongst his most treasured creations.

CHAPTER ELEVEN

IF SHE'D THOUGHT the first days in her grandmother's house with Teo were emotionally strenuous, they were nothing compared to her first week in Teo's Cartana mansion, starting with the harrowing decision to move her things out of Teo's suite and into one of the many luxurious guest suites. The part of her that wasn't furiously trying to preserve her heart had mocked her for attempting to elicit a reaction from Teo.

After her announcement at the breakfast table the next morning about moving bedrooms, he'd remained silent for a full minute. Then he skewered her with one of those hard, censorious looks that somehow also managed to hold shades of perplexity and disquiet. As if her decision had wounded him.

He'd left for the palace straight after. And that had set their routine. She'd work all day in his studio, her heartache temporarily alleviated by creations that were positively bursting free from her sketching pencil. In the knowledge that she'd well and truly come through the fire. She filled sketchbook after sketchbook, and still the ideas poured out.

It was only after she'd completed her fourth that the disturbing truth that Teo hadn't enquired about her work since their arrival propelled her to his suite before breakfast halfway through their second week, her nerves gobbling her as she knocked on his door. To no response.

A throat clearing showed Fernando hovering several feet away. 'Is Teo here?'

He hesitated for a moment before replying, 'His Highness is no longer using his suite.'

Surprise was washed away by all the reasons Teo would abandon his suite. 'Then, where is he?'

Again the butler hesitated for a beat. 'He spends most of his nights in his studio or…in the suite next to yours.'

Her heart soared then dipped, knowing it was foolish to ascribe any reasoning to Teo's actions or why he was choosing to work in his studio only when she was asleep. Maybe he didn't care anymore? It shouldn't hurt that he was avoiding her, especially when she knew he was spending daylight hours with his father. They were rebuilding a relationship long left to fallow. She was happy for him. *And yet…*

The unbearable notion that their connection—as tenuous as it might turn out to be if she wasn't pregnant—hung in the balance wouldn't be dismissed. Berating herself for the selfish thought, especially when Eden had reported during their brief coffee dates that the old king's health had steadied, she turned from the door. 'Is he in the studio now?'

Fernando shook his head, a flicker of a frown marring his brow before disappearing. 'He left on his motorbike before dawn, miss.'

Her spirits plummeted further. 'Oh.'

'Would you like your breakfast now, miss?'

Her appetite was non-existent, but she had to eat. Because if the growing belief that she was pregnant turned out to be true…

If she was going to be a mother…

The overwhelming forces of awe and apprehension shaking through her stalled when they reached the bottom of the stairs and she was confronted with Valenti Domene.

His uncanny resemblance to his twin made her heart flip over. Then it settled because, besides the small scar characterising Valenti's features, his face didn't hold the constant gleam in Teo's eyes that kept her mesmerised.

'Hello,' she said tentatively, suspecting he wasn't there for Teo. This Domene most certainly knew his twin's whereabouts at all times.

'You've been summoned to the *palacio*,' he rasped, his deep voice an octave lower than his brother's.

She fought to quell her heart's stagger. 'By whom?'

'My father.'

Her thwarted elation must've shown, but although one brow quirked, he didn't crack a smile. In fact, during the short journey, she got the distinct impression he was less than thrilled to be in her company.

The chilling gaze he turned on her just before a footman opened the door once they reached the *palacio* further clued her in. 'Word of advice. Do not toy with Teo.'

She bristled. 'Excuse me? What makes you think I—'

He held up his hand. 'You've seen beneath his surface.' Eyes eerily similar to his twin's pierced her. 'You're worth something to him. The question is, are you woman enough to admit he's worth it to you, or are you going to judge him by another's standards until he slips through your fingers?'

Her mouth was still agape when he drove away.

The senior palace staff member discreetly cleared his throat. 'Miss El-Maleh? His Majesty is waiting.'

The prompt refocused her. But she didn't move. Hell, she even went as far as to consider refusing the monarch's request. After a week and a half of living on tenterhooks and not feeling anywhere near assuaged about the distance she'd put between them with her decree of wanting to keep their brief liaison a secret, she was now severely doubting this road she'd taken of keeping her feelings to herself.

Because…

He's worth it. Dear God, he is.

Her insides shook as she was led through the stunning *palacio* to a sun-drenched terrace. And on a wide seat that looked more lounger than chair, festooned with pillows, sat King Alfonse.

Sabeen drew in a breath and dropped into a curtsy. 'Good morning, Your Majesty.'

'Welcome, young lady,' he rasped in a voice much stronger than she'd expected. Maybe it was the lighting, but he looked more robust than she'd expected, too.

He caught her scrutiny, and his mouth twisted, a quirk he'd passed on to his son. 'If you're wondering why I'm not knocking on death's door, I have a secret.'

'Oh? What's that?' she asked, taking the offered seat adjacent to him.

He waited until servers had poured fresh coffee and juice, uncovered succulent platters of food and retreated before he replied, his gaze contemplative. 'I find confronting my past failings, while not strengthening my failing heart, heals my soul.'

'I see,' she murmured. 'Is that aimed in some way at me?'

He reached across and patted her hand. 'It's not a dig, my dear.'

Relief twinned with confusion as she reached for the decaf coffee. If he hadn't brought her here to echo Valenti's indictment, then—

'I invited you here to talk about my son,' he started, his shrewd gaze delving beneath her surface.

She set her cup down without drinking it. She was terrified it would go down the wrong way. But while she was even more terrified of the words she was about to utter, she didn't let that stop her. Maybe it was high time she stopped letting fear win? 'That's lucky because I'm…feeling the need to do the same,' she ventured.

His eyes turned the same quicksilver that, in his son, made her heart jump. Then he smiled. 'Good. Then, I hope this won't be arduous.'

'That's really up to you, isn't it, Your Majesty? Your son has been in knots over you for most of his life. He's not been exactly forthcoming with me as to whether you've made things right yet. Have you? Because he deserves every scrap of attention and love denied to him for whatever reason.'

And because he helped me confront my demons and deserves to vanquish his.

Grey eyebrows rose a notch. Then a glint of respect lit the silver depths. 'He was right to sing your praises. Perhaps you should take your own advice and point all that righteous passion in another direction, eh?'

Her throat tightened. 'I'm not sure what you—'

'You know exactly what I mean. He's caught in anguish that has nothing to do with me or his next collection.'

'And you think I'm to blame?'

'I think you hold the key to ending his anguish. And you're not afraid of a fight,' he tossed in cryptically.

Dear heaven, if the old king was right, if one more fiery battle was what it took, then didn't she owe it to herself to fight for him? For them?

'I—'

'What the hell is going on here?'

They both turned as Teo approached them, his long stride eating up the vast space. His hair was sexily dishevelled, and his leather jacket and dark jeans lent him a rakish look that set her every nerve alight, rendering every argument to deny the pure, profound emotion blazing in her heart to nonsense. She'd foolishly chased after an unworthy man once. And lost. This time she would chase one a million times worthy.

'What does it look like, *mijo*? I'm having breakfast with your guest.'

His frowning gaze rested a beat on his father before settling with unwavering intensity on her. 'Why wasn't I told?'

The old man shrugged. 'Because we were talking about you.'

Teo stiffened. 'Papá…'

The king's expression softened as his gaze moved from her

to his son. 'It's perfectly fine. You can steal her away now if you feel so strongly about it.'

Emotions competed on his face before his eyes darkened. 'That depends on Sabeen. Does she wish to be stolen?'

She rose to her feet, glad her shakiness wasn't outwardly visible. Then prayed for greater composure when Teo's gaze, like clockwork, dropped down her body to her stomach. She saw his father intercept that look, his eyes widening a touch before his introspection deepened. Before he put any thoughts to speech, she stepped away from the table, dropping into another quick curtsy. 'What I wish is to return ho—to the residence. I've had enough of everyone telling me what I should do,' she muttered under her breath.

'Indeed,' King Alfonse said, his tone infinitely amused. 'You have a beautiful voice. And more command at your fingertips than you know. Don't waste them.'

For the second time in a space of an hour, she found her mouth agape in stunned silence as Teo turned to stone.

She did the only thing she could. She fled the royal presence before she did the unthinkable. Like use that power to demand his son love her as she loved him.

He caught up with her before she was halfway to the entrance. For a full minute he walked beside her in silence.

Then 'What was that about?'

'Did you not ask him?'

His jaw rippled. 'He spoke in metaphors and euphemisms, and I'm not in the mood for it.'

Like a moth to a flame, her gaze zipped to him then lingered as they stepped out. Lines bracketed his mouth, and his forehead was pinched in a permanent frown. He looked... haggard. Or as haggard as the most magnificent prince in the world could look.

Her heart dipped. Did it really have to do with her? If so could she...*dared* she take the chance?

She blinked when he handed his helmet to the footman. 'Aren't you riding your bike?'

His eyes lingered on the sleek machine then shook his head. 'I'm taking you home as requested. And since you may be carrying my child, your days of riding with me, while brief, are over. So we'll use the car.'

He opened the door to the town car that pulled up and slid in after her. Thinking he would push for answers, she exhaled slowly when silence reigned on the short journey.

Inside, the staff were absent, probably by some secret palace signal.

They faced each other in the foyer, too many words crowding the air. In the end, she turned to the stairs and climbed, searingly aware he followed close behind. The sound of the studio doors shutting behind him set her heart pounding.

His sharp intake of breath drew her to find him staring at her sketches. The designs she'd been dying to show him. In the light of the gamble she was considering, it felt small. Insignificant.

'Sabeen, these are incredible.'

His praise warmed her for all of ten seconds, before fear crowded in. 'Thank you. Teo—'

'What did you mean?' he sliced in, his own tension mounting.

She knew exactly what he meant. 'Everyone seems to think I'm the cause for your…for whatever is going on with you.'

His eyes narrowed then understanding dawned. 'Valenti?'

'And your father. I took him to task for it when maybe I shouldn't have.'

He didn't answer. His hands propped on his hips, his mouth still tight. 'I thought he'd never been here in this studio or shown any interest in my work,' he muttered. 'It turned out I was wrong.' Her heart caught at the bleakness in his voice. 'About a few things, actually.'

'I'm sorry.'

His head bowed for a full minute. 'Don't be. He's set me straight on some things this past week.'

Sabeen's heart squeezed tighter. Everything about his demeanour screamed a profound discovery. One that weighed heavily on him.

'Wh-what?'

'That I've wasted time trying to prove my existence when I didn't need to. That I was chasing foolish dreams out of...' He shook his head, a tense smile twitching across his face before it died. 'It doesn't matter. Nothing matters.'

His words shut off as a roar filled her ears. If nothing mattered, was she about to risk everything for nothing? 'If nothing matters and everything's fine with you and your father, why does everyone claim you're in pain? Why do you only work in here when I'm not around? Why are you sleeping in the guest suite instead of your own bedroom?'

Bleakness flashed in his eyes before he could hide it. And although his mouth twisted, Sabeen saw his sombreness. Dare she say, his pain?

Even as he scoffed, his hand rose to rub at his chest. In the exact place her own chest ached. 'You think a few changes means you have some insight into me? Perhaps even how to manage me, *tesoro*?'

'They're simple questions, Teo. Answer them and we can move on.'

She'd taken so many bold steps these last couple of weeks. Steps he'd pushed and prodded and dared her into taking. She wasn't going to back away now.

'Move on, or use them as excuses? You already gave your condition about keeping things secret, or have you forgotten?'

Pain rippled through her. 'I haven't forgotten.'

He waited a beat, then spread his arms wide. 'And? Are you about to tell me you've changed your mind? That you care why I can't sleep in my own bed now?'

'Yes. I care.'

With every bone in my body, her heart screamed. But her tongue remained locked, still in full self-preservation mode.

He let out a laugh charged with a thousand currents and a large dose of anguish. All warning her to leave this alone. 'Pick a lane, Sabeen. You've been fighting so hard to push me away. What's changed?'

Because you matter.

And he did. Maybe he always had. Maybe deep down she'd always feared offering her heart might be her greatest risk.

'Because like you, I've learned a few things these past days.'

Shadows winged across his face. 'And what are those things?'

'That whether I'm pregnant or not, I don't owe you authority over me.' She forced her gaze from his, to the beautiful drawings she'd created. At least one thing had gone right. 'You have my contribution to your collection. And hand on heart I can say it's my best work yet, so you should be happy. I'll be present at the launch, of course, and deal with everything that needs to be done leading up to it. But I need to know, is there anything more for me here if I decide to stay?' The words nearly ripped her heart in two. But she didn't take them back. *Couldn't.*

He turned to marble, his eyes unblinking as he inhaled. Exhaled. And said nothing. As silence drummed a death knell. And she had no choice but to turn for the door, her soul shattering as he let her walk out of his studio.

She tore into her suite, her tear-filled eyes unseeing as she snatched her case and tossed garments in. She'd gambled again. And lost worse than before. She wasn't entirely sure she could survive this time. But…

Her hand went to her belly, a feverish hope that the period that hadn't made an appearance last night or this morning as anticipated would mean…

Dear God, she was unashamedly desperate to leave with a piece of the man she loved with her.

Please, please, please—

She whirled when he barged into her bedroom one minute later, silver eyes blazing with purpose. 'You know something? Only yesterday—hell, this morning—I would've let you get away with that. Shrug off the rejection and carry on with my life. I was used to it, after all.'

Her throat closed. 'Rejection? How is asking for more a rejection? I'm…'

His eyes narrowed, flipping from her open suitcase to her face in deep censure. 'It's pretty obvious it's some sort of test! You've shed your baggage and are ready to fly free. Without me? Against my better judgement I agreed to you wanting to keep us a secret. Now you want more? More secrets? More denying?' His gaze dropped to her belly and anguish tore across his face. 'Not even the thought of our unborn child can sway you? Or would you like me to go one better and disavow being the father entirely? Is that how you wish me to prove myself—'

'No! That's not what I want at all!'

He speared frantic fingers through his hair. 'Then, explain. *Por favor.* How do I prove myself?'

'You claimed your child. But you didn't claim me!'

His face clouded. 'What?'

'What am I to you besides a designer? If there wasn't a possibility that I was pregnant, what would I be besides your bed warmer?'

He sucked in a harsh breath. 'A fearless fighter? A strong, courageous woman who goes toe to toe with me and calls me out when I need it? A beauty so incredible she takes my breath away and makes me believe I'll die happy if only I get to spend my last breathless moments with her?'

Sabeen's mouth dropped open.

He closed the gap between them, gently nudged her mouth shut.

'To preclude any doubt, that person is you, Sabeen. I haven't been able to sleep in my bed because you're not in it. I can't stay in this house because I crave you every minute of every day. I filled my father's ears with every crumb of my time with you, then swore him to secrecy because I was terrified it wouldn't fall under your secrecy rule. That you would leave if you found out.'

Her hands rose, reaching for him. 'Oh God, Teo—'

'You want my full surrender? You want more? Well, here it is.' His chest heaved as he stared deep into her eyes. 'I love you, Sabeen. So much I can barely breathe. Can barely function with the thought of losing you.'

Her mouth dropped open again. 'You love me? But...but you—'

He towered over her, a pillar of affronted masculinity, with a blaze in his eyes that snatched her breath away. 'Tell me I can't love you. I dare you. I know I'm unworthy of you. But I have a lifetime to work at rectifying that. If...you'll have me?' The river of self-doubt in his eyes made her want to cry.

A sob slipped free as she hurled herself into his arms. 'Would you stop saying that? Everyone around you believes you're more than worthy. Especially me. God, I was ready to tell you that a long time ago. To tell you more than that. Because you've taught me to be bold. To be brave. To reach for what I want. And what I want, more than anything in the world, is you. I will have you, Teo. Because I love you, too. I think I've been in love with you for years.'

Deep shudders moved through him. He snatched her to him. And an eternity after he'd kissed her, declaring a few dozen times how much he loved her, and then dragging her to bed for lovemaking that made her sob some more, he gathered her into his arms.

He kissed her eyelids, then waited till she opened her eyes. 'I'm warning you now, I'm not wasting time on a long engagement. I need to make you mine as soon as possible before I go insane.'

'I'll marry you tomorrow.'

That soothed him long enough to kiss the sense out of her.

Until she pulled away. 'There's one more piece to go on the kintsugi. Will you do it with me?'

Warmth filled his eyes to the brim. And his nod was a little jerky as he cleared his throat. 'It would be my honour.'

Throwing their dressing gowns on, they walked hand in hand to his studio, and in the early-evening light, they slotted the last piece of the broken teapot they'd brought with them from Morocco into place. Together.

'I lied,' she murmured as they stood, his arms around her, staring at the finished work.

A kiss brushed her temple, her jaw, the corner of her mouth. 'About?'

'About my *jida* not liking you. She would've loved you. Eventually.'

'And I would've welcomed her as the true mother I lacked. But I sense that she will continue to live through you.' His hand dropped to her belly. 'Through our baby.'

'You don't know that I'm pregnant yet, Teo.'

'Hmm, maybe not. But I intend to make sure you are by the time you walk down the aisle and take my name.'

And like a true prince on a mission, he achieved that goal.

'A toast.'

Azar groaned, although a thread of amusement trailed it.

'To Domene X's "Beauty in Dysfunction". And to House of Domene's "Perfection in Chaos".'

The two collections had complemented each other so brilliantly, the result had sent shock waves through the fashion industry. The old king attended, then stood up and applauded long after everyone had finished, the blaze of pride in his eyes something Teo wouldn't forget in a hurry.

Teo grinned now at Azar's visible relief, then pivoted towards his twin, ribbing at the ready.

But his brother was staring at his phone, his nostrils

pinched. Some identical twins were eerily attuned to each other's moods. Teo, although he could broadly decipher Valenti's emotions, had often wondered whether by suppressing his own feelings he had somehow blocked the vital deeper connection to his twin.

It seemed now he'd opened himself up to love and the trove of sentiments it came with, he'd tapped into his brother's emotions too. All humour vanished as he felt terror flooding his twin despite it not showing on Valenti's face. He lowered his glass. 'What's wrong?'

Valenti shook his head, striking for the door. 'I have to go.'

Azar stepped into his path, one imperious hand up. 'Take a half minute, *hermano*. Tell us what's wrong,' he insisted.

His chest slowly heaved, even as he glared at Azar for delaying him. 'Lotte is in trouble.'

Teo blinked. 'Your ward? I thought she was tucked away in finishing school.'

His twin turned his glare on him. 'So did I. Apparently, she's not...' His jaw clenched. 'Look, I don't have time to explain. I need to go,' he insisted.

'Where?' Azar asked.

'Reykland.'

Azar nodded, pulling his phone from his pocket. 'I know you have your plane on standby. But my fighter jet will get you there faster, if you'll use it?'

Valenti exhaled in a rush. Then nodded. '*Gracias.*'

One minute later he was gone. And Azar's eyes were glinting as he winked at his wife.

'What?' Eden demanded.

Azar shook his head. 'I've never seen him so agitated. About anything.'

Teo nodded. 'You know what? Me neither.'

Their eyes met. And when a sly grin appeared on his brother's face, Teo smiled too. Then he gave a different kind of toast. One his twin would've flayed him alive to hear.

'Maybe she'll be worthy of giving him hell...for a while. Then offering him the sweetest heaven.'

His sister-in-law gasped. The love of his life followed with a husky laugh a moment later, playfully slapping his chest before she kissed his jaw. 'You're the worst.'

Teo looked deep into Sabeen's eyes, the only heaven he wanted to drown in. 'No, I'm the best, and you know it.'

She held out for a long beat. Then she sighed. 'Yes, you are, and I love you, for ever,' she whispered.

He winked then gloried in her sweet blush. 'I know, *tesoro.* Now, are you up to the challenge that you love me half as much as I love you? That's the true question.'

EPILOGUE

THE GENIUS PRINCESS and Her Muse.

A picture beneath that headline showed Sabeen sitting in her grandmother's chair with Teo seated on the floor leaning against her right leg. Her fingers were buried in his hair, and he was staring up at her, unfettered love and devotion blazing in his eyes. The image had taken the world by storm three months ago, straight after their spring/summer collection of both Domene X and House of Domene had hit the runways to critical acclaim.

Sabeen gasped as Teo walked towards her, holding the giant version. 'You framed it?' Her heartbeat raced as she examined the picture. Even from the floor his expression owned every inch of her.

He shrugged and set it down on top of the cabinet in their bedroom. 'It's significant. Because standing tall or sitting at your feet, you own me, *tesoro*. Completely. There's nowhere I'd rather be than by your side. Always.'

The simplicity of that answer snagged her heart, but what ignited even more overwhelming sentiment was what was set on the exquisite cabinet, directly beneath the picture.

Her grandmother's teapot. Hot tears prickled her eyes. They travelled with it everywhere they went. She hadn't decided on a place for it since they'd returned from opening their newest flagship store in Rabat.

Their luggage had been brought in while they stopped for

a quick visit with Teo's father, who had bounced back again health-wise shortly after they'd announced their intention to marry. Teo took full credit for that, much to his brothers' griping. Three months after their grand wedding, their father was still in decent health, thank goodness.

Teo approached where she stood and wrapped his arms around her thickening waist. At five months' pregnant, she was only just visibly showing, an outcome he'd been impatient for and now revelled in every chance he got. He frowned and grumbled when she wore dresses that flowed over her belly rather than showcased her pregnancy. He'd gone positively caveman on her, and she loved every second of it.

His hard cheek brushed hers before his breath washed over her ear. 'Until you find the perfect place for it, it would be my honour to borrow it for a time. It, too, is significant.'

'No, I don't want to move it, ever. It's exactly where it needs to be.' Twisting in his arms, she wound her arms around his neck. 'And so am I.'

* * * * *

HIS FORGOTTEN WIFE

TARA PAMMI

MILLS & BOON

CHAPTER ONE

Ares Demetrius calling...
Ares Demetrius calling...
Ares Demetrius calling...

THE INCESSANT RING and the name on the video call flashing on her tablet made Dolly Singh drop the hot cup of coffee in the tiny kitchen of her uncle's home.

Even the shatter of the cup as it hit the floor and the brown liquid pooling into cracks on the already worn-out tiles couldn't unfreeze her from her shock.

Ares Demetrius—the Greek tech entrepreneur who had sold his first app at twenty for a hundred million out of Columbia University, her boss of six years and university mate for three before that—was calling.

Ares calling her at four in the morning wasn't usually extraordinary because her boss was a genius who worked hundred-hour weeks and insisted she be at his beck and call the entire time.

But he'd been in a car accident seven weeks ago while returning to his family's estate in Corfu for the first time in nine years. He slipped into a coma after his traumatic head injury, upending her entire world in one horrible moment.

And the events of the weekend before his fateful trip

had already left Dolly feeling as if their entire relationship had burned down.

Six years of working nonstop beside him, without a life of her own, standing by his side as he revolutionized the tech world, meant her life had suddenly been empty while he lay in a coma.

Seven weeks of not seeing his hard, handsome face, of not hearing his deep timbre, of not meeting that gray gaze that she knew better than anyone else's in the world...it was as if she had been induced into a coma too. But her grandfather falling and injuring his hip within hours after Ares's own accident had made it impossible for her to travel.

"Dolly, *beta*," her grandpa's sleep-muffled voice came from the bedroom. "Your phone is screaming."

"Yes, Grandpa. Getting it now," she shouted back, reaching for the tablet. Her uncle and aunt were on a summer trip financed by Dolly, happy to get them out of the way while her grandfather recovered from hip surgery. The last thing she'd needed was her aunt needling at how morose and depressed Dolly had been for weeks now.

Her hands trembled as she set up the tablet against a pickle jar on the tiny island, her heart speeding up in her chest so fast that she had to rub the area with her fingers.

Outside the jammed-up sliding doors of the living room, she could see dawn paint the sky in splashy pinks and oranges. Soon, the tiny community her aunt and uncle lived in in Brooklyn would come to life in Technicolor: noise bleating from the bridge overhead; smells from the bakery and left-out garbage cans mingling; the tall maple trees painting the streets in deep golds and blazing reds announcing early fall.

It was exactly how she felt at the prospect of Ares coming out of the coma—as if she too were emerging from a deep, restless slumber.

Her finger slipped twice on the screen before she swiped to accept the call.

"*Christos*, Dahlia! How long do you need to pick up a damned call?"

Her heart climbing into her throat, it took Dolly several long minutes to register that he was expecting a response.

How could she when all her other senses shut down so she could focus on the vision before her? When relief that he was better flooded her system in waves?

His rugged face filled the screen and Dolly traced each feature with her hungry eyes as if she were seeing him for the first time, charting every angle and plane.

His high forehead, the long, patrician nose, the thin slash of his lips that denoted his impatience, the divot in his chin that made a god out of him, the square jaw…all as familiar to her as her own strong-angled face and yet now, so achingly different…even new.

Then there were his eyes—a frosty gray that she'd seen warm only once in nine years of their acquaintance.

In spite of her practical, no-nonsense nature, Dolly knew she could drown in those eyes. And had done on that night before the accident, at a very high cost to both of them. Guilt choked any words her brain managed to even make.

"Dahlia? Is it me that has been in a coma or you?"

His gruff question made her snap out of the bubble of longing. "I… You…" A long sigh tumbled through her lips. "I didn't know you came out of the coma," she finally said, sounding utterly stupid.

"How would you, given you cut off all communications with me and the company?"

The uncharacteristically personal tone of that complaint took the wind out of her sails. Until she reminded herself that Ares thrived on routine and efficiency and familiarity and she represented all those things to him.

To wake up in an unfamiliar hospital would have notched up his confusion and his need for control. He wasn't a man who did well with the unexpected and being in a car crash and the subsequent coma had to be devastating.

Despite everything that had passed between them that night, her heart ached for the weakness he tried to hide from the world.

"They couldn't find anything suitable for me at Gen-Tech," she said, mentioning the company he had founded straight out of Columbia with her by his side. "I stayed on doing the minimal for a few days, after the crash. When I wasn't at the hospital with my grandfather." She added the last to fight her own vague sense of guilt for abandoning him.

Clearly, he thought the same. "That's not what Christina said," he retorted, mentioning the third of their college mates—and her childhood friend—who had become CEO of GenTech.

Dolly blanched. And even with her grainy Wi-Fi, which she was mostly stealing off of her neighbor, she knew Ares didn't miss her reaction. Apparently, the man had risen out of his coma with all his superior faculties rearing and ready to go.

Only he hadn't mentioned…their little contract, the big payout he had given her, and the humiliating weekend that had followed.

"I…"

It didn't feel the same without you, the words played on her lips. But she stashed them away, deep in the place where she *should have* stashed the other words too.

"I needed a chance to recover from the anxiety and heartburn six years working with you gave me." In her bid to hide the fact that she had been half-dead herself with him gone, she ended up sounding callous and even irreverent.

"How delightfully practical of you, Dahlia," he said with dry censure that she let hang between them. Maybe it was better to let him think she was cold-blooded. "I see the reason I kept you around all these years."

He sounded like…he used to when they had met during her freshman year at university, he a junior.

Cold and calculating to the last word, brutally honest and painfully reserved, until she had realized that it was a reaction to how he saw the world. With transparent detachment, he compulsively reduced it to a simple equation that his mind could grasp. Emotional complexities made his experience of the world extra messy for him, taking away his sense of control.

It had taken her months to see through to the kindness and generosity of spirit beneath what had seemed like an extremely uncaring exterior.

"How are you, Ares?" she said, wanting to start over.

"I hate everything about this," he responded, without mincing his words.

"Is everything back to…normal?" The word tasted like garbage on her lips because she knew how much he loathed the reductive term. "Christina said you sustained a very severe head wound. When do the doctors think you might be ready to resume usual activities?"

He shrugged. The movement caused the cotton fabric to slide off a muscled shoulder.

Dolly pressed a hand to her mouth. She'd been so caught up in her own tumultuous feelings and shuddering relief at the sight of him that she had noticed nothing else.

Only now could she see past him, *from the new scar on his right cheek*, to the sterile white wall behind him, and the hospital gown sliding off his shoulder to reveal gleaming olive skin and taut muscle. Then there were the multiple machines he was hooked up to, and the people running around him in a flurry of activity.

Her heart made a long, slow dive down into her belly. "Ares…" She wet her suddenly dry lips. "How long has it been since you woke up?"

His gray gaze flicked upward, toward the clock on the wall she assumed. One brow rose, as if he was displeased with his discovery. "Five hours. It took them forever to give me my phone."

Longing flooded her in dizzying bursts, making her tremble on the hard seat. How could she feel this confusing tumble of emotions when he'd made his thoughts on the matter clear? He'd been disgusted by her heated admission that night.

You're like an extra limb to him, she chanted like a mantra now. *Or maybe an administrative robot that's been programmed to do his bidding. Nothing more, nothing less.*

"In about fifteen minutes, I'll be surrounded by my family." Resentment threaded his tone, pulling her back to reality. Obviously, he had told her about some of his family dynamics—given what he'd asked of her—but he'd never let her see his frustration so clearly. "The consulting specialist called my older brother without my permission."

"They had to inform someone, Ares," she said, falling into the habit of pacifying him.

"Especially since you've been MIA," he retorted instantly.

She sighed. "I couldn't abandon my grandpa to strangers' care, Ares."

"So you chose him over me."

"He's the only true family I have and I would do anything for him. Not my fault if you don't get that." She regretted the sharp words immediately.

In the nine years that she'd known him, Ares had rarely, if ever, talked about his family. Given that the Demetrius family was one of the wealthiest, most powerful families in all of Greece, she had simply assumed that it was the ultrarich protecting their privacy. Even though Ares himself had never shown off his wealth.

Only in the last few months had she learned that Ares was actually estranged from them, given the open animosity between him and his two older brothers. Even that admission had only come about because he'd needed her "cooperation."

Naive fool that she had been, she'd readily agreed to his proposal and promptly lost her common sense.

"They must be overjoyed to learn you're awake," she added, trying to be diplomatic. "Your mother definitely." She remembered the fondness in his tone when he'd spoken of her.

"What I know is that they irritate the hell out of me." He swept an expansive hand around himself, gesturing to the chaos. "The worst is that they'll take advantage of my weakened position. The best scenario is this is a fresh opportunity to develop a better relationship. Which is why I need you here, immediately."

"Need me there?" Dolly repeated inanely. *As your wife?* The question danced on her lips, yet something held her back.

She recalled their visit to the county clerk's office, where they signed the marriage contract with two strangers as witnesses in order to protect his wealth, and then the weekend that had followed. The memories drifted through her head like wisps of impressions from her most cringeworthy dream.

"For what?" she forced herself to say.

"As my assistant, what else?" Impatience coated Ares's words. "While the specialist assures me I should recover fully over the next year, he did say that my memory could be hazy and vague for a few months."

"Hazy memories…" Lead settled into her stomach, even as another part of her—obsessed with belated self-preservation—shuddered in relief.

What if he never remembered their arrangement or her foolish admission that she had feelings for him? Could this be the fresh start she needed with him?

Maybe she didn't have to exit his life completely, maybe…

Dolly shuddered at her eagerness that she might not have to remove herself from his life. The time it took for Ares to recover and remember would only be a short respite.

"Are there gaps in your memories? Around any particular time?" she probed.

Ares thrust a hand through his hair, frustration imbuing his every gesture. "If you haven't wiped your memory of everything connected to me and the company, you'll remember that the month before I left for Greece was a particularly stressful time. We had that merger we were considering, and then there was the litigation suit."

"Of course I remember," she said, a thread of anger weaving into her own words now.

"All I remember is being very angry with myself on that flight back to Athens," he said, ignoring her admission, telling her he was in that tunneled hyperfocus mode, "and then through the chopper ride to Corfu."

His gray eyes held hers, penetrating even through the screen. Sweat beading over her forehead, Dolly realized he was waiting for her to fill in the blanks. A very real feeling of horror clamped her gut.

"Did we fight, Dahlia?" he said when she remained silent.

She shook her head. Was it a lie if it had been less a fight and more a fissure in their relationship? The last thing either of them needed right now was a recap of how badly that entire weekend had turned out.

"What else did the doctors say?"

"Why do you care?" he said, sounding like that churlish stranger she'd met years ago.

"Please, Ares. I know that you won't share any of this with your family. So tell me."

He stared at her for a few seconds, his gaze thoughtful. Then he sighed. "The usual stuff about not forcing the blanks to fill, to not rush things. To let my body and mind dictate the healing, mental and physical."

"I can understand that this must feel very…threatening, especially to you," she said, choosing her words carefully. "Losing control of your mind and your body in such a horrible way, but it's important to let yourself heal now. Insisting that it happen on your timeline only defeats the whole thing. Slowly but surely, everything that's important will come back to you."

She knew she was comforting herself along with him, though it didn't really work.

His scowl was so familiar that it warmed her insides more than her own words. "If I need a motivational therapist, I will hire one." His frown deepened. "Is my memory gap that bad or did you feed me this kind of bullshit before too?"

"Fine," she said, her composure snapping. "If you find what I say so…trivial, why are you calling me?"

"I told you, I need you here. Honestly, I'm disappointed that you haven't been sitting by my side night and day, waiting for this moment. Here I woke up with a distinct impression that you were unflinchingly loyal."

"Need me there for what?" Dolly demanded, matching his grumpy tone, knowing that his expectation of her wasn't too far off.

The number of times she'd almost called Christina to beg for a flight ticket on the company's dime was laughably high. Only his sheer contempt for her on their last meeting had stopped her. And the worry that he might work himself up into another bout of fury if he saw her on waking.

The bald reminder of how weak she could be when it came to him made her words unusually sharp. "You've literally just woken up out of a coma five hours ago. A coma you've been in for seven weeks after sustaining a horrible head injury. Your memory is hazy, and you're clearly not in good physical condition. And like you just mentioned, I do not possess any kind of skills that could be of use to you. We both know you don't keep people like me around out of the goodness of your heart." If she was throwing the gist of the things he'd said to her back in his face, there was the relief that he didn't know that little fact.

"Again, have you always been this mouthy with me?" He raised a thick brow, lips twitching. The glint of humor in his eyes took the edge out of his question. "If you have, why do I think you're irreplaceable to me?"

"No one is that for you, Ares. You have always made that clear."

"So we argued about your importance in my life?"

God, the man had a brain like a steel trap. Dolly fidgeted in her seat, holding back the wriggling truth with great effort. "Not really."

Because they hadn't argued. He had simply told her what she was to him and what she wasn't and how foolish she was to harbor feelings for him. And how damnably inconvenient and awkward she'd made everything by actually confessing to them. And oh, couldn't she have just swallowed it all or kept them to herself at least?

But despite her confusion and fear at how tangled things had become between them, *and* annoyance at his current high-handedness that she attend to him, she understood that he must be feeling all those emotions a million times more strongly.

"To tell you the truth, I do not feel like myself," he said, rubbing a hand over the back of his neck. "I do not like that feeling when the entire world is already so strange and alien to me. The last thing I need in this condition is to be surrounded by my…family. But… I can't leave until I solve this litigation suit, once and for all. Wasn't that the reason I traveled to Greece?"

Dolly nodded, even as her pulse spiked like unearthed wire looking to ground. She'd never felt more devious than at the moment, willfully keeping a big secret from him. *Was it willful if it protected them both though?* she wondered, her head beginning to pound now.

"While I understand your dilemma," she said softly, "there's nothing to be done, Ares. Sometimes, life has us by the short and curlies, and we simply have to give in. Trying to wrest control during that time is...counterintuitive, to use your own words."

A smile split his thin lips, changing the very landscape of his rugged features. It even touched his eyes, melting the gray frost. He looked boyishly handsome, so achingly beautiful that the knot in her chest tightened, as if he were holding the threads for it and tugging at them willy-nilly.

Seven weeks of his absence apparently hadn't thickened her armor enough. But caring about him shouldn't necessarily mean that she loved him. The last few months had made her see how terribly tangled her own feelings were.

"Ahh...what a poetic way to put it, Dahlia. Is that why I kept you around, for your no-nonsense approach to life?"

She shrugged, wet heat prickling behind her eyes. "I kept up with your maniacal moods and impossible demands better than anyone else. Maybe that's why."

"So make this period ahead easier for me. Help me catch up to everything. Come back to your job, Dahlia." When she hesitated, he bit out, "Whatever you're making, I'll double it. I'll triple what you were making with me before."

"I'm not working currently," she blurted out before

she could catch the ramifications of admitting that to him. "I told you, I needed a break," she added, hoping he wouldn't read much into it.

"But you take care of your aging grandfather and pay the mortgage on your aunt and uncle's house and pretty much support all of them, don't you? Plus you have those humongous student loans for Columbia that you wouldn't let me clear."

Dolly blinked.

How could he remember that small, insignificant fact but not the earth-shattering contract they had both signed? Had her fervent admission that night been so traumatic that his mind had blocked out the entire week leading up to his accident completely?

"Dahlia?" he prompted, tone impatient.

She cleared her throat. "You paid me well enough that I had some savings. The day after your accident, my grandfather fell and had to have hip surgery. Seemed like a good time to take a break."

"Sure you don't need any financial help?"

She shook her head, shying her gaze away from him.

For all his temperamental moods and ruthless demands on her time and energy, he had always been more than fair to her monetarily.

Then there was the giant payout he had given her for signing the marriage contract, along with stock options in GenTech. She'd used up three-quarters of it to pay toward a long-term care home for her grandfather's foreseeable future. As for the remaining amount, she'd simply written out a check in her aunt's name, which she hoped would cover the meals and clothes and shelter that she and her uncle had given her after her parents had died—

as she had been reminded of constantly after they had taken her in.

It was the only way her self-respect would allow her to take such a huge amount from Ares.

But she wouldn't mistake his caring for her as attachment or more, ever again.

"How long before you can transfer his care to a live-in nurse?"

"A month, maybe. I don't like the idea of leaving his care to some stranger," she said, giving in to the inevitable, but adding a big chunk of buffer for herself.

At some point, she'd have to tell him the truth about what had happened between them. She owed him the truth, even if it meant the end of things between them forever.

The very thought made her stomach cave in.

"That's too goddamned long, Dahlia." His distress came through in his thickening Greek accent. "I need you more."

She laughed past the tears clogging up her throat. "And there's the demanding billionaire baby I know."

"Is this some kind of petty revenge for something I did?" His gray eyes bored into hers. "Did I upset you before I left for Greece?"

And just like that, he came straight to the messy point. "That's not how…" She swallowed. "I would never…"

The words wouldn't come because she was doing exactly what he was suggesting: punishing him—because it was a punishment for Ares to deal with people who didn't know him and whom he wasn't comfortable with. That included his family.

She was punishing him for what he didn't feel for her. Which was so wrong of her.

His mouth took on a tight set. "You're a liar, Dahlia."

Dolly flushed. "I can try to be there in two weeks. No earlier. And you're footing the bill for the live-in nurse."

"Of course." The tension seeped out of him instantly, as if someone had suctioned it out using a tube. Which only made the dark circles under his eyes and the gauntness of his face more pronounced. Guilt stabbed her in tiny pinpricks because she could see that he really did need her. "I'll have Christina send you the paperwork for reinstatement."

"That's not necessary, because I'm not coming to you in a professional capacity."

"I don't need your fucking pity," he bit out.

"There has to be something between pity and being paid for every moment I spend with you, Ares."

"I have been out of it for seven weeks, Dahlia. Christina said the board has been giving her a hard time. Most of the R & D has stalled. I need a bloody assistant to put things to rights."

"Okay, fine," she said, giving in. And then, because she was a pushover when it came to him, she said, "I'm glad you're well. I worried about you."

"Come here and make life easier for me, then."

She laughed at his sheer arrogance and how he didn't see it that way at all. "You can't dictate how I show my... care for you. That's not how this works."

"What use is it, then?" he demanded, a petulant note creeping in.

Tucking her hair behind her ear, Dolly resisted getting into it with him. "I'll be there only temporarily though. A month at the most. My grandfather needs me here."

"It's kind of beneath you, *ne*? Using him as an excuse

to get out of dealing with me and whatever problems exist between us?"

How was the man so perceptive one second and so dense the next? *Because he doesn't understand emotions*, came her own answer. "Fine, you want the truth? I think it's time I moved on from…you, from being your assistant. So I won't be coming back to work for you."

"You make it sound like I tortured you?" The sliver of doubt in his voice—as if it truly were a possibility—pierced her like a needle stabbing into her skin. All she wanted was to reach out and hold him, for both their sakes.

Good thing there was a screen and thousands of miles between them.

"Of course you didn't," she said, threading a smile through her words. "And I wouldn't have stood for it if you had."

"So what was the problem, then?"

Dolly chose her words carefully. After all, she had prepared them for weeks while praying to the universe that he would come out of the coma, healthy and whole. "Working for you meant I had no life outside of the job. I'm twenty-six and have hardly even been in one serious relationship. I had no friends, no fun, no…existence outside of circling you like a planet stuck in orbit. Let's just say my biological clock is ticking and I heard it loud in the last few months."

"Why am I under the impression that you aren't someone who would let society's arbitrary constructs railroad you into following a decided schema for your life?"

Damn it but the man knew her so well.

"You're under the wrong impression. It seems I do

want grand romantic love and companionship and really fantastic sex and friendship and…babies." If she sounded belligerent, it was to cover up the tremors in her voice. But she couldn't hide the heat cresting her cheeks.

While their relationship had always straddled the line between friendship and more, it was the first time Dolly had verbalized her personal desires in such bare words.

Weeks ago, she'd been foolish enough to assume she could have them with him. As long as they were on the path to seeing each other as more than friends and colleagues, she didn't care how long it took to get there.

She couldn't be so foolish again, she reminded herself now. Definitely not with this man who could shred her into pieces with two pithy sentences.

He hadn't just rejected her tender admission of attraction, but called their entire relationship into question.

"Nothing's wrong with it if that's you want, Dahlia," he said, responding to her tone. "Maybe things have changed for you. Or maybe I didn't know you that well to begin with."

She nodded, hating herself for putting him on the wrong foot. Especially when he wasn't completely himself.

"A month it is, then," he said, a steeliness in his tone. "For me to change your mind and make you stay with me. Shouldn't be that hard."

Despite conflicting emotions pulling her this way and that, Dolly laughed. At his sheer arrogance, at his innate confidence, at how the truth of it shone in his eyes.

For a long time, she had prided herself on the fact that Ares needed her, that only she could keep his life running smoothly.

Only to realize that he saw her as no more than a parameter, a constant at that, in the vast, complex equation that was his mind.

"I'll see you soon, Ares."

A sudden rise in the noise level in his room told her his family had arrived. "Not soon enough for me," he groaned, sending goose bumps over Dolly's skin.

She ended the call before he could see how desperately she wanted to soothe him, to be by him. To hold him even, not that she ever had before.

And now she had a month to come clean...

Her belly twisted up in knots as she wondered how she would bring up the small, sticky subject of their having been married in secret. How she would admit that he'd asked her to marry him—to sign a watertight contract to be exact, for a one-year marriage with a huge payout on signing—on one normal Tuesday evening as if it were just a complicated business assignment. And how she had said yes without hesitation and signed the contract.

Because it meant everything to her that he would trust her beyond anyone else, because it meant that, maybe, just maybe, he liked her a little, even. As more than a friend, as more than an efficient assistant.

In her stupid pathetic heart, it had even looked like they were finally taking a step forward in their relationship.

Not that she'd expected Ares to change overnight and fall in love with her just because she was his wife...

There was also the fact that, having stood by him all these years, the lawsuit and the claim on his fortune made her just as furious as it did him. A wife had been the perfect way to protect his assets from his vulturelike half brothers, who had twisted their grandfather's long-ago birthday gift to Ares into a family investment that they also had a claim to.

She was a wife he could sign off his assets to at a moment's notice. As his spouse, her own private assets would be untouchable by his family in the state of New York. But that was the last resort, the final trick up his sleeve, only to be used *if* he couldn't settle the lawsuit outside of court.

The last thing he wanted was for a scandal to touch the Demetrius family.

A week after they had signed the marriage contract, they'd found themselves stuck in a cabin upstate with a snowstorm raging outside. She'd drunk cognac—which had loosened her tongue and her heart, cheap drunk that she was.

And when he had pulled her to her feet and she stumbled into his chest, she blurted out her attraction to him. Her feelings for him that she had tried so hard to nip in the bud but failed.

His rejection had been swift and brutal, leaving her with no doubt of his disgust.

Burying her face in her hands, Dolly let out a half groan, half cry.

It was clear to her that Ares remembered nothing of their arrangement, nor the lurid details of her admission and his swift rejection.

Her time with Ares Demetrius was limited before either the gap in his memories would fill in or she'd tell him the truth. And that difficult fact made her chest heavy and her throat tight.

CHAPTER TWO

Two weeks later

ARES DEMETRIUS WATCHED the weeklong celebration of his grandparents' sixtieth wedding anniversary kick off around him with that same sense of isolation he'd always felt amidst his family.

Although, that particular evening, he made sure to not show it on his face.

Apparently, his traumatic head injury, the subsequent gaps in his memory, and escaping the clutches of death with his body beaten into a pulp meant that he had achieved a mild personality transplant.

He could…tolerate the genuine gaiety around him, and was more than curious about how his grandparents had sustained such a close partnership for sixty years.

But he wasn't overflowing with love for his two older half brothers. He still didn't trust the two of them as far as he could throw them. Not when they were dragging him through a court case for a cut of his tech fortune.

All based on the spurious claim that the check their grandfather had given Ares as a gift for his nineteenth birthday—that he had used to buy a server farm—was an investment from the family fortune.

Given his grandfather had been the one who turned their small export company into a multinational conglomerate, and had been the only source of kindness Ares had known as a child from a man—their father had thought his two older sons' constant meanness was simply boys running "wild"—it felt like even more of a violation to use that check to cause a family rift.

The shameless, conniving bastards...just thinking of the lawsuit made his head pound with renewed rage.

And this was after he had poured tens of millions into the dying family export business over five years to resuscitate it. All without his grandfather's knowledge—the old man would have been ashamed to learn that his two older grandsons had run the business into the ground.

Apparently, his brothers' greed and misdeeds had no end. Even though his investments had paid off and they—and their grasping wives—were now reaping the rewards after a decade-long slump in profits.

As if it hadn't been enough to have tormented him through his childhood and adolescence.

His mother, his grandparents, and his eighteen-year-old sister, Arabella, had begged him to return home for years. Ares's chest twisted at the sight of the latter laughing it up on the dance floor. Examining his life decisions was apparently an ongoing symptom of his current malaise.

Once he'd admitted that he *had* missed them, his entire life seemed to cave in, as if it had been erected on false assumptions. That he had allowed Stefano and Sergio's bullying as children to drive him away from the rest of the family, that he had let them taint his relationship with the ones he did love...was illogical. Especially for a man who thrived on understanding himself well to better operate in the world.

Then there was the other fact that he'd had to face in the last couple of weeks as he'd returned home to the family villa in Corfu to continue his recovery. As a kid who didn't connect to anything mainstream, he had been terrified of his older half brothers. They had been bigger, popular, almost larger-than-life. Now, being back in the family home after nearly a decade and once again in a vulnerable state, it was like living his worst nightmare all over again.

From the perspective of an adult, though, he was beginning to wonder why his father hadn't done more to protect him from his older sons.

But he didn't want to be a stranger to all of his own family. Not anymore. He was a twenty-eight-year-old man who had accepted that he was different and always would be, and he couldn't let it affect how he related to his family and how they saw him.

Not that he had the faintest idea how to go about achieving the close relationship with his family that he craved.

Unless it included writing out a list of Papa's mistakes and missteps. Unless it meant ensuring that Stefano and Sergio ended up in prison for embezzling funds from the family company to support their vices. Unless it meant ripping into his mother and demanding to know why she had been so oblivious to what her stepsons had been doing to her own son.

But he couldn't.

Apparently, he was a weak man when it came to family.

The scandal that would descend on them if he sent his half brothers to jail would be unimaginable. He couldn't hurt his grandparents that way.

Was that why he had gone down the convoluted route of telling his parents that he was engaged to Dahlia minutes before the accident? Because he wanted his brothers to know that someone else had a bigger say in his own fortune? Because the threat of an upcoming legal union between him and the person he trusted the most would deter them from wanting more of his hard-earned wealth?

It was a clever solution and he wasn't surprised that he had thought of it.

Except Dahlia hadn't even mentioned it on the phone call.

Worse, she had made it sound like she wanted nothing to do with him going forward. If his mother hadn't asked him, within minutes of joining him at the clinic, where his wayward fiancée was, he wouldn't have even remembered the plan they had concocted together.

So, not only had she picked her grandfather over him, she had also actively omitted a big truth. Then there was the fact that he had felt every nerve-ending that wasn't battered down by pain come alive at the mere sight of her. It had been an upsurge of sensation, too much feeling, for his confused brain to process.

He wanted to reach through the screen and grab her by her shoulders and pull her to him, to smell her and touch her and feel her breath against his, to relearn how familiar he was with her… The urge had been a reminder that he was painfully alive, bringing with it a deep, visceral response.

An attraction he vaguely remembered feeling before, a shocking primal hunger that had thrown him into a panic and a rage…had that been for Dahlia too? And why did the memory of it make him flinch inwardly?

Christos, not knowing what lurked in the shadows of his mind was both painful and infuriating. Especially with the person he wanted to instinctively trust above all else.

"Won't you dance, Ares?" His mother's voice interrupted his loopy brooding.

Ares fought the nearly overwhelming instinct to step back from the emotion glimmering in her eyes. He identified it to be a combination of guilt and grief and love. And he felt that nauseous resistance to it rise up inside him, filling his veins with something like panic. Especially because of love...which he didn't understand.

Even being able to identify the emotions in his mother's eyes was the effect of nearly nine years with his assistant, Dahlia, rubbing off on him. Not that he was equipped yet to process the first two or return the third. At least in ways that would please his mother.

"No," he said, smoothing out the self-directed ire from his voice.

He was aware that she had barely left his side in the last two weeks. Day or night, she was there when he opened his eyes, more alert and awake than the nurse hired to monitor his state of mind, worry wrinkling her brow. His younger sister, Arabella, had also told him that Mama had barely left his side at the private clinic for the seven weeks he'd been under.

Moving closer, he laid an arm around her slender shoulders loosely. Her smile turned brilliant. "The only person who has successfully dragged me to the dance floor once is Dahlia. She possesses an uncanny knack for making me do things I don't want to or I'm incapable of."

Apparently, he couldn't do small talk but he could

share unnecessary stuff that had hidden import. He frowned.

"She sounds like a very capable and compelling woman, your assistant," Mama said, facing him.

His cheeks flushing, Ares met her gaze straight on. Having holes in his memory wasn't just inconvenient. It made trusting himself harder. "She's been with me in that position for close to seven years. She's been my friend and my...partner for all intents and purposes. It doesn't matter what you call her because no word can encapsulate all she is to me."

He stilled, his own words a revelation to him. They seemed to come from some place deep inside him that bypassed logic and facts, a place he hadn't even known existed within him.

It was the same place that radiated a deep panic when Dahlia had mentioned romance and love and babies.

Had that been because he didn't want to lose her or because he wanted to be able to give those things to her, because he wanted to be the only man in her life? Coupled with the alarming physical awareness that had flooded him at the sight of her, he wondered if he had gone down this route before?

Was that why he had come up with the engagement plan—because it killed two birds with one stone?

"You and this woman..." his mother began.

"Dahlia. Her name is Dahlia," he repeated, feeling a flare of annoyance. "We briefly talked about her at the clinic, remember? About how she's my fiancée?"

"And yet she hasn't visited you once in all these weeks."

"She didn't know about the accident for nearly a week," he said, repeating what his CEO Christina had told him.

"After that, she was caught in her own familial obligations. Then, later, there was no point."

"No point in being by the side of the man she's engaged to while he's in a coma?"

Ares gritted his jaw, since he faced the same question over and over inside his head.

It had been more than simply discombobulating to find himself in a hospital bed, wired to beeping machines, and to have strangers tell him that he had sustained a head injury and had been in a coma for seven weeks.

It had been devastating to find Dahlia absent from the whole scene, anchoring him.

Forget being by his side on the chance that he woke from the coma any moment, she hadn't visited him once. Not once in seven weeks while he lay there.

He had felt…betrayed at learning that little fact from the staff, after clarifying her name multiple times. His own feelings and the intensity of them surprised him too. It wasn't as if her being by his side would have made him better faster or sooner. Or that he wanted her pining away for him.

What was truly shocking, though, was that she'd simply resigned from GenTech and wiped him from her life. It made zero sense when she had a grandfather who depended on her income for his medical needs. A man whom she had adored for as long as Ares had known her.

Like him, Dahlia wasn't sentimental. So why quit a cushy job? Why not coast for a while—Christina was one of her biggest fans after all and knew what a crotchety boss he was—without his demanding ass around? Why not take the break she claimed she needed while cashing in an easy paycheck?

God knew she had earned the right to take it easy ten times over.

Instead, she had sounded as if it had been imperative that she quit. Almost as if she needed to break away from *him*.

He had pondered the why of it endlessly, giving himself a pounding headache more than once in the last two weeks.

"That doesn't sound like a woman who cares about you at all," his mother declared.

Ares didn't miss the thread of hostility in her voice. "Her grandfather had to have an emergency hip surgery." Even that very genuine reason didn't calm the furor in his gut. "She's a very devoted granddaughter. But she will be here any day now."

"I'm curious to meet the woman who's such an integral part of your life, Ares. All these years…it almost seems like she has replaced your family."

Ares nodded.

While he might not like how Mama phrased it—as if it were Dahlia's fault that he was estranged from them, the rest of it was the truth. Dahlia was integral to his life running smoothly and damned if he would lose her at this stage. He had no patience or energy to train a new assistant to cater to his moods and habits, to understand the way his mind worked, to keep pace with his working patterns.

Only a day ago, he had started catching up on work. The alternative was to go mad sitting around, in pain. Especially, since he had to keep on top of whatever new, nefarious scheme Sergio and Stefano were cooking up. The evil two had been far too affectionate and accommodating for him to believe it at all.

And Dahlia knew every inch of his business as well as him since she dealt with most of the personnel and board members and new investors on his behalf.

So every other moment, he found himself looking for Dahlia, a hundred questions pulsing on his lips.

"Come, let's mingle," Mama said, warily extending her arm to him. "There are so many friends and family members that want to meet you after all this time. Remember Athena Skyros?" she said, the words rushing out of her. "You used to be inseparable as kids. She runs her father's fashion magazine now."

Ares looked in the direction his mother pointed to find a tall brunette with an open smile, waving at him from across the large living room. A spurt of affection burst in his chest. "She came by the other day. It was pleasant catching up with her." His easy friendship with Athena was another thing he regretted giving up on.

"She's unmarried, you know," Mama said, catching his eye. There was enough twinkle in hers for him to know that she was teasing for teasing's sake. Testing the waters between them.

Athena's obvious wariness as she approached him made him feel a tightness in his chest.

"Please don't create confusion around this, Mama," he said, making sure there was only gentle rebuke in his tone. "I'm engaged to Dahlia, which means there's no place in my life for another woman." Again, the certainty with which those words poured out of him surprised him. "I am, however, more than happy to catch up with old friends. Although, with my faulty wiring right now, I'll probably insult her with a far too straightforward comment or some such."

Mama slapped the back of his hand. "Don't talk about yourself that way," she said, her rebuke laced with worry.

As they reached her, his old friend's smile broadened.

If he meant to repair his relationship with his family and plant new roots in the place his brothers had driven him from, rekindling old friendships was the best way to go about it.

He laughed when Athena asked his permission to hug him. Her perfume, while subtle, surrounded him like a force field, trapping him inside. Pulling back without looking like he was recoiling from her, Ares answered his childhood friend's eager questions with more than one-word answers. It didn't even require any extra effort on his behalf.

And yet, restlessness skittered under his skin, like a line of marching ants. Which was when he found himself comparing Athena to his missing assistant—*slash-fiancée*—he corrected himself.

Athena's smile, while genuine, was too broad, and she laughed at his nonexistent wit far too readily, and agreed with him far too much. She was, as she'd been as a girl, eager and kind but…*not Dahlia*. And suddenly he knew what the source of the restlessness was.

He missed his assistant with a shocking intensity that he had never known. He missed Dahlia's dry wit and her hard-to-earn smile and how she smelled of nothing but soap and herself—a scent that both grounded and excited him.

That his brain could instantly summon up exactly how she smelled, while he was surrounded by familiar sights and sounds, unnerved him. Because Ares did not like unknowns. Especially when it came to his own mind and emotions.

Christos, why the hell did he miss her as if she were some vital organ? And what had transpired between them that she would give up on him so readily? She'd omitted the truth about their engagement...was there something else that she was holding back?

Dolly stared up at the sprawling villa that looked like it had been carved straight from the limestone cliffs surrounding it. The sky was a brilliant mix of gold and lavender, the sun slowly sinking toward the sea, casting a warm, honeyed glow over everything. Beyond the villa, rolling hills stretched into the distance, blanketed in a patchwork of olive groves and vineyards. Cypress trees punctuated the landscape, their tall, slender shapes standing guard along the hillsides.

She had never seen anything so stunning—or so out of reach.

The warm September air clung to her skin like a silk veil, rich with the scent of the sea and olive trees. Her breath hitched in her throat and she thought she might never forget the sight.

She had known, of course, that the island of Corfu was beautiful from the few pics she had seen on the web but Ares's home was even more grand in real life, and yet still graceful, a fusion of old-world charm and modern luxury.

Her eyes flitted to the swimming pool as she walked up the sweeping staircase made of natural stone—an infinity edge spilling toward the horizon as though it was kissing the Aegean.

The echo of live music and clinking glasses and loud laughter filtering in from the gardens greeted her as she entered the large marble foyer. As she stepped farther inside, the villa opened up to the terrace, where the sun was now kissing the sea.

The grandeur of the villa was overwhelming, almost surreal, and for just a second, she considered turning around and fleeing.

God, she was being ridiculous. It wasn't as if she had to fit into the grand charm of the villa. She was here for a monthlong assignment, her last assignment probably, hopefully, with Ares. She wouldn't be surprised, *and definitely wouldn't mind*, if she was relegated to a tiny outhouse or one of the touristy motels.

Still, the sense of being overwhelmed clung to her. And she knew part of it was seeing Ares after all these months, and seeing him here. In his palatial home. It felt like one of those nature shows she watched on TV—like seeing a wild predator in his natural habitat.

How and why had he left this place at all? Let alone not return for years at a time?

It wasn't just the sheer luxury but the heirloom tapestries on the walls, the deep-gouged wooden beams in the ceiling and the sense of permanence that came with growing up in a place like this. Knowing so perfectly where you belonged.

It wasn't as if her grandfather didn't love her, he adored her. But she had come to him at the age of twelve after her parents' death in a car accident. By then he himself was dependent on her uncle and aunt for his own stability, which meant Dolly had never been allowed to forget the fact her aunt had taken her in because of her generous nature. Despite their own financial situation being hard.

As soon as Dolly had moved in, her uncle had lost a leg in a factory accident and, of course, her aunt had blamed her for bringing bad luck down on them. First her parents, then her uncle, and now her grandfather. For a long while, Dolly had believed herself to be the harbinger of bad luck.

So much so that she had stopped talking to her grandpa for weeks at a time, afraid that contact with her would somehow cause her to lose him. And now with his hip surgery and other health problems, that moment was getting closer and closer.

Could that be the reason she had gotten attached to her boss in the first place?

She didn't hold it against herself for being attracted to him. No woman could resist the man's Greek god–like looks. But this attachment to him…was it because he represented security like she had never known?

If he was anything, Ares Demetrius was constant among a sea of fickle circumstances and unkind fates, a fortress that nothing and no one could budge from its foundations.

Suddenly, the humid September air felt sweeter on her face.

Relief made her steps light as she walked down another set of stone stairs that led her through to an open courtyard filled with blooming jasmine and sweet orange trees. String lights crisscrossed above, draping the laughing and drinking guests in a soft, ethereal glow.

Everyone looked effortlessly glamorous, with rapid conversations in Greek, fluid and full of laughter.

She brushed a strand of hair from her face, feeling heat rise in her cheeks as she ran a palm over her crinkled trousers—no match for the elegant silks and linens that floated around her. Then there was her too-tight lime-green sleeveless top with the tomato juice stain right over her left boob because she'd been sleepy on the long-ass flight.

Not that anyone in the boisterous group paid her any attention.

No sooner had she thought that than she was suddenly flanked by two tall, rugged-faced men with identical features. They wore matching navy suits and leers.

There was no mistaking either of them for Ares, even though they shared the same height, for he would never crowd a woman like that. On second thought, she decided there was no resemblance at all except for the height.

These men were portly and had that prideful, almost predatory, look in their eyes that she usually found in the powerful men she dealt with professionally. Except Ares, again.

For a brilliant affluent businessman, Ares was like a grumpy bear that hid the mushiest heart. Only he didn't use it much.

"The waitressing staff should not come in through this courtyard," one man said while the other sized her up as if she were a hunk of meat. His accent was thick and his expression annoyed.

"Oh, come, Sergio. Do not be such a stuffy boss," the second man said, licking his thick lower lip while holding her gaze. "She's allowed to party after hours of hard work, *ne*? Maybe she has come into the party with dreams of finding a rich man and work of a different kind?" He swept his beady brown gaze over her, taking in her rumpled braid to her sensible flats showing her toes with their peeled nail polish, his mouth turning down. "Although, I have to say the packaging could be better."

Sergio laughed and joined his brother in the disgusting sweep of her body. "You are right, Stefano. There are assets to mine here."

Living in New York was enough to prepare her for men like this. One swing and she could shut up both men in the best way she knew but the last thing she wanted was to create a scene. Here, amidst the Demetrius family and friends. The last thing she wanted to do was to embarrass her boss.

Reaching for patience she didn't have, she took a step away from both men. And instantly regretted it. Now they hovered over her from the top step, looking down her blouse, the creeps.

"I'm looking for Mr. Demetrius," she said stiffly.

Both men chuckled. "That is both of us, darling. Which one did you want exactly," the one called Stefano mumbled while Sergio laughed.

Dolly studied them anew, aghast. Suddenly, she realized these two men were the infamous half brothers who had dared sue Ares, wanting a piece of the fortune he had built by himself. They wanted a cut of GenTech.

Apparently, they weren't just greedy, but creepy pigs who sexually harassed working women. Her fury doubled, surging on Ares's behalf too, aware of how badly they had shaken him up with the ridiculous lawsuit. "As far as I know, there's only one Demetrius man that I or any woman would—"

"Sergio! Stefano!" came another deep voice from behind the two men.

Instantly, the leering expressions disappeared as the men shuffled sideways to make space for the new arrival. "That is no way to treat a guest. Must I remind you to behave like gentlemen?"

Dolly blinked. Tall, with a full head of gray hair and deep brown eyes, the older man who joined their group was incredibly handsome. With strong bone structure and deep-set gray eyes, he was a tantalizing glimpse into what Ares would look like in the future.

"*Kalispera*, Miss…" he said in a deep voice.

Embarrassed heat flushed beneath her skin as she wondered how much he had heard of her taunt. "Miss Singh. I'm looking for Mr. Demetrius. Ares, that is," she said, hating the little quiver in her voice. "I'm his assistant." The little label left out so much but it was also a necessary reminder.

The two bullies shared a glance and a mocking smile. "Ahh…yes, the capable assistant-slash-fiancée that didn't even bother to visit our dear brother while he was nearly dead," one of them murmured with a gleeful smile. As if this wasn't much of a surprise. As if he was disappointed by the outcome.

The comment stung less than the assessing gaze the older man cast her, displeasure at her presence evident in the taut set of his mouth. With one flick of his head, he dismissed his sons.

"I'm afraid you have made a wasted journey, Ms. Singh," he said, confirming her suspicions that Ares hadn't told them of his orders for her. "Ares is not ready to go back to work. His recovery is a long way off."

Dolly straightened her shoulders, knowing that she had to make a stand here and now if she wanted to survive the next couple of months among these people. And not just for her sake either.

She had no doubt that she was going to run interference between them and Ares himself, on top of clearing up the mess between them. Which meant she had her work cut out for her.

"I'm aware of that, Mr. Demetrius," she said, moving up one step so that the man didn't look down on her. Ares might not use his size and glare to intimidate his employees—his cold detachment was enough for that—but she had met enough corporate bosses to know of the technique.

"Think of me as another cog in his recovery. As you must know, he's already restless. My being here will help—"

"He has his family to look after him."

"Ares summoned me here precisely because he needs me."

"It doesn't look like he has any need of you, Ms. Singh. At least not from where I stand."

Dolly turned to look in the direction he pointed. Her eyes widened at finding Ares laughing and slow dancing with a stunning brunette. Apparently, all his numerous social hang-ups and personal space tics didn't come into play with this particular woman, because she had her arms wrapped around his back, and his own clung to her waist.

Even the sight of him dancing with this woman couldn't dampen the overwhelming surge of relief that flooded Dahlia. She greedily scanned the wide breadth of his shoulders and the top of his head—his wavy hair was cropped at the sides like he preferred.

And his profile…with his sharp nose and square jaw and high forehead, it felt as familiar as her own, and yet also…somehow, amidst this new setting and new people, also foreign.

She pressed her palm into the fabric of her trousers, fighting the urge to storm across the courtyard and trace those features with her fingers.

Tears prickled behind her eyelids and she took a deep breath to push them back in. The last thing she needed was to betray her confounding emotions to antagonistic strangers. Nor would Ares welcome her sentimental floundering. The man was lethally allergic to displays of emotion, public or otherwise.

"You see, Ms. Singh, my son is happy and relaxed, surrounded by friends and family. He has spent way too many years away from us. Now he is back where he belongs."

As if aware of her scrutiny, Ares looked up.

His mouth curving, his eyes twinkling, he looked like a different version of himself. A version Dolly had never met and she suddenly wondered if his father was right. If Ares was planning to make his return home permanent.

That's good for you, that rational voice whispered. *You want out of his life, remember?*

Her boss's smile dimmed, just the slightest bit, at the sight of her, though he didn't loosen his hold on the woman or even stop their slow dance. But those penetrating eyes of his…ate her up with that intensity she understood.

Her skin tingled as she stood rooted there, feeling like a pinned butterfly all over again. Her heartbeat thundered in her ears and she was vaguely aware of the senior Demetrius talking at her. Offering to put her on a plane back home immediately. Warning her in no uncertain terms that she wasn't needed here.

The rational, surviving part of her wanted to take him

up on the offer. Maybe even confide in him the ridiculous contract she and Ares had signed and beg him to have it nullified somehow. If anyone could clear up that particular mess, this man could.

Then she could simply walk out of here and never look back, could permanently put Ares out of her mind and other places he shouldn't be. She could start over fresh at some other company, rid herself of this ridiculous attraction to a man who was so out of her sphere, he might as well be from Mars.

One thick brow quirked in Ares's face, his questioning expression clear from across the distance. Even his slow perambulation of the courtyard stopped. The woman in his arms searched and found Dolly, over her shoulder. A frown tied her shapely brows together.

Sounds and feeling rushed back into Dolly's head as if she had surfaced from deep under water. She could run away or she could stand by the man who deserved her support at a vulnerable time.

She shook her head, as if to shake off the temporary cowardice, and smiled up at the older man. "Thank you for your generous offer, Mr. Demetrius. But I do believe I have a job to do here. As soon as that is done—" she refused to shiver at the slow anger unfurling in his eyes "—I will be gone."

CHAPTER THREE

WHEN HER ARROGANT, annoying—how dare he ignore her for two whole hours—ex-boss deigned to approach Dolly, it was past ten. While his grandparents had retired after a short speech and the cutest little dance together, the rest of the family and friends were still partying.

Stifling a yawn, Dolly sank deeper into her chair. She had met far more of his cousins and aunts, and friends of the Demetrius family than she ever cared to.

Somewhere along the long, confusing line of introductions, she had been reduced to "Ares's attendant." Which seemed to be an insult aimed at both of them, especially from his half brothers. As if their brother couldn't function without her constant attendance.

Taking a sip of the chilled ouzo, she gazed out at the hills bathed in the moon's silver light, the dark silhouettes of olive groves and cypress trees stretching toward the endless sky. In the distance, the Ionian Sea shimmered like liquid obsidian. It was a view she could appreciate all night long. And yet, even amidst the glorious setting, she was aware of the tense undercurrent.

Why Ares had decided to fling her to the sharks, only his labyrinthine mind could know.

But she was tired, a little dizzy thanks to the two

glasses of wine she'd downed before she had opted for the ouzo, and was feeling surplus to requirements when he finally joined her at the small table tucked all the way at the back of the courtyard.

Suddenly, even the distant mountains standing watch like shadowy guardians over the star-studded night seemed to pale in significance.

Closing her eyes, Dolly took a deep breath. Her belly quivered with anticipation and relief and...a fizzy joy that she couldn't stem.

Coward that she was, she pretended that every cell in her body didn't stand to attention. That she didn't inhale the earthy, oak moss scent of him deep into her lungs. That she didn't enjoy the way his gaze swept over her face.

The first thing she noticed when she opened her eyes was how the convenient little sconce on the wall illuminated the chiseled planes of his face. Then there was the two-inch-long scar streaking from his hairline down the slope of his cheekbone and across to his upper lip, nearly bisecting it.

Awareness simmered through her, making her skin tingle, as if he were a vast energy source radiating electric pulses, tuned to find and sink into her. Her fingers twitched to trace the uneven, raised skin of the scar.

His jaw had thick bristle and his eyes, while alert, were cradled by dark shadows. The white of his thin linen shirt emphasized the vitality of his olive skin though. She breathed easy, even as a part of her wanted to throw herself at him, wanted to touch him and hold him to reassure herself that he was sitting by her, solid and arrogant as always.

"Does it make me ugly, do you think?" he said, following her glance.

She met his gaze and held fast under the gray storm swirling there. He was…not angry, but he wasn't calm either. Rarely did Ares let his emotions get the better of him. So what was going through his brilliant mind right now?

"I didn't know you cared that much about your appearance," she quipped, glad to find her tone breezy. In any other man, she'd have called it vanity or even insecurity.

"I don't," he said, running a hand over his cheek. "But being here, next to my half brothers, I can't help but remember how it felt to be that scrawny, scared teen again."

Having met the notorious older brothers, Dolly couldn't blame him. She played with the steel bracelet on her wrist, just to give her twitching fingers something to do. "You were called the youngest, sexiest tech nerd on some magazine cover only last year, remember? As for now…scars only increase men's beauty by our society's standards."

"How so?" he said, with that interested gleam in his eyes that said, *Explain the damned world to me.*

She shrugged. "I don't know… I guess they speak to experience and character or some such bullshit."

"And it wouldn't be thought the same for a woman?"

"Most probably not. At best, it would be *a mark of courage* if one walks around without getting cosmetic surgery."

He nodded. "The system works in my favor, for once?"

She laughed at his dry tone. "I don't know about that, Ares. You're a six-foot-four-inch Greek man with god-like looks, an extra big brain and you hail from a powerful, influential family who clearly adore you. Except maybe the two meatheads," she said before she could stop herself. Flushing, she straightened in her chair. "Sorry, I didn't—"

"Don't apologize. I saw that you've had the dubious pleasure of meeting them."

"Yes. And your father. They're quite the…trio." She frowned. "Why didn't you come rescue me?"

"You didn't look like you needed to be rescued." He studied her with that same intensity that had never bothered her before. "It was entertaining to see you take them on."

"Is that why you summoned me here? To be used as some kind of shield against your family members?"

"Not so much as a shield but a buffer. You know this."

Her shoulders rose and fell with her long exhale. "I don't want to get in the middle of your family's dynamics. It's clear they see me as an interloper." Holding his gaze, she hesitated.

"Come, Dahlia, spit it out." Impatience colored his tone. "I have enough with my family pussyfooting around me as if I might fall apart at one honest word. You don't have to treat me with kid gloves too."

"I don't want to stress you out."

"Being here does that to me automatically. It's not just the different undercurrents among my siblings and our parents. All this…the extended family and friends, this celebration, the noise, the constant gaiety, the sheer number of people I don't even recognize coming up to shake my hand, touching me, hugging me…" His already drawn features twisted into a grimace, blunt-tipped fingers showing white against his temples.

Instinct made Dolly grab his wrist. Beneath the face of his sports watch, his pulse thudded a steady beat, her fingers spreading out to touch more of his hair-roughened skin of their own will.

His gaze zoomed to where she gripped him.

Flushing, she meant to pull back but he covered her fingers with his other hand, trapping her there. Even the simple, nonsexual contact made her body come alive, as if a switch had been turned on. Dolly swallowed and searched back through their conversation. "Can't you tell them that the sensory overload is too much? That you need space?"

"And ruin my grandparents' celebration? Arabella told me that they had canceled the celebration because I was ill, that it had been like an endless funeral the entire time. Mama didn't even come home from the clinic except on the weekends." His jaw tightened as he looked around at the laughing, dancing guests and family members. "Honestly, they are celebrating my recovery as much as my grandparents' marriage."

Dolly nodded, even as protests rose to her lips. She wished he would at least let his mother and father see how the raucous celebration affected him. And if he didn't confide in them now, when he was still recovering from a major accident, then when? "Ares, don't you think—"

"Tell me what my father said to you," he cut her off, as if he knew what she was about to say.

"He offered to buy me a first-class ticket to return home. And your mother could barely make eye contact with me."

Displeasure radiated from him. "I didn't think he

would make such a direct move. As for Mama, she worries about me."

"As she should. It's clear your father wants to use this opportunity to reconnect with you. Maybe even heal the rift between you two."

"You've surmised all that in two hours?"

"Unlike the two meatheads, who by the way give me the creeps, your father was genuinely distressed by my arrival." She must be really tired because she was connecting the dots only now. "I'm a mere assistant. Why does he believe I have any say on you staying or leaving?"

"Because I might have intimated something to that effect."

"Intimated what exactly?"

"That you and I have a relationship outside of work."

Lead seemed to sink through Dolly's stomach. Had he remembered everything after all? "What kind of relationship?"

Arms folded on the table in front of him, he studied her for long moments before saying, "I told them you're a conniving, beautiful witch who has chained me with her beauty and did not let me return home all these years. You know, like the siren and Ulysses."

"That sounds over-the-top and…" She shook her head. "Oh, my God! Did you start work on the little droid again? Because that sounds like regurgitated crap that an AI bot would produce."

He laughed and lines crinkled from the edges of his eyes. His white teeth shone against his olive skin and a sheepish grin stretched his lips. "Those lines were the answer from the bot when I asked."

"I'm scared to know what the question was." Then she

gave a rather dramatic sigh. "Your bot is going to sink us all, isn't it?"

His teeth dug into his lower lip as he shook his head. "You jumped ship already. So why do you care?"

"Technically, I didn't jump ship," she retorted. "I didn't go off to another company."

"No, you simply decided to jump into the ocean, *ne*?"

"We're going off track. What did you tell your family about me?"

"That you and I are engaged. To be married," he added, to clarify.

Dolly's belly rolled as if she were lurching on a ship on the high seas, drunk.

"Apparently I told my parents right before the accident."

So he had told them they were engaged before the accident—like they had agreed upon as the first step? But his mother had reminded him. Which meant he didn't remember their plan, the contract they had signed, the confession or his rejection?

"You've gone alarmingly pale, Dahlia."

A soft breeze from the ocean ruffled his collar, giving her a glimpse of the smooth, taut edge of his pectoral muscles. Swallowing, she looked away, pressing her shaking fingers to her suddenly thumping heart. "No wonder they…loathe me. They think I didn't care enough to show up here when you were unwell. But now that you are recovering, I come running back to you."

"You didn't care to be here. That is the truth."

Cheeks heating, Dolly stared at him. "You're angry about that?" she asked, surprise coloring her words. "It didn't make sense for me to fly all the way here, Ares. Not when you—"

He raised a hand, cutting off her apology. "Why didn't you tell me that we agreed to a fake engagement? My mother, of all people, had to remind me what I blurted to her on the phone, moments before the accident."

Shivers coursed through her even though it was only balmy. Dolly rubbed her fingers over her neck. "I…"

"You agreed, right?"

The doubts in his eyes made her feel awful. "Yes, of course."

He sat back. Watching her, drilling holes into her with that gaze.

Lacing her fingers on the table, she sifted through the various options. "When you called me, you'd just woken up after seven weeks in a coma. All I kept thinking was that you're okay. My brain wasn't all there. I was riding the wave of relief and happiness."

Which was mostly true.

He didn't look satisfied but at least moved on. "So, the plan was to use the engagement and the idea of an imminent wedding to encourage my brothers to drop the lawsuit?"

"Yes," Dolly said, past a throat full of thorns. "You thought letting them see that your assets could be mine any day would be a warning. The direct threat would be that you wouldn't let them touch a penny of yours, ever again. That you would never again come to their rescue like you did four years ago."

"You know that I helped the family company out?"

"That you invested twenty million Euros into the export company and paid off the money they embezzled from it, yes." She sighed. "You trusted me."

"I still do."

"But?" she said, her breath hanging on a sword.

He shook his head, shutting her out. "We will follow that plan and make a big show of the engagement, then. Which will give them a chance to plan out some activities for me." A hint of vulnerability flashed in his eyes. "I want to repair my relationship with my parents and Arabella."

"I get that," she said. "But you're starting it with a big lie to them."

He pressed the pad of a thumb to her knuckle. "It's not that much of a stretch, is it?"

Her heart gave a kick against her rib cage, her entire being sinking into that patch of skin he touched. "What do you mean?"

"You've been the only woman in my life for a long while, Dahlia. You know me inside out. And with these damned headaches…" He pressed his fingers into his temples, his mouth bracketed by strain. "Right now, you're the only one I can trust."

"Surely not everyone in your family is like those two?"

"No, but it doesn't mean Sergio and Stefano won't use them to manipulate me. I have to stop them from dragging this lawsuit out, in a way that doesn't hurt the rest of the family. Mama and Papa are, I believe, already at loggerheads," he added. "The scandal of us going at each other will break my grandparents' hearts. It's the reason I stopped it from becoming public."

"They're suing you, Ares. For a huge chunk of your

fortune that they have no right to. At some point, you have to tell the rest of them."

"No. It would only hurt them. Especially Mama and maybe even my father."

The need to question his continued loyalty toward a man who had done nothing to protect him grated on her. Dolly bit back a sigh.

Lies within lies... She was beginning to feel like she had walked into some kind of play, blindfolded, with no memory of how she got there.

Wasn't it better to simply tell him the truth? To get the whole mess out in the open if he was going to be here indefinitely? But if she did, she would have to also reveal what had happened *after*, what had made him look so disgusted with her. Why he'd been so angry with her.

She had no idea where he had hidden the marriage contract they had both signed. If the engagement itself was enough to thwart the meathead brothers as Ares was hoping, could she simply hide her head in the sand about their agreement until they could dissolve the marriage after ten months?

Maybe by then, Ares would not only recover but be relieved that she wasn't his contract wife anymore.

Still, the last thing she needed was to enter a fake engagement with the man she was secretly married to, a man she had too many confusing feelings about.

"Dahlia…" he said, that thumb pad stroking toward her wrist. "What are you not telling me?"

Her pulse spiked as she looked up to meet his eyes. "You're asking too much of me, Ares." It was what she should have said months ago when he'd asked her for "a small favor."

Pulling his hand away, he sat back in his chair, his gaze drilling into hers. "What if I offer to pay for your grandfather to move into that assisted living community that you were checking out last year? For the rest of his life?"

Dolly stared at him, her chest squeezing tight with guilt this time. That was exactly what she'd done with the money he'd given her for signing the marriage contract.

Then there was the shock that he had remembered that her grandfather had been having more and more mobility issues and that, right before Ares's accident, she'd been scouting old age homes. Just when she thought she might be more objective about their relationship... "Are you trying to prove that you can buy me?" The question sounded pretentious and self-righteous to her own ears, because she'd already sold herself to him, even if not for his wealth.

"Buy you?" he snarled, jaw tight.

Heat streaked her cheeks as she tried to cover her confusion. "I don't know," she finally said.

"If I want to take your biggest worry in life off your shoulders so that you can give me your time and focus, is that *buying* you?" Disgruntlement etched his features.

"That was over the line," she said, biting down on her lip. "This whole thing has thrown me."

"Of course it has. Especially since, clearly, you have built this whole new life without me in it."

While she had hoped to find some sense of equanimity about his place in her life, all she had established in the long seven weeks they'd been apart was that she was even more attached to him than she'd realized. She had been lost and confused, even grieving. It had felt as if she had lost a friend and a partner, without ever having enjoyed the actual benefits of either.

But there was no way she could share that with him. He would either laugh at her or banish her again.

He steepled his fingers over his abdomen, his words strained. "Now that I've made the offer, I'll see that it's done."

Her chest rose with her ballooning breath. "That's called railroading. And it's not necessary. As soon as his doctors clear him for moving, he'll shift into a long-term care facility. I was able to get enough funds into place."

"That home in upstate New York?"

God, but the man didn't forget a single detail. "Yes."

"You said the place was prohibitively expensive."

She sighed. "I have savings. You have always paid me well and I liquidated some of my stock options." And before he could probe further, she said, "I'll stay and help you with whatever. I want it noted, though, that I'm agreeing to the fake engagement and everything it entails under extreme resistance."

"Noted," Ares said without missing a beat.

"And I'm going to leave when you figure out a way to beat the meatheads."

Ares was angry enough that he could feel its burn up his throat. To say he didn't like the sensation would be an understatement. He liked the irrationality of her decision even less.

He'd thought seeing Dahlia here, in this environment where he had once been the most vulnerable, would return his self-assurance.

There was a sense of his world tilting right at her presence. Of not being alone, of not being an outsider among familiar faces, a sentiment that had dogged him all his life.

But the fact that she was still insisting on leaving her position, *on leaving him*, made that feeling transient.

He felt like he was struggling for air. A sensation he remembered very vividly from when he had been twelve and Sergio and Stefano had pushed his face into the massive water sump at their farmhouse. Even the passing reminder that he couldn't begin to navigate the world around him without her grated on him.

A pulse of awareness pinged through him as he let his gaze travel over her.

Her tight braid pulled her angular features into focus. A high forehead, the sharp tip-tilted angle of her nose and the thin but wide mouth with lips the color of cherries…nothing about her features was conventional. And yet, mixed together on the canvas of her face, like some artist's individual strokes coming together to paint a vivid scene, she radiated stunning intelligence and subtle beauty.

It was a face one could become obsessed with. The birthmark on the slope of her upper lip, the fragile cradle of her clavicle, the arch of her neck…his fingers tingled with the urgent need to trace every inch of her.

He wanted to dig his fingertips into her flesh, smudge that composure she wore like an armored vest until it crumpled under his fingers. Until she told him why she was so desperate to leave him.

Like so many other emotions clamoring to be heard, this too was raw and persistent. This stringent awareness and dawning attraction to his assistant.

It was the reason he had waited two hours to approach her, even though her arrival had tugged at him as if he were a magnet seeking north.

This attraction was last thing he needed right now, an extra complication when they were caught in a situation that demanded constant proximity. And it made him wonder if he had felt this awareness and attraction to her before.

Had he tamped it down because it was unprofessional and made him feel this…out of control? Had he ever admitted it to her?

Because he was definitely failing now at keeping the boundaries, especially given he was parading her as his fiancée.

"Right," he said, refusing to betray this new awareness just yet, "I forgot about your whole dating, romance and babies plan."

Her shoulders went straight, stretching the soft fabric of her sleeveless top tight across her breasts. The light from the hanging sconce limned her high cheekbones and lips, leaving the rest of her face in alluring shadows. "Mock me all you want. But nothing's wrong with paying attention to what I want from life."

"How did the two unofficial dates go?" The pulsing, pounding pain behind his left eye felt worse as the image of Dahlia with different men moved through his head like a bloody slideshow. "Should I expect one of those men to pursue you across the Atlantic and fight me over you? Do they know that you're engaged to your billionaire tech boss and are playing around with their hearts?"

Swift color rushed into her cheeks, lips parting on a gasp he wanted to catch with his own. "What?" Her voice rose, a half growl, half squeak, drawing attention to them. She laced her fingers on the table. "They weren't even dates. More like coffee at the bodega and sushi at

the hospital cafeteria. Two random guys I met while waiting nights at the hospital. It was more for company than
anything else. H-how do you know?"

"Christina told me."

"She had no right to do that. Are you paying her to
spy on me?"

"We were talking and I expressed my concern at your
irrational behavior. She told me what you've been up to."

She leaned forward, her anger rolling off her in waves.
"*My* irrational behavior?"

A subtle scent of jasmine, deepened by her own, teased
his nostrils. He was claimed by an intense, overwhelming urge to duck his head and bury his nose in the crook
of her neck where the scent would be richer and deeper.
Then he would wrap the braid around his fingers and
pull her closer.

Instead, Ares sat back in his chair, fisting his hands in
his lap under the table. Clearly, something in his head had
shaken loose as a result of the accident because lusting
over his assistant and his one true friend was *so* not him.

Christos, it wasn't just inappropriate but a damned
inconvenience too. Lust and affection and even bonds
of friendship were things that had never interested him
before. And yet now…everything seemed to play out to
the background of Dahlia's presence.

"You're determined to quit a well-paying job to find
romance and love and all that…flimsy stuff. What is it
if not irrational? Clearly, my accident had more effect on
you than you will admit."

"Of course it had an effect, Ares. You were my boss,
my friend and my…" Her throat bobbed up and down.

Despite the cool breeze floating up from the sea, dots

of sweat decorated her upper lip. Again, that urge to lean down and lick at that plump lip, to grasp it between his own and suck at it, filled him. He wanted to touch her, not just to know how she would feel but to comfort her too.

Lust was still a biological function he understood. But this need to comfort her in such a personal way, this anger at what he continued to see as her abandonment of him… *What the hell is happening to me?* Had his brain been completely rewired thanks to the damned coma he'd been in?

With her jaw tight, Dahlia looked as shaken as he felt inside. And that, perversely, grounded him. She was the most sensible, balanced person he knew. Somehow, they would get through this and return to that comfortable, convenient plane of pseudo-friendship. They had to.

Without sounding melodramatic, his survival depended on it.

"I was devastated by your accident and your…coma." Her brown eyes looked impossibly wide in the shadows. "And it made me take a good look at my own life and I realized I don't like the direction it has taken. I want more than eighty-hour work weeks inside a steel-and-chrome office." Her mouth twisted with self-deprecation. "Did you know that I haven't gone on a vacation since I was thirteen? I worked two jobs during high school and college. I had grand plans for a career in business."

"And so?"

"So what?" she said with such fire in her eyes and belligerence in her tone that Ares wanted to taste it straight from her lips.

Was this too a forgotten memory or had Dahlia always been so full of fire?

He had to assume the latter because the one unshakable fact he knew in his gut—which showed how much the accident had changed him, because his gut was suddenly his compass—was that he admired and respected her.

"Did you find the mythical man who's supposed to make these new, feverish dreams of yours come true?" he quipped. "The man who's supposed to give you romance novel–worthy sex and movie-worthy romance?"

Her eyes shied away from his, her anger with him an almost tangible force catching them in a bubble. Outlined against the dark waters of the sea behind her, her profile was breathtakingly beautiful. "You're a bastard, Ares Demetrius."

"Excuse me? I didn't catch your answer," he said, eager to rile her up even more. Maybe then her control would break and he would see what she was hiding. What it was that she didn't want to give him.

"No. I didn't meet half a good man, much less a fully perfect one." Her mouth turned down. "A single hint that I cared for my grandfather full-time, or that I was between jobs, or the fact that I don't like casual sex had them running in the other direction. Apparently, I'm as out of touch with the dating world as you are. There, are you happy?"

"That you have failed miserably at this, yes," he said without an ounce of guilt.

"Jesus," she said, rubbing her fingers over her face. "I've forgotten how blunt you can be."

The chipped nail polish on her nails stood out against her skin, a stark reminder of how far she had come to be here and how she didn't belong here, amidst his contentious family.

The entire world zoomed out and suddenly all Ares could see was how pinched her features looked and how much weight she'd lost. How his rigid, rigorous lifestyle, his accident, his demand that she see to his needs, had affected her.

And now that his focus had turned to her *and only her*, he knew what he needed to do.

"How about I make you an offer?"

"I think you've made me enough offers, thank you," she quipped, sinking deeper into her chair and throwing her head back. The long, graceful column of her throat drew his attention.

Everything about her was a fascinating mystery he wanted to unlock and play with. For the simple pleasure of knowing her like no other man did or ever could.

He shot to his feet, planted himself behind her chair, and gripped her temples. With a surprised grunt, she jerked beneath his touch but he pressed down. "Relax, Dahlia."

Her fingers wrapped around his wrist, the touch jolting through him like the fireworks his cousins had lit an hour ago. "That's not…necessary," she whispered, eyes widening into dreamy pools.

Ares's body reacted with a vivid image of those same fingers wrapped around his shaft, squeezing him hard. *Christos*, he had never reacted like this to a woman's innocent touch. Not that he let any woman touch him, innocent or otherwise.

"As you've made abundantly clear," he said, his words sounding husky, "I demand a lot from you, *ne*? So maybe it's time for me to care for you."

A serrated laugh escaped her lips, coated with disbelief.

He turned his fingertips in tight circles. Her laughter cut off.

"Don't worry, Dahlia. I'm only doing this because I know you will pay it back in efficiency and loyalty."

"Now that's the boss I know."

Smiling, he pressed the tips of his fingers into her temples and dragged them past her hairline into her thick hair. When he rubbed gently, a moan slipped out from behind her clamped lips. The sound pinged over his nerves, shutting out everything else around them.

He clamped his muscles to stop himself from bending down and tasting that moan straight from her lips. It was as if all the hormonal, uncontrollable urges of puberty were hitting him now, in one day.

"Think of the next few weeks as a break, a fun adventure. Who knows? My family might drive me so crazy that even I could join in."

Her brown eyes sparkled with mirth. "You? Fun?"

"Why not? Christina and the new CTO have things well in hand. And I can't manage more than an hour or two of work before these blasted headaches set in. Why don't we treat this…engagement period as a holiday?"

"I'm not sure that's a good idea."

"Give me one good reason you can't spend a month sunning yourself on a glorious beach, eating good food and taking in the sights. You'll spend maybe an hour or two with me for work. When we return to New York, you can begin your perfect man search again. That's my offer."

She sighed and the rise and fall of her breasts mesmerized him. "We'll be muddling all the lines between us. Lines you have always insisted stay in place. Also, I doubt how much fun you can really be."

"Be honest, Dahlia. Are you worried that you might end up realizing that there's no perfect man for you out there but me?"

"What?" Swatting at his hands, she shot to her feet. Her words were a breathy whisper as she studied him. "What do you mean?"

"I got you good, didn't I?" He grinned. "And you keep saying I don't know how to have fun."

Words, and curses he thought, sputtered from her lips as she stepped toe to toe with him. His fingers itched to pull her against him, to absorb all that outrage into his own body. To soothe and pet and coax her into giving him her complete trust again.

Because he had a feeling he'd had it once, utterly. And somehow, had managed to lose it.

Christos, had he ever noticed how perfectly she would fit against him? Was this sudden bout of awareness of her as a woman some byproduct of how close he had come to his death?

It struck him then that he didn't mind this sudden tension between them as much as he should.

All he cared about was that life was both comforting and fascinating when Dahlia was around and there was no way he was going to give her up.

CHAPTER FOUR

Send me your fun list.

WET HAIR DRIPPING from her shower, Dolly stared at the text.

It had been two days since she had arrived at Ares's family home in Corfu. Most of which she had spent unwinding.

Given the fake engagement, it was strange that she had been shown to a separate bedroom from Ares's. But it was a much-needed reprieve.

She still couldn't believe how cunningly playful this new version of Ares was. Neither could she stem the sheer giddy joy she felt from being near him again.

It had been agreed upon with Christina that Ares would work on his droid for the next couple of months. Ares working on the bot and its software meant Dolly wouldn't have much to do except fielding his emails and scanning through weekly reports from different teams.

Dolly stared at her reflection in the mirror and fought silly tears.

Christina and she weren't close—at some point in her adolescence, Dolly had forgotten how to get close to people. But they had grown up in the same neighborhood, so Christina knew how hard it had been for Dolly to lose her parents and move in with her aunt and uncle.

Not only had her aunt made sure Dolly knew that she was a burden on their straining finances with constant diatribes, but the one time Christina had come home with Dolly, she had taken her temper out on Dolly in front of her. When Christina brought it up later, Dolly begged her to never mention it again.

She hadn't wanted her crappy home life to taint anything else. And definitely not her exciting college life with Christina and Ares.

Dolly pumped moisturizer into her hands and began rubbing it into her skin, thinking of what Christina had said last night on the phone. That it was time to think of herself—not her grandfather, not her aunt and not Ares.

Time to think of where her life was headed when this last assignment with Ares was over. Because that's what this was—another assignment, and nothing more.

Yes, she had gone on those two dates but there was no point in deluding herself. The point of the dates had been to prove to herself that Ares didn't mean anything to her rather than to actually explore what she wanted in a partner.

With her grandfather now permanently taken care of, it was time to live her life for herself. And not just romance and dating, but her career too.

Years ago, she had taken on tremendous loans to go to Columbia when she could have easily gone to a community college to pursue a career in business.

With Ares taking over her life like a blazing hot sun, she had let her degree fall to the side. It had served her then to follow his rising star. He had compensated her

TARA PAMMI   67

more than the industry ever paid an executive assistant. Now it was high time she finished her own degree. Although, she couldn't think of any tech company business role giving her as much freedom and as many learning opportunities as Ares had given her, even as his assistant.

It struck her then how she had been the one who had limited herself to that role, not Ares. All he had asked of her was that she be his connection to the outer world. Who was to say he wouldn't have given her bigger projects if that's what she wanted?

And when she thought of it that way, it didn't seem wrong or foolish to have stayed with him for that long. Her faith in him felt very right, in fact.

Send me the fun list.

Send me the Dahlia Needs to Let Loose list.

Send me the Poor Executive Assistant Who Got Stuck with Her Uptight Boss and Didn't Live Life for Six Years list.

Her phone kept pinging with texts from Ares in the same vein.

Despite her resolve to harden her heart, a smile curved her mouth. The man's hyperfocus was the stuff of legends.

An unwise thrill coursed down her spine as she read the texts again. She had been too tired to take him seriously before, but now, wide-awake and rested, she braced herself. To suddenly find herself to be the locus of Ares Demetrius's attention, in a very personal way, was both exciting and scary. For it had always been a project or an app or an algorithm that triggered that hyperfocus.

And if she was honest with herself, it was what she had craved for a long time. That he see her as a woman with her own desires and fears. That it had come about because of his accident was out of her control.

Scrolling to the notes app on her phone, she typed a list of all the things a younger, less cynical Dolly would have wanted to explore in life. She pasted it on the text chain with him and hit Send before she could censor herself.

He would employ whatever means were at his disposal—which was a whole lot of means—to persuade her to stay. This newly discovered teasing charm being one of them.

But as irresistible as this new version of him was, she couldn't forget that the only way to save her sanity, and her dented heart, was in exiting his life as soon as possible.

When Dolly emerged into the white-and-blue bedroom half an hour later, clad in a silk robe that she was definitely stealing from the Demetrius household, she found Ares's very English mother, Juliana, waiting for her.

Standing inside the bedroom with a host of attendants running around her, the older woman looked like a queen visiting a peasant.

Surprise halted Dolly in her tracks. Ares's younger sister, Arabella, stood separately from her mother, looking nervous.

Folding her hands over her midriff, Dolly faked a sweet smile. This woman was a stranger who was trying to protect her son. From Dolly's gold-digging clutches, no less.

"Mrs. Demetrius, how nice to see you," she said icily polite. "I wasn't expecting to have a bonding session with you and Arabella quite so soon. Ares and I have hardly caught up with each other."

If that sounded like issuing marching orders to the matriarch, then so be it.

She was here because she felt obligated to Ares. Even when he turned her upside down, she trusted him implicitly.

In short, she could deal with whatever he threw at her. But his family was another matter. Dolly wasn't going to let anyone treat her as if she was rubbish. She had had enough of that from her aunt.

Juliana flicked her head, which sent the attendants scurrying out of the suite. Arabella lingered near the threshold, seemingly unsure of whether to stay or flee.

"I let you rest for two days, my dear," Juliana began with a saccharine sweetness that made Dolly's teeth ache. "But there is a certain…standard, shall I say—" she paused, as if she had to search for the word "—to maintain when you enter the Demetrius family. Even from the margins. I have come to make sure that you and your wardrobe…" her steely gray gaze, so much like her son's, touched Dolly from head to toe, somehow managing to dismiss her in the same glance "…meet those standards. Our family, friends, even the media will focus on you. I'm sure you do not want to embarrass yourself or Ares in any way."

Flames of anger licked at Dolly, but she held her temper in check. Where had her protectiveness been when her stepsons were tormenting Ares as a confused boy? And what did she think to achieve by alienating her son's fiancée?

"I've been by Ares's side for nine years without embarrassing him or myself," she said, meeting the woman's eyes. "And since you're clearly here to insult me, I'll make this easy. Please don't waste your energy and effort on alienating me. Ares will not like it. I dare say I know him better than any of you."

Without waiting for her response, Dolly marched to the walk-in closet.

Which was twice the size of her bedroom under the stairs at her aunt's house before she had found her own place. Her mind whirred at Juliana's comments as she studied her meager wardrobe.

Granted, her choice of clothes was limited. But if Ares, or his damned family, was ashamed of how she dressed, that was not her problem.

Biting her lip, she rifled through her clothes and picked white linen shorts, and a yellow crop top she'd bought on an impulse. Grinning, she pulled them on. When she cast a look at herself in the full-length mirror, it was to discover that a large strip of her belly was left bare and the stretchy material clung to her small breasts.

Her first instinct was to cover herself up.

Dolly reached for the usual loose T-shirts that she bought in bulk and wore at home. But remembering who was standing outside the closet stopped her. As did the gray gaze of another who took her for granted, and had once erupted quite cruelly at her foolish admission that she was attracted to him.

The knot of hurt from his outburst still pulled at her chest painfully.

Why had Ares been so angry at her confession? Had he also assumed that she was after his wealth, that she truly coveted the status and power that came from being his wife?

Or was it because she had forced him to see her as a woman? Had he assumed that she was like the bot he was designing, that she didn't feel or crave affection?

The reminder bolstered her flagging courage. She quickly braided her still damp hair, swiped on sunscreen and lip gloss and thrust her feet into sandals.

When she returned to the living room, Juliana and her attendants were gone. Arabella, however, lingered.

Dolly's skin prickled as the teenager looked at her with unabashed curiosity. "Please forgive my mother's behavior. She worries about Ares."

"Not your fault," Dolly said, straightening all the things she'd thrown around the room. "I'm a bit surprised that you're being friendly toward me. Was this an order from your pushy brother?"

Arabella's eyes widened. "You're not at all intimidated by him, are you?"

"There's no need to be," Dolly said, half lying.

She was intimidated by Ares, but not for the same reasons as his younger sister.

There's no perfect man for you out there, Dahlia, but me...

His teasing comment had been haunting her.

What if it was true? What if she was never able to connect with any other man like she had with Ares? Where did that leave her?

Whether it was the jet lag or the nightmares she'd had since hearing about Ares's accident, or the fact that her grandfather's health was rapidly declining, her dreams had been far too disruptive and her sleep fretful at best.

Even at his peak health, Grandpa hadn't been an effusive person. At his happiest with her, Dolly would get a slight tap on her cheek from him. Not that she'd ever doubted his affection for her.

But it meant it had been years since anyone had held her properly, or touched her even.

When she woke up from one of those dreams, near tears and shaken, she craved to be held and touched. So badly that it gouged a deep cavern inside her.

And the face she reached for to anchor herself back to the world, the touch she craved was Ares's. It was the same longing that had made her take the drastic step of confessing her desires to him.

His reaction, though, still stung. Still punched hard at the deepest parts of her where she admitted that she was all alone in the world. Had been for a long while.

"Dahlia? You okay?"

Dolly blinked at Arabella's voice. Her throat stung with emotion but she swallowed it all back. "Of course."

He might not be as bad as his family but Ares did like his world just so, like any other rich, privileged man. And for that, he would use any means. The way he was wired, he wouldn't even feel bad about it.

She had to remember that.

"What were we talking about?" Dolly said, forcing a laugh. "I'm still not used to the time difference."

"You were telling me to not be intimidated by my brother," Arabella supplied.

"Right, don't be," Dolly said, straightening the sheets on the bed. "He's as flawed as you and I are. If anything, he's easier to understand if you try too."

"Simpler to understand? His intellect is scary and he left home when I was still a kid. I don't have anything in common with him. And I really want to get to know him before he…decides that he's not happy here and leaves us again."

"That's not—" Dolly stopped herself, catching the look in Arabella's eyes.

Tears shone there but she didn't let them fall. "Thank you for not lying to me, Dahlia, like everyone else." A serrated laugh escaped the young woman. "I want to build a relationship with my brother. But not by manipulating him or emotionally blackmailing him."

Dolly nodded, her heart going out to her. At least, it was what Ares wanted too. Helping Arabella was something she could and would do, happily.

Maybe if Ares nurtured a deeper connection with Arabella, he wouldn't need Dolly so much as his anchor to the outside world.

Maybe with Arabella on his side, he could even convince the meatheads to let go of the lawsuit without further mayhem.

Maybe he would realize that he could function very well in the world without their fake relationship or their very real marriage.

Without Dolly at all in his life.

The idea appealed to her mind and crushed her heart equally.

"How about," Dolly said, forcing breeziness into her tone, "I give you some pointers about his likes and interests? If it's one of his favorite topics, he won't shut up about it, like any other man. But unlike other men, he won't talk down to you if you ask questions. He finds true joy in the art or science behind something."

"Noted." Her expression turned wary before she said, "I'd love to get to know you too, Dahlia."

"Why?" Dolly said, even as her heart warmed instantly at the prospect of getting to know Arabella. She colored realizing how rude her question sounded.

She hadn't been lying when she'd complained to Ares

about not having a life while working with him. Forget romance and dating, she barely even had a friend. If not for Christina—with her unreservedly gushing personality—pestering her at work, no one would know even a hint of what Dolly's homelife had been like for years.

"Other than the fact that my brother thinks the world of you?" Arabella said, smiling.

"You are overestimating my role in his life," Dolly said, stuffing her sunglasses, a hat and a paperback she'd bought at the airport into her beach bag. If she avoided Arabella's watchfulness under the guise of packing, she was only a little ashamed of it. "I'm just very good at what I do for Ares and he rewards that."

Arabella frowned. "You make it sound like your entire relationship is based on work. But you're engaged." She almost sounded sad at that.

Dolly flushed. "No, but…work is the basis of our relationship. There's a certain level of constancy that Ares requires in his life and I give him that. He has very rigid boxes in his head and it's important to not mix them up or he'll explode."

And yet, she had done exactly that.

Just because they had signed a paper contract that bound them together legally—which had affected her way more than she had assumed it would—she had thought it would be okay to confide her attraction to him. Granted, a combination of factors had contributed to her error: they had been stuck because of a snowstorm, her grandpa's health was failing and she had a little to drink. That weekend the tight lock she kept around her heart had loosened.

After nine years of being in a very specific box for him, she'd suddenly jumped out of it and muddied all the lines for him. For Ares, the lines weren't simply lines but deep, solid walls that he lived his life within. He didn't understand nor want to understand the world outside of those walls. And her confession had threatened him— his sense of security, his boundaries—by nearly tearing down those walls.

She knew better than anyone else how he lived his life and yet, she had lost herself in her own feelings, and hurt both him and herself.

"Then there's the fact," Arabella said, bringing Dolly back to the present again, "that you're smart, beautiful and genuine, Dahlia."

This time, Dolly's laugh rang out loud. "Ahh…is there a reason you're sweet-talking me?"

"What? No," Arabella said, a blush dusting her cheeks. "When Mama asked him about the engagement after he woke up, Ares said he's never known anyone else like you. Those were all his words for you, Dahlia. I think I left out *generous* and *kind* too."

Dolly stilled, even as a maelstrom spun through her insides.

She felt like parched earth suddenly facing a deluge of pouring rain. It shouldn't affect her so much that he thought those things about her, but it did. Little filaments of joy seemed to come alive through her body, lighting her up from the inside.

"When he woke up?" she asked, despite knowing not to indulge herself.

Arabella nodded.

She sighed, her head pounding with a renewed ache. These days, she was forever standing at that crossroads of beliefs—one that said Ares saw her as she was, as she wished to be seen and one that said he was ruthless enough to give her whatever she wanted only to keep her close.

Dolly gave herself a mental shake. Going in circles about Ares's motivation would get her nowhere.

She was committed to help him through his hard period of transition after the accident just as she was committed to leaving him. In the meantime, she would enjoy the luxury setting, being looked after morning to night. While keeping a strict, professional distance from him in her head.

Her gaze caught on Arabella's pretty floral sundress. "Can you tell me what the occasion is today?"

"We're going to celebrate Ares's birthday. Don't tell me you forgot?"

"Of course I didn't," Dolly said with a pang. It was the first thing she'd remembered when she'd looked at her smartwatch this morning. *All I wanted to do was to find him and tease him out of a grumpy mood like I did most festive days.* Instead, she had reminded herself that there were others here who had a claim to him more than her. That the little claim she did have to him was fake. "But he thoroughly hates celebrating it. Usually, I'd drag him to my favorite restaurant after threatening him with a lawsuit about employee neglect."

Arabella's pink mouth fell open. "I didn't know that he hates it. I don't think Mama does either."

The girl looked so upset that Dolly said, "Between you and me, we'll manage his grumpiness."

Smiling, Arabella hooked her arm through Dolly's and shuffled her along.

CHAPTER FIVE

ARES STOOD ON the starboard side, his gaze fixed on the rolling waves as they parted around the hull. Away from the loud music and dancing on the main deck. Much as he hated the noisy celebration, he loved being on the water.

It reminded him of the rare occasions he had spent time with his father without Stefano or Sergio around. Something about its blue depths had always calmed him.

That afternoon, with the sunlight hitting it just right, the Aegean glittered like turquoise jewels.

He tried to look interested for Arabella and Mama. The latter, he knew, was aggressively trying to make up for whatever she had overlooked when he had been a boy.

And Dahlia, of course.

Short of ordering her to chain herself to him, the only way he could draw her out was by partaking in as many of the family activities as possible. Plus, there was the fact that he wanted to spoil her. Once, he would have been horrified by the idea of her gaze on him constantly, but now he craved it. Maybe it was the whole nearly-losing-his-life thing but his perspective had shifted on life.

Dahlia had been right about one thing: they had worked far too hard for far too long without enjoying the fruits of that hard work.

Per his plan, he was also supposed to approach his older brothers and begin a conversation about the lawsuit. But every time he laid eyes on them, strutting about like arrogant peacocks, hot fury filled his throat.

He backed off, telling himself that he couldn't ruin the day by starting an argument with them. Plus there was the tiny, infinitesimal chance that his half brothers might back away from the lawsuit, since his accident had turned all their lives upside down. And if they did, Ares would have no reason to keep Dahlia by his side. No reason to keep their fake engagement going.

That he would tolerate Sergio and Stefano's vile claims just to keep Dahlia close for a little longer mildly alarmed himself. For the first time in his life, Ares wished for a friend he could talk to about all the new developments his recovery was bringing.

Christina was a good friend but she cared about Dahlia and would spill his own doubts to her in a second. The only other "friend" he had was Dr. Isiah King who was currently somewhere in the South Pole running a clinic and completely incommunicado. Another university mate.

A dark shadow cut off the direct glare from the sun. He bit back a sigh as he realized it was his parents. Instantly he opened his phone and realized he'd missed a text from Dahlia. Laughter burst up through his belly and chest as he skimmed her list.

Learn to swim. Take a dance class. Climb a mountain. Go for a ride in a hot-air balloon. Act in a movie. Get kissed upside down like MJ. Have an orgasm under water. Go back to school and finish my business degree. Indulge in a red-hot affair with a hot stud. Make a man fall hopelessly in love with me. Marry said man in a grand, beautiful ceremony. Have four babies by thirty-two—two boys and two girls. Live a romance-novel-worthy HEA.

He had no doubt that she had made it as outrageous as possible just to deter him. But after nine years together, she should know him better. Yes, there were things on the list that he absolutely wasn't into, but if it truly brought her happiness, he would try them.

Dahlia wasn't the only one who had let life pass her by.

He didn't know if it was the pain in his hip, like a hot flame licking at him at all hours, or the painful headaches, or the realization for the first time ever that his life was out of his control, but he wanted to more than just function optimally in his own bubble.

Sure, his brain always needed the stimulus of new innovation but he had amassed enough wealth to maintain a luxury lifestyle if he didn't work another day in his life.

He wanted to have new experiences. And he wanted to have them with Dahlia. And he…

The sudden, deafening silence around him finally registered. It was as if someone had muted a loud TV show.

Ares looked up to find his family—including Sergio and Stefano—staring at him as if he'd grown two horns in the blink of an eye. His mother and father looked dazed, as if they'd been frozen in time.

"What?" he barked, his skin crawling at their focused attention on him.

"We've never seen you laugh like that," Mama said, tears in her eyes. "Even as a boy, you were so…serious."

Annoyance prickled through him. But if she opened

the door to his childhood, then he would take it. "I didn't have much chance to laugh like that growing up. And even if I did, you were far too preoccupied with other stuff to notice."

Mama flinched while Papa bit his name through pursed lips like a curse.

"And now? What made you laugh like that?" Mama persisted in a falsely cheerful tone that no one bought.

Her wobbling chin made Ares feel like a monster. He knew she meant well but she and her close-to-surface emotions were beginning to scrape at him like fingernails on chalkboard. As if her misery and grief and guilt were all his burdens that she wanted him to alleviate right now.

He sighed, rubbed his hip, then swept his hand through his hair. One look at the list again and his dark mood lifted like fog under the morning sun. "My fiancée and her demands, that's what made me laugh."

"Her demands," Mama said, somehow managing to sound derisive.

For a man who never got nuance, it was clear what conclusions she was jumping to in that moment.

"Yes, Mama. It's the first time Dahlia has told me what she wants. And I intend to give in to each and every wish of hers," Ares said, just as the loud whir of a motorboat drowned out the silence.

He shot to his feet, ready to take on his dear assistant and all her demands.

It took Dahlia ten seconds to realize that she had cut off her nose to spite her face by dressing like she had. The metal railing was cool against her fingers as she climbed the short, retractable ladder. Her heart was loud in her chest at the thought of a hundred pairs of eyes follow-ing her every step. Grasping the smooth teak deck, she hoisted herself up.

For a few moments, the lavish extravagance of the yacht made her forget her own embarrassment. The main deck gleamed, with its polished teakwood glinting in the September sun, reflecting ripples of sunlight that danced across the sea's sapphire surface.

On the upper deck, elegant, ivory-hued loungers sat with precision, framing a crystal-clear pool that mirrored the Aegean's deep blue. Beyond the smooth, sculpted rails, the vast expanse of water stretched out endlessly. Amidst it, guests flitted about, dressed in pastel linen dresses that made them look like pretty mannequins at designer boutiques.

Dolly had no doubt that she stood out like a sore thumb, with every square inch of her skin exposed by the crop top and shorts.

God, she was stupid. The last thing she wanted was more attention from these people. And yet, that was ex-actly what her stunt had achieved. At least, the gauzy cover-up she had borrowed from Arabella lent her some cover and sophistication.

She was nothing but a guest and these people and their snooty opinions didn't matter to her, she reminded her-self when Ares reached her.

His gray gaze turned molten, like the surface of the ocean during a storm, as it swept over her. A soft grin kicked up one corner of his mouth, and he leaned forward and pressed his cheek to hers in a greeting. For the audi-ence, she assumed, but still, the patch of skin that touched his seared. As if he'd stamped her as his possession.

Was it possible that his tendency for hyper fixation had rubbed off on her?

The pine and mountain scent of his lingered on her as he pulled back, loosely laced their arms together. As if she were a puppet whose strings were in his capable hands, Dolly let him sweep her along.

She had never been gladder for the broad swathe of his shoulders. Seeing him like this, so magnetically alive, brought her earlier realization simmering back to the surface.

She desperately wanted to apologize for messing up, for not anticipating that he might not respond well to her sudden, foolish admission. After all, she knew better than anyone that Ares needed to feel in control at all times, in all situations. Not just in his physical space, but with his emotions too. He was the same man who hadn't returned home in nine years because it messed with his head, even as he funneled millions into the family business.

She wasn't sure if she could ever forget the crushing set-down he'd given her that day—or the hopelessness she'd felt in its aftermath—but she was beginning to understand why he had done it. But telling him that she understood meant telling him what had actually transpired, beginning with their marriage contract. And Dolly wasn't sure if she would ever be ready to bring that up, to render herself that vulnerable to him ever again.

All she had to do was wait out what was left of the twelve-month period, or Ares recovering his memories, and then the contract marriage could be dissolved.

Moving forward was the best. For both of them. Once the headache of the lawsuit was over and his memories mostly returned, Ares himself would not want her around.

The fact that he'd remembered being furious on the flight to Greece confirmed that well enough.

Her breath left in a long exhale and the surrounding opulence rushed back to assault her senses. The main salon they walked through, while Ares nodded at people here and there, was a vision of understated luxury, with creamy leather sofas, polished marble floors and floor-to-ceiling windows, which framed the brilliant seascape outside. Dolly felt as if she was gliding through an ever-changing painting, while the guests were nothing but avid, covetous spectators.

Still, no decadent view could dim her zinging aware-ness of the man himself.

Finally, he led her down a spiral staircase to the lower deck. Glass doors opened to a cozy sun-drenched lounge that seemed to melt into the horizon, while the yacht sliced effortlessly through gentle waves, leaving a trail of white foam.

The guests could still see them from different nooks if they wanted, but the lounge provided a modicum of pri-vacy. A part of Dolly wished he didn't have to parade her in front of his brothers and family, but it was the whole point she was there.

She let out a shaky laugh, rubbing a hand over her belly. "When Arabella mentioned a picnic, I assumed a beach and a rug and some wine."

"I've never seen you so nervous before," he said with a wry twist to his mouth. The full impact of his gaze landing on her was like a shot of adrenaline straight into her veins.

"What? You've suddenly grown receptive antennae to others' moods and emotions?" Dolly retorted.

"I've never been…unaware of your moods and emotions, Dahlia." When she didn't answer, his jaw tightened. "Or was I?"

Dolly sighed. The last thing she wanted was him to regret things he couldn't change about himself, then or now. Or for him to feel responsible for the misery she'd brought on herself.

Whatever he saw in her expression prompted him to say, "Don't sugarcoat reality for me, Dahlia. I couldn't bear it if you lied to me."

Her stomach twisted into such a tight knot that she could barely form words for several long moments. "Insofar as they affected your well-being, you could read me well."

Her sarcasm kicked the corners of his mouth into a soft grin. He poured her a glass of champagne and handed it to her. Head tilted to the side, he studied her while she sipped.

A boozy brunch on a yacht with views that belonged in a travel magazine…when was she ever going to get a chance like this again? Plus, she always actually enjoyed Ares's company. No man or woman she knew had his blunt wit, the fresh way of seeing things that he did. So she needed to stop fighting this and exhausting herself, at least for now.

She cast him a sidelong glance, unable to help herself, as he raised his face to the sky.

"You look…different," Ares said, catching her lingering glance. "I guess that outfit means you finally got the memo that you should see this as a vacation."

Shaking her head, she leaned against the glass door leading onto the outer deck. "I never thought I'd see the day you would try diplomacy."

"What do you mean?"

"I look like a cheap hooker who returned after a botched job to fight over her payment," she said, wanting to provoke him, unbalance him. Wanting to test this new dynamic between them. "Points to you for not saying it."

Throwing his head back, he laughed uproariously, the sound swathing her from all sides like a baby's worn-out blanket.

She gave up all pretense and just stared, longing flooding her.

His jet-black hair wind-ruffled, his gray eyes warmed up, the corded column of his throat inviting her touch…he looked so achingly gorgeous that her heart gave a weak thump. With the blue polo shirt hugging his lean, wiry frame, and in white shorts that made him look young and carefree, this was an Ares she'd never seen before, and therefore had no defenses against.

Even as laughter softened the harsh angles of his face into stunning beauty, the deep lines of pain etched near his mouth betrayed him.

Before she could think on it, she was tracing the grooves around his mouth in a featherlight touch. A gasp at her own audacity escaped her. "I'm sorry. I don't know what I was thinking."

His long fingers enveloped her wrist before she could jerk away. "It's okay, Dahlia."

"It's not," she said, tugging out of his hold. She felt his touch everywhere and yet not enough anywhere. "You look exhausted and I…forgot myself."

"I don't mind your touch," he said, bending his head, as if in supplication. As if he needed her touch rather than just tolerating it for the sake of pretense.

Her fingers tingled with the urge to sink into his thick hair. "Ares…"

A naughty grin curved his lips as he looked at her. "So we have never even thought of doing this before?"

Her cheeks flamed. "Doing what?"

"Touching each other. In comfort or passion or—"

"No! And you said you have memory gaps about the time before the accident," she said, her heart in her throat. "Are your memories coming back? Do you remember something specific?"

A frustrated grunt fell from his lips. "No. But I…"

"What?" She had never seen him hesitate ever before and she was beginning to hate all the half-truths surrounding them. "Is this some kind of test of my loyalty?"

"Of course not." He looked thoughtful, as if he was trying to figure out the conditions for an algorithm. "There's a lot of confusion in my head about you. But I can see that I have horrified you by asking if we've ever been involved." Alarm flashed in his eyes. "Or is it that you didn't trust me to not take advantage of you in some way?"

Dolly swallowed the ache that was beginning to feel like a permanent resident of her throat now. "Of course you would never take advantage of me."

The vehemence with which she said it clearly wasn't lost on him either. Her champagne flute rattled as she placed it on the side table. Suddenly, the yacht felt like a cage more than anything because she couldn't run from herself.

She turned away from him, wishing there was a way to purge her awareness of him. "I think we should stop talking about this. There's nothing to be achieved by focusing on the past."

"I hate not knowing," he bit out at her back, confirming her theory that his memory holes were contributing to his sleeplessness and agitation more than physical pain.

"Have you thought that if your mind's blanking things out for you, then maybe they are not worth remembering?" she said without turning. It cost her so much to say that.

"So I should just focus ahead?"

"Yes."

"Right, forget what we did or didn't do in the past, *ne*?" He stepped in front of her again, blocking her view of the sea. "Fine. But I want to test a theory I do have about the present. About you and me."

Her heart beat so loud that even the waves of the sea seemed to dim in her ears. Dolly pressed her palm to his chest, wanting to push him. Which was ridiculous because she might melt if he made skin contact with her. "This isn't really the time for one of your experiments, Ares. We're surrounded by your family and friends."

"Who are all curious about how I act with you. I might as well be a wild animal let loose among innocent lambs for their viewing pleasure. And since my mother gave you a different room, we didn't get any time to practice our newly engaged act."

There was frustration and something else Dolly couldn't pin down in his tone. Something almost like… anger. Also, now she understood another source of his mother's doubts about her.

"You're saying you want to share a room with me?" Although now that she knew the size of the villa, sharing a room might be like sharing a small-sized New York apartment.

"Isn't that what engaged couples do?" he quipped, studying her intently. "Now you've got my entire family even more curious about us."

"That's your problem," Dolly retorted, irritation making her response short. "They don't know the little fact that you don't like anyone in your personal space, Ares. I was trying to not step on your boundaries. And I haven't been sleeping well anyway."

It was the wrong thing to say to him. And in that miserable tone. It was as if she were the innocent lamb who not only had made eye contact with the wild animal but had decided to run. It was in the nature of the wild animal to give chase then.

First and foremost, Ares Demetrius was a problem solver. And she had just presented him with a very personal one, especially when he was looking for openings to persuade her that she was better off with him.

He turned fully, the heat of his body a welcome blanket against the briny breeze. "What's wrong? Why aren't you sleeping well?"

She didn't miss the grimace that crossed his face at the sudden movement.

"Dahlia?"

Knowing that he was like a dog with a bone when he spoke in that tone, she gave in. "I've been having nightmares."

"The same ones you had after your parents died in the car accident?"

Her head jerked up so fast that she pressed her fingers to the back of her neck. "How do you know that?"

"That one time at college, you slept at our apartment when you were dating Tony. When I came in from a midnight session at the computer lab, you were thrashing around in his bed. He had gone off to smoke."

Shock pummeled at Dolly. "That was years ago and I dated him for like two measly weeks. It's how I met you." A spark of happiness lit up within her chest at the memory. "I don't remember telling you about their accident."

"You didn't, at that time. I was your boyfriend's freaky roommate, obsessed with order and silence, remember?"

Dolly shook her head. "I never thought that of you."

"No, you didn't." A warm glow suffused his expression as if he too cherished the memory. "The next night, I started putting insulation around Tony's room to stop the noise from seeping out. And you dressed me down. Saying I wasn't just rude but insensitive. It was refreshing. You treated me like you did everyone else. Instead of making passive-aggressive comments, you told me why what I was doing could be perceived as wrong."

Dolly laughed at his phrasing while her stupid heart did that flip-flop thingy again. "The next evening, you brought a psych resident to talk to me. You know, Isiah checked on me the entire semester." For a moment, Dolly blanked out at the memory of Isiah King, the one man who could be loosely called Ares's friend. A preeminent expert in the field of psychology, Dr. King had spent the last seven months at the South Pole for some secret project. "I still don't understand how you know about the accident."

One finger on his brow, Ares pursed his lips, then blew out a breath of air. "Promise you won't go off on me here? If you do, I'll have to pretend it's a lovers' tiff and then we'll have to make up for it. I've read that couples have a lot of fun—" he raised his brows "—when making up from arguments."

Dolly didn't know whether to laugh or run as fast as she could. Or maybe she could jump into the sea and start swimming toward North America. "I won't. So tell me."

"Isiah told me you had trauma from your parents' sudden death, nothing more, which you admitted yourself. You told me about the car accident a few years later. At that time, I was paying him and wanted to make sure he was treating you right."

"You paid Isiah to talk to me?"

"You needed an objective listener with the right background."

"Why?"

"Like I said, you needed someone you could trust, Dahlia. At that time, he was the only one I could afford to pay. You already told me you had minimal insurance and—"

"Why did you pay him to help me?" Dolly said, feeling as if she were drowning.

Ares stared at her as if she was stupid. Which he had never done before—to his credit, given the brilliant brain *he* possessed. "I wanted you to feel better. Seeing you in pain made me very uncomfortable," he added in his usual matter-of-fact fashion.

The memory seared through Dolly.

She had forgotten that, after a few weeks, Ares began coming to her own dorm room and sitting in the armchair next to her tiny bed, working away at his laptop until the small hours of the dawn while she tried to sleep.

The move to the college, a new environment with

strangers, and being all alone all over again, had triggered her nightmares, she knew. Leaving her grandfather behind had been one of the hardest things to do. She'd worried about herself and worried about how he would be looked after in her absence.

With Ares standing like a sentinel in her room, the nightmares hadn't returned. She had felt safe and cocooned, more than she had ever felt at her aunt and uncle's place. When she had offered feeble protest on the second night, Ares had claimed that he never slept anyway and that her dorm room was more peaceful than the lab or his own apartment.

She and Ares had been inseparable after, even though they had been pursuing completely different majors. And when Ares's app had taken off in his senior year, selling for millions, and he'd asked her to come work for him, she had ditched her business degree and never looked back.

Even more than the generous salary and stock options, which she couldn't deny, the idea of working at a start-up tech business with one of the most innovative, brilliant minds she had ever seen had made her follow him.

A soft gasp escaped her lips as Dolly stared at him now. All these years later, it was almost as if her mind had smudged that memory. Worse, it had also skewed her point of view since his rejection, muddying everything that had been good about them.

It wasn't just his exceptional good looks or his wealth or his brilliant brain that had lured her into falling for him. It was the generous heart that he hid beneath it all. The realization made her feel a little less foolish.

"So why are the nightmares back now?" Ares demanded, with his one-track mind.

Dolly blinked, still lost in the past.

"There must be a reason." His jaw turned granite hard as he stepped back from her. As if to study her better. "Is it my family and their open animosity that's triggering them? Or is it that blasted aunt of yours again?"

"No, the nightmares have been on and off for months now. Although, yes, a new, strange location always throws me off."

"Tell me what you think might have triggered them this time."

She sighed. "My grandfather's health has been declining for a couple of years now. You know that. When he broke his hip, I thought I might have lost him. Then you and I...there was news of your accident and coma...it was a lot. It's one of the reasons I quit too. I was desperate enough to change something, anything."

"And now?"

She shrugged.

His finger lifted her chin, his gray gaze an ocean she could willingly drown in. "I'm here, Dahlia, and not going anywhere."

Tears filled her eyes. Shaking her head, Dolly stepped away from him, even as he ate up the distance she wanted to put between them. "I know that," she said, the words coming in a shout through her thick throat. "I see you and I..."

"It's okay, *agapi*."

It felt as if he were flaying her skin off to see the vulnerability she hid beneath. As if the loneliness and grief she had felt at learning that he was in a coma couldn't be contained by her body anymore.

And then there was no gap between their bodies, nowhere for her to go. And she wasn't sure she even wanted to escape.

When his hands landed gently on her shoulders and pulled, Dolly gave in. His arms were like tight vines around her back as he squeezed her close. With her face buried in his chest, her tears turned to sobs, wrecking through her with the force of a storm.

All the loneliness she had known when he was comatose came pouring out of her.

She clung to him, inhaling the scent of him deep into her lungs, burrowing into his hard, lean muscles, letting her heart have its fill of him. She had no idea how long he held her like that, letting her grief and fear run their course, and she didn't care. Most of her life, she'd craved to be touched and held like this, to be loved. And the longer she'd worked for Ares, the more vividly her dreams began to take his form.

This wasn't that, she reminded herself, but just for a second, it was everything she had ever wanted.

"And here I thought you were a smart woman, Dahlia," Ares said in a dry voice, her head tucked under his chin. As if they had done this a hundred times before. His fingers kneaded the tight knots at her shoulders. "You could have told me you weren't dealing with it well, you know. Asked me to hold you like this."

"That's like asking a cactus to grow colorful flowers. And you hate any touchy-feely stuff, Ares. That can't be news to you."

"I apologize if you have never been able to depend on me before." He frowned, and all the small scars and nicks on his face looked deeper. "I'm beginning to see the seeds of why you want to leave me."

"It's unfair to make you think you were a bad or un-caring boss, Ares. I just want different things now. Be-ginning with a full night's sleep."

He nodded. "Will you ask for help at least while you are here, Dahlia? I don't like to see you in pain. Not when I can do something about it."

"Not all of my troubles can be solved by you," she said, smiling.

For the first time in days, it felt as if that pressing weight on her chest had been lifted. There was no bet-ter proof than his thumping heart in her ears to know he was well. God, she hoped her mind got the memo and let her have one peaceful night.

His hands moved over her back with infinite tender-ness before he released her. And the loss of his warmth, of his hardness, of him, was instant.

"I don't agree. I'll bloody well solve anything for you. You should know that."

"Thank you," she whispered. A sudden burst of awk-wardness filled her, and her hands and her body felt ex-traneous to her feelings.

"Ares?" came Arabella's tentative voice from the spi-ral staircase.

Dolly could have kissed her for interrupting at that exact moment, before she blundered her way into an-other cringey deep confession. Maybe she should pay his sister to interrupt them every fifteen minutes while she was here.

"I'm sorry for disturbing you," Arabella said, blushing prettily. "Mama sent me. Everyone's waiting for you."

Pulling back, Dolly straightened her wrap. "We should go. I can't monopolize you like this."

"You can, anytime," Ares said, grinning.

Dolly blushed. If he kept up this relentless charm, no one could save her from herself. "Aren't you the one who wants to reconnect with his family?"

"Making me cut a cake like a child and stuffing themselves with processed sugar, and buying me nonsense gifts that have nothing to do with my interests, is the way to do it?"

"Hey, no sugar-shaming," Dolly said, loosely lacing their arms together. "They want to celebrate you, Ares. And I want to too," she said, clearing her throat. "Please let us. I'll even eat your share of the cake and save you from it."

CHAPTER SIX

DOLLY STARED, EYES wide in wonder as they arrived at the main deck. She made a conscious effort to untangle herself from Ares's side. Even without the animosity aimed at her by his parents, it was clear that they were desperate to spend time with him.

All around her, the world seemed to shimmer in turquoise shades.

The yacht had veered away from the busier parts of the coastline, and they were now approaching a secluded cove nestled between jagged cliffs. The cove, almost invisible from afar, opened to reveal a small, crescent-shaped beach with powdery white sand and lush greenery spilling down the rocky slopes.

Dolly scrunched her toes in her flip-flops, desperate to feel that sand. Although she didn't want to explore it with so many eyes on them.

Leaning over the railing on the yacht's side, she noted that the water was crystal clear, shifting in shades from bright teal to deep blue, with gentle waves lapping softly against the shore.

"Careful," a voice said at her ear. "We don't want you to fall overboard. At least not before you learn how to swim."

She barely processed Ares's words past the stinging waves of pleasure radiating from his fingers on her bare flesh.

Damn her and her crop top. If she had thought getting that pent-up grief and tightness out of her chest would give her relief, she was wrong. It seemed like it had created even more space in her body for that zinging awareness of him. Somehow the hug had been exactly what she'd needed—comforting and warm—while this touch on her waist felt different.

"I made up that list to show you that you can't give me everything," she croaked out.

"You should have known better than to challenge me, Dahlia." When she took a step back, the rogue laughed. "We're engaged, remember?" His warm breath coasted over the shell of her ear, making her shiver. "You can't jerk like that every time I touch you."

"And you can't use me as an excuse to miss the celebration," she said, for once getting the upper hand.

He groaned. "I'd rather explore that cove with you."

Her chest and neck heating, Dolly remembered the earnestness in his sister's eyes that morning. "I have something to make this easier."

She opened the small beach bag she had brought with her. Reaching past the various sundry items, she finally found a pair of sleek, top-of-the-range noise-canceling earbuds she'd ordered before leaving New York, among several other items for him. They looked like tiny worms in his large palms.

"I've given Arabella a few pointers to give you when you talk to different cousins. She knows to prompt you with details that you can ask about." When he looked doubtful, she tsked at him as if he were a recalcitrant child. "Come, Ares. Remember the time your young cousin Darius sent you that hand-drawn card after you did a video call with his entire class about computers? You said it would have been nice to talk to him properly. You won't get this chance again. Also, remember Darius's mother told you that he's a geeky kid who gets picked on a lot and that it would mean the world to him if he could bring his brilliant computer-billionaire cousin Ares Demetrius to talk to his class?"

"You're right." An instant calmness settled over his expression as he tucked the earbuds inside his ears. Leaning down, he pressed a soft kiss to her temple that made her heart stutter. "What would I do without you, Dahlia?"

Pretending as if she hadn't heard him or felt those words deep in her core, she angled her head toward the waiting crowd.

Stefano, Sergio, his grandparents, his parents and some cousins she had met the night she had arrived, surrounded a festive-looking table arranged with cake and drinks.

When Juliana extended a glass of wine to Ares, Dolly reached out to take the glass from her. "Ares doesn't drink alcohol."

Juliana stilled, cast her son a glance that betrayed her anguish, and then jerked her hand back. As if Dolly's touch might poison the drink.

The crowd around them got louder, raising their glasses in toasts as Dolly shifted so Ares's father could stand next to his son.

Raising her own flute, Dolly stared around the smiling, excited faces even as their lengthy toasts flew over her head. It was clear that the Demetrius extended family was a very close-knit one, and most of them genuinely wanted to celebrate his well-being.

More than one cousin she had dealt with on the phone or email—usually to execute some order Ares had given regarding donation or scholarship or financial loan— came to greet her and congratulate her, remembering her better after this second meeting.

Ares himself made rounds to greet each guest, with his father as chaperone.

Curiosity lit a path through Dolly as she noted the pile of smartly wrapped presents waiting for Ares. What kind of presents had his family chosen for him? And for just a second, her mind wandered to that forbidden place she had locked the doors on and thrown the key away.

What if she and Ares were truly an engaged couple and she was meeting his family for the first time? If things were not distant between him and them, and if they could see how much she cared about them, would they like her too? Would they have welcomed her into the family with the warmth with which they greeted Ares after all these years? What would it be like if Juliana wanted to help her upgrade her wardrobe because she wanted to really help Dolly? What would it be like to get to know Arabella, as she'd hinted at?

"Is it true that Ares does not like to celebrate his birthday?" Juliana said, reaching her.

It was a nod to the high-pressured environment Dolly had worked in for so many years, driven by Ares's stringent demands, that she didn't startle at the older woman's whisper.

One sidelong glance at her told Dolly that she might as well be a search engine about her son when it came to the older woman. And that made it easier to see her with compassion. "No, he doesn't. Although it's not that he has anything against his birthday in particular. He doesn't like the pomp and the cheer, I believe."

Tears lingered at the corners of Juliana's eyes. It could be the suddenly fierce breeze causing it, but Dolly knew that wasn't the case.

"When he sold the app in senior year, we had all been working round the clock. My job was literally to feed him at appropriate intervals, get him to move, hydrate him, force him to catch sleep, while Christina, our other friend, negotiated contracts and translated the legalese for him. When the sale was done and he'd signed on the dotted line, do you know what he wanted to do?"

"What?" Juliana said, her fingers clasping Dolly's forearm tightly. As if she couldn't take the chance that Dolly might leave the story incomplete and disappear.

"He wanted to work on the next version of the app. Christina and I and our friend Isiah, we had to drag him to the restaurant and demand that he enjoy a nice dinner with us. It was only when I nearly fainted out of hunger that he came out of the trance."

Juliana sniffed loudly in resonse. "I saw you hand him the earbuds and the prickly ball in his hands," she said next.

"The earbuds are top-of-the-line noise-canceling. This way, the noise is more of a background buzz. And the prickly ball in his hand grounds him, tethers him to the people around him and the conversation. He really has a brilliant mind. But on a social level, he's a little high maintenance."

For the first time since Dolly had arrived a few days

ago, Juliana turned and looked at her. Took in Dolly as a woman *and* maybe even as an actual person. The stare, while much softer, reminded Dolly of her son's. "You knew today wouldn't be enjoyable for him?"

"It's not just today, Mrs. Demetrius. This anniversary celebration, these guests, the constant cheer and music, everyone circling him…all of it disturbs Ares. Especially now, when he's not himself a hundred percent."

"Why didn't he tell us to cancel the whole damn thing then?" Juliana said, an ache in her voice. "Why doesn't he ever tell us anything?"

The second question was rhetorical and not for Dolly to answer. But she tried to address the first one. That Juliana ached to get to know her son was obvious.

"As much as the noise and the crowds bother him, he wants to spend time with you all. He wants to build a connection with Arabella and you and his…father. The accident and the coma, I believe—" Dolly had to swallow her own ache here "—have shaken him up, forced him to see his life from a new perspective. I think he misses having you all in his life."

If possible, Juliana looked even more miserable at the last thought. She nodded. "Apparently my eighteen-year-old daughter, Arabella, has more sense than me."

Dolly raised her brows at the sudden turn in the conversation.

"I'm sorry for being so uppity to you, Ms. Singh. It's clear you care about my son."

Mouth falling open, Dolly stared at the older woman.

"I just don't understand how you didn't visit him all the weeks he was in hospital," Juliana said, confusion clouding her words. "I mean, yes, Ares has made excuses for you, but still…"

To that, Dolly had no reply. She simply took a sip of her drink, which turned out to be some kind of strawberry-flavored cocktail.

Whatever she saw in her face, a soft smile broke through Juliana's serious facade. "I don't know how much you and Ares have talked about this, but we could do a Christmas wedding, you know. Whatever you want, big and grand or small and elegant… I could arrange it all for you. And since it's a few months away, it could give your grandfather time to recover from his surgery so that he can attend too. Please, consider having the wedding here. His grandparents would be heartbroken if they missed it."

The glass flute in Dolly's hand cracked, spraying the cocktail and glass shards everywhere. Even the cold splash of the drink on her chest and the prick of glass against her finger couldn't compete with the deafening pounding in her ears.

A Christmas wedding...

Ares and her wedding at Christmas...

Ares and her wedding at Christmas with her grandpa and his family and Christina and Isiah present at the beautiful villa...

The visual was far too vivid and heart-wrenching and captured her deepest, darkest wish perfectly.

She was still standing there as Ares, a fierce scowl tying his brows, pushed through everyone and reached her. He wrapped those familiar fingers around her wrist, pulling at her hand until he could examine her palm closely.

"It's nothing," Dolly whispered.

"Your pulse is racing, Dahlia." A filthy curse she'd never heard before fell from his lips. "What did you say to upset her?" he bit out at his mother, uncaring of the avidly watching guests.

Shock held Dolly in its grip. She'd never seen such anger in his eyes before and it was all on her behalf. Shaking her head at her fanciful thoughts, she said, "Ares, she didn't…"

Juliana raised her palms in a conciliatory gesture, her face pale. "I didn't say anything to upset her, Ares. I swear. Only that I was happy to help her plan a Christmas wedding, big or small."

His eyes sought Dolly's as if seeking confirmation. With a sigh that rose up from the depths of her soul, she nodded.

With her other hand, Dolly reached for Juliana. God, the woman must think Dolly was the strangest creature. "It was nothing you said," she whispered, hating the fact that she had only ended up causing a bigger scene. "I just squeezed the flute too hard."

Juliana nodded and turned to Ares. "Why don't you and Dahlia go explore the cove by yourselves? I'm sure you have both had enough of all this noise and are dying to be by yourselves now."

Ares's face gleamed with satisfaction. Without letting go of Dolly's hand, he leaned down and kissed his mother's cheek. "Thank you for arranging the party for me, Mama."

"Happy birthday, Ares," Juliana said, tears in her eyes but a smile curving her lips.

Ares did not remember another occasion when he had felt so grateful for his mother's presence of mind. Granted, he'd been reminded, again and again, of her devotion to him when he was in the coma but her actual interaction with him had always felt like it was scripted. As if she'd put his name as the heading and written down a list of questions she should ask him. As if she were fulfilling a checklist as his mother. Except today.

Today, she'd seemed to see him, recognize that what he wanted at that moment, more than anything, was to be alone with Dahlia. He made a mental note to seek Mama out that night and spend a few minutes in her company.

It wouldn't be too much of a hardship, especially since he had learned from Arabella that reading romance novels was Mama's secret pleasure. He could tease her about it before thanking her for giving him the most fantastic idea of all.

He couldn't betray to her or Dahlia that she had planted the idea in his head. Especially since he'd have muddled his way to it if he hadn't been operating sub optimally.

Now he had the perfect solution to his problems—Dahlia and he would simply marry. He had expected to spend his life alone, in the rare few moments that he had thought about the future. Innovations in his field, his company continuing to prosper, and Dahlia by his side were the only constancies he'd ever wanted.

But the world and the people around him operated at a different level. For reasons he didn't understand, he was able to see the gap in his perception and the world's much more clearly since his accident.

Even now, his chest felt tight as he remembered how Dahlia had sobbed earlier. Her grief, over the possibility of losing him, had provoked an equal amount of pain inside him. Precisely like those moments after he had crashed into the cliff, pinned under thousands of pounds of hot, angry metal, every breath more painful than the former. Passing out eventually had been a blessing.

How typically arrogant and blind of him to assume that she hadn't felt his loss at all. Clearly, it had affected her more than she could put into words. It had taken a taste of her pain for him to realize how deeply she felt, and how wounded she still was beneath the easy efficiency she showed the world.

How lonely she was.

And in the moment when he had woken up from the coma, not knowing where he was, not finding her nearby...had been the loneliest moment of his life too.

It was ridiculous to struggle separately when they could be together.

Dahlia needed constancy, a place of belonging, a life where she was wanted and needed and loved. Ares could and would give her all of it. Except the last.

Love was a thing that had always been beyond his un-derstanding. His parents had fallen in love while Papa had still been married to Sergio and Stefano's mother, which Ares remembered, had torn the family apart. And then Mama had spent the rest of her life trying to make it up to his half brothers, just as Papa had, by letting them run wild.

He wanted nothing to do with love when it only hurt others. All he wanted was to take care of Dahlia and he would make sure that she had everything.

Apparently, they even had his mother's blessing now. Not surprising that Mama had done a one-eighty regard-ing Dahlia, but then she wasn't cruel. He had hoped that she would see what Dahlia really was, sooner or later.

Which only made his two main goals easier to achieve:

sustain a closer connection to his family while keeping Dahlia by his side forever.

As they anchored just outside the cove, the crew prepared a sleek, inflatable tender boat. He held her waist as Dahlia took off her spiky sandals and stepped into the boat. The air felt invigorating against his face as Ares joined her and took the controls. Salty spray misted their faces instantly.

Dahlia's laughter as the boat zipped across the short distance stole through his aching body, jolting awareness through him.

His senses had always been attuned to the outside world's clamor, but this...this felt unbearably good to experience and he wanted to chase every inch of it with her. He felt free and excited for the future again. Something he didn't remember feeling in the last few years. When they reached the beach, they hopped off the boat, feet sinking into the cool, soft sand.

Dahlia's eyes went impossibly wide as she took in the private paradise surrounding them. Her lovely too-wide mouth fell into an O, and Ares decided he wanted a taste of it today. He hadn't missed how she shivered at his touch, how her breath became shaky when he touched her.

The yacht glided away and she jerked around to watch it, a sudden urgency marring her movements.

With the apex sun painting her golden-brown skin with its loving fingers, her toned thighs moving like animated notes of a tune, she looked beautiful. Ares looked his fill, feeling that tightness all over his body again.

While it had punched him that first night out of the blue, desire was now an ever-present hum in his blood. When she wasn't near, he occupied himself with all the things he would do to her, beginning with kissing the thick bow of her upper lip. When she was near like this, he felt a mad, heart-racing urgency to make sure she stayed by his side through whatever means possible.

The glance she cast him over her shoulder as the yacht moved away was filled with panic and excitement. He chose to focus on the second.

"Why are they leaving us here?" she said, a thin sheen of sweat coating her face. The flaps of her gauzy wrap played with the breeze, giving him tantalizing glimpses of taut flesh. Everything about how she was made suddenly a fascinating mystery to him. He wanted to unravel it all, until she was laid naked for him. In all the ways possible.

"I thought you might like to explore this cove out of the spotlight," he said. "Plus I wanted to be alone with you. Bring you out of hiding. Don't worry. They won't come back. A motorboat will pick us up later."

"Oh."

Ares willed her, with everything inside him, to ask what he meant by it. Instead, she let the sandals fall to the sand and pulled the ends of the wrap together. At least, she wasn't denying him her company.

Reaching her, he gave her his hand.

She only hesitated a moment before she took it. Her touch soothed the scraped, out-of-control parts of him instantly. The compulsion to place the pad of his thumb over her raging pulse won.

But her wariness was like a shield around her, warning him to take it easy with her. There was no doubt in his mind of her reaction to his idea. While he had his own hang-ups, Dahlia had been through much worse in her life, beginning with losing her parents at such a young age. And having to live at a home where she was constantly told she wasn't wanted. Even that, he'd learned through Christina.

He'd always seen Dahlia's efficiency, her competence, but not the vulnerable heart she hid beneath. And now, he would never make the mistake of taking her for granted in any way.

They walked the beach, with warm water gently lapping at their feet for a long while. The silence that surrounded them spoke of that familiar contentment that had been missing without her, but there was also a tiny, constant crackle under his skin. As if this new awareness between them was building up with every breath.

"Does your hip hurt less the more you walk?" she asked, breaking the silence after they had nearly walked for fifteen minutes. The pain in his hip, as she'd apparently guessed, felt bearable. When he didn't answer immediately, she said, "I also noticed that you favor your left side sometimes?"

"Yes to both."

Out of his periphery, he could see her chewing on her lower lip. "Does it come and go, or is it always there? The pain, I mean."

"The second," he said, without looking at her.

"I'm sorry you're in so much pain, Ares." Something almost like guilt punctured her words.

"It's not your fault, Dahlia."

The silence that followed was fraught with something he couldn't recognize. It was almost as if she held herself responsible for his accident. Which was the most ridiculous thing he'd ever heard.

"Ready to tell me what we argued about before I left?"

She stumbled so badly that she nearly hit the sand before Ares could catch her. With a grunt—because she was on his injured side—he pulled her up. Her breaths were harsh pants as she clung to him, her face buried in his shoulder. So his suspicion was right.

They *had* argued and he had left New York either angry or upset with her. And it had to be something personal or it wouldn't have lingered in his head, messing him up, distracting him on that drive when he'd crashed.

But racking his brain about the reason or thinking of those few days before the accident only made his headaches worse. Which then made him wonder what horror was waiting for him when those memories did come back to him.

Had she threatened to leave then too? Had she betrayed him in some way? Or had he done something so unforgivable that she'd washed her hands of him when he met with the accident?

CHAPTER SEVEN

ARES HAD NEVER gotten over his half brothers tormenting him as a teen, over his parents not protecting him. The very idea of Dahlia somehow betraying him too brought the sensation of his chest caving in with a vengeance.

When she opened those big brown eyes and he was caught in them, he told himself to see the truth cemented deep in his bones. That Dahlia would never do anything to harm him in any way.

Her long lashes fluttered, as if she needed to hide away her expression. "I'm sorry. I nearly dragged you down."

"Enough apologizing, Dahlia," he said sharply, frustrated by her wariness.

She straightened herself, her eyes taking him in greedily. "Is there anything I can do to help with your workload? I feel like I'm really doing nothing."

There was that thread of guilt again. He decided to ignore it for now. "You're kidding, right? I couldn't have gotten through this morning without you. And that's not counting all the paperwork and documentation of months that you're sorting for me."

She nodded but didn't look convinced. Her fingers lingered around his mouth, her finger once again tracing some imaginary lines. "I don't like seeing you like this. You're limping, and Arabella said you look deathly pale after a physiotherapy session. And clearly, you aren't sleeping well either."

"Recovery will take as long as it will. It's frustrating, yes. But my body has its own rhythms and needs that I must respect."

A soft, tremulous smile curved her lips. "I thought I would find you flipping out that you aren't healing faster or that things are not getting resolved quicker."

He shrugged. "I think nearly dying and then being out of it for almost two months has given me a different perspective on life. Isn't that what you're always moaning at me to develop? Asking me to stop and smell the damned roses wherever they are?"

She scowled. "You make me sound like a nagging wife."

He grinned, finding the idea of Dahlia nagging at him day and night quite delightful. She had been like that once, he realized with a frown.

Their early years at GenTech, she had been more playful and snarkier and just more...open with him. In the last couple of years, all of that had disappeared.

Why? Had he discouraged it? Or had he done something else to make her close herself off to him?

Another thing to figure out and return to how it used to be. He added it to the endless mental to-do list with her name on it.

He didn't know whether it was healthy or not, but she was definitely becoming an obsession to him. And he found it mildly alarming that there was nothing he could do to stop it.

"Why did you want to spend time alone with me?" she

said, raising her chin. Suspicious little creature knew he was up to no good.

Slowly, pushing away the edges of her wrap, he reached for her waist. He wanted to touch the tight dip and the silky skin there. Her breath hitched audibly. "I noted that you didn't bring me a birthday present this year."

Soft pink dusted the tops of her cheeks while loose strands framed her fragile face. She rolled her eyes and Ares wanted to tug her braid and kiss the sarcasm out of her. "You hate it when I drag you to a restaurant and present you with a gag gift every year. You moan for days about it after as if I tormented you. You tell people who visit you at the office horrible stories about my gifts."

"Yeah, but now I'm used to it. I look forward to it even."

She folded her arms at her midriff, unintentionally emphasizing the upper curves of her breasts. Ares kept his gaze on her eyes through conscious effort while his fingers itched to trace those curves. "Okay. What do you want?" she demanded.

"Come closer. You aren't scared of me, are you?"

"Of course not," she said, her brown eyes turning a deeper amber in the sun.

"And you will tell me if anything I do is not okay?"

"Yes." Her eyes flitted between his. "Ares, what is it that you want?"

"I want to touch you."

Dolly wondered if somehow Ares had figured out how to tap into the deepest part of her psyche and decided to persuade her by using that. "Touch me how?" She blurted the question before she could curb it.

A grin danced at the edges of his mouth. The rascal

pretended to frown, as if he was giving it a lot of thought. But she knew his tells from years of watching him and his answer was ready.

"Like a lover," he said, his eyes darkening.

She pulled back as if she could read his intentions.

He held her gaze without looking away, as if he didn't care what she saw in it. She licked her lip and swallowed and like a laser pointer, it focused on her mouth. His hand reached out, gently wiping the beads dancing over her upper lip. She felt like a pinned specimen, every breath and movement under complete scrutiny.

Then there was the fact that she had waited for so long for him to feel like this. To want to touch her and kiss her and…to want her, simply.

And yet, when she'd admitted something similar, he had been so *angry*. So put off. So was this change because of the new Ares the accident and the coma seemed to have unleashed? Or was he testing her to catch her out?

No, that was too cruel. Even for how blunt and cutting Ares could be.

"Dahlia?" he prompted, something careful in the way he said her name.

"Let's get this straight. Just so I'm not floating around in some feverish, fantastical dream," she said, voice turning hoarse, "you want to touch me like a lover would?"

"Have you had feverish fantastical dreams about me?" he pounced, that bad-boy swagger back.

"That's not the answer to my question."

"Yes, I want to. I want to more than touch you, Dahlia. I want to kiss you and pleasure you and…do other filthy things to you."

Her heart gave a wild kick in her chest, her belly

churning. "Since when?" she said, unable to hide the flicker, no, the live flame, of interest that lit her up.

Now his frown was real. "Why does that matter?"

"Because," she said, nearly shouting the word, "I want to know if this is some kind of game you're playing. You know, to…" The sudden hard glint in his eyes made her choose her words carefully. "Change my mind. To stop me from leaving."

"Wouldn't wisdom advise the opposite?" he said, bitterness punctuating each word. "That entangling sexually with your executive assistant—the woman you're fake-engaged to and one who knows all your professional secrets—is the most dangerous thing to do?"

"It would," she said, heat streaking her cheeks. "I just…" She stared at him, the words refusing to come. She was too tempted.

But there was also the reminder of how she'd barely survived his rejection before the accident. Tangling with him now was like playing with fire.

And yet, surviving his rejection and the last weeks where she'd thought she'd forever lost him had given her new perspective on herself too. Why should she not reach for what she wanted, when he was offering exactly that? Why couldn't she have a fun fling and work him out of her system? Why shouldn't she have this, if she already knew she could stay standing when it ended?

"It's not a game, Dahlia," Ares said, pulling her closer. The more he touched her, the easier her surrender would be and he knew that too.

"How are you flipping the switch to this so easily?" she whispered, sounding helpless but drawn in.

"Have you ever known me to question why my mind operates the way it does?" he said.

A swift, loose kind of heat was spreading through her limbs, pooling in her lower belly. The brush of his engorged shaft against her belly was its own torment.

All he wanted was to push her into the sand and sink into her so that he could relieve the ache. To discover if she would feel as good as he was beginning to believe. "All I know is that you've taken it over entirely. Like today, when you walked in…" Gently, he nudged her a step back and ran his gaze over her. "You've never dressed like this before."

Ares wrapped his fingers around her waist. Like an invading conqueror refusing to give up hard-won ground.

For once, she met his eyes straight on, not hiding the naked desire thrumming through every inch of her. It was a trip in itself, to let him see all of her like that. To let him see how she trembled from head to toe when he was near.

Desire spun through her at the simple eye contact, making her dizzy. Because he rarely, if ever, let anyone look into his eyes.

"Don't you want to hear what the sight of you, dressed like this, does to me?" he said, each word dripping with his hunger.

Like her, he was taking down the last of the armor between them and surrender, Dolly decided, had never felt sweeter.

"I want to know," she said. "Even though the sensible part of me is screaming that we're crossing a line that can never be uncrossed."

"Are you worried that I'm taking advantage of you?" Belying his question, his grip on her hips tightened. And she wondered if he even knew. But there was no doubt that he wanted her as much as she did him. His words, his body language, and the tension gripping him told her that. He nuzzled her nose and Dolly thought she might melt like ice cream under the hot Greek sun. "Does this scare you?" A thread of vulnerability he couldn't mask echoed through the question.

"Let's get one thing clear, Ares," she said, clasping his cheeks. "I've never, nor will I in the future, be scared of you. I just think…we're complicating things."

He shrugged. "It doesn't have to be complicated. Right now, I'm attracted to you. That's all. Then there's the fact that you're determined to leave me soon. So you see, I would be a fool to not make this move right now. When you consume every waking thought. We both know it can't be anything more."

She nodded, not surprised that he was thinking along the same lines as her about this…affair. With his usual blunt honesty, telling her what it would be and what it wouldn't be. No more foolish dreams, no weaving extra meaning into every gesture. "Wow, if only I had your logical brain. Your persuasive words. Your utter arrogance that the world will arrange itself to your needs," she said.

His gaze ate her up as he dragged his fingers down to her clavicle and the hollow of her throat. When he notched his thumb into it, her pulse rocketed. Satisfaction blazed in his eyes, turning the irises molten.

"You're so responsive to my touch, Dahlia. It's the most primal thing I've ever known." His mouth joined his fingers, tracking warm trails down her jaw. "Should I tell you how I want to explore all this silky-smooth skin with my lips and tongue? How much I want to dig my teeth into the tight dip of your waist? Or how sexy your thick, toned legs look in those shorts?"

"God, Ares. Let a girl catch her breath," Dolly murmured, her body bowing in his arms however he wanted it. Fantasy blended into reality and she lost her foothold on both. For just a second, fear swamped her. With her wrapped around him like a vine, would he remember that fateful moment when she had confessed something similar to him, though not in such blatant words?

"Shh… Dahlia, I've got you," he said, pressing his fingers into her lower back. "This is me, *agapi*. There's no need for fear between us."

Dolly buried her face in his neck, afraid of what he might see. But she refused to let his previous rejection ruin it for them now, refused to let the shadow of a future that had never been possible blur the present. "I know," she said, as much for herself as for him. "But it's hard to reconcile this man who can so easily give words to his wants, who feels such naked desire, with the man who never even noticed that I was a woman, much less a desirable one."

It was a question he had asked himself numerous times.

"I can only surmise what the past me, who by the way sounds like a dumbass, was thinking."

She smiled then, even though it was the curving of her lips against his neck that he sensed. It felt like a ray of sunlight touching his face after standing in musty darkness for too long. Even this hunger for her touch, this new need to bind her to him…all of it was like standing in brilliant sunlight after living in a cave all his life. "I might agree with that."

He buried his face in her hair and the familiar scent calmed him. "All I can say is that I must have wound myself up very tightly around the boundaries between us. And given how important you are to me, didn't wish to cross them."

"Okay," she said, still shaking.

Ares knew how much of a chance she was taking on him, how brave she was being by exploring this thing between them. "Put your arms around me, Dahlia," he said, not giving her an inch.

The few seconds before her arms came around his neck, fingertips creeping upward into his hair, felt like a thousand eternities to Ares's impatient mind.

And when she went on her toes and pressed herself deeper into him, near-violent shivers racked her strong frame. So much vulnerability wrapped in strength. But even he, with little knowledge of how this worked, understood that these shivers spewed from a different source. Her breasts rubbed up against him in a delicious glide that made his eyes nearly roll back.

He grinned, his attention drifting to the rise and fall of her chest and the nipples poking through the crop top. She was aroused by his nearness, by his words, by him. Having that proof was so much better than the speculation. He wanted not just her kisses and her passion, but all her deeply held secrets.

But he couldn't dwell on this when she rubbed her lips against his and whispered, "No more questions. No more analysis or warning or caveats. Please, I just… I want this. Isn't that enough?"

"More than enough," he whispered in her ear just as she buried her entire face in the hollow of his neck. "I've got you, *agapi*."

A guttural groan fell from his lips as she dragged her teeth up and down his Adam's apple, her fingers tightening on his scalp. His heart beat so loudly that it wouldn't be a surprise if it thumped out of his chest, suffused with wanting. As if she understood what he needed, Dahlia brought her lips to his chin, and then to his mouth.

Her own moan joined his inhale, and his entire body— every cell and sinew—came to a stillness at that first contact. As if to savor the taste and feel and scent of her. She pulled away, just an inch, and settled in with a deeper press this time. Sweet and tart, with a hint of strawberry, her taste sank into his every pore.

With a rumbling groan that made his chest shake, he pressed and pulled back, pressed and pulled back, tasting her over and over. She groaned, clasped his cheeks as if to stop him from pulling back, and rubbed her lips over his.

Pleasure poured in like an avalanche through Ares, spinning through his limbs, as if he were an endless algorithm that had been plugged into a supercomputer.

His brain struggled to keep up with the sensory receptors, struggled to note what action of his caused what reaction in her.

It was an endless feedback loop anyway, he told himself, eager to evoke more of those hoarse, husky, hungry sounds out of her.

On and on, he kissed her, their lips finding a frenzied rhythm. She nipped at his lower lip and the slight hiss of pain made his cock throb. He returned the favor and when she moaned, lapped at her lower lip.

The more he tasted her, the more he needed. While he nipped and licked, optimizing for a better, deeper fit, drowning in his own savage need, she wrapped herself around him like a string of lights around a Christmas tree.

Her warm pants, the glide and slide of her soft flesh, her nails digging into his scalp, it was a symphony of sensations inside him. A harsh breath escaped him as she nibbled his lower lip with her teeth. That she was as mindless as him in her need was like pouring gasoline on the flame of his desire.

The silent cove, the crashing waves, the stretch of endless blue, everything disappeared as their tongues tangled and their bodies writhed and glided against each other. But it wasn't enough. Filling his hands with her buttocks, Ares lifted her.

Long legs wrapped around his ass, Dahlia clung to him like she never wanted to let go. And the feel of her heated core against his cock was heaven. "Oh, God, Ares. Right there. Just there," Dahlia murmured, her lips swollen, strands of silky hair falling loose from her braid.

The searing heat of their bodies turned into a flame, even with their clothes on.

Holding her like that, despite his body protesting at the sudden movement, Ares thrust his hips up into her. She bounced in his grip, following the rhythm by grinding her hips down. Her mouth ran down his neck, teeth and tongue licking and nipping at his skin.

His injured shoulder strained at her weight, his hip was nearly crying in pain, and Dahlia… *Christos*, her head thrown back, she was making those breathy little sounds that narrowed his entire world to her. He'd woken up wanting this with her, needing to see her like this…finally.

"Tell me what you need, Dahlia," he commanded through gritted teeth.

"Something more. Just a little more. Please, Ares…"

Bending his head, Ares closed his mouth over her tight nipple, over her crop top, and sucked on the peak. Her breath hitching, her hips ground down on him in a frenzy and then Dahlia fell apart in his arms with a soft cry.

Unable to bear her weight any longer, he sank to his knees and crumpled to the sand with her. His hand automatically went to his hip, as if to clutch down on the pain, but still, he couldn't stop looking at her.

With the sun blazing above them, the faint sheen of sweat coating her skin like glitter, she looked like the mermaid in the poster that Arabella still had up on her wall. For just a moment, he wondered at the ending of that story.

"Are you okay?" he asked gently, when her eyes popped open.

She licked her lips, turned to look at him, and sprang into a sitting position. Her hand covered his on his hip, regret and guilt painted like neon signs across her face.

"Don't start, Dahlia."

"I—I'm not a lightweight and that must have—"

"Was it good?" he asked, eager to see the flushed desire in her face again.

"I think I nearly blacked out. And I'm not usually… I didn't mean to demand it like that. I completely lost control."

"I like it when you lose control or when you demand things of me, Dahlia." He pushed completely onto his back and patted the space next to him. When she hesitated, he frowned. Why did she distrust him so? "You just dry-humped your way to an orgasm while riding me. Lying down next to me is that much of a stretch?"

"That was sexual and it has been a long-ass dry patch for me. This…is much more intimate. You don't understand."

A familiar despair took root in his chest but he refused to let it grow. "Maybe I don't. However, I do understand that a woman might want to be held after an orgasm like that, instead of a pat on the head for a good job."

"Did your AI bot tell you to say that?"

He shrugged.

Her eyes glowed with warmth. Gingerly, she lay back down. On her side, with her palm flat on his abdomen, her warm, soft flesh snuggled into him. Her nose tucked itself somewhere between his neck and shoulder, though she was very careful to not lean into him.

Ares closed his eyes, and the scent and feel of Dahlia, all wrapped around him, magnified. With her taste lingering on his tongue, he felt engulfed by her in the best way.

He had no memory of ever feeling such contentment in his life before. Of clicking into his place in the world. Of not wanting anything more in any way except to lie like that with her.

"Why do you like it when I demand things of you?" she whispered after a long while. "That's like the opposite of everyone I've ever come across in my life."

He lightly slapped her hip. "For a smart woman, you're also a silly woman."

"Hey! That's mean," she said, returning the slap on his chest.

He circled her wrist, keeping her palm there. His heart thudded under her touch.

"You should know by now that I'm not like anyone else you've ever met, Dahlia."

Raising herself on one elbow, she grinned down at him. It rivaled the sun's own warmth. "I will give you that." Her nose scrunched.

He stared at her, taken in by the breathtaking shine in her eyes. "When you demand things of me, I can give them to you. And then when I see your surprise, I feel like I could own the entire world."

"You would hate owning the entire world. That's a lot of admin logistics and dealing with people."

He gave a mock shudder and she laughed and this too, he realized, could become addictive. Making Dahlia laugh without restraint. Making her happy. Making her come.

Her laughter dwindled quickly. Her gaze drilled into his, her other hand tracing his scars with a proprietary gesture. "What does this mean, Ares?"

"It means that I desperately want to have sex with you, Dahlia." He caught the pad of her palm with his teeth and bit into the flesh. Her lithe body shuddered next to him, her breasts rubbing against his side again. "I've been through so much trauma with the accident and the coma and all of it, you know. It could prove healing."

"Oh, my God, you're so bad, Ares. Where did you hide this wicked side all these years?" Then she was falling onto him, her carefree laughter sweeping him up into its warm embrace. When she began kissing him, Ares knew it was the best birthday he had ever had.

And as long as he could keep Dahlia by his side and the world at bay, he didn't mind celebrating them.

CHAPTER EIGHT

BETWEEN HOT-AIR BALLOON RIDES, swimming lessons, shopping trips with Juliana and going running with Arabella at the crack of dawn, in addition to the acquisition meetings she attended with Christina and Ares for a company he was buying, Dolly wanted to tell herself she was too busy to think of his outrageous proposition that they indulge in a red-hot affair.

She kept using *outrageous* every time she thought of it, because she needed her mind to keep thinking of it as such. Her heart and body, the traitors, had already discarded the word and adopted *delicious* instead. Especially when she remembered the heady free fall of her orgasm while she rode him.

She still couldn't believe that she had been that wild, wanton creature who had simply demanded and then taken what she needed. Every time she thought it, her cheeks flushed and a pulse seemed to come alive at her core.

Now, in moments when she didn't actively work on resisting the thoughts, she was reminded that it was her deepest fantasy coming true. God, she'd even crushed on him at Columbia. Nine whole years…

Spoken in such bare terms, the proposition should

have felt anything but romantic. And yet, Dolly had never heard such naked, honest wanting before. Had never seen that need for her. And that it came from Ares still boggled her mind.

She kept wandering through her days, head in the clouds. While Ares hadn't asked her again in the following week, he had kissed her at every opportunity.

Like during the hot-air balloon ride, when they were literally floating above the clouds. When she'd teased him that he was turning green and didn't have to be all macho when he had a fear of heights.

Like when she'd panicked during the swimming lessons, had swallowed too much water and couldn't breathe.

Like when she had drifted off during the virtual quarterly meeting with shareholders—imagining introducing Ares to her grandpa and letting his strategic mind beat Ares at chess—and he'd pulled her off camera with her braid twisted around his fingers and kissed her upside down…just as she'd put on the list.

Then there was the time just two nights ago when she had found him immersed in the Jacuzzi, his complexion deathly pale after a brutal physiotherapy session. Knowing that he didn't like to see her worry over him, she'd joined him, hoping to distract him. Of course, the man had other plans. As he always seemed to do, when it came to her these days.

Instead of giving him solace, she'd ended up with his fingers inside her, working that glorious, deep spot that turned her into sheer sensation as if he was already a master at finding it, while his thumb tap-tapped against her clit relentlessly, urging her toward ecstasy. Teeth digging into his shoulder to lock away her moans, she had come so hard that she'd nearly blacked out, *and* had needed his help to get out of the tub.

She should have known better than to challenge him with the list. Although, with each item he crossed off on it, she couldn't help wondering how he would tackle the rest. Especially the romance-and-marriage-and-babies part.

Obviously, he couldn't make them come true, but with Ares and his single-minded focus…anything was possible. She shivered as her mind went to forbidden zones made of foolish dreams.

And the crux of the matter was that she couldn't deny him anything.

With each day and heated encounter dragging her deeper and deeper into falling for him, her fear about what would happen when he discovered the contract marriage also escalated. She wasn't even sure why she was hiding it anymore—it wasn't as if they weren't already involved.

Or was it the fear that when he learned the truth, he would feel betrayed? Or that when his memories returned and he felt whole, his current attraction to her would fade completely and he would want things returned to as they were before? That he would have nothing but scorn and contempt for what he would see as his weakness?

Like when her aunt had shown her true feelings about Dolly coming to stay with them *after* her parents' insurance payout had dried up. Overnight, Dolly had gone from a cherished niece to a painful burden, with reminders that every meal, every pen and notebook she needed for school, every piece of clothing she was bought, was a result of their generosity.

Losing her parents had been bad enough, but that rejection—having her aunt turn on her overnight, had hurt worse than any pain she'd ever known. She'd never quite recovered from the abandonment, had only tried again and again to please her aunt. To gain back her approval. That was why she had used some of the money from the marriage agreement to reimburse her aunt.

Which was the saddest thing ever. Because her aunt would never be happy with Dahlia, not even if she kept her in luxury.

Even her battered heart knew that Ares could never be as willfully malicious as her aunt. But he could hurt her worse than her aunt ever had or could.

She needed to remember that after the accident and the coma, he was on a novelty kick, that his interest in her would reset back to her being an efficient assistant to him. To a necessary cog in the complex machine that was his brain.

That, even if she slept with him, which she so desperately wanted to, she needed to remember that nothing could change when the month was over. It would simply be a fling.

It was inevitable that Ares would return to his previous hyper fixation on work and innovation, and she would become an afterthought in the margin. Already, she could sense the restlessness in him, even though he claimed that his hip pain and headaches were getting better. Could sense that he was feeling caged, either by the villa and his family or the restrictions put on him by his health.

In two weeks, she would be leaving. Her grandpa needed her assistance to make the permanent move to the long-term facility. Ares, she knew from experience, would be more than glad to uncomplicate this whole tangle between them, whatever he said now. Time was ticking down. Which meant time was running out and it was foolish to not reach for what she so desperately wanted.

"Come in," came his command when she knocked at his door.

Just that phrase seemed to reverberate through her. Once she had made the decision, it had been impossible to wait for a moment. Still, she'd given him enough time to recover from the evening session of physiotherapy. The last thing she wanted to do as his lover was to become a bumbling mess at the sight of his pain.

Running a hand over her abdomen, where butterflies seemed to be having a parade, she opened the door and walked in. Her fingers lingered on the doorknob as she took in the gray and navy furnishings of his suite.

It was five times the size of her bedroom and done in a very masculine scheme. Dressed in gray sweatpants and his chest bare, Aries was standing by his desk with his glasses on, peering at some notebook. He turned when the door clicked shut behind her and his eyes swept over Dolly from top to toe. She was very glad for picking the emerald green pj's. They were one of the most luxurious things she'd ever owned, and as she stood there, she realized she had been saving them for him.

The silk robe she'd worn over the pajamas fluttered against her freshly shaved legs as she moved into the room. As if following her steps, the recess lights flicked on and a gasp escaped her.

His bare chest was littered with so many tiny scars that instant tears prickled behind her eyelids. Then there was the network of deeper scars and burn marks that littered his right hip. "God, Ares. You must have been in so much pain. I wish I could take it from you. Because I would." Her impassioned declaration hung in the silence but Dolly refused to take it back.

The fact of the matter—that she kept trying to fight—was that she would do anything for this man.

Walking around the bed, Ares plopped at the edge of it. Long legs kicking out in front of him, he crossed his arms at his abdomen and the sight of his hair-roughened forearms and the lean definition of his chest made some of her ache recede. "That's a ridiculous idea. You can't take my pain away, Dahlia. And even if you could, you're the last person I would give it to."

Folding her arms at her midriff, she half laughed, half nodded. "I know that it's not possible. It's something you just want to do for someone you care about."

"So you do care about me, then?"

Her impatient exhale came out as a whistle. "Of course, I care about you. I'm here, aren't I? Trapping myself deeper and deeper into your web."

He frowned. "I'm not a spider nor are you a nasty little bug."

"It's an analogy, Ares," she said, walking deeper into the room. "If I had any sense, I'd be miles away. If I had even an ounce of self-preservation, I would not be standing here in your bedroom."

"You need self-preservation only if I were somehow harmful for you." His frown deepened, highlighting the lines of pain around his sharp features. "You think I would hurt you?"

She shrugged, refusing to get into an argument with

him. Especially one that was beyond the scope of his understanding of emotions. And it came to her then.

Ares could absolutely shatter her into so many tiny pieces but he would do it without meaning to. It was just how he was built.

"I do accept your proposition. On the condition that when I leave here, we can still remain friends. Even though we won't be colleagues, or fake engaged anymore." It was more than a little pathetic but she wasn't sure she could stay sane and functioning if she didn't see him from time to time. At least, this way, she could ease herself out of his life slowly instead of taking herself out at the knees.

Instant tension suffused every muscular inch of his body. Shoulders straight, his flat abdomen rippled with his angry breaths. "Let me get this straight. You are agreeable to having sex with me, posing as my fake fiancée, and at the end of all of this, you still plan to walk away but want to remain friends?"

"Something like that."

He shook his head, dislodging a thick wet strand onto his forehead.

Dolly's fingers tingled as she imagined pushing that lock back.

Why was she just imagining it? Through some twist of fate, the man she had pined after for years wanted her and she was in his bedroom. She was allowed to touch him.

He was hers, even if only for the next couple of weeks. He was hers without any doubt tonight. Covering the distance between them, Dolly stepped up to him and pushed that stubborn lock of hair back.

He caught her wrist, stopping her from coming any closer. "Why not come back to work for me, then?"

"Because unlike you, I won't be able to separate the personal and the professional. Not after tonight. It's messy and will disrupt my work."

"Because you will have feelings for me after having sex with me?" he said, watching her with an unerring intensity. God, the man had lashes she would die for.

A knot of tears and an unbearable ache sat in her throat. *Too late*, her heart whispered. "Possibly," she said, forcing a laugh.

"But you're very sure that I won't?"

She clasped his cheek, the stubble rasping against her palm. "You like people to stay in very specific, separate boxes, Ares. You need your world to function in a particular way. We have complicated this too much anyway." Her thumb moved over the jut of his cheekbone. "You will find all this tedious soon."

He nodded, as if she was imparting a very important lesson. "So after these few weeks of having sex with me and pretending to be my fiancée and shedding tears over how much pain I was in, you will leave me like you left the company. And go back to the search for the perfect man to fall in love with?" He pressed his cheek deeper into her palm and rubbed, even as his words aimed to cut. "Clearly, you operate in the same way I do, Dahlia."

Dolly flushed. "What are you saying?"

"I think if you leave, you and I are done. It is as simple as that."

"You're kidding?"

"Not at all."

Widening his thighs, he pulled her close. The swipe of his straining cock against her inner thigh made her gasp. As if pulled by a string, her gaze dipped to his crotch.

The thick outline of his erection made hot pulses run up and down her entire body. She licked her lip and a rumbling sound came from his mouth.

"See, this is getting messy already," she said hoarsely. "I'm here, desperate to kiss you and touch you and… you're making this about how you want this to play out."

"Are you? Desperate for me?"

Leaning forward, she buried her face in his throat and breathed in deep. It might be her safe place in the entire world after all. "I can't sleep for wanting you. The whole world, all these experiences that you have laid at my feet, everything feels colorless when I imagine touching you."

His mouth found hers in a violent frenzy. She gasped as he devoured her, as if she were his last meal.

There was no soft claiming or learning or exploring, like their kisses of the last week. No waiting for her to feel comfortable or familiar with his particular brand of need.

This was a pure devouring hunger, spreading to every limb, shaking her from within. His hands were everywhere—in her hair, stroking over her shoulders and back, cupping her hips, grabbing her ass and pulling her fully into him. The press of his cock against her heated center made her throw her head back and moan like a wanton creature.

Ares dragged his teeth down her throat, leaving a trail of scorching heat behind. "Wrap your legs around my waist."

Dolly had no idea how she got her limbs to follow his command, but the next thing she knew, his erection rubbed against her core with the exact amount of pressure she needed. She sank her fingers into this thick, damp hair, eager to touch him everywhere. She wasn't going to leave an inch of him unexplored tonight, she promised herself. She would glut herself on him so much that he would remember tonight forever too.

The bright recessed lights in the ceiling made her blink as her back hit the cool sheets. Even the silky glide of her robe against her fevered flesh was too much sensation.

His torso looming over her, Ares looked down at her, taking in her shaking form with a fascinated gaze. The sensuous thrust of his lower lip made her want to bite him. Hard. "I wondered how you would look with all that efficiency and composure stripped from you," he whispered, pushing away damp tendrils of hair from her forehead.

"I thought my efficiency and composure were what made me such a model assistant," she croaked out.

"Not in every context." One long finger rubbed at her lower lip and then drew down her neck and chest, stopping at the V-neck of her pajama top.

His gaze burned with molten desire that Dolly couldn't have imagined in her wildest dreams. But there was also something more there that she couldn't identify.

"Why are you looking at me like that?" she said, unable to hide her vulnerability from creeping into her tone.

"You are beautiful, Dahlia." He shook his head, spraying her bare skin with tiny droplets of water that should have sizzled against her skin for how hot she felt. "Your mouth, your breasts, your curves, your legs…everything about you is hot. And you tell me, in nine years, I never had the guts or urge to tell you this? Much less act on it."

Dolly swallowed. What could she say to that? How could she convey to him how afraid she was that this Ares, who saw her, wanted her, touched her like this, might disappear in the blink of an eye? How did she explain to him that she was existing on the razor's edge of fantasy and reality, afraid of both?

"No. You—you didn't like dating, and for the big charity events, you usually hired someone professional, from like a dating agency. I always had the impression that you were not into…physical stuff. As for me, I was very much a tool in your kit, Ares. A very important one, mind you, but an accessory. I don't think you saw me as a…" *Person*, she'd been about to say but caught it at the last second.

He had paid Isiah years ago just so she could have someone to talk to about her nightmares and he hadn't even had that much disposable cash at that time. He *had* cared about her pain. About her happiness.

About her.

Confusion filled her. But still, as always, she tried to navigate this, both for him and herself.

"Some of your irrational dislike for relationships, romantic or otherwise, your refusal to feel emotional vulnerability… I understand those things better now, given your childhood and your family. Of course, I think it was easier for you, than anyone else, to shut down all that stuff. To not let yourself go down that route at all. Your willpower, your ability to focus, shutting everything else out is, as you know, your superpower." She added a little laugh to her words. "And superpowers have downsides too."

Ares frowned, even as his broad palm pushed her top up, his fingers rubbing every inch of flesh he uncovered. Her nipples beaded as his fingers moved under her breasts, and in between, and over and around, but never touching the aching buds. How he could make her analyze him even as he drove her crazy…she didn't care to know, as long as he kept doing it.

"Clearly, I was a foolish man," he said, grabbing the neckline with both hands. Anger punctuated each word. The fabric ripped with a hiss in the thundering silence. Dolly wondered if the entire world could hear her thumping heartbeat as his penetrating stare moved to her bare breasts.

She thought his fingers might be trembling when he cupped her breasts, his thumbs now tapping and tracing and drawing mindless circles around her nipples. Her spine arched off the bed, and she would have flown away, if she didn't sink her fingers into his hair and anchor herself there.

"Tell me, Dahlia. Tell me what you need. I have some ideas, but I want to hear what you want. I want those delicious sounds you make when you come. Only a thousand times louder. I want to leave you soaking so that when I come inside you, I can take you as roughly as I want." He whispered the words against her breast, the rasp of his stubble deliciously scraping the sensitive skin.

She pressed her hands on top of his palms covering her breasts and squeezed. "My nipples… I would love your mouth here." She closed her eyes, whatever little courage she had used up in saying that.

His pine scent surrounded her, his heart was thumping against hers but she still couldn't believe that she was saying these words to the man who she had worshipped first as a friend, then as a fantasy lover.

"Your wish is my command," Ares whispered as he sprinkled soft, slow kisses all over her breasts as if he had some great plan in his head. He kept kissing in concentric circles around the needy tips.

She tugged at his hair, impatience making her rough. "My nipples, Ares. Give me what I need."

His husky laughter rumbled against her skin. And in the next breath, he flicked at one nipple with the tip of his tongue and then wrapped his lips around it.

Dolly held his head to her breast and moaned so loud that it wouldn't be a surprise if everyone heard her. Not that she cared.

The way he gave his thousand percent to any task he undertook, Ares licked and sucked at her nipple, as if it was the most delicious treat he had just discovered.

When one side felt over sensitized, he switched to the other one and laved it with the exact same attention. On and on he circled her, inside his mouth, the tip of his tongue tapping against her in some rhythm that tightened the knot in her lower belly.

Dolly arched and moaned as his mouth moved down her belly. Her hand stretched out on the bed, reached something…that felt like a notebook. Without thought, she grabbed it, distracted.

Usually, the man was as careful with his notebooks as a dragon would be with its treasure. They were his necessity and his one luxury vice. He ordered the most expensive hand-stitched ones, made endless, copious amounts of notes for different projects in them and didn't let anyone, even her or Christina, so much as get a peek inside.

She was about to put the notebook on the side table when she caught her own name written on the white label in his neat script. Her breath was rapid and her gaze more than a little blurry as she opened the notebook.

Flow charts, and names of body parts, and sketches and instructions written out in his methodical handwriting jumped at her.

For just a second, she wondered if this was some kind of master plan to seduce her into staying with him. It wasn't that much of a stretch because she'd seen his notes for companies he was about to acquire and so on. A hard nip at her hip had her look away from the notebook, into the deep gray gaze that instantly took her captive.

"You're not here with me," he said, digging his teeth deeper into the flesh of her hip. Even as his fingers busied with the hem of her panties. "You know I demand a hundred percent of your attention, Dahlia. Now I'll have to punish you."

Dolly smiled at his impatient tone. Clearly the man was as bossy here as he was in a boardroom. "What is this?" she said, shaking the book in her hand.

"Oh, I made some notes." As if that answered enough, he played with the tiny bows on the seam of her panties.

Dolly tapped his shoulder with her foot, even as part of her was horrified that she was touching him like this. And when he didn't look up from humming against her skin, she put her other foot on his other shoulder and tapped again. He looked up, his mouth curving in the most wicked smile she'd ever seen.

"Notes about what? And why are my name and different body parts in here?" she said, almost losing her line of thought when he moved that delicious mouth down to her mound, still covered by the thin mesh of her panties. The kiss he placed there made her arch her hips into chasing his mouth with wanton abandon.

He laughed then and patted her, as if promising her

that there was more to come. She held her breath with anticipation as his lips hovered over her aching flesh.

"Please, Ares. Won't you tell me what this is about?"

"I've been watching certain kinds of videos. There's so much bad stuff out there, Dahlia, you won't believe it. But I finally found some tasteful stuff, catered toward women and I have been taking notes. You know how much I hate a job done shoddily."

"You watched videos and took notes?" she said, pushing herself up onto her elbows. It was hard enough to process when his delicious weight pressed her down into the bed, much less the mind-boggling things he was saying. "What do you mean?" The moment she asked the question, it came to her.

But of course, he possessed an analytical mind that was constantly finding the best ways to learn new things. And only Ares, so secure in himself, would admit all that he had done to make this better for her. God, would there ever be an end to the ways this man could surprise her? An eternity with him wouldn't be enough. Wouldn't be boring or safe or dull, all things she had made her own life.

Her chest rose and fell, even then she couldn't get enough air into her lungs. "Christ, Ares. Are you saying you've been watching porn?"

"Yes. Although it's interesting how much of it is actually aimed at men looking like studs and women just giving in to whatever their fantasies are. Still, I got some pointers. But as you know, nothing is better than your personal feedback. All you have to do is tell me what you want and where and how fast or slow. Like everything else, your pleasure is in your own hands and I'm here to give it to you, however you need it."

She laughed and her heart slipped just an inch into love with this man. Tears leaked from the corners of her eyes. "You watched porn and took notes and drew flow-charts so that you could do this correctly with me? Am I getting this right?"

"Yes," Aries said, holding her gaze, his fingers busy rolling down her panties.

"Were you aroused by it?"

"At first, it felt clinical, even boring. Some of those videos are very badly done. Then we kissed and I started imagining doing those things to you. When I heard the sounds you made when you came and how sweetly you squeezed my fingers as if you couldn't bear for me to leave you, it became real. I didn't even need to watch after a while. My mind was more than ready to imprint you in those delicious scenarios and my imagination ran with it."

"I don't know what to say."

"You don't have to say anything," he said, with a kiss over her belly. "Just tell me what you want more of. I don't like not being good at anything. And I have zero field experience with this stuff."

Dolly wondered if one's heart could expire out of shock and sweet discoveries. Although she had wondered about it before. Given the man worked hundred-hour weeks and barely tolerated more than two and a half people, it hadn't been that much of a jump. "Are you telling me you've never done this before?"

"No. And I hated the thought of being at a disadvantage."

"And kissing…was I your first kiss too?"

A dark shadow seemed to fall over his eyes but he shook it off. "For all intents and purposes, yes."

Before she could catch her breath and probe what he meant by that, he was pushing her knees indecently wide and lodged those broad shoulders between them and… his mouth delved there. At that spot that was pulsing for his attention.

"Apparently this is called 'eating you out' and ever since I read about it, I have been dying to know what you taste like."

Dolly could barely breathe at the wolfish grin he seemed to have conjured overnight. And his filthy intentions put in such bare words made arousal spike through her. His endless curiosity, his keen mind…she should have known he would put all of that toward unraveling her at every level possible.

He took a deep breath, pushed her panties aside with one hand and then unerringly found the sensitive bundle of nerves that was screaming for attention with his other.

Feet on his shoulders, she tilted her hips into his touch in an instinctive movement.

When he licked her slit and then tunneled his tongue deep, she let out a keening cry. Sensation upon sensation curled through her lower belly and she wanted to fly right out of her skin as it built and built. It was too much and not enough. Her skin felt too puny to contain the avalanche of pleasure he was bringing down upon her.

"Mmm…you do taste perfect, *agapi mou*," he whispered, rubbing his sinuous lips up and down her. "Sweet and tart and just mine."

His fingers began to pinch and tug and flick at her clit and she half laughed, half sobbed as she remembered his notes about adding stimuli from different sources.

"I can't wait to feel how eagerly you will squeeze my

cock, Dahlia." He penetrated her with one finger and then two, and Dolly nearly came off the bed.

His lips pursed and released her clit as if she was his favorite squeeze toy. On and on, he tormented her with his tongue, his fingers and his lips. Sweat coated her skin as she moaned and writhed under his firm grip.

And soon, Dolly was flying. So far and so high and so bright that she started sobbing. The pleasure was unbelievable, unbearable even. He kept her there, at the peak, never letting up his sensual assault. Her orgasm thrashed her around, and before the first one could recede, another smaller one took hold of her just as his fingers sound that spot inside of her.

Pleasure crested and waned and crested again.

One hand tugging at his hair, one hand bunching the sheets around her, Dolly let go as pleasure she had never known overwhelmed her. Tears soaked her neck and the sheets beneath her as Ares urged her on and on with sweet words and filthy kisses.

Even through the indescribable haze, Dahlia felt a sinking sensation in her stomach that by allowing herself to have this intimacy with him, she'd opened a door. And she was hurtling past the last line of defense against falling irrevocably in love with him.

If she wasn't there already.

CHAPTER NINE

ARES CRAWLED ONTO the bed on his knees to watch Dahlia in that vulnerable moment.

He found he was even hungrier for this than to bury himself inside her.

Tears had drawn tracks down her cheeks and neck, and her lips trembled uncontrollably, as if she was keeping some big storm contained inside. Incredible tenderness he had never known encompassed every inch of him. "Dahlia, open your eyes. Tell me what's wrong." As always, when he felt threatened, his need to fix everything around him came to the fore. "Was that too much? I did read somewhere that some women find orgasming painful, but I thought you would tell me something like that." Maybe he should modulate his tone from scolding but he was painfully hard and seeing her like this was doing something indescribable to his insides.

"Of course you didn't do anything wrong. How could you?" she said, opening those doe-like brown eyes. The rims were just a little bit pink, as was the tip of her nose. "It was just that good, Ares."

He grinned, that tenderness now joined by a savage kind of satisfaction that he had pleased her. "Good. I always do like a job well done."

She giggled, her stomach rising and falling under his palm.

He found that he really liked touching her—the slight curve of her belly, her long, sleek thighs, and the curvy parts of her like her breasts and her hips. He liked hearing her heart thump-thump under his palm, liked hearing her breath rush out of her, in different tempos depending on what she was feeling, what she was saying or what he was doing to her.

He felt close to her at that moment, or rather he felt that she was finally completely bare to him. All her armor and walls were in rubble, as she stared up at him as if he was made of the stars and the sky.

It was a feeling Ares had never known and it crept under his skin because before he could examine it, like an insidious worm tunneling deep into his insides, making him feel all warm and glowing from the inside. And in that moment, he realized he would do anything to hold on to that feeling, to have her look at him like that. As if he was her entire world.

"I would worry that your ego would get bigger about this but—" Dahlia pushed up on one elbow and kissed the corner of his mouth, and then lay back down on the bed with a sigh "—I think you deserve to develop a big ego about this. That was…amazing." She stretched like a cat, her foot rubbing against his shin, and he decided he liked being touched in this way too. "And I thank you for all the research you've put into it."

He laughed. "I've just had my tongue inside you and you sound way too formal about it."

A shocked gasp escaped her puffed lips. "Jesus, Ares. You go from brooding, stubborn, have-to-have-my-world-just-the-way-I-want to this dirty-talking stud? If I faint one of these days, you're to blame."

He cupped her shoulders and pressed himself to her side, his need for her a simmering buzz in his veins. The sight of her dewy skin gleaming under the lights, her breath still coming in pants, everything about her fed his suddenly voracious need. A hiss left his lips as he rubbed his cock against her thick hip, even as pain from his injured side contrasted shockingly against the pleasure.

Her movements were hesitant as she lifted her hand and pushed a lock of his hair back. From there, her touch drifted down, tracing his clavicle. He didn't miss the wariness in her eyes, as if he might explode if she did something wrong.

Again, that missing memory nagged at him. "Dahlia?"

Her shimmering gaze met his. "May I touch you?" she said, her throat bobbing up and down nervously. "I mean, I understand if you like doing things, but don't want me to do things to you," she clarified in a rush.

Excitement was an electric spark inside him. With a rough moan that he could not curb, he nudged his cock between her hip and the bed for deeper friction. "Dahlia, does that feel like I don't want to be touched? You keep saying what an impatient man I am, but waiting for you to come to me has turned me into the most patient man in the world. So, yes, put your hands on me. Touch me however you want."

She swallowed and nodded, still looking fairly apprehensive. He pushed his sweatpants down and kicked them off while she turned to lie on her side, facing him. His cock was screaming for her attention, but she didn't start there. The need to command her attention there rode him hard, but pushing up on his elbow to cradle his head, he waited.

It felt like an eternity passed before her soft fingers clasped his cheeks and she pressed a multitude of kisses to his face. With each kiss on each scar, like that grief she let him see, a wealth of regrets seemed to pour out of her. If it helped her to feel better about his pain by doing this, then he would subject himself to a thousand tormenting kisses from Dahlia's lips.

Soft, slow rumbles emerged from his chest and throat as she did a thorough job of kissing every inch of his full shoulders and chest and even his abdomen. Her fingers were featherlight and in turn, his muscles clenched in agony, needing a rougher touch.

His breath turned serrated when she pushed him onto his back and straddled his hips, taking care to not push her knee into his injured side. Something about the way she looked at him made his chest tighten. No one had ever seen past his eccentricities before. Then there was the lust shining in her eyes, which distracted him from the deeper pull of emotions at that moment. He wasn't sure whether he was glad or not, only that he was buzzing with need. The tips of her silky hair kissed the tiny patches of his skin that her very efficient mouth might have missed.

His breath became shallow when she, with delicate efficiency, took his cock into her hand and squeezed. His arousal oozed out of the head and Ares groaned. "Move down, Dahlia. Let me feel you," he commanded.

She played with him for a few more breathtaking moments before she scooted down. The press of her damp folds against his engorged cock, and the way she leaned back to sink deeper onto him, made his breath punch out of his chest in staccato gasps.

"Dahlia…" He gripped her hips with his fingers. Her wetness coated him, and it was the most decadent sensation he had ever known in his life. "Undo your braid. I want to see your hair," he said, his arousal spiraling with each downward roll of her hips.

The visual of her gently heaving breasts as she did the rolling thing with her hips again was the most erotic picture he had ever seen.

Holding his gaze, Dolly undid the braid, sank her fingers into her hair and shook it loose.

"Lean down and kiss me. Rub those plump nipples against my chest. I want to know how every inch of you feels against me."

A tremulous smile curved her pouty lips. "For a man who wrote down instructions on how to please me, you seem to know exactly what you want."

"I do know what I want. I just wanted to make sure that it is pleasurable for you too and not just me. So, stop talking and come kiss me."

Smiling, she moved her hips in the back-and-forth motion that dropped her wetness up against his cock, and he groaned out loud. Then slowly, like a cat stretching, her palms moved up his abdomen, his chest, and then gripped his shoulders as she leaned down. He ravaged her mouth. There was no other word for it. And the more he got of her, the more he wanted, as if it were nothing but a slippery slope toward some unknown destination. Even that couldn't shake his lust.

He slipped his tongue inside her mouth, and licked and nipped it as if he was laying siege. He swallowed her moans and groans and mewls and still he couldn't get enough. He sent his hands exploring every curve and dip of flesh, wanting to push her to the edge again. With deft, hard strokes, he touched her everywhere, squeezed her breasts, until her nipples dipped into his mouth. He caught one aching peak with his lips, slightly grazed his teeth and she reacted like lightning painting the sky.

He loved how responsive she was to everything he did. They rolled and rubbed their bodies, seeking a deeper touch, needing more and more, breaths mingling and separating.

The surge of sensations was stifling and he waited for his mind to want to separate itself from the feelings crowding him. But it never came. And he knew it was because this was Dahlia, a woman he trusted like no one else. The one person in his entire world who saw him, knew him and wanted him. Who had stood by his side through so much.

"I want to touch you again," she said, and then her fingers came around his cock again and all thoughts fled.

He thrust his hips into her hold, and covered her hands with his, showing her that he needed a firmer grip and quicker strokes. Like the efficient assistant she'd always been, she took instruction well in this too.

And when he knew he was going too far, he pushed her onto her back on the bed. Her thighs fell away, instantly creating a cradle for him. He notched the tip of his cock at her folds and rubbed himself up in her wetness. Heat gathered in his balls, begging to explode. "There are some condoms behind you in the drawer," he said, somehow managing to remember it at the last moment.

"I get tested regularly and I'm on the pill. You?" she said, her voice husky with desire.

"I've never wanted to do this with anybody else, Dahlia."

"Then we're good," she said, palms stretched over his chest.

"I want better than good. I want everything." He plunged into her in one stroke.

Having fixated on bringing pleasure to Dalia, he had watched endless amounts of porn in the last couple of weeks. He had taken himself in hand and gotten off so many times that he felt like a teenager. And yet nothing could equal the pleasure of her squeezing him as if she was made for him. Pleasure pounded at Ares from all directions and he felt like he might drown if he didn't move. Still, he somehow managed to catch his breath and looked down at her from his perch on his elbow.

"You okay? Did I do that too roughly?"

The sleek muscles of her thighs trembled as she gave a slow thrust of her hips while he ground down into her.

"No, it's perfect, Ares. It's better than anything I have ever imagined. It feels like you're here," she said, bringing his palm to her chest. Her heart thudded madly.

He caught her lips in a rough kiss. "I want to come, Dahlia, so badly. And I'm not sure if I can be gentle."

"Yes," she said, wrapping her fingers around the nape of his neck. Dragging her nipples against his chest in a delicious glide. "Whatever you need…please take me and use me as you want."

There was no turning back after that.

Ares found the rhythm he liked and pounded into her

mercilessly. Her groans only added to the surge of heat tunneling down his spine, into his balls.

Cupping her knee, he pushed her leg into her chest as far as he could. "Keep your eyes on me," he said, when she closed her eyes for a moment. "I need you here with me, Dahlia. I need you."

She raked her nails down his back and the hiss of pain only added to the pleasure chasing him. "I am here, Ares. I'm here all the way with you."

"Come with me," he said as his climax began to light a trail down his spine. He wanted to feel how her orgasm felt around his cock. He wanted her so delirious with pleasure, that if somehow, she managed to leave him, he was imprinted in her heart and soul.

With his finger on her clit, he tilted her hips and angled his thrusts until he hit that point that had made her scream just minutes earlier.

And soon, she was shivering around him, squeezing him like a vise, for everything he could give. Then she fell apart with his name on her lips, her nails digging into his flesh.

Ares came in a mindless rush, heart pounding in his ears, his entire body, jerking and shaking as his orgasm crashed over him. It was unlike anything he had ever known, the pleasure that rushed at him.

And in his heart, he wondered if this moment was the culmination of nine years of knowing her. Why had he waited this long to make her his?

CHAPTER TEN

THEIR GRANDPARENTS' ANNIVERSARY had been celebrated. Even his birthday had been marked and gushed over, like it had never been before. Most of the extended family and friends had taken their leave and hopefully, the grand loving-family showboating that his parents excelled at was over. It had only been close to four weeks but it felt like an eternity.

Ares could breathe again. When he wasn't in danger of losing that very breath as he and Dahlia explored each other's bodies with increasing fervor. It had become a sort of game between them, as to who could bring the other to their knees with pleasure first.

Although the time she'd gone down on her knees and taken his cock in her mouth, she had definitely won. Even losing could become addictive if it was to Dahlia and her far too efficient mouth and fingers.

The villa was quiet and peaceful, except for the pounding of Arabella and Dahlia's shoes in the early mornings when they went running in the grounds. Or when they giggled and generally created mayhem in the kitchen, experimenting with new recipes because his sister wanted to train to be a chef and was using Dahlia as her guinea pig.

And since she was acting as such, Dahlia had roped

Arabella into her own activities. Ares hadn't missed
Dahlia's strategy. She was trying to be the bridge between him and Arabella, taking out the awkwardness of
what they would talk about on his side, and the pressure
of disappointing him from Arabella's.

His sister, he was learning, was shy, kindhearted and
witty, and obsessed with everything to do with New York.
Her round features grew animated when she hounded him
or Dahlia for details about Central Park or Times Square.
And then a wistfulness would take over her young face
when she said Papa might not let her travel that far for
college.

Dahlia would cheer her up by promising her that Ares
would convince their father to let Arabella come live with
him for an entire summer and that Dahlia herself would
show her all of New York.

Empty as her promises to Arabella might be—for
Dahlia reminded Ares every chance she got that she was
leaving at some point, although she said it with less and
less conviction each time, and Ares had no inclination to
take on Arabella's responsibility nor to talk to his father
about it—he would be forever indebted to her for how
she looked after his sister in those moments.

In the evenings, the two women attended a tango dance
class that he'd arranged—with the charming dance in-
structor he'd hired usually flirting outrageously with either or both of them. Or the three of them lounged around
the pool while he taught them the rudimentary principles
of chess. Dahlia, to his delight, was bloodthirsty with her
attacks and barely gave strategy a thought, while his sister was far too scared to make any bold moves.

And while his headaches weren't getting better, they

weren't getting worse, though his memories of before the accident remained hazy. He was even able to fall asleep for longer than he had in a month. Especially if he tired himself out by trying some new position with Dahlia. Even sharing the bed with her, with her arms and legs thrown around him, was a novelty and a much-needed anchor for both of them—he with his pain and she with her nightmares. Which were getting less frequent.

It was comforting and exciting to have her so close, depending on whatever his mood, and hers, dictated.

The last board meeting with his shareholders, where he had presented his face and reassured them that he wasn't dying yet, could be called a success.

And while he hadn't yet proposed making their arrangement permanent to her, he had noted that Dahlia was smiling more these days.

Her grandpa, she had told Arabella one morning with a loud squeal, had been able to stand unsupported for a whole minute and was doing well on his road to recovering full mobility. She'd even let Ares say hello to the older man quickly on a video call, which she hadn't in nine years of their knowing each other.

She'd lost that haunted I-don't-belong-here look. Of course, he wanted to believe that he and the kisses he stole from her every chance he got, had something to do with the new pep in her step. And *Christos*, he couldn't get enough of the little sounds she made when she climaxed and how responsive she was to his every touch. Making her come, while denying himself over and over, was now his favorite obsessive game. Until she decided that she wanted him to lose his mind too.

He was perpetually in a state of arousal but he liked

that too. He liked being so preoccupied with planning what he would do to her next or how he would take her when she came to him finally, that everything else fell by the wayside.

It was as if he was living out nearly a decade of leisure and luxury and all kinds of sensual pleasures he'd never really wanted before, in a few weeks. Neither was he sure if he would ever be able to see his parents' villa without her in it.

He'd always hated the fact that Sergio and Stefano had driven him out of his own home and yet he now wondered what home truly meant. A foolish part of him even hoped that the lawsuit might quietly go away, without shaking up the current situation.

Some evenings, his parents joined him, Arabella and Dahlia by the pool, apparently content to watch them from a distance. While Mama did her best to engage Dahlia in conversation, Papa continued to remain stubbornly silent. Ares didn't have to wonder about what kind of poison his ears had been filled with by his half brothers.

Sergio and Stefano—and their uppity wives and their whining, spoiled children—had thankfully left for their own residences in a nearby island. It was another side effect of the new perspective he had on life. He was more than happy to go down the route of "out of sight, out of mind" with his brothers.

Except he knew, and Dahlia kept reminding him, that some kind of resolution needed to be achieved regarding the lawsuit. *Before* everything went public, triggering a scandal. It was time to settle the score with his brothers, one way or the other.

He had never in his life resisted something that needed doing as he resisted this confrontation with them. In the deep dark of the night, when he couldn't sleep for his hip pain, he had even wondered if he was still scared of them, wondered if he had let them become so large and ugly in his mind that he couldn't tackle them head-on.

Still, he should have known that Sergio and Stefano, being insufferable asses, would bring it to a boiling point themselves.

One evening, he was panting through his stretching routine up on the high terrace of the villa. Near the end of his routine, he caught Dahlia swimming slow laps in the pool below, while suddenly Sergio and Stefano crowded her from either side. They were far enough away that Ares couldn't hear their words. But he could read Dahlia's rigid shoulders and deep scowl well enough.

Adrenaline flooded him as if he was once again facing the jagged, twisty edge of the cliff he was driving around, his speed too much to control in the last split second. His ire spiraled as he discovered his father standing a few feet away from the scene, arms folded at his midriff, watching quietly, as if the whole thing was unfolding just as he pleased.

Ares was a mass of fury as he took the winding stairs down to ground level and then passed rows of neatly manicured gardens.

The last of the sun's rays were shimmering across the surface of the water and Dahlia's shoulders as he reached the group.

"You are both worse than I could have ever imagined." Dahlia's words were gritted out between clenched teeth, eyes flashing like rare gems. She kept her voice low, he knew, for his benefit. "And if you repeat any of this vile, slanderous nonsense you're spewing in front of Ares, so help me God, but I'll do bodily harm to you."

Stefano had the grace to look dumbstruck at her outburst while Sergio simply laughed, splashing water onto her face and shoulders. She calmly wiped the water and began swimming towards the edge.

Ares grabbed a towel, approached the pool and stood waiting for her. Immediately, the meatheads' expressions changed while out of his periphery, he saw his father approach the pool.

"Hey," Dahlia said, looking up, the word pitched a little high.

Ares gave her a nod and a hand as she pulled herself out of the pool. Water sloshed down her body in rivulets, wetting his sweatpants. When he held the towel aloft and stretched his arms, she walked into them. He wrapped it tight around her, noticing that she was shivering and trying to hide it.

He enfolded her in his arms, expecting her to pull away. That she tucked her wet forehead against his shoulder without resisting his protective gesture only set his already boiling temper ablaze.

It was clean and clear, the surge of anger that filled his limbs and fired his blood. He had ordered her here, against her own wishes. While she had repeatedly reassured him that she could handle Mama's microaggressions, her having to put up with his half brothers' cheap comments was too much.

"Are you okay?" he said, pressing his mouth to her wet temple. The scent of her sank into his pores and centered him.

"I'm absolutely fine." She looked into his eyes and swallowed. "They didn't scare me. And honestly, it wasn't even about me."

"Then why do you look like you've swallowed something bitter?"

"Doesn't matter. I handled it. This is why you brought me here, remember?"

Something about the way she said it pricked his chest. "To help me find common ground with them. Not to absorb all the crap they level at you because you are with me."

"It's nothing like you're imagining, Ares," she said, clasping his cheeks. "The big macho man that you are, you're still their target. Not me."

He frowned. It was the last thing he'd expected her to say. "What do you mean?"

She shrugged.

"Tell me, Dahlia. Or we will be here all evening. My hip is on fire if that makes the decision for you."

"I don't want you to be affected by their nasty words."

A strange tightness coiled in his chest. But the feeling wasn't quite what he would call discomfort exactly. He chuckled, even though the last thing he felt like was laughing. "They took everything they possibly could from me when I was a vulnerable boy." He didn't bother to keep his voice quiet. He wanted his father to hear it, understand it. He wanted regret—if he could muster up any at this stage—to haunt his father as his brothers' taunts and bullying had haunted him as a boy. "There is nothing more they could do to me now. Except hurt you."

"They didn't hurt me," Dahlia said, eyes shining. "But, Ares," the very universe itself seemed to dwell in how she said his name, "how many times have you or Christina or my grandpa told me that I shouldn't let my aunt or her cruel words get to me? That there's no rhyme or reason to how she speaks to me, despite everything I have done all these years to please her? To get one measly word of approval?"

He clasped her cheek and let his thumb rub up and down her cheekbone. "What are you saying, *agapi*?"

"That their words can still have the power to hurt you and it's nothing to be ashamed of."

"I have, hopefully, left shame behind, Dahlia. Also, are you worried that they might beat me up in a physical confrontation? I'm not a vulnerable runt anymore."

Her palms shifted over his shoulders, squeezing, and then landed on his chest. "No, you're not. I just…"

"What did they say to you, Dahlia? I need to understand if anything I have said to them about backing out has sunk in. Unless you want to spend the next few months here, stuck with me. Mama will surely have us married by Christmas, then."

"Now who's using scare tactics?"

"Is it such a scary prospect, then? To live in the lap of luxury as my wife?"

"Is this some kind of damned test?" she said, panic filling her eyes.

"That was the original agreement between us, right? That we would fake an engagement to scare my brothers off. They'd know that, once you are my wife, I could transfer all my property and stock to you if it came to a real, dirty court battle between me and them? So you must have at least imagined what being my wife for real would entail?"

She jerked, as if he had scalded her. Her lips trembled. "You really can't think all this wealth and luxury would sway me?"

"No, of course. You want fairy tales and true love. Even though we both know it probably doesn't exist," he said drily. "Come, Dahlia. You're wet and shivering. Out with it. What did they say to you?"

She sighed, bit her lip, then nodded. "For two meatheads, they seem to be pretty shrewd when it comes to us. They wanted to know what you were paying me to…"

"To what?"

"Sergio asked how much I was charging you to be your whore. Then he did his cringey villain laugh and said there was no way any woman would devote herself to you, except for your millions. I had the pleasure of correcting him to billions." Her little satisfied smile reminded Ares to breathe. Neither did he miss the fact that she was trying to manage him. "Stefano, for all he follows Sergio like a blind dog, apparently has a little more class and substance than I gave him credit for. He asked me if my loyalty was up for sale. Promised me they would double whatever you're paying me if I walked away from you and the whole wedding. Even better if I make our breakup into a huge scandal, say you abused your position of power to lure me into an affair and engagement. But of course, the villain that you are, you ditched me when you didn't have use for me. All that will obviously add more dirt and weight to their lawsuit against you."

She was right and he, Ares discovered, was disappointingly wrong.

He could still be cut by their words. Especially Sergio, who seemed to understand the deepest wound that Ares had never healed from. The same wound that pulsed and raged when he couldn't get his mind to calm. At those moments, even the pain pulsing through his hip was a welcome distraction. Through sheer will, he refused to let his mind give a form to that wound.

"I'm hoping you refused their offers, *agapi*," he said, baring his teeth. Much like a wounded animal, he assumed.

"Of course I did," Dahlia said, bristling. The little shake of her head sprayed droplets onto his cheek. Sudden shadows danced in her eyes. "And clearly, they aren't going to listen to common sense. The next step I think is to appeal to your father to talk to them. Put the fear of scandal into him. Seems to me he's the only one who can control them."

"I will decide the next step," Ares said, suddenly feeling exhausted. "You should get out of the wet suit and take a hot shower."

"Walk away now, then," she said, her mouth at his jaw. "I will shower and be in your room in ten minutes."

He wrapped his fingers around her nape and took her mouth in a rough, possessive kiss that he wanted to deepen. His erection throbbed for relief and her breath came in warm pants when he released her. "I don't like conditions, Dahlia, or caveats. You know that." And before she could say anything again, he tightened the towel around her and gave her a push toward the house.

His father reached him on hurried footsteps as he turned to look at his brothers. Sergio and Stefano jumped out of the pool and grabbed towels, leering at him. Challenging him to come at them.

His father barked something at them that Ares couldn't

hear through the deafening roar in his ears, his hand on Ares's shoulder. The meatheads exited, tame as well-trained dogs. The extent of his father's control over them made the antics they had taken up against him even more tragic.

Ares jerked away from the older man's touch, resentment coating his stomach like acid. "Don't touch me," he bit out, angrier than he had ever been in his life. "How dare you stand there and let them bully her? She's an innocent woman. How would you feel if someone did that to Arabella? What the hell is wrong with you?"

"They were simply talking to her, figuring out what her game is. Whatever that woman told you about your brothers—"

"Don't talk about Dahlia. She's got more integrity in her pinky finger than the whole lot of you."

"She's an outsider, Ares. How can you—"

"Then, by all accounts, I'm an outsider too. The only time you or your sons remember me is when they need money."

"Ares…"

"Did you know that they've stolen thousands of euros from the family company before they came up with the idea for this lawsuit?" he bit out. Another serrated laugh escaped him as the man he'd once idolized stared at him without blinking or even a hint of regret.

And then he saw the truth in those eyes. "Of course you knew. You sent them to me. Didn't you?"

"You had the means to help them and the company, Ares. That's what family does. Imagine how it would have broken your grandfather's heart to know that we might slide into bankruptcy."

Ares turned and covered the distance between them until he was face-to-face with his father. "And what do you call turning a blind eye to your older sons beating the shit out of your younger one? Or leaving him locked for an entire night in the tool shed? Or dunking his face into the water sump for long, painful minutes?"

"They were just being boys, Ares. And you needed toughening up. If it wasn't them, you would have been subjected to it at the boarding school that you begged to be sent to. If you hadn't left and stayed away, all that would have been settled among the three of you a long while ago."

"You..." His throat felt like it was full of needles and thorns. "I see how foolish it was of me to expect that things had changed here. You are the same old fool who ran the business to ground, and they are the same greedy, cheating, thieving bullies who will take whatever they can get their hands on. And Mama...she refuses to see any of this."

"Don't bring your mother into this, Ares."

"And the lawsuit? Am I allowed to bring her into that?"

His father flinched. Resignation filled Ares. It felt the same as the metal that had dragged itself through his hip as he tried to crawl out of the flaming mess of his car. "So you know about that too and haven't done anything to stop them."

"You have billions and at the end of the day, they are your brothers, Ares. Settle some money on their children, stock options in your company maybe, and I promise I will get them to drop the lawsuit."

Ares laughed and rubbed his hand over his hip. "You think they will be happy if I simply settle some stock in their names? You think they won't come at me and my company again?"

"Not if you give them enough," his father said without a pause. "Or the entire family gets dragged through the press and the scandal will be horrible. You owe it to this family, Ares. Without your grandfather's gift—"

"No, I don't owe anyone anything," Ares said. "I will not give them or you a penny. Let them do as they will."

"No, Ares." Panic seeped into his father's features and suddenly, he looked old and exhausted. Whatever pity Ares might have felt leached out of him, leaving a hollow in his gut. "Think of what might happen if they win? All the assets you might lose. The check your grandfather gave you for your nineteenth birthday…officially, it can be shown that it came from the family money."

"I don't care what they or you can prove, Papa. I know how to protect myself and the company from your grubby hands. Tell your sons to do their worst."

As an eight-or nine-year-old boy, Ares had learned to not show his fear, to let no tears fall when Sergio or Stefano played a particularly nasty trick on him. Forget pity, it had only made them feel as if they'd won over him.

And that early learning came in handy as he mindlessly walked around the grounds in relative darkness. The feeling of loss and pain remained the same though. But he wasn't alone this time as he had been back then, he reminded himself.

He had Dahlia on his side now and while the thought didn't take away the disappointment and the pain, it steadied him.

CHAPTER ELEVEN

DAHLIA WAITED ALL night for Ares. First in her bedroom, then in the gym, then in the sauna, then in his own bedroom. Had even crawled into his bed past midnight, desperate for a whiff of him. Buried her face in his pillow and around dawn, she'd fallen into an exhausted slumber.

He had never come to bed.

There had been no sign of him the next morning either. When she'd asked Arabella about it, the girl's eyes had filled with sudden anxiety, provoked by Dolly's fervent question. Finally, the girl had admitted that she had seen her brother that morning and that he had looked extremely agitated. When she'd begged to know what was going on, Ares had admitted that he was going to visit their grandfather who lived in a nearby village. Then there was the fact that their mother had gone off to London early this morning.

Dolly's heart had sunk to her toes, her own agitation on behalf of Ares rising. Clearly, something big had happened with his father and brothers after he'd ordered her to leave. The villa was eerily quiet, as if in anticipation of the incoming storm. And yet Arabella looked alone and small and afraid and she hadn't wanted to abandon the girl.

God, how had she grown so fond of the teenager? And

what was she going to do when it was time to bid good-bye to her too?

The last thing she'd wanted was for Arabella to live through the fraught, even toxic fallout of her brothers' actions. It was only a momentary reprieve since Dolly couldn't protect her from the consequences forever.

Still, she understood why Ares hadn't wanted to open a vein of poison straight through his family.

So, Dolly lied that she was taking the day off—as if it had all been planned with Ares, and begged Arabella to take her sightseeing. She texted Ares several times throughout the day, even knowing that his cellphone was usually a second thought for him and he hated to be harassed through texts like that. She'd happily bear his ire and irritation if it meant knowing that he was faring okay.

It was late evening when they returned to an empty villa.

Her body humming with alarm now, Dolly took a quick shower, and pulled on a worn-out T of Ares's from Columbia.

Her hair in a braid, she was coming down the winding stairs on bare feet when she heard Ares and another familiar voice from the large study. For just a second, she wanted to run back up the stairs to her bedroom and hide there.

Pressing a hand to her abdomen, she walked into the living room to find Ares and his entire family assembled. Including his parents, the meatheads, his grandparents and Arabella. The tension in the room was cloying enough that she hesitated.

The conversation ground to a screeching halt as all heads turned in her direction. But Dolly had eyes for no one else, nor space in her heart to register anything beyond Ares.

Her gaze collided with his and for a moment, all the breath whooshed out of her. Anger and something more shimmered there, before he cut eye contact completely. Thoughts flocked through her head at an alarming rate, making her dizzy. But all she wanted, her stupid heart wanted, was to go to him and hold him and have him hold her tight.

And yet, the gap between them felt like it was wider than ever.

"Oh, don't run away, Dahlia. We've been waiting for you to arrive. There's important family stuff to take care of."

"Ares…"

"Sit down, Dahlia," he bit out in a soft tone that made alarm bells clang in her head.

Something was very wrong.

A moment later, Ares flung a sheaf of papers onto the middle of the coffee table, the movement ringing with impatience and barely suppressed fury.

"Here are the papers I had drawn by my lawyer today. And some other important documentation that I should have acted on, months ago."

Eager greed danced in the meatheads' eyes while the rest of them looked baffled. "What are they, Ares? What's going on?" Juliana asked him and then turned to her, as if Dolly would know the answers. Something about the trust in her eyes made her stomach tight.

"Oh, my sweet, wonderful wife doesn't know much about it," Ares said, in a mocking tone. "At least not what I've been up to in the last day."

A single bee's buzzing would have been loud like thunder in the ensuing silence.

"Wife? What do you mean?" Juliana said, looking between them.

Everything inside her came to a standstill, a cold fist at the center of her. He knew. How? Had he remembered everything? What did that mean?

Dolly understood what it meant to want the ground to open up and swallow you whole. Her cheeks burned at the scrutiny from everyone.

"Ares…" she tried but he cut her off again.

"Turns out Dahlia and I are already married."

Arabella jumped up, clapped and hugged Dolly with genuine happiness while the rest of them stared at her and Ares. His grandparents wished her a happy married life and Dolly, for the life of her, couldn't even respond to that.

"I…" Dolly said, not knowing what she wanted to say. "Please, Ares. Let me explain."

"But you said you were engaged and we thought…" his mother began, but Ares cut her off with a raised hand.

"Dahlia was clearly trying to protect me and my feeble mind, Mama."

"That's ridiculous. I never thought of you as feeble," Dolly snapped, feeling defensive.

Ares didn't even look at her. "The point is I've had enough of trying to do the right thing. Of trying to feel like I could be a part of this family." Standing up, he pushed one folder toward the sofa where his father sat with his brothers standing behind him. "That folder has all the accounting documentation about how Stefano and Sergio stole thousands of euros from the family company, leading it nearly to bankruptcy. And how much money I've injected to save the company and the employees from their crimes."

A collective shudder seemed to go through the room. His mother and sister looked devastated, and Ares...there was only a blankness in his expression that tugged at Dolly.

"I've gone through it with my lawyers and grandfather," he said, motioning to the older man. "I also have a document from him attesting to the fact that the money he gave me as a birthday present for my nineteenth birthday came from his own pocket and not the family business. It clearly stated that you two," he said, pointing a finger toward Stefano and Sergio, "have no right to even a cent from my company, much less the millions you're suing me for."

This time, Juliana's "Did you know about this?" addressed toward her husband was loud and full of outrage. Arabella looked like she might simply crumple while Ares's father stared at him in shock.

But Ares didn't wait for his father to reply to his mother. His answer was written on his face.

It was as if Ares had lost all hope of fixing the fissure in his family. Of receiving the amends he deserved from that man and his brothers. "Then there's the little fact that my darling Dahlia and I are married. Legally. If you don't desist with the lawsuit, I have papers here that I can sign which will transfer all of my personal wealth to her name in a second. All of it."

When Sergio and Stefano and their father burst out at once—the former two shouting threats at him, Ares raised his hand, palm out. "I'm not done," Ares said, his nostrils flaring. "Not that I don't trust my wonderful wife, but that is only an extreme measure I had to have in place because I wasn't sure if I could trust anyone in this family, including my own parents."

Juliana's soft gasp made Dolly's throat ache. The men stared at Ares, red-faced.

"I have Grandpa's permission to turn you in to the authorities for embezzling funds from the family company. I've already turned in another set of these documents to the police. They should be coming for you any moment. Please don't ask me for funds for the lawyers. You're on your own now." Finally, Ares met his father's gaze. "If they find you an accomplice to the embezzlement, you will be taken in too." His throat moved in a hard swallow, his jaw so tight that a vein pulsed there. "It's what you deserve for enabling these two all these years and for not protecting me when I needed your protection. But since it will break Mama and Arabella's heart, I have instructed my personal lawyer to look into it, as a favor to me, that you don't end up in jail."

Pandemonium erupted in the wake of this declaration. His grandfather patted Ares's shoulder, standing tall and dignified among the rubble of his son and grandsons' tempers.

Juliana and Arabella were openly crying, and Stefano and Sergio were screaming at their father now, blue in the face, while their father stared at Ares, as if he couldn't believe what he had unleashed.

Standing amidst all of them, Ares looked alone and unbending and unshaken.

And all Dolly wanted to do was go to him and hold him in her arms. For even as he looked like none of this cost him, she knew that he was devastated. That he was angry and hurting. But she also knew that he was angry with her too, that whatever they had built in the last month was hanging by a thread.

And that she had brought that on herself through her own fears.

Dolly was sitting in the veranda attached to Ares's suite, watching the sun begin its descent in the sky when the door finally opened. The chitter of the cicadas and the scent of jasmine kept her company as if they were old friends. God, even the villa, so overwhelming and grand at first, felt like a dear friend now. For she had spent the happiest moments of her life here.

But she also was beginning to see that wherever Ares was would be home to her. Somehow, the realization felt like it was late, or rather inopportune, after the worst had occurred.

She had been sitting like that, for hours, desperate for him to come back. *Come back to me*, her heart said, but she was afraid to admit it, even to herself.

Her legs felt leaden as she pushed up to stand and face him. She'd pretzeled herself inside out to never let her aunt find fault with her. She'd studied hard, worked harder, sacrificed so many of her own personal desires to pay back what her uncle and aunt had done for her by giving her a home. She'd not given them a single chance to find fault with her in any way.

And yet, now she was facing Ares with a truckload of lies and half-truths nearly bowing her back, making her actions with him wrong in so many ways. God, she was such a fool to have waited this long.

Who hadn't she trusted—him or her own feelings? What was scarier to believe—that he wouldn't love her or that she didn't deserve to be loved?

Her arms and legs trembled with the need to go to him but she resisted. "Ares, I'm so sorry. I…know how much you wanted it not to go this way."

He came to the veranda and leaned against the arch, without looking at her. His other hand was wrapped around the nape of his neck. Moonlight created deeper grooves of the lines pain had etched into his face—both physical and emotional. "It was foolish to hope for a better, a different resolution."

"No," she said, turning toward him, her throat filled with tears. "It's not foolish or shameful or weak to want to be seen and loved and understood, Ares. Never that. In fact, I think it takes uncommon bravery to want to mend relationships, to come to the table, willing to forgive and wanting to build something new."

He laughed and the sound rippled out to her, full of sarcasm. "Forgive me if I'm not in the mood to put too much stock into your words right now, Dahlia. I'm tired."

He seemed to barely get out the words. "Ares, please let me explain."

"It's a little late for explanations, no?"

"Will you please look at me?"

He turned, and there was none of the wicked laughter or the teasing glint in his eyes. No asymmetrical tilt of his lips or the flash of his smile. Not even the basic recognition she'd always seen in him at the sight of her.

"It was foolish to hide the truth from you. I understand how strange it must have felt to you—"

"Strange to have Isiah call me and tell me the marriage contract I sent him by mail has followed him around the world as he traveled?"

Dolly sighed. Of course, Ares would have trusted only

their old friend with the contract once it was signed. No wonder even his lawyers had only assumed that Dolly and he were engaged, but not married.

"And that I'm already married to the woman posing as my fiancée, the woman I trusted more than anyone else? And that I made a ten-million payout to you for being my wife for twelve months? No wonder you left the company the moment you heard of the accident. You'd had everything you could get out of me and didn't need my overbearing, rigid, arrogant self in your life."

"That's unfair!" Dolly shouted, outrage taking the space of guilt. "Ten more minutes and you will say I caused your accident to retire as a filthy rich widow. Please, Ares... I understand that—"

"Feeling like I can't trust you hurts me more than you could even imagine, Dahlia."

That one guttural admission wiped all her anger, filling her with regrets. "You know, deep inside the place that you've been trusting more and more, that I didn't do it for the money. I was devastated by your accident. I felt as if I'd lost my own—"

"Enough, Dahlia! I don't want more lies about how much you missed me."

"No, you have to listen to me today," she demanded, going toe to toe with him. "You can't seriously think, after everything we've been through together, that I married you for money?"

Cutting eye contact, he rubbed a hand over his temple. Even when he spoke, he sounded so rational, so calm that Dolly's temper spiraled in contrast. "Maybe you didn't."

"Maybe? You railroaded me into the payment! You told me it was better to term it like a service done."

"Fine. But I still don't see why you wouldn't tell me that we were actually married. Why didn't you tell me that you're my bloody wife for real?" A rough groan escaped his lips. "You know how I tormented myself that I must have done something awful to you? That I had to be the reason you abandoned a relationship that we built for nearly a decade?"

Dolly shook her head, considering and discarding where to start, what to say. God, she'd made such a mess out of it, and a very real panic was beginning to brew in her stomach.

What if she lost him over this? Just when she was gaining the courage to believe they had another chance? To reach for what she had always felt for him, deep in her heart, from the moment he had sat by the chair near her bed in her dorm room, making sure she wasn't alone with her nightmares?

"I have a reason for why I didn't tell you. And like you, I hoped that your brothers would come to their senses and drop the whole lawsuit. Which is the only reason we married, Ares. To protect the company from their grasping hands. If they dropped it, the twelve months would pass, and our marriage would be dissolved legally. Nothing to give a second thought to."

"That was before we decided to have sex with each other, Dahlia," he said, sounding extremely tired. "Now it will have to be a divorce after twelve months because the marriage was consummated. And don't worry. My lawyer said there's a nice payout for you however it ends too."

"Stop! Stop saying that," she said, grabbing his shoulders.

He stared at her, finally making eye contact, confusion and something else painted across his features. His lips twisted with bitterness. "What I can't stop wondering is why you did it." The more emotional he got, the lower his voice fell, until it was a soft rumble that pulled at her. "Was it out of pity? Did you feel sorry for me?"

"What was out of pity?"

"Sleeping with me."

She pushed at his chest, beyond anger or rage now. "You know that's not true. I did it because I wanted to. So much. I've always wanted you like that, Ares."

"I don't believe you."

"It's the truth, late as it might be. Do you want to know what it is you forgot? Why you were so angry with me when you left for Greece? Why I had to walk away from you and the company even though an hour didn't go by when I didn't think of you?"

"Yes, I want to know."

"That weekend, the weekend after we signed the marriage contract, we got caught up in a snowstorm upstate. There was a citywide power outage and I was chilled to the bone. You poured me cognac, I believe, to get me warmed up. I had never drunk anything more than maybe one beer in my life. It went straight to my head, cut through every rule and boundary I lived by. I…" she licked her lips, feeling her heart bottom out of her "…I told you that I had feelings for you. That I had never felt like that before. That being your wife on paper made me want the real thing. That you had always made me feel safe and needed."

The words nearly made her choke on their way out but she released them.

Ares said nothing, watching her with that impenetrable look in his eyes.

Dolly pushed the heels of her palms against her eyes, feeling as if she was splaying herself open. Her palms came away wet. "God, I don't know how long I went on for or what else I said. When it was morning, I woke up with a headache and a hangover. Your coat was across my shoulders and the scent of it, of you, more than anything else, brought it all back to me. Your silence in the wake of everything I'd said, how you carefully untangled me from you because I put my arms around you and my head on your chest. I was…embarrassed, terrified. Before I could sort through things in my own head, you—you went off on me.

"You said I crossed lines I should never have. That you were disgusted by my unprofessional behavior. That I had ruined our relationship. That you couldn't trust me anymore."

Whatever remnants of shame were still stuck in her got washed away in the retelling. He had been brutal on her, but she should have never let him make her feel ashamed of her feelings. Maybe getting drunk and admitting that you had feelings for your boss to his face was a big no-no. But she hadn't started out to hurt him or demand anything of him. "And the fact that I might have ruined our friendship devastated me."

Like she'd just told him, there was no shame in loving someone, or wanting to be close to them, or telling them the truth of it. "It's only after coming here that I realized that I must have thrown your entire world out of order by admitting to it. You dropped me off at my studio, told me to take a couple of weeks off while you decided what to do with me. You said you were stuck with me, even if you fired me, because of the contract we signed. You wouldn't make eye contact with me as I got out of the car. I had never felt such pain in my life, and this is counting my aunt's endless rejections of me. My head hurt from the hangover and yet I felt like I had been dealt a body blow. I…felt crushed, heartbroken. I don't know if I expected you to return my feelings. I was drunk. But I never expected such swift, brutal anger from you."

Her throat, her body, her heart, every inch of her felt sore.

"Dahlia—"

"No, let me finish. Because I don't want to go through this again. I never want to relive that moment." She wiped at her cheeks roughly with the back of her hands. "So yes, when you said you forgot what happened before you left, when I couldn't find the damned piece of paper we both signed, I felt…relief. If you didn't remember that it had happened, maybe I could forget that it had too." She laughed through the tears. "Within hours of waking up, you demanded I come here with your usual arrogance, and I couldn't stay away from you. I told myself it was better that the contract was forgotten. You had this new perspective on your family and life and I thought you might be able to convince them to drop it, that the fake engagement might be enough. I thought when you had them, you would forget all about me. Then you'd never need to know that we were married. When the twelve months had passed and it was time to dissolve the marriage, I didn't think you would care that it had existed at some point as it would all have been old news by then."

"All you had to do was tell me the truth, Dahlia. You knew how much I agonized over what had happened. How much I hated being in the dark about my own behavior. How much I tormented myself about how I must have hurt you."

"You did hurt me," Dolly said softly, giving voice to that small truth too. And somehow saying it made her feel lighter. Made the hurt less sharp. "It felt like I'd lost the one person that I thought I would never lose. It felt like I was all alone in the entire world. Because your friendship mattered to me more than anything else."

"Then why not tell me what I did when you were here? How badly I hurt you?"

"Can't you see, Ares? Then I would have to tell you what had brought it on. I was trying to get over you. Telling myself that they weren't real feelings. That it was attachment or codependency or some such nonsense. I never wanted to give you that power over me again."

"And then when I suggested that we start a sexual relationship?"

He wasn't saying it like that to hurt her, Dolly knew that. Still, the bare truth of his words helped her hang on to her own clarity. This could have gone so much better if she'd had the nerve to own up to the truth but the conclusion was always going to be the same.

"I'm attracted to you. I always wanted you." She shrugged. "A fun fling is all you wanted and honestly, after everything that happened, it was what I wanted too. I wanted whatever I could get of you. I even justified it to myself that it could help me get over you, given I had an exit strategy. And I convinced myself that you're on a novelty kick, that sooner or later, it would fade too and you would revert to the Ares who didn't see me as a person. I won't let you make me feel wrong about that."

"And yet, it does, Dahlia. All of it feels wrong. Feels

distorted. You're my wife, in every way possible. And now, I don't know if anything you said or did these past few weeks was real because you were lying to me the whole time. It feels…dirty."

"It doesn't matter anymore, does it?" she said, cutting him off before he said something that would crush her all over again. "It didn't get resolved the way you wanted it to but it's done. I know the contract stipulates that we remain married for another nine months, and I will honor it. But there's no need for us to pretend to anything anymore, Ares. Not an engagement, not friendship, not even a work relationship. You have a lot of fallout to deal with, after what you've set in motion. I will not add to your burden."

"So understanding, always, Dahlia."

"I'm doing my best here, Ares, to make this easy for you."

He nodded, as if coming to a conclusion. "Easier for me or for you, Dahlia?" Then he straightened and nodded, as if coming to a conclusion. "I will have someone take you to Athens first thing tomorrow. Pack your bags and be ready."

And there was the final blow. Because the truth was he didn't need her anymore, did he?

Dolly left without another word, her heart in tiny fragments.

CHAPTER TWELVE

FIVE WEEKS LATER, Dahlia was surprised, no, shocked, that her electronic pass allowed her entry into the private elevator that rode up to Ares's penthouse in Manhattan.

She'd come prepared with an elaborate story to beg the doorman to let her in. Instead, he'd given her a nod, greeted her by name, and before she knew it, the doors to the elevator were swooshing open.

Sudden panic rushed at her as the initial obstacle she'd prepared so much for didn't even materialize. She focused on the increasing floor numbers but nothing helped cut through the worry about seeing Ares.

Although the plan was that he wouldn't be here at this precise moment. The elevator doors swished open before she even finished reassuring herself. The dark marble floor gleamed, making her nearly dizzy as she walked into the large foyer.

She had been at the gorgeously designed duplex penthouse multiple times before and yet…everything felt strange and new and alarming.

Her eyes automatically drifted to the life-size cutout she'd had blown up from one of the tech magazines that had featured Ares only last year. God, how he'd hated the sight of it. And yet, he'd let her hang it. Let her decorate the place with a piece here and there—with input from him, when she'd said it looked bare and soulless.

Standing there, gazing at all the memories collected over the years, made every breath painful. What a fool she was to want a glimpse of this, as if it would fill the bottomless pit in her heart that he had left behind.

But five weeks of not seeing him had felt like five painful eternities and Dolly was so eager for even a scrap of information about him. Christina had called her a few times and then stopped when Dolly wouldn't answer. Her loyalty to Ares would still be absolute. Unlike Dolly, Christina would never be foolish enough to fall in love with a man who would never return it. And somehow, she'd kept herself from finding out how he was faring.

Even though it ached to imagine him navigating this new rift in his family, all without her.

Of course the scandal that had touched his family, with the meatheads facing prosecution for embezzlement, had reached New York too, given Ares had made it his home for nearly a decade. Anything more personal than that wasn't public knowledge. Just how he liked it.

Letting Arabella tempt her into coming here had been foolish. But when the girl had texted Dolly that she was in New York and begged to meet, Dolly hadn't been able to resist. Yes, Ares had thrown her out of his life but she cared about Arabella. Especially given the aftermath of everything that had happened in her family. If Arabella needed her, Dolly would be there. But she should have insisted that the girl meet her downstairs, or at a café somewhere. Anywhere else but here.

She'd just fished her phone out of her bag, intending to text Arabella, when she felt him standing at the top of the stairs, glaring down at her. It was as if the very energy in the air had been charged up. The phone escaped her graceless fingers, thudding to the floor as Dolly looked up, as if drawn by a string.

Her neck ached, her heart thrummed at a dangerous beat, her belly sloshed as if she was riding that elevator down at dangerous speeds, but she couldn't look away. In a white linen shirt and black trousers, with scruff making his jaw dark, he looked painfully, achingly gorgeous.

And he was looking straight into her eyes, as if he meant to drown himself in there. The intensity and intimacy of it was as shocking as his rough kiss. Her spine straightened, and her tongue swiped over her lower lip before Dolly realized what she was doing. Embarrassment flooded her cheeks and she looked away, panting.

Rubbing a hand over her forehead, she said, "I'm sorry. I shouldn't be here. Arabella said…" She swallowed the knot of tears in her throat. "I'm leaving."

"Don't move," Ares said, in that commanding tone of his just as she turned.

And her stupidly in-love body listened as if it were one of Pavlov's dogs.

Dolly bit her lip, hard, hoping it would propel her out of the lovesick daze.

His feet made barely any sound on the floor as he reached her. The scent of him—soap and pine—came at her first, nearly knocking her out at the knees. Then his clever hands were on her shoulders, turning her around.

Dolly dropped her gaze, afraid of what he would read there.

His fingers caressed her cheek, then tipped her chin

up. "You have the very bad habit of apologizing for things that aren't your fault, Dahlia."

Taking a deep breath, she swatted his hand away. "I just… I can't do this, Ares. I simply wanted to check on Arabella."

"Can't do what, *agapi mou*?"

His voice so infinitely tender that heat prickled behind her eyes. Why was he being so kind after sending her away? Why wasn't he angry with her for invading his privacy? "I can't be near you. It's…unbearable."

His throat bobbed as his gaze flitted between her eyes. "Not even for the few minutes it will take me to tell you that I was an ass and a coward and a fool? I shouldn't have sent you away. Nothing has been the same since."

She laughed then, through the tears. His brilliant eyes and stunning beauty were easier to bear through the fog of her vision, dulled and dimmed just a little. "Both of us made mistakes. Without the intent to hurt each other. I can see that after all these weeks. So this is not necessary."

"Dahlia—"

"I know you're not used to affairs, but you don't owe me anything, Ares. You never promised me more. It's okay to let this go."

"But I promised myself more, *agapi*. And you know the whiny baby I become when I don't get what I want."

"What do you mean?"

"Did you know that when my mother asked if she could plan a Christmas wedding for us, I almost said yes to her right there?"

"Don't play with me."

She almost turned on her heel when, in one swift, sudden move, his arm was at her midriff, he was bending his knees, and two seconds later, Dolly was slung over his shoulder in a fireman's carry.

A giggle erupted from her mouth and she covered it with her palm. "Ares," she said, beating at his back, very half-heartedly. "Your hip! Oh, my God, this must be killing you."

He proceeded without a break, to carry her to one of the bedrooms at the back of that floor. "Wait, where's Arabella?"

"I sent her shopping."

"What? So you knew I was coming?"

"Yes."

Once again, the recessed lights of the different ceiling hit her eyes and Dolly found herself on her back. Staring up at the man she'd love forever.

"That's not nice of you. To make me come here without asking me yourself."

"Would you have come if I had asked?"

She shrugged.

He sighed, long and deep. "Just hear me out, okay? If you don't like what I say, I will never show you my face again."

"I like your face," she blurted out before she could stop herself.

He grinned and then sobered. "I like yours too, *agapi*. In fact, it's quite stupid of me that it's taken me this long but I more than like you. I love you, Dahlia, and I never should have sent you away, wife or not."

Tears swam in her eyes and hope unfurled like some slumbering beast, ferocious in its bite. But Dolly fought it back, for now. Fear had a deeper, fierce hold on her.

And she knew it would hurt him but she couldn't help it. "I want to believe you. But, Ares, I understand if you're simply unable to do without me at work. You're a creature of habit and nine years is like a lifetime to you."

Hurt flashed in his eyes but he didn't chase it away or cut eye contact. He let her see everything that traversed his beautiful features and Dolly stared as if she were a starving man offered a feast. "I can see why you would think that."

Putting one knee on the bed by her thigh, he bent until his forehead pressed against her lower belly. Something about the supplication in the gesture nearly broke her heart all over again, even as it patched up the fragmented pieces. "In five weeks, I've tried everything to remember that scene at the cabin, during the blackout. And it won't come to me. It's as if my mind has decided to cloak it in darkness forever. Ashamed of itself."

Dolly couldn't help it. She might as well stop breathing than stop herself from sinking her fingers into his hair. His confusion, his ache, it was an open book to her. "It's okay, Ares."

"It's not," he said, placing a kiss on her belly. "I hurt you. And I can't fathom a version of me that would do that to you. The only answer I have is what you surmised so cleverly. I never realized how well you truly know me, Dahlia. I think my brain couldn't make the jump, couldn't sustain the idea of losing you. Then there was the way my parents and their so-called passion ruined so many lives. I convinced myself that I didn't need passion in my life and nothing could distract me from that stance. Until you. And even that night at the cabin, I would have been afraid, Dahlia. So afraid that I couldn't be all that you would need in a man. All my life, I've been told again and again that I fall short and you…you were the most important thing in my life.

"So, I chose contempt to hide my own panic beneath. I'm so sorry for thrusting that on you."

"I had just confessed to loving you, Ares. Why would you lose me?"

His lean shoulders rose in a shrug. "I've never wanted a woman as a lover before, Dahlia. The one time I had kissed a girl, the meatheads had paid her to kiss me when I turned sixteen, and then to tell me that I was the worst kiss she'd ever had. It only cemented the feeling that something was wrong with me."

"God, I wish I had punched the daylights out of at least one of them at the pool that evening."

His laughter reverberated against her flesh. "That would have been something to see."

Now she glided her fingers from his hair to his forehead and he looked up. "As clichéd as it sounds, I didn't know what it was to be loved or how to do it in return, Dahlia. You, your friendship, even if we didn't call it that back then, was the only constant in my life. And when you confessed your feelings to me, I think my entire world was hit by an earthquake. My own family, who was supposed to love me, had mocked me, ignored me, abandoned me. I didn't trust that love wouldn't take you away from me."

His gaze cut to hers then. "I hate the idea of hurting you again by bringing up that moment."

She nodded. And then made up her mind. "I think I trust you and myself enough this time to know that you're only doing it because it's necessary. Because we can put it behind us, then."

"I don't want to put it behind me. Because I never want to hurt you like that again."

"You won't, Ares," she said, that hope gaining force inside her.

"The anger as I was driving to Corfu, the distraction, it wasn't at you. It was at myself. I think the moment I left you and got on the plane, I realized how badly I had erred. How I ruined any chance I had with the person I truly adored. Your stricken face... I kept seeing it when I tried to sleep. You were right that I crushed you. I was driving so recklessly because I wanted to come right back to you, Dahlia. I wanted to tell you I was sorry and I hated myself with an intensity I've never known before."

"Shh," Dolly said as his voice quivered. "Please, Ares, I don't want to think of the accident. I felt so guilty that I drove you to it."

"You didn't, *matia mou*," he said, now pressing kisses to her upper belly. His tears drenched her skin, washing hers away. "And when I woke up from the coma and I saw your face, it was all crystal clear. The thought before I crashed...that I couldn't lose you, no matter what."

"You promise?" Dolly asked, like a little child demanding forever.

Ares kissed the corner of her mouth. As if he understood exactly why she was asking. "I do, sweetheart. I was angry and hurt that you didn't tell me about the contract. Coming on top of what my father did, and refused to do, it felt like another betrayal. It felt like nothing in my life was worth caring about. That I wasn't worth caring about. Processing emotions healthily is obviously not one of my brilliant qualities," he quipped. Dolly knew what he was doing and she hated everyone who had taught him to minimize his pain.

"No," Dolly said, pushing up and planting her own kisses all over his face. "Don't you dare say that, Ares Demetrius. You're mine and you're the most wonderful, arrogant, wickedly charming man in the entire world, and you're worth more than a hundred men together because you're also the kindest. I love you, Ares. I've loved you since you sat by my bed those nights in college, because you made me feel less alone in this world. I will always love you."

And as if the moment had been orchestrated, their mouths found each other, and communicated deeper than any words could.

It was a long while later and they were both panting, their clothes strewn about the bed, when Dolly remembered that his sister was visiting. Still, she was loath to disturb the moment by bringing up painful stuff for him.

She placed her palm on his bare chest. Under her touch, the steady beat of his heart felt intimate. As if the beat belonged to her.

Not as if. It *was* hers. He was hers. Although it would take a while to fully comprehend it.

Five weeks hadn't dimmed their physical connection one bit. If anything, they had gone at each other with a voracious need, eager to cement the tenuous emotional connection.

Every inch of her felt deliciously sore. And yet, inside her chest, her heart glittered as if it had been imbued with magic.

Pushing herself up on her elbow, she studied Ares's face.

Eyes closed, hair thoroughly mussed by her fingers, he looked peaceful.

"I can hear the gears in your head turning," he said, one corner of his mouth lifting more.

Leaning down, Dolly pressed a kiss to that tiny imperfection. "I'm happy. Bursting with it. And a little scared that this might be a dream."

Taking her hand in his, he placed a kiss to the center of her palm. "It is real. You're never leaving my side, Dahlia, ever."

"Ares..."

His gray eyes popped open and held hers. "Yeah?"

She licked her lips. "I was really happy to learn that you brought Arabella here. She must be devastated by everything that happened. She's not angry with you?"

"Not at all. Mama's here too."

"What?"

"She left my father. At least temporarily, I think. And she asked me if she and Arabella could stay here with me for a few months. Until she figures out what she wants to do."

"She did?" Disbelief pulsed through Dolly's tone. "I don't mean to doubt her but—"

"Don't apologize, *agapi mou*. It was a shock to me too. Turns out my mother's biggest sin was being completely unaware of how badly Stefano and Sergio had treated me back then. She had a really difficult birth with Arabella and went into a depression, she told me finally. And by the time I left home, she was just getting better. She promised me that she would spend the rest of her life trying to make it up to me."

"Oh, Ares. I'm so glad. Aren't you?"

Instead of answering her immediately, he searched her eyes, his grip tightening over her wrist. "You don't mind?"

"Don't mind what?"

"If they live here for a few months?"

Dolly laughed. "This is your home and I'm just so glad—"

Pulling her down to him, Ares took her mouth in a possessive kiss that left her panting. "Our home, Dahlia. You aren't going back to that studio apartment. And as soon as your grandfather is able to stand without being in pain for more than five minutes, I want to marry you again in a proper celebration."

"We're already married," she said, sniffling.

"Not the contract stuff. This will be a grand, traditional wedding wherever you want to have it. This time, I want it done right."

Dolly made a pout of her tingling lips. "Maybe you should start it right by asking me properly instead of commanding me."

Pushing her onto her back, he pressed his lean body down into hers. Her breath shivered out on a pleasurable sigh. "Dahlia Singh, will you please be my wife forever this time? Because you're my entire world, *yineka mou*. Without you, I'm lost and lonely and nothing and I—"

Dolly didn't let him finish. She kissed him, her very heart in the touch. "Yes, Ares. I will marry you forever and ever, because I adore you too."

"You still want those noisy, crying babies?" he asked, his eyes shining with pure adoration.

Dolly laughed and nodded. "I want a big family."

"Then let's get started on them right now," he said, pinning his hips into hers and kissing her with that intense devotion that only he could show.

She laughed, wrapping her arms around his shoulders. "Maybe after I finish my degree? You know, the nonprofit charity project we spoke of starting years ago? I was thinking of something like that."

"Right. Humanizing me a little more, Dahlia?"

"Not to prove anything to the world but for ourselves, Ares."

"That sounds perfect."

And Dolly knew that she would never doubt her place in the world again. She would be Ares Demetrius's wife and she would be needed and wanted and loved for the rest of her life.

* * * * *

Did His Forgotten Wife *sweep you off your feet?*
Then don't miss these other spicy stories
from Tara Pammi!

Twins to Tame Him
Fiancée for the Cameras
Contractually Wed
Her Twin Secret
Vows to a King

Available now!

MILLS & BOON®

Coming next month

KING'S EMERGENCY WIFE
Lucy King

'I'd like you to draft an announcement regarding the imminent change to my marital status.'

If Sofia was startled by his request, she didn't show it. She barely even blinked. 'Have you finally made your choice?'

Ivo nodded shortly. 'I have.'

'I understood none of the current candidates were deemed to be suitable.'

'That's correct,' he said. 'I had to think laterally. Outside the box. It turned out to be an excellent move.'

'Then may I be the first to offer you my congratulations.'

'Thank you.'

'The palace will breathe a sigh of relief.'

'I can almost hear it now.'

'I'll draft the announcement immediately and email it to you for approval,' she said, glancing down briefly to jot something in her notebook. 'It will be sent to all major news outlets within the hour.'

'Good.'

'The people will be ecstatic.'

'I certainly hope so.'

'Just one thing…'

'Yes?'

She lifted her gaze back to his, her smile faint, her expression quizzical. 'Who's the lucky lady?'

'You are.'

Continue reading

KING'S EMERGENCY WIFE
Lucy King

Available next month
millsandboon.co.uk

COMING SOON!

We really hope you enjoyed reading this book.
If you're looking for more romance
be sure to head to the shops when
new books are available on

Thursday 25th September

To see which titles are coming soon, please visit

millsandboon.co.uk/nextmonth

MILLS & BOON

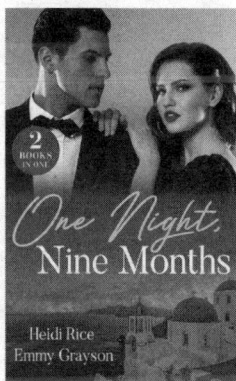

afterglow BOOKS

Afterglow Books is a trend-led, trope-filled list of books with diverse, authentic and relatable characters, a wide array of voices and representations, plus real world trials and tribulations. Featuring all the tropes you could possibly want (think small-town settings, fake relationships, grumpy vs sunshine, enemies to lovers) and all with a generous dose of spice in every story.

For all the latest book news, exclusive content and giveaways scan the QR code below to sign up to the Afterglow newsletter:

SCAN ME

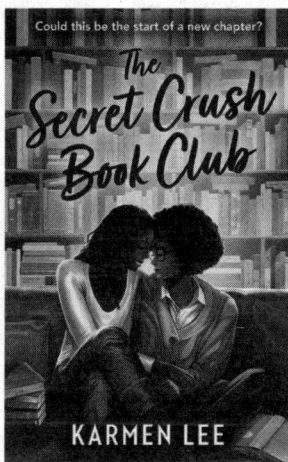

LET'S TALK
Romance

For exclusive extracts, competitions and special offers, find us online:

f MillsandBoon

X @MillsandBoon

⊙ @MillsandBoonUK

♪ @MillsandBoonUK

Get in touch on 01413 063 232